A PASSEL OF HATE

JOE EPLEY

ISBN-10: 1461075939

ISBN-13: 9781461075936

Library of Congress Control Number: 2011905717

Foxwood Press
Tryon, North Carolina

This book is dedicated to
America's Citizen Soldiers,
past and present,
who preserve our freedoms.

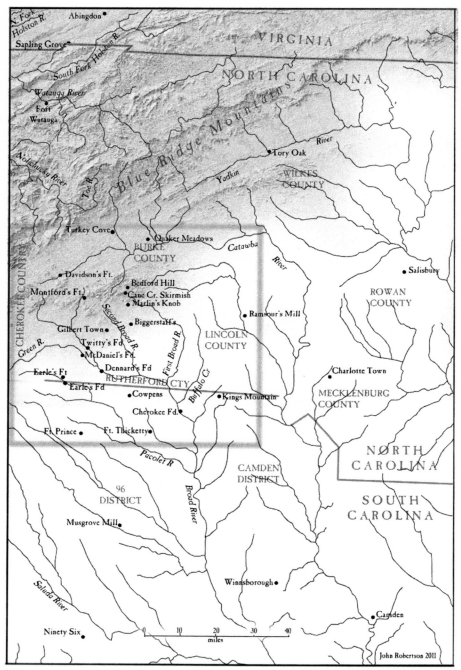

Western North and South Carolina, 1780

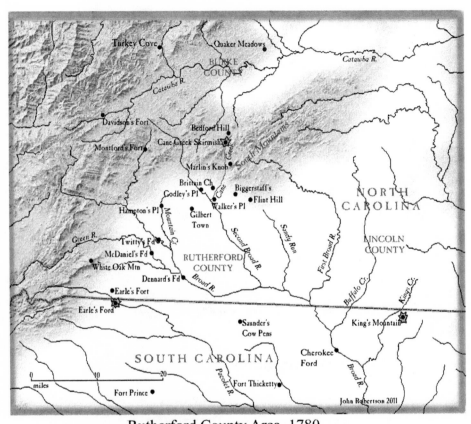

Rutherford County Area, 1780

Note: Rutherford and Lincoln County were considered by Tories to be Tryon County.

Author's Notes

Although a work of fiction, this book is based on what history has recorded about the people and activities surrounding a campaign that significantly affected the outcome of America's War for Independence.

Kings Mountain was the largest American-versus-American engagement in the war. Only one British soldier was there, Patrick Ferguson. It also was the first significant battle in which the rifle played a prominent role.

The events leading up to the battle at Kings Mountain flamed a civil war within the interior of the two Carolinas, creating a chasm of ideologies and animosities that caused bitter splits—oftentimes brutal hatred—among families and neighbors. Among the two thousand or so participants in the Kings Mountain battle, there were at least forty-two sets of brothers, eighteen father–son groups, and many more extended family clusters. Not all members of the same family fought on the same side.

Many of the characters within this book appear in their historical roles, but their dialogue and individual actions are speculative and based on assumptions gained from research into the events, personalities, and circumstances of that time. The Godley, Pearson, Foreman, and McCracken families described within are fictitious but represent a composite of life in the 1780s. Rance Miller and George Bluebird are also fictitious characters.

In researching the book, I found that history seems to have ignored Colonel Andrew Hampton, commander of the Rutherford County militia (Liberty Men) and, who at sixty-seven, was the oldest person known to be in the battle. The monuments on the battlefield omit his name from the list of commanders, but carry the names of Charles McDowell and William Hill, neither of whom was at Kings Mountain. We know from memoirs, pension statements, and letters that Hampton was there. This book presents my theories on his role.

"This brilliant victory marked the turning point of the American Revolution." —President Theodore Roosevelt

Quash the Rebellion
23 August 1780

The stench was overbearing, even on the upwind side of the battlefield. It had been seven days since the rebel army was decimated here. Most of the bodies were now buried. A few body parts and dead horses were not. The rebels not killed, wounded, or captured were sent running in panic after tasting the steel and ball of the highly disciplined British regulars of His Excellency the Most Honorable General the Earl Cornwallis, commander of His Majesty's forces in the southern colonies. The rebel commander, General Horatio Gates, led the rout, abandoning his troops in the field as he fled north from the South Carolina countryside.

The sticky, humid August heat was discomforting as Major Patrick Ferguson, Inspector of Provincial Forces, guided his horse around the debris of war and the fetid, bloated horse carcasses. A combat veteran of battles in Europe as well as in America, the wiry officer ignored the smell and battle litter, but he could not ignore the heat.

He was in dress uniform, a bright red wool and linen coat with the white facing of the Seventy-first Foot—Fraser's Highlanders—his home regiment from which he was detached to recruit, train, and lead Loyalist militia units of the western Carolinas, a task most career officers did not understand and avoided like the plague. His breeches were dazzling white, thanks to the two new female assistants who traveled with him on campaigns to keep his clothing and body in good condition. Free of dust and dinge were knee-high, black riding boots, shined to a gleam. The long black ostrich feathers sprouting from the top of a red-and-white-checkered bonnet fluttered as though alive. With his head uncomfortably hot, he refused to wear the traditional wig favored by British officers.

Protocol for meeting with the commander-in-chief required senior officers to be in full-dress uniform, no matter how inadvisable such garments were for the insufferable heat. A spotless, black stock encircled his neck outside a tight, white linen collar. Dangling from his neck was a highly polished silver gorget signifying his leadership position. The sun reflected upward from the gorget into his eyes, adding yet another nuisance to the occasion. With each prance of his horse, his sword and scabbard smacked against his leg.

Ferguson was apprehensive about the meeting. His right arm permanently bent and mostly useless from a gunshot wound received three years earlier in the battle at Brandywine, ached constantly, but he ignored the discomfort. He had withstood the surgeon's probe for the ball that went into his elbow and then a second operation without antiseptic. More than two years were spent in painful recovery. It was a wound that would cause most soldiers to be medically discharged as an invalid and be sent home a hero, away from the blasted colonies where backwoodsmen fought as barbarians and not with the civility of the European military. Such a wound was a ticket back to the cool highlands of Scotland and away from the wretched Carolina heat.

His pride refused any thought of being a cripple. He rebuilt his strength and learned to write, shoot, and use a saber with his left arm. Before his right elbow was shattered by a rebel ball, Ferguson was considered the best shot in the British Army. He probably still was. However, on this day, these personal skills were not on his mind.

Recently, the British Army had accomplished a series of stunning victories that left South Carolina free of most rebel forces—the rout of Gates at Camden last week, the capture of Charles Town in May, and just a few days ago, Lieutenant Colonel Banastre Tarleton's decimation of Colonel Thomas Sumter's South Carolina militia at Fishing Creek. Survivors of those battles had fled in terror to North Carolina.

Yet, after Sumter's defeat, about sixty miles to the west on the banks of the Enoree River, one of Ferguson's units met disaster at Musgrove's Mill. Ferguson was not at the Musgrove battle; he would not have let his forces be lured into a trap that killed sixty Loyalist soldiers and wounded another ninety. The Whigs captured seventy of the Tories and left only four of their own dead on the battlefield.

At the time of the deadly ambush, Ferguson was only a few miles away looking for Colonel Charles McDowell, who commanded western North Carolina's partisans. Although the battle was not his personal failure, Ferguson could only assume that those headquarters staff officers, far from the backwoods battle site, would think the worse. All commanders had to answer to the failure of their subordinates.

Before they could reorganize after Musgrove's Mill to take advantage of the defeated Loyalist forces, the rebel field commanders received word of the Continental Army's devastating loss at Camden. They were ordered to retreat swiftly to Gilbert Town north of the Carolina border.

As the rebel militia, with their prisoners each riding double with a partisan horseman, sped northward, Ferguson was consolidating his widely separated units into a unified force to pursue the notorious backwater warriors. But as he was readying his force to give chase, the summons came for him to report to headquarters,

The core of his command was a cadre of veteran Provincial troops, well-trained, disciplined, and battled-hardened. Most of them were from New York and New Jersey and wore the red coats of the British Army or the green jackets of the elite Queen's Rangers. Although his militia of farmers, tradesmen, and hunters had no uniforms, they knew the terrain and were not reluctant to fight anyone who defied the king.

Militiamen were mostly undisciplined and wildly independent, all factors Ferguson was trying to change. A few were little more than bandits and marauders. Many would fight like savages. Most could be brave and effective in battle if there was time to whip them into shape. Some would run at the hint of trouble. With good training, they were suitable for irregular warfare where identifying enemy from friend was often difficult.

Although emotionless in outward appearance as he rode beyond the battlefield, inside he was still seething at not being able to go after the rebels who had been so near. He had a sufficient force to render the fleeing backwoodsmen impotent. So now, he wondered, is it back to the spit and polish army, rigid in tradition and protocol?

A young subaltern, barely seventeen and sweating profusely in his impeccable uniform, ran up to Ferguson as he arrived at the plantation house commandeered for the British headquarters near Camden, the largest community in South Carolina's interior. "Major!" the subaltern shouted as he doffed his tricorn in a rushed salute to the senior officer. "Lord Cornwallis has been asking for you. You are to go in right away, sir."

Ferguson dismounted as a young Negro boy who served the plantation took the reins of his horse. He paid little heed to the dozen or so other officers hanging around on the porch and under the shade of the giant water oaks just outside the headquarters entrance. Here, the battlefield stench was only a faint whiff and present only when the wind was blowing southward, yet several of the pompous staff officers were using dainty handkerchiefs to cover their noses.

Gleaming white in the midday sun, the colonnaded plantation home had been confiscated from a rebel government official who had fled the British Army's advance. It was large and well appointed with quality furnishings. A center hallway extended the full length of the house to an open back door in a vain attempt to capture any breeze to cool down the interior. On the left, an ornate staircase led to the upstairs bedrooms. On the right, double doors opened into a parlor where the adjutant's staff was busy writing orders, reading reports, and dispatching expresses to outposts throughout the colony.

The headquarters minions did not pay the intruding major any attention until Ferguson said loudly to the full room, "Sir! Major Ferguson to see Lord Cornwallis."

The adjutant looked up from his reading and responded in an aloof attitude. "Oh yes, His Lordship is expecting you. Stand easy; I will let him know you are here."

The colonel slid open the doors that normally led to a dining room, now seconded as the commander's private office, and quietly entered and closed the doors behind him. After a few minutes, the adjutant returned and told Ferguson to enter.

Ferguson removed his bonnet and tucked it under his right arm. He stiffened his body as he entered to report to the man who could make or break his career with a single word. He walked purposely to the front of the table used as a desk by Cornwallis and snapped to attention. "M' Lord! Major Patrick Ferguson, Inspector of Provincial Forces, reporting as ordered."

Although a brevet lieutenant colonel in the British Army and a full colonel of the militia and Provincial troops, Ferguson made it a point to refer only to his permanent rank when addressing senior British officers.

Cornwallis was coatless as he worked in the stifling heat, his white shirt showing a slight stain around the armpits. "Ah, my roaming partisan fighter," he said with a smile as he looked up at Ferguson, and then let the smile fade. "I was looking for you earlier so that we could have dined together."

"I came as soon as I received your express, sir. It was a day-and-a-half ride to get here," Ferguson replied, still standing at attention and bristling inwardly at the rebuke.

Only in the last two months had Ferguson earned the begrudging respect of Cornwallis. The general initially did not know that Sir Henry Clinton, the supreme British commander in the colonies, had complete confidence in the auburn-haired Scotsman and had given him the mission of organizing Loyalist militia. Despite the general's early misgivings, Ferguson amazed Cornwallis by successfully recruiting and training more than a thousand militiamen within a few weeks. Ferguson had gained a glowing reputation for the use of his trademark whistles of silver and brass as effective tools to communicate orders in fluid situations. The whistles hung around his neck today.

"Relax, Major, relax," the general said as he rose from his chair and walked over to a large map pinned to the wall. He was tall and fit for his forty-two years and had a pronounced tilt of his left eyebrow, the result of a hockey stick blow when he was a student at Eton. "I hear good reports about your work with American Loyalists, except, of course, for that foolishness up at Musgrove's Mill."

Ferguson winced inwardly at the reference to the failed battle that occurred in his absence.

Cornwallis continued. "I have met with the militia commander from Tryon County up in western North Carolina. Uh…what's his name?"

"Colonel Ambrose Mills, sir." Ferguson replied.

"Yes, yes, good man. He owns property near here as well as up on the frontier. I knew some of his relatives back in England. He admires your combative skills and says that his militia will follow you anywhere. He thinks he can get a thousand more volunteers from the back country to join the king's service."

Although pleased with the compliments, Ferguson said nothing. He respected Mills, but had strong reservations about the Tory leader's ability to recruit that many volunteers in the sparsely settled mountains and foothills seething with rebellion and unruly partisans bent on terrorizing their Tory neighbors. He shared Cornwallis's belief that the militia was almost useless on the modern battlefield but was good as cannon fodder and in making a show of force to the populace. He quietly questioned the belief held by the British high command that the majority of North Carolina residents were loyal to the king and would help them finally put an end to the rebellion, now in its fifth year.

Cornwallis motioned him to the wall map. "Let me tell you about our plans and your role in them. With our victory here at Camden and Tarleton taking the wind out of Sumter's band of rabble on the eighteenth, the organized rebel army in the south is no more. Still, there are a few pockets of banditti and ragtag militia lurking about. Gates and his cowards, those who are left to him, are racing back to the north with their tails between their legs. We have an open road into North Carolina. It is my intention to take the army all the way to Hillsborough by winter. There is strong Loyalist sympathy in North Carolina, so we shouldn't have much trouble. However, there's still some pesky rebel sentiment that we must take care of around Charlotte Town and in the western regions."

He continued as he pointed to the map, "I will take Charlotte Town and then Salisbury, a two-day march farther up the road. These two towns are key to pacifying the West. From there, we are only a few days' march to Hillsborough and the headquarters for North Carolina's insurrectionists. I'm sure their so-called government leaders will have fled by the time we get there. Else it will be the hangman's noose for them."

Cornwallis turned and looked at Ferguson. Using the Scottish officer's familiar name, the commander said, "Now Pattie, your command will provide the main army with a screen on our left flank. Along the way, I want you to calm down the countryside. Lieutenant Colonel Tarleton will take care of my eastern flank."

Ferguson personally liked Tarleton and respected his fighting abilities, but he did not care for the dragoon's arrogant and flamboyant style. He could not help resenting that although ten years his junior, Tarleton held a senior rank.

Cornwallis continued with his orders. "I want you to rein in some of your lads who are roaming the countryside and hanging anybody they see fit. They are causing us to lose friends. I'm getting complaints about them, especially brutes like Cunningham, Miller, and their ilk."

Cornwallis was referring to Bloody Bill Cunningham and Rance Miller, both Tory militia captains who often acted independently of the British command structure. They had become notorious for savage assaults on anyone who refused to honor England. Their cruelty included burning homes, hanging or flogging opposition sympathizers, destroying crops, and stealing horses, cattle, and anything else that suited their fancy. More than one wife or daughter of independence supporters suffered sexual humiliation from rogue Tories.

"We must treat those loyal to the government with kindness and respect. We should do the same to the neutralists who cooperate with us. Treat harshly those who openly defy the king's representatives, but stop making war on women and children. Make it known that I will hang anyone who is ungentlemanly toward women and children.

"Be judicious in requisitioning horses and food. Make sure that you only confiscate property of rebel sympathizers; we don't want to make new enemies. If you need to forage from our Loyalist families or even those expressing neutrality, make certain that they are left enough provisions for their own needs. All Loyalists are to be given full receipts for items taken so that they may receive compensation when this unpleasantness is over.

"As for those rebels who take up arms against the king, show no mercy, and particularly no mercy to those who violate the parole we gave them after capture."

Ferguson looked at the map and mentally traced his operational area that included the Pacolet, Broad, and Catawba River valleys, an area running westward into the mountains, a hundred miles or so from Charlotte Town. There were few roads in the western frontier region; the population was sparse, with only one little place in Tryon County called Gilbert Town. There were a few plantations in the backcountry. These were far apart and small in comparison to those in coastal South Carolina, but some were prosperous and had numerous livestock and large acres of food crops, all necessities for an army living off the land.

Ecstatic with the news he would continue his independent command free of interference from staff officers who did not understand that partisan warfare had neither a front nor rules, Ferguson responded enthusiastically. "Thank you for this honor, sir. My lads will protect your western flank, and we'll eliminate sedition along the frontier. With my Provincials providing the backbone and leadership for the militia, we should have little trouble in quieting the countryside. ·

"In another three to four weeks, I can have the rest of Colonel Mills's backwater militia and our new South Carolina recruits ready for battle," Ferguson added.

"You don't have three weeks, Major," Cornwallis responded sternly. "You need to get your people moving north quickly. Training will have to be done as you go. After all, your opposition is only misfits and undisciplined ruffians."

Although Ferguson did not openly dispute his commander, he knew differently. As he was preparing to take his leave to begin planning his new mission, Cornwallis continued, almost as an afterthought. "By the by, I have reassigned the South Carolina Royalists to new missions. I'm going to have to take your New Yorkers as well."

That news stunned Ferguson. Nine months ago, prior to the invasion of South Carolina and capture of Charles Town, Ferguson had recruited 175 select volunteers, mostly of the Queen's Rangers and Loyal American Regiment from New York and New Jersey. He had formed them into a Ranger company that proved most effective in the Charles Town campaign. When he took command of the militia, they had agreed to stay with him to train the short-term Loyalist volunteers. After Charles Town fell, Ferguson also took over the South Carolina Royalists, a sizable provincial force that was trained and disciplined. Although no match for British regulars, the uniformed provincial troops were experienced and better equipped than militia.

Ferguson momentarily lost his demeanor. "But, M'Lord, I need the Provincials! We have a huge territory to cover. Militia fighters come and go almost at will. Most are brave, but they are irregulars. They don't have the skills needed for today's battlefields. Less than half of the new men have any training at all. The Provincials are the only disciplined veterans I can trust to hold fast in battle.

"My New Yorkers have over three years' service, much of it in combat, but there are little more than a hundred of them, and some are detached to Ninety Six. Without their experience and the trained South Carolina Royalists, it will be difficult to teach basic tactics and musketry to backwater militia in a short period while at the same time securing the area."

"Calm down, Major," Cornwallis said, shifting into a more formal stance. "I'll see if we might let you keep the northern Provincials a while longer, but I need the South Carolina troops now to help secure Ninety Six and the Georgia border country."

Speaking emphatically, the British Army commander added, "But regardless of whom you have in your corps, Major, your mission is simple. Move into the backcountry of North Carolina and quash any and all signs of rebellion. I want you to stay close enough to me to provide protection for my western flank, and, if need be, where we can reinforce you. I will be marching the army toward Charlotte Town by week's end."

These Terrible Times

3 September 1780

It may have been September already, but Mary Pearson did not know for sure. She had no calendar, but although the leaves had not begun to change, she recognized other signs that summer was almost over. Yet, with no breeze, the air was hot.

She sat on a stool in the shade of her log home, weaving with her calloused hands thin, wooden splints evenly into a basket. Dozens of two-foot-long splints curled on the ground beside her; still more were soaking in the rich brown dye from the bark of a white oak tree. She used the darker strips to add a little decoration to her handiwork.

In the bottomland below the house, her husband Michael and her son Patrick were harvesting a field of sorghum to be rendered into molasses. Her baskets would be traded for clay jugs at the mill, where liquid was crushed from sorghum canes and boiled into sweet, thick syrup. Several full jugs would serve their cooking needs until the next harvest.

Paddy, the name she called her son, had developed into a lanky man with a chiseled face like his father and flaming red hair like she once had. He had a gentle disposition and, *thank you, Lord*, had come home from the war mostly unscathed. He was shirtless in the heat, and both he and his father wore wide-brimmed hats made shapeless by months of use in abusive weather.

Her sixteen-year-old daughter Rachel and eleven-year-old son Sam were off in the woods nearby trying to find the family cow that had again broken through the split-rail fence earlier in the morning and had wandered off. She had three other children, but she had lost two in childbirth and the third had died from snakebite when he was only two.

Guiding the light yellow-tan splints in among each other with her nimble fingers, she barely noticed the dust coming from the south end of the lane leading up to her home until horses and riders were almost upon her. Mary thought it strange for a dozen horsemen to be there, a good two miles from the main road to Gilbert Town. She called to her husband who looked up from his stooped position with the sickle poised to cut another stalk plump with sweet nectar.

Patrick, who was guiding a weary horse pulling a rough-hewed sledge laden with cane stalks, raised his hands to shield his eyes from the late-morning sun and wondered who the armed riders could be and why were they coming to this out-of-the-way farm. *Are they Tory or Whig militia?* He asked himself.

Both he and his father eyed the rifle leaning against the cabin behind Mary. They had not carried it to the field with them since they were so close by and now regretted that careless decision.

The riders had no uniforms, but most had muskets cradled in their arms. They rode at an easy gait, but with purpose in mind. The Pearson men began walking the one hundred yards back toward the house, keeping a wary eye toward the intruders.

Mary stood, placing her half-finished basket to her side as the horses stopped in front of her. Three of the horses took their riders on past the house by several paces. Although the men held their weapons casually, their hard eyes betrayed peaceful intent. Leading the group was a stout man in his mid-thirties, better dressed than the others, but like the others, he was covered with red dust of the dry Carolina clay.

Despite the dust, she could see that the leader wore a good-quality tricorn hat with a dirty white lace trim and two colorful pheasant feathers. A wide red sash was tied around his middle under a belt carrying a cartage box and knife. A white leather belt, holding a scabbard with saber, was slung diagonally across his chest. His horse was jet black, a Spanish Barb gelding with a shiny coat, a breed not common in these parts. He sat on a dragoon's saddle with matching pistol holsters on the front flanking each side of the saddle. She did not know that the rider had taken the horse and saddle from a dead Continental cavalry soldier at a skirmish near Moncks Corner, just north of Charles Town.

"Mornin', ma'am," he said, doffing his hat in a respectful salute. "I'm looking for one Patrick Pearson. Might he live here?"

"Who wants to know?" she asked, her concern clearly understood in tone and manner. Fear was in her eyes.

"Captain Rance Miller of the Royal South Carolina Provincials, at your service, ma'am."

Without thinking, Mary gasped, "You are Tories! We are in North Carolina. What are South Carolina Tories doing here, and what do you want with my Paddy?"

Patrick walked to join his mother as his father began to sidle toward the rifle leaning against the cabin, a sickle still in the father's hand. Two of Miller's men maneuvered their horses quickly to block the senior Pearson from reaching the rifle; another two rode behind Patrick and dismounted.

"I'm Patrick Pearson," the son stated, darting his eyes back toward the men who had dismounted behind him. "What can I do for you?"

"Not for me, Master Pearson," Miller said in a condescending manner, "but for your king."

"I don't have a king; I'm my own man." Patrick responded.

"Did you not swear loyalty to the king when you were captured last spring near Charles Town?" Miller snapped. "Did you not agree to serve your king so that you could be paroled for your sin of rebellion and go free instead of rotting in a prison ship?"

Proud to have been a Liberty Man, Patrick Pearson had volunteered for duty with the Rutherford County Whig militia in February and marched south with Colonel Andrew Hampton's regiment to participate in the defense of Charles Town when the invading British Army began encircling the city. He was with a small detachment trying to capture some enemy supply wagons when his unit was overpowered by British soldiers. Two of his comrades were killed and four others seriously wounded in the short skirmish.

He and three companions were captured unhurt and were harassed by the British soldiers with threats of hanging or prison ships. By swearing allegiance to the Crown and pledging under penalty of death to never again take up arms against the English government, he was granted a parole.

"Your oath obligated you to serve the king when called upon in time of need. That time is now. You are needed by the loyal militia to help put down this damned rebellion," Miller declared, his voice rising as he continued.

"But, sir, I've seen enough fighting. I want no more of it. I have kept my word and have not taken up arms against England. But I ain't going to fight my friends," Patrick replied.

Quiet until now, Michael Pearson shouted angrily, "You have no call to come here. We ain't in this war. We are neutral. Now get off my land and leave us be!"

Miller stood up in his stirrups, towering over the Pearsons and his men on foot. In a severe and forceful tone, he responded. "First, I do have call to be here because young Master Pearson took an oath. If he reneges on that oath, it means he is a liar, and he is siding again with the rebels. Second, I'm here on order of Lord Cornwallis, the commanding general of His Majesty's forces in the Carolinas, as well as that of Colonel Ambrose Mills, the commanding officer of Loyalist militia for North Carolina. So, Mister Pearson, I advise you to keep a civil tongue and not interfere with the king's business. We have every lawful right to be here."

As Miller spoke, three more of his men dismounted, the one closest to Patrick carrying a length of rope. Another two shifted their muskets to a more ready position.

Miller turned to face Patrick again. "You have two choices. You can come willingly with us and do your duty, or come with us under arrest and face the consequences of aiding the insurrection. Give me your answer now."

Patrick put his fists on his hips. "I will not go with you, sir! You can't make me fight my neighbors."

"Arrest him for treason and violating his oath," Miller shouted the order to his men and withdrew one of the pistols from a saddle holster.

The man with the rope looped it over Patrick's shoulders before the young farmer could move. Another militiaman standing behind Patrick put the barrel of his musket against the back of Patrick's head. "Stand still, rebel."

Patrick's father reacted quickly. Raising the sickle, he lunged toward the raider with the musket pointed at his son's head and sliced the man's arm to the bone, causing him to drop the musket and howl in pain. Only seven feet away, Miller swung the pistol around and fired into Michael Pearson's head, splattering blood and brains onto Mary Pearson's face and dress as she stared in horror.

During the sudden action by his father, Patrick slipped from the rope before it was tightened around him and smashed his fist into the Tory militiaman standing next to the rope man, forcing him to stumble back and drop his musket. Patrick reached for the falling Tory's weapon and never saw the musket butt that slammed into the back of his head, knocking him unconscious.

Mary screamed and lunged toward Miller's gun arm, drawing blood as she bit into his hand before he jerked it free. Miller yelped. "Damn you wench!" He swung the heavy pistol barrel down across her forehead. She crumpled next to her husband's body, blood gushing around her face as she tried to focus and grasp what was happening to her family.

As his raiders began tying Patrick's arms behind him, the militia captain shouted orders to his men. "Hang that insolent bastard for treason and attacking soldiers of the king! Burn the house! Get what they have of value. Be quick about it!"

Four men wrestled the bound Patrick to his feet as he slowly regained confused consciousness. They hustled him over to a walnut tree as one man stood up on his horse's back to tie a rope to a limb about ten feet off the ground. Another brought over the stool Mary had been sitting on only a few minutes before. With his arms tied, Patrick was hoisted up on the stool as the hanging rope was looped twice around his neck and secured with two half-hitch knots.

There was no slack remaining in the rope between him and the tree branch overhead. He quieted in shock, not from the rope but from seeing his mother and father bleeding on the ground. Without ceremony, the stool was kicked out from under him; and Patrick Pearson, eighteen years young, was strangled slowly to death.

The Tory militiamen gathered the white-oak splints and baskets and threw all into a pile inside the house door. Miller's sergeant went behind the house to the shed with an outside cooking fire and ignited a torch that he carried inside the home and began setting fire to the bedstead and highly flammable crushed baskets and splints.

They confiscated Pearson's horse that had been left in the sorghum field still hitched to the sledge. They also took Pearson's rifle, an ammunition pouch containing fifteen lead balls, a horn half-filled with powder, and a block of lead for melting into shot. They missed the second rifle and powder horn hanging inside over the entrance door.

As he reloaded his pistol, Miller watched his men go about their tasks with practiced efficiency gained over the past year from plundering and destroying dozens of homesteads belonging to rebel sympathizers. He didn't look forward to having to explain his actions to his immediate commander, Patrick Ferguson, the British officer in charge of the Loyalists fighting for the king. He felt confident that he could easily justify why he had to kill these rebels and burn their farm.

Two days ago when the British commander had told him to start recruiting paroled rebels in North Carolina, he also warned Miller against using what he called excessive force. "Honey catches more flies than vinegar," Ferguson had said.

Within five minutes, Miller's company completed their work. They didn't bother moving their victims farther away from the fire. Mary was beginning to recover from the concussion Miller had given her, but was inactive with shock as she tried to take in the burning house, her dead husband lying beside her, and her son hanging from the tree just forty feet from her. Her mind could not yet absorb the tragedy that had befallen her family. She did not see the assailants ride away from her shattered life.

Rachel Pearson was thankful that their old cow had run off again. It gave her an opportunity to escape the boring and mundane chores that her mother had for her around the house. At sixteen, a month past fifteen, she cherished the rare moments of freedom. The forest was cool, the ground soft under her bare feet as she mindlessly wandered through the woods. Approaching one of her favorite spots, a pool at the bottom of a small cascade on Mountain Creek, she spotted a man who looked like he was washing himself. While her instinct for self-preservation told her to turn and run away, her curiosity took over, particularly after seeing that he was not an Indian.

Instead of slipping back into the woods, she sneaked closer and kneeled quietly on the ground behind some bushes to watch the stranger. He was young, lean, and had long brown hair. His shirt was draped over a rock, and his back showed a maze of jagged pink scars. He was sitting with his bare feet in the water and was bending to wet the knife he was using to scrape a scraggly beard off his face. Lying beside him was a long rifle with metal ornaments meshed into the stock of the weapon. A hatchet, shot bag, powder horn, and deerskin possibles bag were only inches from the rifle. A few feet farther back was a blanket roll, tied and ready to carry on his back. She wondered who he was.

Jacob Godley was enjoying the warm sunshine and cool water. After more than three months of serving as a Ranger guarding the frontier from marauding Cherokees, he was tired. He was on his way home by way of a back hunting trail he had heard would get him to the Gilbert Town road when he spotted the pool and decided to clean up and to get rid of the beard he had grown during his wilderness duty. Since the Cherokee began raiding frontier homes years ago, the county's men not off fighting the war were subject to serving three-month tours on the Indian line. They patrolled between a series of small forts, mostly fortified homes or blockhouses five to ten miles apart, stretching along the foot of the eastern edge of the Blue Ridge Mountains. Some, like Jacob, made clandestine trips deep into the mountains to spy on Indian trails and camps.

In the early 1760s, the mountain-ridge boundary had been established by a treaty with the Cherokees, angry because continued excursions by white men into their territory had pushed them out of the piedmont. The British colonial government agreed that white settlers would stay east of the mountains. It was an agreement ignored by both sides. Many settlers did not know about any agreement or, if they did, did not care about it and crossed over to hunt and trap. Some even foolishly tried to homestead. Indians came east of the mountains to trade, hunt, or raid farms they felt were too close for comfort. Murder by both sides was commonplace.

Since 1775, when open rebellion broke out in the American colonies, British sympathizers had been furnishing the Indians with weapons and military advisors. Along the frontier from Virginia down into Georgia, they encouraged Indian attacks on the remote homes. However, most Cherokee had no idea who was Whig or Tory among the whites; all looked alike to them; all were targets.

Over the past four years, since age sixteen, Jacob had served short stints in the militia, defending against Indian raids. He preferred the solitary wilderness duty to getting involved with the war against England.

This current tour completed, he was making a long walk home. Without any further delays, he should be with his parents by nightfall. It would please his mother immensely if he came home with a clean body. So with the inviting pool on a hot day in the waning summer, he stopped to wash his shirt and shave his unkempt beard.

As Jacob scraped the last of the long hairs from his face, he tensed. Through his warrior senses, he felt someone looking at him. He carefully washed the hairs from his knife, dried the blade on his buckskin trousers, and placed the knife beside his shot bag. With the suddenness of a lightning strike, he lurched into a swift roll, grabbing and cocking the rifle during the maneuver. His Pennsylvania long rifle was always loaded and primed. As he rolled into a little shelter behind a small boulder, he aimed his flintlock and shouted, "Show yourself or die!"

The quickness of the man's movements startled Rachel, as did hearing his warning and the cocking of the rifle. Seeing the weapon pointed straight at her, she pleaded loudly, "Please, sir, don't shoot me! Please. I mean no harm."

The sound of a girl surprised Jacob. He yelled. "Come out so I can see you."

She slowly stood up from behind the bush, her arms outstretched at her sides, and walked a few feet toward Jacob.

"Who's with you? Why are you spying on me?" Jacob asked, still lying in his defensive position, leery of possible danger.

"I'm Rachel Pearson. Nobody's with me. I live just over the hill. I wasn't sneaking up on you; I was looking for my cow." Then feeling bolder, she asked in a demanding tone, "And just who are you, and what are you doing on my family's land?"

Jacob relaxed a little and sat up, but still held his rifle at the ready. "I'm Jacob Godley from up on Second Broad River. Don't mean to trespass. I've done my time on Indian line duty and heading home. This trail leads to the Gilbert Town road. Our place is a half-day walk north of Gilbert Town."

Looking at his scars on his back, she asked, "How did you get your back all cut up?"

"You are a sassy thing, aren't you? If you must know, I got it wrestling a bear."

"Who won?"

"Well, I'm here." Jacob answered jokingly as he placed his belt and knife around him. He began looking at Rachel in a different light. He had not seen a girl so lovely in months. He found himself warming to her and her to him when they heard the faint crack of gunfire. Jacob tensed, but Rachel said, "That's probably my pa or brother shooting a critter for supper."

Jacob sat down and began lacing up his knee-high moccasins. Habit made him always to be ready for anything. Rachel sat beside him in an unladylike position, bunching her dress up between her knees as she put her feet into the creek. She was fascinated by this young Indian fighter and felt a kindred spirit with him.

They fell into conversation like old friends, talking about their families, their likes and dislikes. He amazed her with descriptions of the high, granite cliffs and the soaring waterfall in the foreboding Broad River gorge less than a day's walk west of them and of the vast wilderness he had seen over the mountains.

He became mesmerized by the sparkle in her bright, brown eyes and the freckles that enhanced her smile. Her long, auburn hair had natural curls that flowed down over her shoulders. A free spirit, she was not wearing a mob cap normally worn by women who felt it proper to keep something over their head. She wore a plain, unadorned apron over her dress.

Forgetting his own desires to reach home before dark, Jacob asked if her folks would be worried about her being away so long. "I haven't heard Mama yell for me yet." Rachel laughed. "You can hear her screech a mile off when she wants us young'uns."

She chatted about neighbors living along the creek, Colonel Hampton's grist mill about four miles upstream, McFadden's Fort nearby that had been burned last year by Tory night riders, and the farm closest to theirs. She turned to point in the direction of the Foreman place when they saw black smoke billowing above the trees. "That smoke is coming from our house!" she screamed.

Rachel jumped to her feet, keeping her dress and apron bunched in her hands so her legs would be free for the long strides needed to run unencumbered through the woods, and raced up the hill toward boiling, black smoke. Jacob quickly gathered his belongings and sprinted after her, impressed with her swiftness.

When he passed over the crest of the hill, Jacob saw Rachel leap across a rail fence without breaking stride. As he got to the fence that surrounded a long, sloping meadow down to the Pearson home, Jacob stopped and quickly accessed the scene. A log house was engulfed in flames. Only a few feet from the fire, a woman was kneeling over a man's body, trying to pull it away from the flames. Both were bloody. Beyond the couple, a shirtless body was hanging from a tree.

Jacob paused and took time to carefully scan the area, looking for actual and potential threats. He saw Rachel running across the field toward the couple on the ground, but he could see no one else. Still, he cocked his rifle and ran to the tree line by the meadow before moving quickly, but cautiously at a crouch, down the forest edge, guided by his survival instincts. By the time he had worked his way down to the track that led to the Pearson home, Rachel was already helping her mother drag the man's body farther away from the fire.

While inspecting the tracks of a dozen or so horses coming and going, movement from the woods beyond the fire caught Jacob's eye. He dropped to one knee and raised his rifle, aiming at the emerging figure. It was a barefooted boy who ran out of the woods yelling, "Mama! Papa!" Jacob lowered the weapon and uncocked it.

The boy stopped short of his mother and father. Grasping that his parents were all bloody and his father deathly still, he seemed to enter a trance, unable to say or do anything.

Jacob rushed to Rachel, who was trying to comfort her mother by brushing away the blood on her face. Mary Pearson was holding her husband's bloody head in her arms, close to her bosom. Rachel stared beyond Jacob, pointed to her brother hanging from the tree and screamed, "Get him down! Get him down, now! Sam, help him."

Satisfied that there was no imminent threat, Jacob went over to Patrick's body whose feet dangled less than eighteen inches off the ground. He called to Rachel's little brother, who was just staring at his sister and parents. "Come here, boy. Help me cut this fellow down."

Sam ran over as Jacob pulled out his knife. Jacob told the boy to climb on his shoulders while he held Patrick's body. Looping his arms around the hanging man, Jacob recoiled from the strong fecal odor caused by bowels relaxed in death.

Sam began crying after he stood on Jacob's shoulders and recognized his brother hanging there. While he sliced through the rope, the boy tried not to look at Patrick's bulging eyes. The cut made, Sam jumped off Jacob's back as Jacob lowered the body gently to the ground. Jacob concluded the assailants were not Indians; Cherokee did not waste rope or time with hangings. They would not have left the woman alive and would have collected the victims' scalps.

As he walked back to Rachel, there was no doubt that her father was dead and her mother hurt badly. He asked about Mary's condition; Rachel answered that the wound looked worse than it was. "Who could have done this?" he asked.

Both Rachel and her brother shook their head, saying they had no idea, but their mother hissed seemingly to no one. "Damned Tories! They were led by Satan's disciple...Rance Miller, that's who!"

Jacob knew many of the Tory names who were active in the region, but not Miller. He walked quickly around the house but could do nothing to stop the fire; it would have to burn itself out.

Since their meeting on the creek, Rachel had transformed from a flirtatious teenager to a serious-minded woman. She took charge of her family's situation and instructed her young brother to run to John Foreman's place about two miles away to get help. Foreman was their closest neighbor.

Mary regained some composure and, like Rachel, assumed the practicality essential for backwoods living. Rachel introduced Jacob to her mother and explained that he had taken care of Patrick's body. Having cried out all her tears, Mary looked at him with sad eyes. She pointed to a tree up in the meadow. "Let's bury them up there under that big maple. Mick always loved to sit up there under that tree. It's so peaceful." Looking at Jacob, she asked, "Will you help us bury them?"

The shadows were getting long, but the heat had not abated much when Jacob completed digging a hole six feet long, four feet wide, and four feet deep. Sweat poured off him as he climbed up from the grave, hoping that the hole would be large enough for the two victims and that the survivors didn't mind the one grave. He had found a spade and pickax in an outbuilding away from the house which now was nothing but charred, smoky embers. He watched Rachel, her mother, and her brother with another man and woman coming up the hill. The man was leading a saddled horse hitched to the sorghum sleigh on which the two bodies lay.

Jacob put his shirt on and tied his hair back with a bandana that he usually wore tight over his head when walking through the woods. He did not have a hat.

As the assemblage arrived at the grave site, the man introduced himself as John Foreman. Jacob noted he had only one arm. Now wasn't the time to ask why. He would learn later that that Foreman lost it in battle three years before at Monmouth Courthouse in New Jersey while fighting with the North Carolina Continentals.

They gently laid the bodies into the ground. Foreman said a few words about the Pearson men being good people and "struck down in their prime by heathen Tory raiders" at such an unfortunate time. He quoted from memory a biblical passage of Daniel, but added his own interpretation: "Our brethren who sleep in the dust of this earth shall awake and shall live forever. But their killers' lives shall be an everlasting horror and disgrace. God, grant no mercy to them."

Foreman's wife, Rebecca, had her arms around Rachel's mother, trying to comfort her. Mary stood stoic, gazing down into the grave where there was no shroud for her dead husband and son. Looking childlike, weak, and vulnerable, Rachel held her brother's hand as Jacob covered the bodies with earth. She did not notice that the cow had wandered back into the field.

The burial complete, Foreman turned to the women and said, "Mary, you and your children will stay with us as long as you like. Sam, go get that cow. We'll take her with us, but we've got to get going. It will be dark before we get home. We'll come back tomorrow and see if we can salvage anything and finish harvesting the sorghum."

Foreman then looked at Jacob. "You are welcome to stay the night too. In these terrible times, we need a good rifleman around."

NEIGHBOR VERSUS NEIGHBOR

3 September 1780

A pair of ungainly oxen strained at their double yoke, goaded by a long cane wielded by fifteen-year-old Wayne Godley. Stretching from the yoke were four chains tied to a large, chestnut tree stump nearly four feet in diameter. Wayne's oldest brother, Robert, was using a locust pole to help pry the stump of the two-hundred-year-old tree from the ground. It was the last obstacle on the new five-acre clearing that would soon be producing barley and corn.

Two other Godley brothers, William and Andrew, were chopping at the root tentacles stubbornly refusing to part from the hard, red clay. They began working on the stump yesterday and had renewed the effort at sunup, and now at midmorning, it looked like the chore would soon be completed. They just hoped the chains would hold, and they would not have to forge more links, a task that would take several hours.

Wayne and Andrew needed to get back to their father's place to help him with the sorghum harvest. Their other brother, Jacob, was away in Indian country, somewhere in the west. He preferred hunting or chasing Indians to doing farm work with the rest of the family.

Since this was Robert's land, and he was not only the oldest, but also the biggest of the brothers, he had the hardest job of leveraging a ten-foot, locust prying pole up under the stump's roots. In one mighty lunge, the beasts finally pulled the stump free of the earth's grasps. Wayne led the animals as the beasts pulled the wooden clump over to the edge of the field where tree debris was piled. All would be burned after the next rain.

They decided to break for the day and to return the oxen to the pasture up near Robert's new clapboard house, built from wood cut last year and sawed into planks. He had been successful with his new farm and new family that now included two youngsters under the age of three.

As they were walking back to the house, four riders trotted up the road toward them. Robert recognized the lead man as his wife's uncle, Aaron Biggerstaff. In addition to owning a large plantation on a knoll above Robertson Creek, he was also one of the leading Tories in the area and a captain of a newly created Loyalist militia company. Robert, a sergeant, and William were among the volunteers in Biggerstaff's command. Neither of the older Godley brothers was anxious to go to war, but each had married into a Tory family, and both were convinced that they would be better off under Crown rule rather than that of an undisciplined and untried government.

The horsemen stopped in front of the Godleys. Biggerstaff dismounted and exchanged quick pleasantries before getting to business. "Boys, we've been called to active service. We muster with other Tryon militia down on the Broad River day after tomorrow. Bring your own rifles, horses, and bedroll. Don't know if they will let us take the horses with us, but Colonel Mills will let us know for sure after he talks to a Colonel Ferguson. He's the British officer who commands our militia.

"But first we have a more urgent problem that needs taken care of." Biggerstaff motioned back to one of the riders. "Martin has just come from the east side of Flint Hill. A bunch of Whigs are plundering our friends there. We got to stop 'em. Get your rifles and horses; we're going there now."

The commander then looked over at Andrew Godley. "Andy, I know you fought the British down near Charles Town and your sympathies probably still lie with the rebels, but when you took a parole, you swore allegiance to the king. I've been ordered to call all of you parolees to service."

Robert looked at his nineteen-year-old brother and joked, "Damn, little brother; now that you've seen the light and are one of us, that means we can't wrestle over politics no more!"

Andrew and Robert almost came to blows earlier in the year when Andy volunteered to go with the Liberty Men to Charles Town after the port city came under British attack.

After less than two months with the Liberty Men, Andrew's detachment lost a skirmish outside of Charles Town when he and several others, including Patrick Pearson, were captured. He accepted a parole in lieu of prison for the duration of the war and was forced to walk barefooted 245 miles back home.

Hearing that he was drafted into the Tory militia shocked Andrew. He told Biggerstaff, "Well, Cap'n, I did take the oath to the king, but I don't like this one bit. As much as it pains me, I will accept my fate and go with you if you let me serve with my brothers. But you got to know, sir, my heart ain't in it."

"Just do your duty, Private Godley, for you are with us for the duration. I hear there will be pay from the British Army, something the rebels don't get," the captain stated.

Andrew and Wayne had ridden double on their father's horse from the family home, a few hours away up the Second Broad River from Robert's farm. Andrew said to their youngest brother, "Looks like you have to walk back home, brother Wayne. Tell the folks what's happened. I'll be back when I can. You tell Papa I didn't volunteer, but I had to keep my word as promised."

"Why can't I go with you?" Wayne pleaded with Biggerstaff. "I can shoot as good as my brothers can, maybe even better."

All of them laughed. Wayne was on the cusp of turning sixteen, but looked younger. Thin and impulsive, he was envious of his brothers' adventures on the Indian fronts over the past few years.

"You ain't going," Robert told Wayne. "You are too little and too young. Besides, somebody's got to help the folks. Who knows when or if Jacob will be back?"

"Jake and Andy both were only sixteen when they joined the militia and went off to fight Indians," Wayne argued. "I'm as big as they were then."

"I like your spunk, boy, but I need experienced men already hardened to fight," Biggerstaff said. "And there are other reasons why you ain't going. We need able-bodied men to stay here to protect folks from rebels and Indians. Besides, your folks would never forgive me for taking four of their boys away to war. It's going to be bad enough with them for having to lose these three."

"Sergeant Godley," Biggerstaff turned and addressed Robert. "Get your section ready. Go by the Peterson place and Winlow's and collect them. I'll gather a couple more men and meet you at the mouth of Cathey's Creek before the sun reaches its highest." With that order, he remounted and rode off, seeking the rest of his command.

"Damn!" William said. "Lucinda is going to be boiling mad." William's wife was known for her sharp tongue. No one doubted that she was the dominant one in that marriage. Her arguments had convinced Will to embrace the Tory cause instead of staying neutral as his father had.

William turned to his younger brother. "Wayne, before going home, go by and tell Lucinda that I've been called to duty."

"I ain't going to have her hollering at me!" Wayne protested. "I'll let Mama tell her. I still don't see why I can't go along with you. I ain't never seen a real fight before."

It was late in the day, the sun about an hour from touching the mountains when Biggerstaff's militia company approached the farmyard of Joshua Clemmons. The small one-room cabin was in a wooded grove, barely visible about a hundred yards' distance from the Salisbury Road. When he saw the gristly scene in the Clemmons front yard, Biggerstaff quietly ordered his men to dismount and advance on foot toward the cabin while he rode behind them into the clearing.

They became more cautious when they saw that Clemmons was unconscious, held more or less erect by a strip of rawhide that tied his arms to a tree limb. His shirt was ripped from his back, which was bleeding from multiple lashes. His wife, Helen, was lying on the ground just a few feet away with her dress torn and body bruised, her breasts clearly visible. The side of her face pressed into the dirt as she sobbed hysterically, her hair badly jumbled with twigs, and abrasions showing through the dirt on her face and arms.

Unaware of the approaching militia, three men came staggering out of the house laughing lustily. They were drunk. The largest had a jug in his hand; the other two were in their mid-teens and were carrying some bedding in their arms. When they saw the armed men approaching, they ran for their weapons leaning against the cabin's side. Robert fired his rifle at the group as he walked. The ball smashed into the musket closest to the assailants. Robert cursed. He should have stopped and taken better aim, but instead of hitting the biggest man, the shot only smashed into the flintlock, but it scared the culprits and forced them to stop.

"Cease and desist this moment," Biggerstaff ordered loudly as he galloped up in front of the trio. He was wearing his gorget, denoting his authority as a military commander. "William, you and Mister Winlow get that man down from the tree and treat his wounds. Andy, look after the woman."

He then turned to the three staggering suspects. "Who are you and what is going on?" Biggerstaff demanded. There were six militia rifles aimed at the barefooted drunkards who were quickly sobering. Robert quickly reloaded his rifle.

The oldest of the three was in his late thirties, with an unkempt beard; yellow, rotting teeth; and a dirty, slouched hat. He tried to stand up straight but had difficulty with his balance. His clothes were torn and dirty. "I'm Richard Pounds," he declared. Pointing to the whipped man being untied and lowered to the ground, he slurred his words as he arrogantly boasted. "And this Tory bastard stole my cow. We been making him pay for it. Now just who the hell are you people?"

"We are the militia established by legal authority in Tryon County to protect the citizenry from blackguards like you," Biggerstaff answered back. "You are under arrest."

"This here's Rutherford County. It ain't Tryon no more, and you goddamn Tories got no rights here," Pounds spat.

When the captain asked about the whipped man, William Godley answered, "It's Josh Clemmons! He and I were on the Indian line together at Montford's Fort. He's a Quaker and never hurt nobody. And Pounds was there too. He's no good."

"I've heard of you, Mister Pounds, and your reputation," Biggerstaff said. He then turned to Robert. "Tie up these three and let's sort this mess out. How's the Clemmons woman doing?"

"She's calming a little, but still hurting," Andrew said.

"Well, get something to cover her, boy," Biggerstaff snapped.

Joshua was barely alive. He had been flayed viciously with a whip. His wife had been beaten and raped. She did not say anything about a sexual assault, although they readily saw the marks on her breasts and arms where she had been brutally squeezed and hit. Bloodstains were splattered on her torn dress.

Andy searched through the ransacked cabin and found a cloak, which he brought outside and wrapped around the woman, who still seemed to be in a daze but had stopped sobbing. He had been to war but had never seen anything like this before. The brutality of the assaults angered and disgusted all of Biggerstaff's men.

Biggerstaff dismounted and bent over to inspect Clemmons's injuries. Peter Winlow, who had a knack for wilderness medicine learned from living with the Cherokee for two years, was down in a marshy area near the house gathering green cattail plants to make a poultice from the honey-colored paste that grew between the plant's young leaves. The jelly would not only ease the pain from Clemmons's back but would also help minimize infection.

Speaking softly, Biggerstaff asked the wounded man what had happened. Joshua said that the Pounds's cow had wandered onto his property earlier in the day. He was getting ready to go see who it belonged to when Pounds and his boys came staggering up, calling them insulting names. It was obvious the three had been drinking whiskey. Pounds had a distillery up on Flint Hill.

"I didn't steal his cow," Joshua protested in a loud whisper and then cried louder, "Helen! What did they do with my wife?"

Andy was trying to wash away the dirt and tears from Helen's face. He whispered softly that she was now with friends and everything would be all right. He turned to her husband and said, "She'll be fine. She ain't in as bad a shape as you."

The militia leader stood up, walked over to the prisoners, and spoke to the bound teenagers. "Who are you two?"

"They's my sister's boys," Pounds answered. "Lazy as hell, they are. They're the ones that played with the woman. Just feeling their manhood; no harm meant."

"Liar!" both boys shouted in unison. The oldest looked up and pleaded to Biggerstaff. "Honest, mister, we didn't touch that woman 'cept to hold her back when she hit Uncle Dick with a stick when he was whupping that cow thief. He's the only one to pleasure himself with her."

When Pounds tried to shout down the boys, Biggerstaff, who was nearly two hundred pounds of hard muscle, smashed his fist into the surly man's face, knocking him over with such force that it dislodged two of his rotting teeth and bloodied his mouth.

Robert walked over to Biggerstaff. "Well, Uncle, what are we going to do with them?"

Not over his anger at Pounds, the captain turned to Robert and said more sternly than he meant, "For the duration, Sergeant, you will address me as Captain. Never call me *uncle* in front of the men again."

"Yes, sir!" whispered Robert.

"As for these vermin, I've seen enough. We'll try them and then hang 'em," Biggerstaff said.

The boys began to whimper. The youngest cried out, "Please, sir, we didn't do nothin'. It was Uncle Dick that beat up on these people."

Pounds snarled at the boys, "Shut up, you sniveling brats!"

"Quiet!" Biggerstaff shouted sharply.

After conferring with Robert and another older member of his company, Biggerstaff ordered that straw be put onto the bottom of Clemmons's two-wheeled cart and that the wounded man be put in it, lying on his stomach. Helen and Winlow would ride in the cart with Joshua and try to keep him as comfortable as possible. "We'll take them to Red Chimneys. Mary and my sister Martha can take care of them."

Biggerstaff's plantation was named Red Chimneys because the two large chimneys anchoring opposite ends of his home consisted of bright red clay packed around stone and wood.

James Withrow had served in the Whig militia under Colonel Andrew Hampton for more than four years. They had been on expeditions together against the Indians, against the British at Charles Town earlier in the year, and, during the past four months, fighting Tory marauders in upper South Carolina. In July the two officers had helped capture Fort Thicketty and fought at Earle's Ford.

Withrow was home only two days when Hampton sent word for him to start patrolling the First and Second Broad River basins for Tory brigands plundering the countryside. Hampton's spies had told him that Ferguson, with British regulars, was just south of the main Broad, probably already in Rutherford County. A Whig home had been torched on Puzzle Creek, and Withrow was trying to pick up the trail of the villains as he led his thirteen men toward Flint Hill.

They were on the narrow wagon track that led toward Ramseur's Mill when he bumped into Biggerstaff's Tory company. The forest was thick along both sides of the road, limiting visibility. The sun was low in the sky, plunging the forest into a false twilight. Leading his company, he rounded a sharp bend and came within 120 feet of Biggerstaff, who was as startled as much as Withrow was in finding themselves so close.

The two men were neighbors and had known each other since Withrow started developing his plantation on Cane Creek four years before. In the early years, they had been good friends who enjoyed spirited political arguments. They served together in Rutherford's expedition to the Smoky Mountains against the Cherokees in 1776. In the past year, however, they drew apart in the rift between Liberty Men and those maintaining strong allegiance to the mother country.

Biggerstaff was the first to raise his right hand, palm open and out. He shouted, "Truce!"

Recognizing the peaceful signal and his former friend, Withrow repeated the gesture and yelled, "Truce!"

As they rode toward each other, lifting their hats in a brief salute, about half the men within each column slid off their horses and took up defensive positions with rifles cocked and half-aimed at their adversaries. They did not share the same trust their commanders had.

"Lower your rifles," Withrow shouted to his men.

Biggerstaff turned and repeated the command to his soldiers, who reluctantly obeyed.

"What are you doing out here, Jim? Thought you were down letting Ferguson kick yours and old man Hampton's arses all over South Carolina," Biggerstaff asked with a thin smile.

"Our time was up, so we came home. Then we heard that a gang of Tory banditti was terrorizing innocent folk around Puzzle Creek. We are trying to run them down. That wouldn't be your boys, would it, Aaron?"

"No sir! We might not see eye to eye politically, Jim, but damn it, you know me better than that. I don't believe in plunder, and I certainly don't make war on women and children," Biggerstaff said indignantly.

He then turned in his saddle and pointed to the Clemmons's cart and the three men tied behind. "We just caught some of your Whig brethren beating a Quaker family nearly to death back on Flint Hill. Come on back and see for yourself."

Withrow rode with his counterpart to the cart. He saw Clemmons' face twisted in pain as he looked up from the straw. Helen and Winlow were applying more cattail jelly on her husband's back.

"That you, Josh?" Withrow asked the wounded man.

Clemmons recognized his former commander. "Yep, Cap'n Withrow. It's me, or what's left. That son-of-a-mangy-bitch Dick Pounds jumped Helen and me. Just about killed us, they did."

Biggerstaff quietly told Withrow the details as they rode on behind the cart to look at the prisoners who were sitting on the ground, their wrists tightly bound. Pounds looked up and recognized Withrow. He staggered to his feet and said, "Glory be, Cap'n. You're a sight for sore eyes. These Tories were getting ready to murder me and my nephews 'cause we are Liberty Men, true as can be. You come to save us, Cap'n?"

"You do that to Josh and his woman?" Withrow demanded.

"Well, sir, he's a dirty Tory. And he took my cow," Pounds answered arrogantly. "Me and the boys had to teach him a lesson. We could've shot him, but felt he just needed a whupping. His woman turned into a banshee and started beating on us with everything she could get her hands on. A wildcat, she is. We had to stop her."

"Did that include violating her?" Withrow asked angrily.

"We didn't do nothin' like that! No sirree, Cap'n. We just wanted to let Tories know they couldn't go 'round stealing stock, that's all," Pounds protested.

"Dick Pounds, you were a scoundrel, a bully, and a coward when you were with me at Fort Montford. And a liar to boot," Withrow said with disgust. "From the looks of things, you haven't changed a bit."

"Now there ain't no call for that," Pounds squawked indignantly. "I been faithful to the liberty cause, I have. And I ain't never turned my back on anyone who believes that way."

Withrow spun his horse around and told Biggerstaff, "He might be a Whig, but he is no friend. He's the worse kind of scoundrel there is."

Riding back to the front of the cart, Withrow recognized William Godley, who also had served with him on the Indian frontier. "How you doing, Will? What do you know about this situation?"

"Evening, Cap'n. We found poor Josh tied up to a tree with his back all cut up from a thrashing by a mean ox-whip. He'd be dead if we hadn't got there in time. His woman was on the ground all beat up and crying with her clothes torn half off. Those three bastards were drunk as sows, plundering the cabin and laughing about it."

Withrow turned to Biggerstaff. "Will here was with me on the Indian line with Pounds and Clemmons. I found him and Josh to be honest, God-fearing men, but Pounds was useless as teats on a boar hog. We had to give him a taste of the whip for meanness and insubordination. I ordered him discharged in disgrace. Are you going to hang 'em?"

"Thought I would try to get some legal authority to try them first," Biggerstaff said. "This is not political, Jim. Those three are criminals of the worse sort. They need hanging."

"Well, hang 'em. Until this war gets out of the area, there's nobody but us to enforce order. Let me discuss it with my boys, but I think we all are in full agreement on this situation," Withrow said. He then asked, "You need us to help string 'em up?"

"Just so nobody gets the wrong idea, I'd appreciate it." Biggerstaff responded. He didn't want the reputation of hanging Whigs for their beliefs. He ordered two of his men to get some rope and find a suitable hanging tree. Withrow called four of his militia to help. The two teenage boys began begging loudly for mercy and to be turned loose.

As they prepared for the hanging, Withrow spotted Andrew Godley looking sheepishly at the ground. "Andy Godley! Now what in tarnation are you doing with this bunch?" Withrow demanded. "I know your two brothers married Tory women and are so henpecked they don't know any better, but you know right from wrong. Hell, boy, you fought with us Liberty Men against the British at Charles Town. You told me you wanted us free of the royal shits."

Biggerstaff and some of his men gave Withrow a hard look for those remarks, and he harshly challenged his neighbor. "You also married into a Tory family, Jim. There is no call for insults and name calling."

"Yeah," the Whig captain shot back, "I did. And I reject their beliefs. My wife knows who rules in our household, so she keeps her mouth shut when it comes to politics. I don't jump sides."

"I swore to stand by the king, Cap'n," Andy responded, "when the British gave me parole. It was that or the prison ship or hanging. You wouldn't want me to go back on my word, would you?"

"It's not right," Withrow spat in disgust and turned as the three prisoners were pushed up on top of three horses. Enemy militiamen joined together in a common cause as they put looped ropes around the necks of Pounds and his nephews.

Although working together, the two militia groups had hard feelings for each other. The militiamen ignored the cries of the boys and the hate-filled glare from Pounds; they were more leery of their armed adversaries.

Biggerstaff called back to Joshua. "You want to see vengeance done, Josh?"

The wounded man struggled to push himself up enough to look over the cart sides. His wife buried her face into the straw and cried, "I never want to see 'em again, except in hell."

The condemned men continued to plead for their lives up until their captors led the animals away with the culprits tied by their neck to the tree. As they slipped from the security of the horses, the men began kicking and struggling, but soon were limp and lifeless.

Withrow turned to Biggerstaff. "Damn it, Aaron, I don't want to have to fight you and those Godley boys. But if you join up with Ferguson and his South Carolina banditti, fight you I will."

"I wouldn't like us fighting either, Jim, but seems we are on a course we cannot escape," Biggerstaff said. "I just hope we don't see each other until after the war is done and we can talk again as friends."

"Keep safe," Withrow said. He signaled his men to remount, and they rode on east. The two militia units wouldn't see each other again until an afternoon five weeks later on a ridge top thirty-one miles to the southeast at a place called Kings Mountain.

The Loyalist Leaders

3 September 1780

That evening as Jacob Godley and the Pearsons walked solemnly to the Fore-man home, Rance Miller arrived at a hunting camp on the side of White Oak Mountain, thirteen miles to the southwest. Miller joined Patrick Fergu-son and a gathering of ten senior officers serving under the British inspector of militia in their first meeting since Lord Cornwallis had issued orders to quell the rebellion in the frontier regions of western North Carolina.

As guest of Colonel Ambrose Mills, the senior militia officer in the west, they dined on roasted beef culled from a local rebel's herd and washed it down with hard cider.

While Miller cut off a chunk of beef from the spit, Ferguson asked for status reports from each his officers. Although only a major in the British Army with a brevet lieutenant colonelcy, Ferguson outranked the militia and provincial colonels and was addressed by all except the British as colonel. His second in command was Abraham DePeyster from a prominent New York family and a veteran provincial officer from the Royal American Volunteers. Although a captain, a provincial officer outranked the militia colonels.

DePeyster reported that most of the South Carolinian militiamen were trained and had been issued British muskets and bayonets, but most were still south of the Pacolet River. "Unfortunately, the recent recruits, including

Colonel Mills's North Carolina militia, need several more weeks of training. They appear to be brave lads, but I'm not confident they can perform as needed on the battlefield. We're waiting on the supply wagons now so we can issue them their muskets, although some brought their own weapons with them."

Turning to Captain Miller, Ferguson asked, "And how did you do in enlisting parolees?"

"We got two to come along voluntarily today and one under arrest," Miller answered. His independent unit was tasked with finding former captured rebels who had been released on parole after they swore allegiance to the Crown in lieu of going to prison or facing the hangman's noose.

"Any problems?"

"Only one, a Pearson boy refused to come with us. When we placed him under arrest, his father went berserk and nearly cut off the arm of one of my men. The old man would have killed him for sure if I hadn't shot him dead. The prisoner broke free and attacked another of my men and tried to take his musket. We hanged him. His ma jumped me like a wild panther and bit my hand…and drew blood!"

Miller raised his hand, wrapped in a bloodstained bandage, to show the others, several of whom snickered aloud. "I had no choice but to hang the boy for violating his parole and assaulting representatives of the king. I ordered their house burned. We confiscated their horse, rifle, and what food we could carry."

"What about the woman? Were there any children around?" Ferguson asked.

"No brats that I saw. The woman has a sore head where I hit her with my pistol, but she's still alive, I guess."

Miller, now at thirty-six years of age, was not always mean-spirited. He once was a devout Anglican Church member and had a prosperous plantation near Wynnsborough, South Carolina. Although outspoken in his Tory beliefs, he was not militant about it and was generally respected by both Whig and Tory neighbors. Nine years before, he married a woman, engaging in stature and demeanor, from one of Charles Town's most prominent families. They were devoted to each other and wanted children, but she had miscarried twice. By late 1775, they believed that they would at last have their first child.

Shortly after the Royal Governor of South Carolina was forced to leave the colony that year, a provisional government was established to rule without England's guidance. A group of young Liberty Men, celebrating their province's newly declared independence, accosted a carriage in which Miller's pregnant wife was riding. The rowdy teenagers were abusive as they teased the mother-to-be of bringing another Tory bastard into the world. They began singing and dancing around her. As their taunts grew louder, they spooked her horse and caused the woman to lose control of the reins. When the runaway carriage reached a high speed, one wheel hit a rock and the vehicle flipped over, throwing Miller's wife into a pile of logs alongside the road. She died two days later from complications created by the forced stillbirth of her six-month-old fetus. Rance Miller would have fathered a son.

Miller's life was shattered. After learning who the miscreants were, he waylaid three of them in separate attacks over a two-day period and stabbed each to death, getting his revenge up close and personal. When it became known who had killed the young men, the local Whig militia went to Miller's plantation to arrest him, but Rance had learned from a neighbor that the militia was coming. He escaped into the forest with his gold coins and strongest horse.

Several of the murdered boys' family members were among the militia. Enraged by Miller's escape, the vigilantes ransacked his house before burning it to the ground. The court confiscated Miller's twenty slaves and sold them at auction to pay restitution to the families of the three men killed by Miller.

Miller fled to Florida where he was commissioned as a lieutenant in Thomas Brown's Kings Rangers. When the British retook Savannah, he organized a Ranger company that created havoc in Georgia's interior and aided in the retaking of Augusta. By mid-1779 and until after the capture of Charles Town, his Rangers conducted guerrilla raids on plantations and rebel stores throughout South Carolina, including making several excursions into the Wynnsbrough area, where he continued to settle old, personal scores. In the most gruesome raid, he killed the brother and father of one of his wife's tormentors and, as a special message to his former neighbors, left their severed heads on spikes in front of the ruins of his old plantation.

After being formally promoted to captain by the British Army, he joined Ferguson in July 1780. Miller's group operated as an autonomous special unit to spread terror and intimidation in the backcountry areas not yet under British control. There were several other irregular units like Miller's, including Bloody Bill Cunningham, whose Bloody Scouts also created a reign of terror with murder and arson on the civilian population throughout upper South Carolina.

Colonel Mills was visibly upset with the news about the Pearson family, but bit his lip for the moment as Ferguson continued with the another officer, "And you, Captain Dunlop, how did your recruiting of parolees go along the Broad and Green Rivers?"

A New Yorker, James Dunlop had fought in numerous battles in the north since 1776 after he was commissioned a captain in the Queen's American Rangers. This was the same Ranger unit created originally by Robert Rogers in the French and Indian War more than twenty years earlier. He still wore the green Ranger uniform.

"We collected three repentant rebels who are honoring their oaths and came with us peaceable. And I picked up four additional volunteers," Dunlop responded.

"But we had one incident. When we approached the McFadden plantation on Mountain Creek, some rebels shot at us from the trees. We returned fire and gave chase, but the waylayers got away. One of my boys was hit in the arm, but nothing serious," Dunlop stated. "No one was at home. As Colonel Mills will tell you, the McFadden menfolk ride with Hampton's renegades and are notorious for badly treating their neighbors who continue to support the king.

"We couldn't let that ambuscade go unpunished. I ordered the place destroyed. We burned the house, crops, and all outbuildings. Their horses were gone, but I did liberate ten head of beef and two sheep."

Dunlop had a reputation of being the most vicious provincial officer serving the British in the Carolinas. He had participated in the capture of Philadelphia, the battle at Brandywine, and the fighting at Monmouth Court House. He hated rebels with a passion and had no tolerance for any of them, military or civilian. At every fight, he was always in the forefront and had the scars that attested to his bravery. Ferguson recruited him for the South Carolina invasion and now used him for the most risky of assignments where gutsy leadership and unquestioned loyalty were essential. Unlike Rance Miller, Ferguson trusted Dunlop.

"Burning houses isn't making us friends," Mills said emphatically. "I realize the McFaddens are traitors to the core, but the Pearson family is well liked in these parts. We are sending the wrong message if we want get people to embrace our cause."

"We have to be judicious in our efforts, gentlemen, but we cannot tolerate armed resistance," Ferguson responded sharply.

The British leader was silent for a few minutes as he savored his cider and then said, "Gentlemen, I have heard all the boasting about how much Loyalist sentiment there is in these parts, but from what I gather, only about a fourth of the population in this area truly support the Crown."

Speaking in unison, the militia officers tried to protest the statement, but Ferguson waved them down as he continued. "I suspect there's no more than a quarter of the people in open rebellion. That means half the people living around here are staying neutral or waiting to see which way the wind blows. It's that half we have to persuade to support us.

"Burning farms and hanging people will not win converts. As Colonel Mills aptly said, it deepens the resolve of the less violent Whigs and their neutral friends. Now, in both of the cases that you two got into today"—Ferguson pointed at Dunlop and Miller—"I find your actions justifiable, but, gentlemen, we must refrain from creating unnecessary hardship on the countryside."

Speaking to the group as a whole, Ferguson continued. "I have no doubt that we will prevail in this expedition. The rebels are a nuisance, but they are no match for the king's trained soldiers. Still, if we can capture or kill their leaders, everyone will be better off. My spies tell me that as we speak, many of them are fleeing over the mountains. Let's make sure that those who don't run away either surrender or die."

Mills stood and addressed the British officer. "I appreciate what you said about stopping unnecessary terror, sir. These are basically good people who live around here. Some are misguided politically, but still they're decent God-fearing folk. They shouldn't all be painted with the same brush as Hampton's rebels. I hope we don't have any more hangings or burnings."

"Colonel Mills." Ferguson turned and faced the Tryon County commander. "All officers are under orders to be tolerant…to a point. Now, I need to know where the local rebels are, including their leader Andrew Hampton. I want his hide before he causes more trouble."

Without waiting for Mills to reply, Ferguson continued. "I understand you have a number of your militia already patrolling about."

"Captain Biggerstaff's company has twenty men up in the Flint Hill area," Mills answered. "Rebel barbarians are on the rampage up there, plundering and killing innocent people. I have another company operating along Sandy Run and the First Broad River, putting down pockets of insurrection there. I've sent additional militiamen who are familiar with the Indian line to look along Cove and Mountain creeks west to the high mountains. Most of them have done Indian line duty there. Colonel Hampton, by the way, lives on Mountain Creek. Captain Dunlop didn't know it, but earlier today, he was within a few miles of Hampton's plantation."

"How can you be sure of your men's loyalty, Colonel?"

"They are men of their word, and most have already proven their worth in battle. Many of the Indian line volunteers don't want to be involved in the war against England. I imagine most will stay neutral or join us, but we will spy them out. My men are true to our cause."

Mills then cleared his throat. "I would like to recommend, Colonel Ferguson, that Biggerstaff's company continues to be mounted. These boys have their own long rifles and good horses. They know how to fight the Indian way. They can be more effective as Rangers than as routine infantry."

"I'll give it consideration when I see what they do in the next few days," Ferguson responded. "I know the rifle has greater accuracy and distance. Perhaps your lads might be useful as scouts, skirmishers, and snipers."

A native of England where his family was prominent, Mills was old for soldiering. At fifty-two, he had been aggressively opposing the revolution since Governor Tryon put down the Alamance Regulators in 1771. Short in stature, he was in good health and could hold his own campaigning with young warriors who were barely shaving. One of the few Anglican Church members in the frontier area dominated by Scots–Irish Presbyterians, he had long been one of the most vocal supporters of the monarch.

Twice over the years, he was arrested by Whigs. In 1776, he was taken to Salisbury, the closest town and more than ninety miles east, where he was jailed for his Tory convictions. Imprisoned only a few weeks, he was released after signing a loyalty oath to the rebel government. Then two years later, he was again captured while raising a five-hundred-man militia in North Carolina to fight for the British in Georgia. He was again sent to Salisbury, but had escaped after his friends attacked the only prison in western North Carolina to liberate him.

Some accused him of helping the Cherokee raid settlers along the frontier, even though he and his son had participated in punitive forays against the Indians. His loyalty to the mother country was influenced by a ninety-thousand-acre land grant that his family received from the king, much of it mountain forests deep within Cherokee territory.

Mills had wanted this meeting with Ferguson to be at his nearby home, Valle Temp, along Green River, only a short distance from where it flows from deep coves on the back side of White Oak Mountain. However, rebel spies were constantly snooping around the area. It could be disastrous if the traitors decided to attack this group of senior officers while they were meeting at his home. Several weeks before, a band of rebels occupied his house for a few days while Mills and his son were serving the British Army down in South Carolina.

Ferguson continued with his orders. "We need to intensify the training for the new militia. Let's bring in as many recruits as you can get over the next couple of days and be vigilant for any rebel threats. All of us are to gather in Gilbert Town five days from now. That will be my new headquarters. I expect all of Tryon County to be back in the fold of His Majesty's government by week's end."

Ferguson stood up, indicating an end to the meeting. "Thank you, Colonel Mills, for your hospitality, good food, and drink."

There was a chorus of "Here! Here!"

Ferguson turned to his two most aggressive captains, "Dunlop, you and Miller patrol in force around Gilbert Town. Colonel Mills, give them a few of your boys to serve as guides. I want the place cleared of all rebel bushwhackers. If you see a large concentration of rebels, back off and report their disposition back to me. Otherwise, be firm in your actions with residents, but you must also be fair. Let's win friends while we destroy our enemy."

"Yes sir!" Dunlop responded. "You can be assured that any waylayers practicing their cowardly trade will taste my sword or swing from the closest tree."

BUILDING A NEW WORLD

3 September 1780

It was well after dark when the Pearson survivors, the Foremans and Jacob Godley arrived at the Foreman home, all exhausted and emotionally spent. Mary Pearson went straight to bed with no thought of food. The others sat on the front porch in the cool of the evening. They ate cornbread and molasses and drank cool milk fetched from the springhouse.

For a long time, no one talked. Then John Foreman told Jacob that he should take one of Foreman's horses at first light and ride to warn the Whig militia of Rance Miller's raid. He felt that Jacob would become lost on the back trails at night. *Who knows what Tories might be lurking around to ambush him?*

He then asked Jacob, "How did you happen to be at the Pearson place this morning?"

☙❧

1759 – 1775

There was a vicious storm bouncing the transatlantic, three-masted schooner the night that Jacob was born. His family was traveling to Philadelphia and the new world in 1759. George and Agatha Godley had bonded themselves for five years to a prosperous farm family near Lancaster, Pennsylvania, as payment for their voyage to the new world, including passage for their two young sons, Robert and William. They hadn't expected Jacob to arrive in the world until after they had reached the colonies, but since he popped out of his mother's womb three days before the ship docked, they were required to pay a few shillings more for his passage.

Ten years later and after five more children, the Godley family had scraped together enough resources to buy a wagon, a pair of oxen, a horse, a milk cow, a rifle, and a few farm implements. Like most self-sufficient men of that era, George made what little furniture and tools that they had. They joined other families in similar circumstances, packed all their processions into a sturdy Conestoga wagon, and migrated south along the Great Wagon Road toward Salisbury, the westernmost town in North Carolina. They had heard of good and plentiful land in the Carolina frontier regions.

Following a rugged Indian trail westward about ninety miles from Salisbury to the headwaters of Second Broad River at the foot of the Blue Ridge Mountains, they found a three-hundred-acre valley of rich top soil that they leased from an absentee landholder still living in England. Once Godley cleared the forest and put the land to use, the land agent would come by each year to collect rent. The Godleys were given two years before the first rent was due.

Their homestead was in the newly created Tryon County, named for the province's royal governor, William Tryon. The frontier county included an area covering the southern piedmont from the Catawba River westward into the Blue Ridge Mountains and the Indian territory beyond, and from the South Carolina border, still not fully defined, northward to the South Mountains. To the Godleys, the county's name was meaningless. The closest communities were Salisbury and Charlotte Town, both a three-day walk east.

George cleared much of the land himself, with the boys helping as they developed in size and strength. Occasionally a neighbor lent a hand. The crowded wagon served as home for several months until a one room, dirt-floor cabin was built. Three years later, when they built a two-story, hewed-log house with a cooking shed out back to replace the cabin, neighbors from up to ten miles away came by to help hew and place the logs and planking used on walls and floors, erect the framing, and nail in the red oak shingles on the roof. Their prosperity at farming enabled them to buy glass window panes brought in from Charles Town. George made the nails in his own forge and carved more than two-hundred wooden pegs to hold the house together.

By 1775, they had a thriving and diversified plantation with cattle, sheep, hogs, geese, apples, corn, flax, sorghum, and grain. A summer and winter garden occupied a small plot near the smokehouse. On a nearby creek flowing from the mountain behind their house, George built a small gristmill. Since they were so close to Cherokee territory, they were constantly on alert for Indian raids. The Godleys had been spared any direct attacks on the family, but occasionally they saw an Indian hunting party cross their land. Once in a while, a horse or cow went missing. Several farms within two hours' walk had been struck more violently by Indian raiders who, on more than one occasion, killed the residents and burned their houses and crops.

George taught his sons to shoot as soon as they could hold a flintlock. He encouraged their roughhousing, much to the consternation of their mother. They competed in knife and hatchet throwing, for the threat of Indians was of far more concern than the open rebellion against Great Britain that they heard was breaking out in the northern colonies. George told his family the rebellion was none of their concern, yet on the first of September 1775, all the family went to a meeting at Brittain Presbyterian Church over on Cane Creek to hear Tory and Whig neighbors argue through the day about what they would do if war came to their part of the Carolinas.

Officially, under British rule, the Presbyterian gathering place could not be called a church and in most communities was identified only as a meeting place. In this remote region, residents openly called it their church as well as the only central gathering place for the region's populace.

"The desire for liberty is already here," Andrew Hampton, one of Tryon County's more prosperous planters and a stalwart of the Whig party, told the crowd. "And I for one am for telling the Royals to sail back home."

At sixty-three years of age, he had the vigor of men half his age and had earned high respect for his campaigns against the Indians.

Both loud jeers and cheers of support clashed as Hampton continued. "Just two weeks ago, as a member of your Committee for Safety, I joined with Colonel John Walker and forty-eight other good men of this county at the Tryon Courthouse. There we signed a resolve that we will no longer be beholden to the Crown. We believe this is the only sane course we can take during these troubling times.

"Our neighboring county of Mecklenburg has also made a similar declaration. These resolves have been sent by express to the congress meeting up in Philadelphia.

"What can a royal governor do for us when he is sitting down in New Bern over three hundred miles away riding around in fancy clothes and carriages? Nothing but levy more taxes on us! We must support our fellow citizens in New England and break the yoke of tyranny dictated from across the Atlantic Ocean."

"Not so fast," James Chitwood demanded. At fifty-seven and with a booming voice to match his dominating stature, Chitwood was five years younger than Hampton. He was also a successful, though smaller, plantation owner. Known for being a man of ill temper, he spoke passionately and was easily heard by all at the outdoor gathering, "The Crown has provided us with stable government, and for the most part they leave us alone. Hell, most of us live so far back in the wilderness that the tax collector can't even find us.

"How can this rebel congress help us? They know nothing of governing. Some of us were born in England, and we are duty-bound to honor the king and our mother country. To speak against the legitimate government is treason. There is no justification for it. There is no forgiveness for it. And, Mister Hampton, we gave you no authority to make such a declaration in our behalf!" he added.

Chitwood now received the jeers and few cheers from the opposing camps.

Hampton signaled the crowd to settle down. "Mister Chitwood, you must make your own decision and live with it. Four years ago, we saw how brutal the Crown smashed a peaceful organization of law-biding citizens down in Alamance County simply because they had concerns about unfair taxes and laws not being enforced. Since the government authority was so far away, they just wanted a little self-regulation. Some of you may have been there."

"I was!" someone from the crowd said in a loud voice.

Another piped up, "Me too."

"Some of the Alamance leaders were hanged because they had the fortitude to stand up to the governor and simply ask for fairness, nothing more. Dozens were shot dead. Murdered where they stood." Hampton's voice had risen to a high pitch, which he now lowered a little. "They were not rebelling against England, yet Governor Tryon, the scoundrel, squashed that citizen movement without mercy and forced many, including several people here today, to flee their homes and make a new life elsewhere.

"That cruel action was only in one small community, but the movement for self-rule started then and today it covers the colonies from Massachusetts all the way to Georgia."

His neighbors listened intently as Hampton continued. "Back in April of this year, our British overseers dissolved the North Carolina Citizens Assembly. That arrogant dictatorship got the people down east so riled up that they stormed the fort where the governor was staying. He was forced to scurry out to sea on a British warship. He will not come back on our shore." Laughing sarcastically, Hampton added, "Now, some of you are still quaking in fear of these English lords. For shame!"

The audience standing out under the shade trees by Brittain Church was about equally split three ways. Some were vocal for independence movement, some solidly for status quo and the remainder, the largest group of all, wanted no part of the political wrangling. Although they wanted to be left alone, many enjoyed watching the verbal bickering. Some of the Quakers left the meeting early, mostly in disgust at the entire situation, endless pontification, and uncivil debate.

Although George Godley was among those who didn't care one way or the other, he stayed. He wanted to know what future his family could expect.

Looking directly at Godley, Hampton acted as a charged-up preacher, reeling in sinners for salvation as he pleaded. "Some of you still live on land taxed both by the royal government and greedy landlords who have never seen this country and who don't know what it is to clear trees, till the land, and fight every day for survival. All they want, all they care about is your last shilling. You, more than any others, should be fighting to get that yoke off your back and lay claim to your own property."

Godley said nothing. Like others at the meeting, he knew that if he was overt in the independence movement and it failed, he and his family would be kicked off the property with nothing. It was not a risk worth taking, even if the rents were becoming more horrendous.

Some of the few members of the Church of England who lived in the county refused to come to the gathering at a Presbyterian church, even though this was a community event more than a religious one. Once a month, a Presbyterian circuit pastor visited for several days of worship, fellowship, and weddings. The royal government only sanctioned the Anglican weddings, which was another bone of contention among the Scots–Irish settlers. Brittain Church provided a social atmosphere for the sparse population to come together and for the militia to muster at the adjacent Fort McGaughey.

A few Anglicans favored rebellion, while most all the Scots–Irish Presbyterians were for independent rule. Animosity between the two faiths added to the tension. Both partisan groups proclaimed that God was on their side and that those who disagreed would burn in hell.

Ambrose Mills, the wealthiest and largest of the landholders in Tryon County and a devoted member of the Anglican Church, was at this session. Quiet during most of the oratory, he succumbed to the urging of his Tory friends and stood before the assembled neighbors, telling them that they needed to pull their energies together to oppose Indian raids instead of insulting their English protector. His short speech was booed by the Liberty Men, the name that the independence craving Whigs gave themselves. Some accused Mills of being in bed with the Cherokee. Others chastised him for backing the royal governor against the Alamance Regulators five years ago.

As the day progressed and whiskey jugs were passed around, the arguments became more strident. By late afternoon, after more of the older men and women drifted away, the Liberty Men began to jostle physically with their adversaries until eventually isolated fistfights evolved into a widespread brawl.

Robert Godley, who was engaged to a Biggerstaff girl from a Tory family, stood with her and her parents. The eldest of the Godley siblings, he reluctantly avoided the fight. William wasn't so bashful and joined the fray until his father cuffed him on the back of the head and pulled his son away. George told the family they were all going home; they would have nothing to do with either side. Visibly disgusted, George proclaimed that it was sinful to be in a melee on church grounds. Although he had been raised an Anglican and his wife a Presbyterian, they tended to act more like Quakers.

Jacob, now fifteen, and his younger brothers were disappointed at having to leave. The young teens were enjoying the excitement, the magnitude of which they had never witnessed before.

A little later that month, as tensions continued to mount between Whigs and Tories, a new Tryon County militia was organized by Hampton and other signers of the Tryon Resolves for the protection of the area's Whig revolutionaries. They called themselves Liberty Men. Some, like Hampton, had commissions first offered by the royal governor. After signing oaths of loyalty to the new government, most had those commissions transferred to the fledging province's Committee of Safety.

Hampton was a lieutenant colonel and his friend Colonel John Walker was the new militia's commander. Both had already served five years with Ambrose Mills as officers in the local Royal militia, sponsored by the British government primarily for protection from raids by the Cherokee. In 1770, Hampton was commissioned a captain by the royal governor and rose in rank over the years.

Walker, equal to Mills in prominence in the county, but the most influential Whig, would soon leave the local militia to become a colonel in a regiment of North Carolina Continentals. He and few other volunteers from the county, mostly landless young men looking for adventure, went north to join General George Washington in his struggles against a growing professional army being reinforced from the mother country.

Robert and William Godley were already part of the local militia and veterans of several jaunts against Indian raiders. They regaled Jacob and the younger boys with their exploits against the Indians and adventures into deep black forests, of climbing mountains reaching beyond the heavens, and of struggling across cascading rivers flowing westward. But they were becoming leery of the officers who seemed more concerned with rebel politics than protecting against a common enemy.

When it came to fighting Indians, Whig and Tory settlers more often than not acted as one. Politics were pushed aside when it came to facing threats from the Cherokees, who considered most white settlers on the frontier fair game in their quest to preserve their ancestral land. However, when life at the isolated frontier forts became dull and boring, many heated arguments erupted between those loyal to the king and those wanting an independent nation.

Although the two older sons did serve on Indian duty, they and the senior Godley flatly rejected Hampton's attempt to recruit them into the militia formed by the rebellious Liberty Men to take the battle for independence to their Tory neighbors. George also told Hampton, and later Ambrose Mills, that he would not join in any Tory militia either; his family wanted to be left alone. There was no justification for neighbors to have such animosity toward each other.

The two oldest boys had different feelings but did not openly defy their father at that time.

CHEROKEE EXPEDITION

Summer 1776

With support from Tory agitators, deadly Indian raids along the frontier intensified during 1776, so much so that the new provincial congress ordered Brigadier General Griffith Rutherford to activate a militia army from throughout western North Carolina for a punitive expedition deep into the western mountains to the heart of the Cherokee country. Similar expeditions were launched in Georgia, South Carolina, and Virginia.

In August 1776, Jacob Godley, now sixteen, joined his two older brothers at the Tryon County muster of all able bodied men at Fort McGaughey near Brittain Church. Their father refused to go and had urged his sons to stay home. Robert was excused from service because he had broken an arm four days before by falling off the roof of the house that he was building for his new bride.

At first, the older brothers told Jacob that he could not go, that he was too young, barely sixteen. Jacob went directly to General Rutherford and pleaded to be included; he wanted to fight, but if need be, he would go as a drover.

"If you have your own gun, we'll take you," Rutherford told the boy.

"I got my flintlock," Jacob answered. His weapon was an old fowling musket loaded with buckshot, but still functional and good for close-in fighting.

Jacob hated farming and would often slip away to hunt, trap game, or explore the forbidden mountains to the west. Excited by the possibility of going even deeper into the high, blue-hazed mountain wilderness, Jacob was intrigued by thought of engaging Indians in deadly combat.

The Tryon militia, with Jacob tagging along blissfully, marched to the headwaters of the Catawba River where they joined other militia at Davidson's Fort. After leaving men behind to rebuild and strengthen the fort, Griffin led more than twenty-four hundred volunteers over Swannanoa Gap into Cherokee country, territory forbidden by treaty to white settlers.

They marched down the Swannanoa River valley that was flanked on the north by the towering and foreboding Black Mountains, forded the wide French Broad River, and followed a trading path up Hominy Creek before crossing the ridge into the Pigeon River valley. They marched through Balsam Gap, blanketed with lofty fir trees, and trudged on to the Tuckasegee River basin deep in the Smoky Mountains before advancing up the Little Tennessee River toward the middle towns of the Cherokee.

Similar armies advanced into Cherokee country from South Carolina and Virginia. The Virginians, including the far northwestern district of North Carolina called Watauga, advanced southward along the western slopes of the Blue Ridge, razing overhill Indian towns along the Holston, French Broad, and Nolichucky rivers.

Each militia group experienced occasional deadly skirmishes, but no major battles. One of the largest nations among the eastern Indians, the Cherokees were scattered from Georgia to Virginia in dozens of autonomous town-states. They had no concentrated warrior band of a size sufficient to repel the large, heavily armed invading armies from the East.

Over the past forty years, smallpox and other white man diseases had taken more lives in the tribe than all their battles of that time, about half the population. Many Cherokees were not in favor of war and the sacrifices that it brought. When the ravages of war threatened their villages, most ran away, seeking refuge in the deep-forested wilderness.

Jacob was thrilled with the adventure as the militia penetrated the remote mountain valleys. He couldn't understand at first why most Cherokee didn't fight and why they abandoned their towns and crops, which the raiders looted and burned. The few Indians who tried to resist were killed or captured to be sold into slavery.

Rutherford's brigade was guided by Catawba Indians, bitter, longtime enemies of the Cherokee. The Catawbas, whose homes were on the river by that name, just south Charlotte Town, told harrowing tales of murder and slavery at the hands of the mountain Indians. One of the piedmont Indians, George Bluebird, took Jacob under his wing early in the trip and taught him how to track and to move stealthily through the lush mountain forests. The Indian guide showed Jacob how to walk parallel to trails so he could avoid being seen, yet not get lost. Jacob learned more about field craft in a few short weeks than he had learned throughout his sixteen years. Although Bluebird was almost as old as Jacob's father, they became inseparable friends.

Jacob's first exposure to a deadly clash with Indians came on a trail by the Tuckasegee River when he was in a squad scouting ahead of the main force. Sneaking along a small stream were two armed men and an Indian woman trying to hide from the invaders. Once detected, the Cherokees tried to surrender. Instead, nine militia rifles fired into them almost at once. Jacob thought the action was murder and was further shocked at the savagery of his fellow whites who ruthlessly scalped their victims. It was his first witness of violent death.

By late September, Rutherford met up with Major Andrew Williamson, whose South Carolinians had encountered little opposition in their punitive raids. Together, the two brigades destroyed every significant Cherokee town in the southeastern Smokey Mountain region. What trophies of war they could not carry, they burned or destroyed. The destructive campaign put to waste the winter storage of corn, dried meat, and fish; tanned hides; pottery and baskets. Burned were all the permanent log dwellings in the middle towns of Cowee, Echoe, Sugartown, Quanassee, Hiwassee, and Nikwasi.

With the days getting shorter and the air more nippy toward the end of September, Rutherford declared his mission a total success and turned his men east to retrace the 150-mile trek back to the civilized foothills before the first snows fell. Since the campaign start, he had received no word from the Virginia expedition against the overhill towns west of the Smokies. Rutherford asked for volunteers to go down the French Broad through hostile territory to the Nolichucky and Holston rivers, find the Virginians, and give them news of the North and South Carolina victories. The patrol was to bring back to Rutherford a full report of the Virginia expedition.

Jacob was among the first of thirty volunteers to step forward. William tried to pull him back, but Jacob argued that he wanted to see where the back rivers flowed. Rutherford refused the married men and those with responsibility for aging parents, ordering them to move back into the ranks. This left only eight volunteers, including Jacob and George Bluebird.

Arthur McFall, a veteran explorer and hunter from the North Fork of the Catawba River, led the small group. At twenty-six and more than six feet tall, the unfashionable bearded McFall struck an imposing figure. He was said to have stared a panther down from a tree with his piercing blue eyes, causing it to slink away rather than suffer McFall's wrath. He was patient but had little tolerance for anyone making unnecessary noise or questioning his decisions. As they made their way westward, McFall taught his men the skills that made good Rangers. Jacob was elated with his on-the-job training.

Bluebird had been a captive of the Cherokee for five years and was familiar with the French Broad region, including the trails that bordered the river to the west of the mountains. McFall also had visited the area with some friendly Cherokees a few years ago on a fur-trading expedition. They took turns guiding the others.

It took three days to walk along the banks of the French Broad River to the mouth of the Dumpling Creek where the group turned north, following a mountainous trail over to the Nolichucky. The trek was, for the most part, uneventful. They ate cold jerky and nuts, refusing to make a fire lest they be detected. Twice they skirted small parties of armed Indians and hid to avoid contact. They passed a cluster of five Indian huts, all burned and abandoned.

On the fifth day, as they approached the Nolichucky and looked downriver, they spotted flumes of heavy smoke boiling above the trees some distance away. Gunshots echoed through the trees. They made their way to the site to investigate, moving cautiously first down the southeast side of the Nolichucky and then up a small tributary.

Jacob kept his old musket primed and ready to fire; the shotgun was ideal for short-range work in the dense forest. The others had the long rifles made famous by the Pennsylvania German gun makers. These rifles, with a smaller caliber ball, had three times the range and accuracy of the smoothbore muskets used by the British military and many of the Indians. Unlike the fowling gun, usually only one projectile left the rifle barrel when the trigger was pulled. Jacob figured that most times in the forest, one could not see much more than fifty yards anyway, so his shotgun would be fine. With a half-dozen or so metal scraps crammed down the barrel, he was sure to hit something and cause serious damage.

Approaching the burning village, they spotted Indian women and children running in terror through the forest about them. They had found Colonel William Christian's expedition.

Jacob saw an armed Indian man, trying to protect his family, stop and shoot toward the attackers only to fall from a rifle ball. Steering clear of the fighting, Jacob and his group crawled through dense laurel toward the conflagration. As they neared the burning structures, they saw other frontiersmen running through the village, some with lighted torches, some shooting at the fleeing natives, and others methodically destroying anything useful. Jacob watched in horrid fascination as a white attacker picked up an axe abandoned next to a burning hut and severed the head from an old Cherokee woman who was on her knees singing a sad chant of death. Someone shouted, "Quit that senseless killing!"

As the excitement died down, McFall called out to the militia group nearest him and identified his company to avoid being killed by fighters who usually shot first and asked questions later. Keeping their weapons cradled and pointing downward as they walked into the soot-smeared frontiersmen, Jacob tried to remain calm as McFall explained their mission. Commander of the Washington District militia company was thirty-one-year-old Captain John Sevier, whose face and clothes were covered with sweat and dirt. The knife and hatchet in his belt dripped blood. He was quite happy with the morning's work.

"We sure got those heathens a-running, Jack," one of his militiamen yelled. Sevier was called Chucky Jack by his men because of his fondness for the Nolichucky River valley, a favorite hunting area and a place he said he wanted to develop for his own home as soon as the Indian troubles were past.

Sevier had twenty-two men with him; the overmountain men's main force was down beyond the confluence of the French Broad and Holston, another two days' walk. After McFall relayed Rutherford's message, Sevier said the overhill expedition had also been successful and they were going after more towns further down the Tennessee River on the western side of the Smoky Mountains. Christian's brigade had killed more than a dozen Indians and three of their Tory advisors. Another white Indian ally was hanged on the spot, despite having surrendered without a fight and begging for mercy.

The Sevier party was escorting several wounded and sick men back to Fort Watauga when they discovered this small out-of-the-way Indian village.

As trophies for their work, they had ten captured horses heavily laden with food supplies, tools, hides and other valuables taken from various towns that they had destroyed.

Sevier scribbled a message for a rider to take to Colonel Christian reporting the day's successful raid. McFall offered to go with the messenger and take General Rutherford's report directly to the Virginia leader. After selecting two men from his patrol to go with him, McFall ordered Jacob and the others to proceed with Sevier's men back to the Watauga. McFall would rejoin them within a week or so and then lead General Rutherford's men back home.

When Sevier's group camped that evening, Jacob developed a friendship with Matthew McCracken, a boy his own age and who had accompanied his father on the expedition. Young McCracken criticized Jacob for bringing a smoothbore fowler on a fighting expedition. He talked into the dark about the virtues of the long rifles made by his father, the Watauga settlement's leading gunsmith. They talked into the night about the Indian raids on both sides of the mountains, about their families and their prowess as hunters. Then exhaustion overtook them, and they slept on the ground.

The October air was cold, waking Jacob before sunrise. He had only his hunting shirt over a linen shirt his mother had made just before he left home. He also had a piece of sailcloth that he used as a shelter and wrap. It was not much good at providing insulation from the cold ground or for keeping dry, but it was better than nothing.

He was grateful that Bluebird had given him knee-high, deerskin moccasins taken from a dead Indian back near Nikwasi, a Cherokee town on the Little Tennessee. The Indian footwear was warmer and more comfortable than the old shoes that he had at the start of the campaign, but which had torn apart back on the rock strewn trails before he had reached the Tuckasegee River. For more than a week, Jacob had to walk barefooted before his friend confiscated the more durable footwear.

In the emerging half-light of predawn, Jacob rolled up his bed roll and tied it for carrying over his shoulders. He did not stand until after careful searching his grey-shrouded surroundings. He slipped his powder horn, shot bag, and possibles bag over his shoulder and picked up his musket, ensuring that it was primed. With weapon in hand, he crept over to a small branch and then followed it upstream beyond where the horses drank and pissed, before bending down, washing the sleep from his eyes, and drinking deeply from a clear pool. The cold water was erasing the last vestiges of sleep when he heard shouts and shooting in the main camp.

Jacob double-checked the flint and prime in his musket as he began running toward the noise. Rushing into the clearing where he had slept, he saw a Cherokee warrior knock down Amos McCracken and then raise a war club to smash the gunsmith's head. Jacob barely slowed as he half aimed and fired only twenty feet away from the attacker, hitting the Indian in his upper back and head, blowing him away from his intended victim, the upper third of his body shredded into a bloody pulp.

Lying semiconscious in a fetal position a few yards to the left of the senior McCracken was Matthew, suffering from a knife wound. Another Cherokee whooped and grabbed Matthew's hair for a trophy. Before the Indian could slip the knife blade under the boy's scalp, Jacob rushed forward, flipping his musket around to catch hold of the barrel as he ran. Ignoring the barrel's heat, he swung the weapon like a club, smashing the stock into the Indian's head with enough force to crack the wooden stock of the old musket and nearly separate it from the barrel. The blow opened a cavity in the Indian's skull, splattering brains and blood onto Matthew.

Jacob was oblivious to the shouting and shooting around him. In his peripheral view, he saw two more Indians running toward the river. He picked up Amos McCracken's rifle, praying that it was primed for firing. He cocked the hammer, aimed, and pulled the trigger. Despite more than one hundred yards' distance and before the roar from the shot left Jacob's ear, one of the escaping Indians yelled in pain, grasped his shoulder, and then slowed to a staggered trot as the second warrior vanished into the undergrowth.

Trying to make sense of what had just happened, Jacob watched, almost unseeing, as other militiamen ran past him, chasing the surviving Indians who were involved in the predawn raid. He learned later that two militiamen had been killed along with six Indians, including the two he had slain.

"Praise God! Praise God!" Amos McCracken yelled as he saw his son sit up, clutching the bloody shirt where he had just missed a fatal knife plunge.

"And you, young Jacob," Amos said as he got to his feet. "You saved my boy's life! You saved my life! Praise God! Glory Be! You are the David that slew Goliath!"

Off in the distance, they heard more yelling, then three roars from militia rifles. As Captain Sevier ran up to check on the status of the situation, his younger brother Robert, pointing at Jacob, yelled, "Jack, you shoulda seen this wildcat here! He killed two of them bastards while they were trying to take McCracken's hair... and then he shot another at two hundred paces! Ain't seen nothing like it."

Sevier looked over at Amos, "Is that right?"

"Sure is, Captain. That scrawny boy is a natural-born Injun fighter. And a damn good shooter too!"

"How's your lad?" Sevier inquired about the gunsmith's son.

"Looks like he'll live, but he's gonna have a good scar to tell his grand-children about."

Sevier looked now at Jacob who had yet reloaded the rifle and was still trying to comprehend what he had done. The militia captain asked, "Where did you learn to fight like that, boy?"

Jacob had no idea how to answer the question. The enormity of his actions had yet to be understood. Slowly realizing that he had killed his first humans, Jacob answered quietly, "Wrestling my brothers, I guess, Cap'n."

He looked at two militia privates, each rising from an Indian body and waving a bloody scalp taken from Jacob's victims. The older militiaman, toothless Paul Adams, was all smiles as he offered the messy glob of hair, blood, and skin to Jacob, "You earned these, boy. Good trophies. Ain't never seed two Injuns kilt by the same man so fast and then shooting another 'un on the run.

"Don't want 'em," Jacob said as he pushed away the hand carrying the scalps. "Appreciate you offering, but I got no use for things like that."

He had already taken a dislike to the barbaric custom. Jacob also real-ized now that he did not like killing either. Adams, however, was happy to keep the bloody trophies.

The men who were chasing the Indians that ran away from the camp now returned, both carrying blood-crusted scalps. They reported to Sevier, "That'un shot by the lad fell about four hundred paces out. All the fight was out of him 'fore we kilt him for good. Pete shot the other 'un trying to get across the river."

For the rest of the morning, it seemed that every man in the camp came by to congratulate Jacob for his bravery and skill. He was an instant hero, yet embarrassed by all the attention. It felt strange, unreal. Obviously proud of his pupil's abilities in his first battle, George Bluebird told Jacob, "You did the right thing. Otherwise Mister McCracken and his son would surely be dead. Accept what happened. It was good."

In gratitude for saving his and Matthew's life, Amos gave Jacob his own rifle to replace the ruined shotgun. Jacob was touched by the gesture, although, at the time, he did not recognize the weapon as an original Dickert rifle made by the most prominent gunsmith in America.

The militiamen were in jovial spirits as they continued their journey home while escorting captured contraband plus their wounded and sick comrades who were unable to stay with the campaign. The men kept up their good-natured praise of Jacob for his alertness and the feat of downing three Indians just seconds apart. "Sure don't want ye mad at me, boy," said a heavyset man with enormous whiskers and a thick Scottish brogue.

They fed him from their own food supplies, mostly potatoes, corn, and half-cooked meat taken from Indian huts.

After four hours moving along the trail, the column stopped to rest. Jacob felt his bowels growl. Although many of the men would drop their breeches and shit in sight of each other, Jacob wanted to be alone. He followed a little steam along a wooded hillside and then turned up the slope bypassing a chasm through which the stream tumbled. Enjoying the solitude of the forest, he climbed up a steep portion of the mountainside and behind a thicket of rhododendron, where he stripped some of the fat, green leaves from the bush and wadded them in his hand to clean his behind. He leaned his new rife against a beech tree, untied and lowered his breeches, and then squatted to relieve himself.

A black blur and rustling bushes caused Jacob to turn his head. He only saw a glimpse of the black bear that jumped him from behind and swiped him with her huge claws, sending him tumbling down the hill. His breeches were still around his knees as he pushed himself off the ground and tried to crawl away, yelling and slapping ineffectually back at the enraged animal. He screamed as he felt the pain of sharp claws dig into his back a second time and continued to scurry away from the bear, hoping to escape the teeth that had already clamped once into his upper arm. He did not know that this mother bear was fiercely protecting her two cubs that had been asleep only a few feet from Jacob when he had stopped to defecate.

Half erect as he stumbled from the attacking bear, Jacob tripped again and fell over the edge of a deep, rocky bank above the cascading stream bed nearly fourteen feet below. One leg jammed between a large rock and a fallen tree trunk as he cart wheeled down. He heard his leg break before he felt the pain shoot through his body. Fear of the bear was greater than that of any broken bone. Jacob twisted free and fell six more feet into the shallow water below. Struggling to get up again, he saw the bear stand on its hind legs and roar at him from the top of the embankment. Jacob had never been more scared in his life. He was petrified by the animal's scowling order for the human to never trespass her turf again. He tried to lunge further downstream, but fell face forward over the rock-filled streambed, unable to put any weight on his leg.

Panic enveloped Jacob as the first shot exploded just a few feet away from him. Militiamen, hearing his screams, came charging up the hill. They began shooting at the bear as soon as they saw her swatting Jacob over the ledge. He heard still more shots and then felt arms lifting him up, carrying him to the water's edge. He didn't know which pain was worse, the bleeding cuts on his back, the bites on his arm, the broken leg, or the manhandling by his rescuers. Then the pain from all took over as he lost consciousness.

When he regained awareness of his situation, Jacob was lying on his stomach, his shredded, bloodstained shirt wadded in a pile near him. One of Sevier's men was tying two sturdy tree limbs, about an inch and a half in diameter, against his left leg to immobilize a broken bone. Bluebird had made a poultice from the pounded inner bark of a hickory tree and was applying the muck to Jacob's back and arm to stop the bleeding and relieve pain. The Catawban spoke soothing words as he worked. "Don't worry, young Jacob. You'll live. We are fixing your leg and the scratches and bites so they will heal better." With a smile, he added, "You are just too skinny and ornery to make a good meal for that bear."

Jacob heard the laughter of the dozen or so men standing around staring at him, all openly relieved when they saw the boy's eyes open.

The Scotsman who had praised him earlier laughed the loudest and shouted, "Well, laddie, that'll teach ye not to fornicate with our Watauga bears!"

The crowd roared again with laughter.

"Yes siree," another chimed in, "those Cherokee women are just too tame for him. He had to go dancing with a she bear! Boy, don't you know them mountain she bears think flatlanders are just too ugly."

Still another yelled out, "She just got mad at him 'cause his doodle ain't big enough!"

Jacob was in tears from pain and the mortification of the laughing insults. He cried back in a loud protest, "Damn it! I didn't do nothin' to that damn ol' bear!"

Sevier kneeled down next to Jacob. He too was chuckling, but spoke softly. "Calm down, young fella. If the boys weren't a-funning you, it would mean they didn't like you. You have earned their respect. We want you whole again." As he stood, Sevier added a little louder, "Now, you have made enough attention for one day, behave yourself."

Jacob, not knowing if the commander was joking or serious, buried his face in the ground.

A litter was rigged between two horses, one of them Sevier's, to transport Jacob to the McCracken home where he would stay to convalesce. Bluebird told his young friend that he would go see his family and tell them that Jacob was all right. He would also tell them about Jacob's extraordinary bravery in battle.

By November 1776, more than forty Cherokee communities from Georgia to Virginia had been razed and their supporting crops and animals captured or destroyed. Despite the magnitude of the four-pronged operation, casualties from fighting were relatively light. However, the deaths and illness from starvation and disease during the following winter were enormous and severely crippled the proud Cherokee nation. Except for a breakaway group led by Chief Dragging Canoe and a few other renegade warriors bent on revenge, the will of the Cherokee nation to make all out war had, for the most part, evaporated.

In the north, the war for independence was not going well.

COMING OF AGE

1777-1779

My dear family,

I pray this letter finds you in good health and spirits. My broke leg is mended & the bear bites healed up good, but I got scars.

Mr. & Mrs. McCracken took me in & give me real good care. Mrs. McCracken mothers me like her own. She teaches me better reading & writing & figuring numbers. I read some in the Bible near every day.

Mr. McCracken teaches me how to make rifles. He's letting me stay here to learn this trade as long as I earn my keep. I want to make Papa a new rifle.

Their son Matt & me work at the forge. We hunt & wrestle a lot. Matt's got 3 sisters & 2 brothers younger than him. They fuss & fight just like we did at home, mostly all in fun.

It's pretty country here & best of all, there's much game. I got me a new rifle that is true for over 200 paces.

I hope the Tory & Whig bickering has calmed down over there & everybody is getting along. Most folks here think like Papa & hope the war goes away. Some Tories live around here, but mostly they stay low. A few men from here have gone north to join Gen. Washington.

I'm in the militia, but the Indians don't bother us much since we burned their towns last year.

Don't fret about me not coming home right away. It's nice here & I am learning a honest trade.

Your obedient son and brother,
Jacob

After the painstaking task of penning his first letter, Jacob asked John Sevier if it could go with some dispatches that his father, Colonel Valentine Sevier, sent over the mountain every month or so to North Carolina authorities. Sevier said they would get the letter to a Colonel McDowell at Quaker Meadows and perhaps McDowell could forward it on to Jacob's parents. Jacob folded the two-sheet letter into thirds and wrote on the back:

Mr. George Godley
2nd Broad River
Brittian Church Community
Tryon County, No. Car.

The family received the letter four weeks later, delivered by Andrew Hampton himself. He had been visiting McDowell on militia business at McDowell's Quaker Meadows home and agreed to deliver it to the Godleys, even though he was upset with the family for not siding with the cause for independence. "Helping them get a letter from their boy is the neighborly thing to do," he said. He also had heard of the unusual exploits by young Jacob over on the Nolichucky last October and wanted to know more about the Godley boy.

George insisted that Hampton stay over for dinner and listen as Agatha read the letter aloud to the family after the meal. Robert, now married with his own home, was not there. He would not read it for another week. Although disappointed that Jacob had decided to stay over the mountains, the family was pleased to hear that he had recovered from his injuries, was with a loving family, and was learning a trade. The brothers wished there was more in the letter about Indian fighting and the encounter with the bear.

Over the next three years, Jacob grew in size, skill, and self-confidence. He lost his boyish awkwardness, and although he remained slim, his muscles hardened from handling heavy iron around the forge. No one would let him forget his prowess as an Indian fighter, although he continually tried to downplay the episode as an accident.

Except for a few warriors bent on revenge, the Cherokees now wanted peace. Occasionally, however, a white settler would be found murdered in the backcountry or an isolated cabin burned and livestock stolen. The militia was sent to find the culprits and bring them to justice.

In the spring of 1777, Cherokees returned to some of their burned-out villages along the Holston and Nolichucky and rebuilt their homes. There were much fewer of them than before. To demonstrate that they were no longer enemies, the main clan helped the militia find renegades who attacked white settlers, or at least they went through the motions. They did not want a repeat of the 1776 decimation of their homes and crops.

A significant exception was Dragging Canoe and his breakaway band the Chickamauga Cherokee who raided homesteads in the more remote frontier regions claimed by white settlers, but he never was able to mount as strong an offensive as that which occurred in the summer of 1776.

Jacob reported for militia duty more than a dozen times over the next three years, usually for periods of between one and three weeks. As a Ranger, he would often go on solo or two-man patrols deep into the wilderness to discover whether Indian parties were hunting game or plotting attacks on settlers. Like a ghost, he took pains to leave no trace of his travel or allow himself to be seen by adversaries. He perfected the stealth techniques the Catawba warrior George Bluebird had taught him, and quickly became known as one of the best spies and trackers in the Watauga area.

During his first year over the mountains, Jacob met Isaac Shelby and his father, Colonel Evan Shelby. Isaac and John Sevier had been close friends since each had served as a lieutenant under their fathers in the 1774 Dunsmore War against the Shawnee and Mingo Indians out in the far western reaches of Virginia. Both young men proved themselves capable leaders, though a bit brash in their actions as many aggressive young officers tended to be.

When he was not taking supplies to the Continental Army or surveying in the new wilderness called Kentucky, Isaac was a frequent visitor to McCracken's forge and often gave orders for several rifles at a time to resell to his friends. He was a close friend to Daniel Boone and brought the famed explorer by to see Amos McCracken after Boone had lost his trusty rifle and a year's worth of furs to a large Indian hunting party in Cumberland Gap.

The heavily armed Indians "traded" a rusty musket that had seen better days for Boone's well-cared-for Dickert rifle.

Boone stayed with the McCracken family for several days while the gunsmith custom-made a new rifle for the frontiersmen. Jacob and Matthew spent as much time with Boone as the senior McCracken would permit. They were mesmerized by the explorer's many stories. The boys went hunting with Boone one day and received practical lessons about patience, tracking game, and making each shot count.

Amos McCracken was glad to see Boone and his enticing charm leave so that the boys could get back to reality and concentrate on their chores. He was also disappointed that Boone had nothing to pay for the rifle he had made for Boone except a promise to bring some beaver pelts next season. It was a promise never kept. McCracken did get the old, rusty musket that Boone got from the Indians who had waylaid him. The gunsmith melted down the old barrel and made new andirons for his wife's cooking fire.

Jacob's first job at the McCracken forge was chopping wood to make charcoal used to heat iron to a point that it could be molded into gun parts, cooking pots of all sizes, plows, hinges, chains, or tools. He then spent tedious time making rasps, ensuring a uniformity of etched lines in the files. It showed Amos that Jacob had the patience and attention to detail needed to make guns.

Crafting a rifle was no easy job. It usually took two or more days for a trained gun maker to produce a weapon from a bar of wrought iron. First, they had to get the iron, which came from a bloomery located up Gap Creek, a stream that flows into the Watauga below the fort and a few miles from the McCracken homestead. The first time Jacob visited the iron works, he thought they were burning dirt. Men were dumping what looked like dirt and charcoal into the top of a towering rock chimney built into the steep side of the hill. Melting iron flowed from the bottom of the glowing chimney.

Large pans pulled by a stubborn ox skimmed limestone and the reddish-brown Oriskany iron ores from the mountainside surface. After a pan filled, it was emptied on to a pile at the top of a nearby twenty-five-foot-high rock furnace. The iron stone, as they called it, was dumped into the top of the furnace along with limestone and charcoal. Down below, a water wheel powered a large six-foot-long leather bellows that continually forced air into the furnace base, feeding oxygen to the burning charcoal and creating the immense heat needed to smelt the earthen mixture and separate the iron from iron oxide. In a semiliquified state, the iron oozed to the bottom of the furnace and flowed out into sand molds before cooling and hardening into four- to five-foot-long bars of wrought iron, each weighing twenty to twenty-five pounds.

McCracken usually took two pack horses to the bloomery each month or so and bought ten to twenty bars of iron at a time to take back to his forge.

Having worked in the small family forge back on the Godley farm, Jacob knew the basics of blacksmithing and molding iron into implements. He adapted quickly to Amos McCracken's patient instructions and constant admonitions. "Always make sure you are right the first time; then you don't have to redo it. You certainly don't want to get a bad reputation for doing shabby work. Lose your reputation and nobody respects you. Nobody will trust your rifles," he cautioned.

There were three outbuildings used by McCracken for his gun making, all within a hundred yards of his house. These were three-sided sheds, two with large, waist-high open hearths, fixed bellows, and long work benches. Wood-shingled roofs kept rain and snow out of sheds. In each structure, two side-window openings, which could be shuttered in foul weather, were usually kept open for air circulation to cool the workers. A wide array of tools needed for their craft were stored in a protected area at the back of each shed.

Rifle barrels and other large, metal implements were made in the larger shed. The second and smallest shed was for more intricate work, such as cock and trigger mechanisms for weapons, small tools, hinges, and cookware for the kitchen. It had a grinding wheel for knives and axes. The third shop was for woodworking, including carving and finishing rifle stocks and crafting furniture. It had a foot-powered lathe and wood drills.

Jacob did mostly menial tasks during his first year with the McCrackens as he looked over the gunsmith's shoulders and watched each move he made, mesmerized at times by the constant rhythm of the hammer on iron, always exacting in force and striking point. He marveled at how easy it seemed for Amos to hammer out a bar of iron to a four-inch-wide metal strip that was four feet long, and then mold the heated metal, a few inches at a time, around a hardened mandrel, fusing the edges of the flattened iron together to complete the first stage of the rifle barrel. During this process, he shaped the outside of the barrel as an octagon.

When asked by Jacob, "Why eight sides?" Amos replied, "'For one thing, it makes it easier to hold the barrel when we bore it and put in the grooves. For another, it makes the barrel lighter and easier to steady when you are propping it up for a shot. And because that's how they are supposed to look."

The iron had to be kept hot during the process so that it was malleable, yet cool enough to hold its shape. Jacob quickly learned that keeping the charcoal at the right temperature was critical to working iron efficiently. It took Jacob more than thirty tries before he produced his first barrel to the satisfaction of the gunsmith. Through the training process, his skill and his eye improved.

The next phase, called the anneal process, was getting the iron tube ready to bore. Placed into the heated charcoals, the barrel became a dull red before being allowed to cool slowly. Boring the barrel to the desired diameter usually took more than a dozen bits made from water-hardened iron, each slightly larger than the other. They started with the smallest bit first and gradually moved to the larger bits. Amos repeatedly would push the barrel up a wooden carriage as Jacob or Matthew turned the drill crank until the inside of the barrel was smoothly polished and consistent throughout.

The gunsmith constantly checked the barrel for straightness and made precise hammered corrections where needed.

The most crucial part of making a true-shooting rifle, and the most difficult for Jacob, was putting the rifling grooves inside the barrel. The grooves caused the ball to spin when fired, giving the projectile greater accuracy at longer distances. Each groove made one spiral turn in the four-foot length of the barrel. McCracken made some weapons with five rifled grooves, but occasionally he produced the seven-groove weapons that gave more spin and accuracy to the ball, but were more difficult to fabricate.

In the woodworking shop, Jacob learned to make a rifling guide by using a round hardwood pole shaped by a foot-powered lathe. He then took narrow, six-foot oak strips and wrapped each around the four-foot pole, equal distant from the other throughout the spiral. This served as a guide for a cutting blade to create grooves in equal-spaced spirals down the length of the barrel's interior.

By the time a barrel was finished, the original twenty-four pound iron bar weighed less than nine pounds. The remaining iron scraps were melted again and were forged into the flintlock, flash pan, frizzen, trigger, screws, and bands that secure the barrel to the stock.

Jacob enjoyed the more challenging work required for making the metal trigger and hammer parts that produced the sparks that ignited the powder in the barrel. Using smaller hammers, files, and chisels, all made at the McCracken forge, he worked the individual parts to a finish so that each worked with precision. Each rifle had its own set of tools and two bullet molds made exclusively for that gun. The molds ensured that the right size lead ball would be produced to fit perfectly within the barrel.

Matthew was more talented in the woodworking area than Jacob. He enjoyed whittling various sizes of wood into useful objects like furniture, forks, bowls, children's toys, and stocks for the rifles.

McCracken rifle stocks came from walnut wood, which was preferred to maple or hickory because it held up much better in all types of weather and use. There was an abundance of walnut trees on his property. A standard pattern was used to shape the wood into a one-piece stock on to which the metal parts of the rifle were fixed. Once shaped into a rifle stock, the wood was generously treated with linseed oils, hand-rubbed into the grain to preserve the wood and bring out rich walnut tones.

Unlike the German gun makers of Pennsylvania, McCracken did not put any brass or silver ornamentation on the stock. His rifles were simple in design and contained no carved patch box. Most frontiersmen preferred the utilitarian design. It made the rifle cost less and easier to keep clean.

Amos explained to his young apprentices that while the Dickert and other rifles produced in Lancaster, Pennsylvania, were prettier than his weapons, his would match the others in quality, accuracy, and range. "Deer and Indians don't care how fancy the rifle is that kills them. Accuracy is most important," Amos said. "A hunter always has to trust his rife to shoot straight. Nothing else matters."

Each rifle had a fixed rear sight about twelve inches forward of the breech. Dovetailed on top near the barrel opening was a thin forward sight made from silver. This provided a fixed sight for sixty paces; however, by using judgment, the seasoned shooter could assure accuracy from one to two hundred paces and, in some cases, longer distances, much farther than the standard smoothbore musket. The fun part of the process for Jacob and Matthew came after a rifle was assembled. Both fired each weapon six times, twice at sixty spaces, twice at one hundred paces, and twice at two hundred. Then they compared results. They shot from a prone position with the barrel resting in a sturdy Y-shaped tree branch secured in the ground.

If the shot pattern deviated too much, then the weapon went back for more work. Some time it took only a minor correction, but occasionally, it required redoing the entire barrel. Thanks to the precision and attention to detail drilled into the boys, such rejections were rare, except in the first two years of Jacob's apprenticeship. Only after the rifle proved its accuracy during the test firing would the gunsmith etch his initials into the barrel. No unsigned barrel left the McCracken shop.

It was during the test-shooting phase that they determined the correct amount of black powder needed for each weapon. A measured cup was then carved from a horn tip to make it easy for the shooter to have the ideal charge poured into his flintlock muzzle.

The shooters placed strips of cloth, lathered in animal grease and cut into small squares, over the barrel opening after the powder was poured into the weapon. A ball was placed on the patch and inserted into the barrel; the ramrod then pushed the patch and ball down to form a tight seal with the powder. A touch of powder was placed in a pan under the hammer and frizzen. Once the hammer was pulled back into a cocked position, the trigger was pulled, causing the hammer, which had a piece of flint attached, to spring forward, the flint striking the steel frizzen, creating a shower of sparks that ignited a small amount of priming power in a pan just opposite a tiny touch hole at the right rear of the barrel. The resulting flame from the primer shot through the hole and ignited the powder in the barrel, causing it to explode and propel the ball out the muzzle and toward a target.

Most of the McCracken rifles were about .45 caliber, ideal for deer and human targets. A smaller and lighter .35 caliber was made for boys learning to shoot. The smaller shot was better suited for small game like squirrel, raccoon, and rabbit. Occasionally he would make a heavier .60- to .75-caliber rifle specifically for bear and elk hunting. One-fourth of the weapons made by McCracken were smoothbore fowling pieces, shotguns with better than a half-inch-diameter barrel.

Jacob also gained a positive reputation for making knives from the heavy butcher knives to the small patch and folding knives for detailed cutting and carving. For fighting and heavy cutting around a campsite, he favored the larger blades that were thick and strong enough to withstand rugged use, yet still hold their edge. The strength of the blades, Jacob learned, came from mixing powdered charcoal in with molten iron, which was water cooled to produce stronger steel. He honed all of his blades to a razor-sharp edge. For the butcher knives, he usually used deer antlers for the hilt, although some hilts were from walnut or hickory wood. A Godley knife became the envy of all who saw one.

When Jacob completed his first rifle that met the rigid specifications of Amos McCracken, the gunsmith told him it was his. "Your life depends on having a perfect weapon," Amos advised. "You made it, you use it. You live or die by your handiwork."

Jacob used his first-made rifle from then on, rarely taking the prized Dickert out in foul weather, on long overnight hunts, or on militia duty. He was intensely proud of the new weapon and named it Liz in honor of Elizabeth Proctor, a girl who lived about two miles from the gun shop and in the shadow of the battle-scarred Fort Watauga along the Watauga River at Sycamore Shoals.

Jacob met Liz at a monthly militia muster during his first summer in the Watauga settlement. After completion of formal training, usually a half hour or so of drills, the younger militiamen often held a series of competitive events that included marksmanship, hatchet and knife throwing, foot racing, and wrestling. Most times, Jacob took top honors in marksmanship. As he was getting ready for the hatchet throwing, he caught sight of the teenage Proctor girl staring at him. She smiled when he grinned at her, but he felt foolish when he was eliminated in the first round by bouncing the small axe off the target board instead of cutting into it.

The girl, full-bodied at only fifteen, had bright brown eyes and raven hair. She had an easy laugh and a bouncy spirit that caused some of the older women to frown; they felt Liz was no longer a girl, but a woman coming of age and destined for trouble if she did not abandon her flirty style.

Jacob was determined to impress her with his wrestling skill. He had honed those abilities through hours of painful lessons at the hands of his older brothers back across the mountains. Thanks to their aggressive play, he had the quickness and agility to throw men of much greater size. He did that with the muscular Sam Perkins, a twenty-eight-year-old planter from Stony Creek who was a full head taller than Jacob. Perkins rushed at Jacob, hoping to get him in a bear hug and crush him into submission. As the brawny man approached, Jacob dropped to the ground, rolled up under Perkins, trapping the bigger man's legs in between his and tripping him, causing him to fall flat on his face to the howls of laughter from those watching.

Jacob jumped up and strutted with more haughtiness than was his normal, more humble character. He noticed that the young lady was pleased as well. He beamed with pride.

Jacob was confident that he could take his next opponent, Roger Earnest, a likeable lad, although some thought him to be a bit slow. He was younger and smaller than Jacob. However, Jacob didn't know that Roger had four older brothers who delighted in besting him in forced wrestling bouts.

As the two circled each other, looking for an advantage, Jacob kept glancing back toward Liz and then made a quick lunge at Roger. Roger ducked and twisted around, and then using Jacob's momentum to his advantage, flipped Jacob over a hip and flat on his rump, making him now the target of a loud round of laughter. Humiliated, Jacob looked up and saw Elizabeth laughing with the other onlookers. He felt like crawling under a rock as he turned on his belly, burying his face in the grass.

Matt plopped down beside Jacob and laughingly chided him, "If you paid as much attention to Roger as you did that Proctor gal, you could have beaten him."

"The devil with you!" Jacob retorted. "I wasn't looking at no girl."

"Sure, and it snows in July."

After a while, Jacob got up and walked away from the competition area. He leaned back against a beech tree, closed his eyes, and rested his head against the smooth bark, trying to escape into his own world of make-believe. He had begun to doze when startled by a feminine voice.

"Would you like some water?"

Jacob looked up at the shapely silhouette against the sun. She was holding a dripping gourd of water. He took it and mumbled, "Thank you."

"You are that boy who likes to wrestle bears and shoot Indians, aren't you?" she asked. "Mister McCracken's apprentice?"

"Yeah, I work for Mister McCracken, but I don't wrestle bears. In fact, I ain't much at wrestling anything it seems," Jacob said gloomily as he drank from the gourd that had been shaped into a long-handled cup. "I'm Jacob Godley."

When she sat down beside him, Jacob quieted as he recognized her as the girl with whom he had been smitten.

"Well, Mister Godley, my name is Elizabeth Proctor, though most folks call me Liz. My father is the cordwainer in these parts. You do wrestle pretty good when you pay attention to what you are doing."

"What do you mean, pay attention? When I wrestle, I always pay attention, or I get beat."

"Like today?"

A sheepish grin came over his face as he lowered his eyes, "Yes, like today. Guess I was asleep today."

"Or making eyes at me," she said teasingly.

"I'm sorry. I didn't mean to offend you," Jacob sputtered.

"To the contrary, sir," she replied with a coy smile, "I'm flattered that you did."

GOING HOME

1779

From the first time he had talked with her, Jacob used every excuse he could to be near Elizabeth. He spent a few days each month at her house on the pretense of working for her father, including making some chains, cutting tools for shaping leather into shoes, new door hinges, a new hammer, and scores of shoe buckles. Liz and Jacob became comfortable with each other but never were able to steal more than a few moments alone. Usually her younger brother or sister would tag alone, at their parents' insistence, when they went on a walk away from the Proctor home.

One morning over breakfast in the early summer of 1779, Jacob asked Amos McCracken for permission to go help fix up the shed that had collapsed during a freak storm the week before at the Proctor place. "Confound it, boy," McCracken blurted out. "Why don't you just go marry that girl? You spend all your time over there anyway. Let her people feed you."

Jacob blushed and barely muttered, "Well...I...I haven't thought about it. And besides, I have to finish my work for you. I can't think about marrying anyone until I get my own place and can support a wife. Anyways, she might not have me."

All but Jacob laughed as Amos continued his good-natured ribbing. "Don't tell me you haven't thought about marrying that Proctor girl. You sure ain't keeping your mind on the hot iron. Damn, boy, you spend much more time with that gal, and the first thing you know, you'll have her in a family way!"

Jacob jumped up from the table with an unaccustomed anger. "Sir! I resent that! I mean you have been real good to me, Mister McCracken, like a father. I haven't messed up a rifle in months, and you know it, sir. I would never ever do anything untoward to Liz!" He looked at McCracken's wife and pleaded. "Please, ma'am, you know I wouldn't, don't you?"

Ruth McCracken glanced over at her husband and playfully slapped at his arm with a wooden serving spoon, "Amos, stop teasing Jacob. He is a good boy. If he and Elizabeth want to hitch up, I say let them. Though they are a might young."

"I'm nineteen and she's almost eighteen. We're old enough," Jacob protested. "But I got to support her before I can marry her. I can't impose on y'all by bringing her over here, and we shouldn't be staying with her folks either."

A few days later, Liz and Jacob walked along the riverbank as had become their custom most warm Sundays. Nearby, her young brother fished and her sister picked wild flowers. He told her about the conversation with the McCrackens and, for the first time, he described how she was constantly on his mind. "Is that what they call love?" he asked.

"Well it's about time, Jacob Godley," she replied. "You are a nice escort and all, but I need something more than another well-worn shoe around the house. So if you love me, what are you going to do about it?"

Jacob was used to Liz's bluntness. He responded that if she were willing, he would ask her father for her hand. "Before I can marry you, Liz, I got to provide for you. That means getting a place with a plot of land to raise food," he said. "We can't live off your folks or the McCrackens."

He told her that if he continued his apprenticeship for another year, Amos would let Jacob work off payment for a cabin and twenty acres of bottomland that the gunsmith had traded for two rifles and a fowling piece. The log cabin had not been lived in since its former owner abandoned it last spring. It was only one room with a loft and needed some repairs. Jacob offered to take Liz up to see it if she would be his bride. Her response was a shrill "yes" as she wrapped her arms around him and kissed him for the first time since they had met two years before.

Her little sister spied the embrace and, giggling, yelled to her brother, "Come quick, Liz is a-kissin' her feller!"

When walking back to the house, they boldly held hands in public for the first time. Jacob was rehearsing exactly how he would broach the marriage subject with Liz's parents when a rider galloping up the road and interrupted his thoughts. The running horse responded to a yelled "Whoa!" and skidded to a halt in front of the couple.

"To arms, Jake!" Lieutenant Jesse Beam shouted. "There's trouble on the 'Chucky now! Major Sevier wants us Rangers there quick as greased lightning. Get your horse and gun. Let's go."

Jacob's militia commander usually was not excitable. Today, however, he was flush with insistence, and his horse had a heavy lather of sweat. "Got a lot of other things I need to do today, Jesse," Jacob answered. "What in tarnation is so all powerful urgent?"

"Injuns on the war path ag'in. They done burnt a house near the major's plantation," Bean responded hurriedly. "No time to waste. Do your sparking later. Meet me and the rest of the Rangers at the fort. Now kiss her and move it, boy!"

Bean spurred his horse into a turn and rode off to gather more of his men.

Jacob noticed Liz's parents on the front porch staring at the commotion caused by Bean's sudden arrival. He turned to Liz. "I do love you, Liz, but I have to go. We'll talk to your papa when I get back."

"You take care of yourself…and stay away from them she-bears," she said jokingly as tears began to form in her eyes. "I'll be here waiting for you."

She kissed him again quickly before he turned and ran back toward the McCracken home to get his rifle and horse. On the way, he saw Matthew riding toward him with two rifles slung over his shoulder and Jacob's horse carrying his bedroll. Ranger duty demanded swift responses.

There were only ten in the Ranger band as it galloped fourteen miles to John Sevier's new home on the Nolichucky River. More mounted militia joined them along the way. They passed a few volunteers on foot, moving at a steady trot. The sun was fading when they arrived at Sevier's place where about a hundred other men had already gathered and were preparing to go on the offensive.

Sevier called his officers together. Most of the other volunteers crowded around to hear what was happening. There was little formality.

"OK," Sevier said, "we got two problems. First, a bunch of Indians hit the Johnson place downstream on this side of the river this morning. I think they are part of Dragging Canoe's savages. They killed Johnson's six-year-old daughter and badly cut him up before his sons came a-shootin' and ran them off. We got about a dozen of our boys already at Johnson's place, and we need to get more of you there now.

"To make matters worse, that son of a bitch Arthur Grimes and his Tory horse thieves are roaming the countryside causing bad trouble again. They hit the Kilpatrick place yesterday. Grimes was spotted this morning about five miles upstream near the 'Chucky. Lieutenant Beam, you take your Rangers and about ten other mounted militia and go get them. Bring 'em back dead or alive.

"Captain Williams, your company will set up a defense position here. The rest of you men will come with me to the Johnson place. Let's catch and skin some Indian vermin," Sevier ordered.

Riding eastward, Jacob learned that Grimes was a notorious outlaw who had come over the mountains from Tryon County about three years ago. Most of Grimes raids occurred at night and usually while the militia were off chasing Indians. One of Sevier's spies had located the Grimes lair in a secluded cove not far from the treacherous Nolichucky Gorge, a twisting, ten-mile canyon with roaring rapids and flanked by steep, forested walls.

With the spy as a guide, the Rangers moved slowly through the night, carefully traversing a narrow, rocky trail. It was too dark to see the trail from horseback, so they walked and led their animals. A hard rain began shortly before dawn. The heavens emptied with a deluge for several hours, a weather pattern seen off and on for the previous three days. The group, with clothes thoroughly soaked, took refuge under a large rock shelf where someone else had recently camped. Jacob felt the ashes that still had a trace of warmth.

Scouting at first light, they found the washed tracks of six horses leading southeast. Without orders, the men mounted and rode back into the rain, following a trail obvious to experienced trackers. At midmorning, the rain slackened and they spotted wispy white smoke hovering over the trees ahead, clinging to the treetops as though afraid to go higher. The Rangers dismounted, spread into a wide skirmish line with rifles at the ready, and moved stealthily toward the smoke. Grimes and his men were cooking some beef over an open flame protected by an overhanging rock.

The Rangers silently added dry primer to their flintlocks and began to crawl toward secure positions to surround the outlaw gang. Their trap was just short of being ready to spring when Peter Grimes, younger brother of the gang's leader, ventured out to relieve himself. He spotted a Ranger crawling through a laurel thicket, raised his rifle, and shot at the intruder, hitting him with a nonfatal blow in the hips that caused the Ranger to scream out in pain.

"To arms!" Peter shouted, "Militia!"

Arthur Grimes ordered his men to scatter into the forest. Some of the outlaws shot at the moving shadows of creeping Rangers. Grimes took aim and shot Matthew McCracken in the shoulder, then mounted his horse and spurred it past the tightening human noose, ducking a flurry of ball from the startled militia. As others shot at the running fugitives, Jacob was not able to get a clear shot. He ran toward Matthew screaming, "How bad are you hit, Matt?"

"Smashed my shoulder bone, damn it!" Matthew responded. "Get that sum'bitch for me. Shoot him dead!"

Beam shouted to Jacob and the two men next to him to go after Grimes. The remaining Rangers began chasing down the other escapees, leaving two men to look after the wounded.

Heavy rain returned with intensity as Jacob chased Arthur Grimes through the thick forest toward the Nolichucky. He put Matthew out of his mind and concentrated solely on his quarry. The trail was easy to follow, with many bent twigs and visible muddy hoofprints.

Speed was more important than stealth for Grimes now. However, because of the rain, the poor trail conditions, and the steep, rocky terrain, no one could move faster than a walk without risk of slipping and falling. Grimes knew he had to escape or be hanged. He barely took time to stop and reload his rifle.

It took nearly an hour for Grimes and one of his companions to reach an old Indian ford just downstream from where the Nolichucky spews from the gorge. Already the churning, murky water was too swift and deep for a man on foot to wade across. Believing that horses could still get them safely to the other side, Grimes and his follower urged their mounts into the flooded torrent.

As Jacob and the other Ranger broke through the woods into the open space above the river bank, Grimes was pushing his horse toward the far side of the river that threatened to swallow riders and mounts into its roaring grasps. Just over halfway across, the horse carrying Grimes's companion lost its footing and plunged under the flood before it then bucked up out of the water, its rider trying desperately to hold on to both his rifle and reins. The frightened horse whinnied in panic as it reared, causing its rider to lose his grip and slip into the frothy brown roil. Grimes had all he could do to keep his own horse on course and under control without looking back or trying to help.

Jacob saw the hapless man carried away by the swift current. Still clutching his rifle, the outlaw bobbed above and under the water several times before disappearing under a massive standing wave. Looking back across the river, Jacob saw Grimes splash into a calm eddy and gingerly step his horse toward the shore. The two Rangers jumped from their mounts and took aim. Jacob's rifle misfired; the powder in the flash pan was too damp. The other shooter missed his mark as Grimes dodged jerkingly before losing himself into the hidden folds of the rain-clogged forest.

The Rangers looked eagerly at the menacing river, debating whether to risk their lives to keep up the chase. Seeing the fallen horse roll over in the angry river as it washed downstream, they decided not to try.

Dejected, the Rangers retraced their steps and met up with three other militia and the two wounded Rangers. Jacob inspected Matthew's wound as the others sought dry wood to start a fire. A lead ball had smashed into the bone and ricocheted out of Matthew's body, leaving two gaping holes. The other man only had a grazing wound along his hip, and although it still hurt, he was able to walk and ride.

The rain was only a mist when the rest of the militia arrived. They had in tow two of the Grimes gang, their heads bloody, their arms bound tightly together, and their legs tied under their horses' bellies.

They knew that Grimes would probably take a dangerously steep and rocky trail up the south side of the Nolichucky gorge and then make his way over the mountain to the Catawba valley and the protection of Tory sympathizers. There was no way to follow him at this time. It would be at least two, maybe four, days before the river would be safe to cross.

Wet and disappointed, the Rangers took their prisoners and wounded back to Sevier's plantation. Although they were crestfallen for letting some outlaws escape, Sevier was elated. Two bandits were dead, two captured, and the rest on the way out of the area, therefore, no longer a headache.

Suffering a twisted ankle, the militia commander had just returned home from chasing Indians at the Johnson homestead. He designated four older militiamen to escort the wounded Ranges back to their homes. Jacob asked to go with Matthew, but Sevier replied, "No. Only men hurt or with families go home first."

With the wounded taken care of, his troops rested and their bellies full of roasted groundhog, Sevier called for the magistrate to try the two captured brigands for high crimes. The prisoners pleaded that they were only soldiers for the Crown just doing their duty trying to quell the rebellion. "Reason enough to stretch their necks," one of the militiamen yelled.

Sevier ordered the man to hush. The next morning, Abraham Kilpatrick testified that the two prisoners were among the party that beat him and his wife after bodily throwing them out of their house and stealing their belongings, including their rifle and horse. He added that Grimes and the two accused captives destroyed the family's meager food supplies and left them destitute with nothing to eat.

No one doubted the verdict would be anything but guilty and the sentence of death by hanging. Even the prisoners were resigned to their fate before the trial began. Someone produced two, twelve-foot-long leather straps. The condemned men, their hands still tied behind their backs, were each hoisted onto a saddleless horse, facing the animal's rump. As the strips of rawhide looped around their necks, one asked if he could write a farewell letter to his wife who lived in Salisbury. "Tell us her name. I'll take a message to her myself," one of the executioners laughed, "and then I'll pleasure her more than your sorry arse could ever muster up."

The condemned man spat at the speaker and yelled, "I'll see you with the devil, you rakehell!"

The taunting militiaman snorted and led the two horses away from the tree, leaving their former riders kicking and jerking in the air until life choked from them.

Jacob and his fellow Rangers were emotionless during the hanging, although Jacob wished he never saw another one. As the dead men were cut down from the tree, a company of militia arrived from chasing the Indian marauders further south. They reported killing two but had to give up the chase when the other Indians escaped in canoes down the rain-swollen river. A friendly Cherokee who worked at the Johnson homestead verified the raiders were from Dragging Canoe's Chickamaugas.

Sevier told his militia that Colonel Evan Shelby would be arriving soon with a party of several hundred Virginians to go down to the Chickamauga country and put an end to Dragging Canoe. He asked for volunteers to accompany Shelby. About half agreed to go, but Jacob surprised the officers by refusing to volunteer. He missed Liz and wanted to see how Matthew was doing, but instead, Jacob was ordered to spend the next several days scouting the area for Indians.

Jacob's clothes were muddy, his hair matted and tangled, his body bone tired when he rode up to the Proctor home. He knew he should have gone back to the McCracken house first to clean up and check on Matthew. It had been ten days since he was last at this spot where Liz kissed him good-bye. After the chase and execution had ended on the Nolichucky, she was all that Jacob could think about.

The early summer sun was bright and warm. He expected to see her running out of the house at any moment. Instead, it was her mother, Inez Proctor, dressed in black, who emerged from the house onto the porch. She looked sadly at Jacob as he walked toward her and said, "Howdy, ma'am. Where's Liz?"

Liz's mother broke into tears. "Oh, Jacob! Our Elizabeth is gone!" She sobbed.

"Gone? Where?" he asked, not believing what he had heard.

"Yes, gone. She's…she's dead."

"But…but how? Why? What…what happened?" a bewildered Jacob stammered.

"Damned hornets stung her to death just four days ago," Inez blurted. Choking back tears, she continued. "She must have disturbed their nest and they swarmed her. Stung her so much, we couldn't count all the whelps on her poor body. She tried running away from them, but collapsed down by yonder beech tree. She was dead before we got to her."

Jacob plopped on the ground, dropping his rifle. He hung his head between his legs. "But we were going to marry," he moaned.

"I know, Jacob," Inez said. "Liz told us. She was so happy to be with you. We would have welcomed you into our family. But God saw things different. He took her away. We had to bury her the next day because it was too hot to wait any longer."

Liz's mother moved next to Jacob and put her arms around him as he began to sob aloud, the first time he had cried long and hard since he was seven years old. Zeb Proctor walked over and gently helped Jacob to his feet and said in a slow, solemn manner, "She told me you were going to ask me for her hand but got called to militia duty. Take comfort in knowing that I would have readily granted your wish."

The Proctors led Jacob to a small plot by the tiny church near the fort and the fresh grave with a makeshift, wooden cross and wilted wildflowers strewn about. "We will get a stone marker soon to put there," Zeb said.

"It ain't right," Jacob said, just staring at the mound of dirt as he shaked his head back and forth.

"We can't question's God's judgment," Liz's mother said, rationalizing the event. "She is in heaven with Him now."

"I question His judgment!" Jacob screamed. "She belongs here with me!"

Jacob turned abruptly and tramped off, retrieved his rifle, and began leading his horse to the McCracken home, angry and feeling as though most of his life had drained from him.

Five months after her death, Liz's memory still monopolized much of Jacob's thinking, no matter how much Ruth McCracken and others had tried to console him. When she urged him to find solace in the Bible, he refused. He had not looked at the Good Book since learning of Liz's death. He did not want to. He did not feel that God had played fair with him and Liz.

After the first October frost, he and Matt, whose shoulder had healed, went bear hunting. They found some bear scat that was still soft, probably not more than an hour old. After hobbling the horses, Jacob and Matt tracked the animal and stumbled upon him after only twenty minutes of stalking. The old boar was napping in a sunny clearing, but awakened as Jacob moved into position about fifty yards uphill among some boulders. Sensing danger, the bear stood on his hind legs and roared.

Jacob forgot his fear of bears as he steadied his rifle by bracing it against a tree. When the four-hundred-pound animal dropped onto four legs and charged at him, Jacob fired the large-caliber weapon, hitting the bear in the head. At the same time, Matthew fired his rifle, its ball smacking into the bear's chest.

The three-day trip netted one bear and three deer. The hunters gutted and skinned their prey on-site, then cut the meat into manageable hunks which were wrapped in the animal hides. These were lashed to the rack on a pack horse.

Back at the McCracken place, Jacob and Matt scraped the lingering meaty pieces from the hides and prepared the skins to be cured. The bearskin would make a nice robe for sleeping during winter's bitter-cold nights. The deer hides would make hunting shirts, gloves, trousers, and moccasins. The McCracken girls used big iron cooking pots to render the bear fat into grease to make pemmican. The excess fat would be used for cooking and to help prevent rust from collecting on their weapons and other iron products. The meat was cut into strips and hung in the smokehouse to be cured as jerky.

Engrossed with their work, they did not notice the horse coming toward the house until they heard its rider shout out, "Hello at the house. Where can I find one Jacob Godley?"

Jacob turned to the figure silhouetted against the sun, "And who wants to know?"

"I'm Andrew Godley from Second Broad River of Rutherford County."

"That you, Andy?" Jacob responded as he realized the stranger was his brother who was only a year younger than him, "I hardly recognize you all grown up."

Andrew dropped down from his horse and ran to his brother, wrapping his arms around Jacob in a tight embrace. "You all beefed up too, brother," he exclaimed as he hugged Jacob and spun him around. "You look fit as a fiddle, that you do."

"What brings you over the mountains? How's Mama and Papa and the family?" Jacob asked without pausing for Andrew's responses.

"Mama sent me to fetch you, Jake," Andy said, his face losing its grin and turning serious. "It's Papa. A tree fell on him about a week ago when we were clearing land up on Little Camp Creek. He's hurt bad and can't move about any. He wants to see you before he dies."

"Then he's still alive?" Jack asked. "How's Mama taking it?"

"He was alive five days ago when I left. But he's weak. Mama's strong. You know how she's the rock that holds the family together. She's worried, and that bothers me. Thought it would take longer to find you, but everybody around here knows where the McCrackens live."

Jacob introduced his brother to the McCrackens, who had many questions for Andrew. They wanted to know about the war and about how Tories and Whigs were getting along. They talked on through the night as Jacob started gathering his belongings. His adopted family told Jacob he should go to his father. Amos said, "There will always be a place for you in my home, my shop, and my heart. Come back when you can."

The gunsmith gave Jacob the horse that he had been riding for the past year as an additional payment for his services. Jacob had one extra set of clothing, the leather shoes made by Zeb Proctor, two knives, and a razor he had made for his father. He was wearing his hunting smock over a wool shirt. He also wore deerskin trousers and moccasins. On his belt, he had his shot bag, hatchet, and butcher knife. Around his shoulders, he carried a full powder horn and a possibles bag that contained a ball molds, rifle tools, extra flints, a wedge of lead to be melted into shot, and the militia wife, a rudimentary sewing kit. Around his neck hung a shot board holding six balls for quick access, each wrapped in a greased cloth patch, and a small knife for cutting swatches and other intricate jobs.

With the weather turning bitter, Jacob tied a wool scarf tightly around his head for warmth. Tied to the saddle was a misshapen hat used for protection from the elements and wrapped in an oilcloth was a heavy linsey-woolsey cape that Ruth McCracken had made for him last winter. Lighter than bearskin and almost as warm, it also served as a sleeping robe. Jacob strapped his rifle named for Liz over his shoulders. He carried the Dickert leisurely, but at the ready.

Ruth gave him a sack filled with potatoes, corn bread, bear meat, and pemmican for them to eat on their journey.

Jacob had a tearful goodbye with Ruth and the young girls. Matt looked as if he would tear up when they hugged and wished each other well. "Tell 'Chucky Jack that I'm sorry to leave the militia. Hope I'm back soon," Jacob said.

"You are a good rifle maker, Jacob," Amos told him as he gave his apprentice a firm handshake. "Don't give up the trade. And thank you again for saving Matt and me from them heathen Indians back in seventy-six and not letting those Tory bastards kill him last summer."

With little small talk, they shook hands again before Jacob mounted and waved one last time before he and his brother rode off. They stopped by the Proctor house to say good-bye before heading toward the windswept Yellow Mountain Gap.

After three days of steady travel, the brothers rode up the wagon track by Second Broad River to the Godley home. George Godley was sitting on a bench outside the front door and basking in the sunlight. His arm was in a sling, blooded scabs crisscrossed his face, and propped on a stool, his left leg had two splints that ran from his crotch to his ankle. He smiled and waved as Jacob and Andrew rode up, then yelled, "The prodigal son returneth! Come here, boy!"

"Papa! I thought you was near dead, you old rascal!" Jacob cried as he rushed to his father and put his arms around in a light hug, being careful not to aggravate any of his father's injuries. "It's damn good to see you doing so well."

"Taken up cussing, have you now?" the senior Godley retorted, wincing from the hug that caused pain from three broken ribs that Jacob did not know about. "And you've done grown a head taller and a bunch of new muscles as well. You look good, Jacob. I'm glad you come home. Mighty glad."

Looking over at Andrew, his father said, "Thank you for bringing your brother back, Andy."

Josephine, Jacob's ten-year-old sister, rushed up, hugged Jacob, and then ran around to the back of the house to the cooking shed yelling, "Mama! Mama! Jake's back. Jake and Andy got home."

Agatha ran to her son, tears streaming as she hugged and kissed him, crying. "We have missed you so."

The following Sunday, Robert and William with their wives and children crowded in the Godley home to enjoy the first full gathering of the family since Jacob and William marched off to fight the Cherokees three years before. Jacob described his experiences fighting Indians, making rifles and the ill-fated romance with Liz Proctor.

They told him about how the county was renamed Rutherford in honor of the general and that the home of William Gilbert nearby was the new county seat and called Gilbert Town. Robert snorted. "It's blasphemy to name our county after a rebel. To us, this will be always Tryon County."

William Godley talked about how the Tories and Whigs in the area were still arguing politics except now there were more bloody confrontations, usually at night by banditti, as George called them. Now that the British had retaken most of Georgia, the rhetoric among neighbors of differing philosophies was more strident and, more frequently, downright ugly and violent.

Andy had already told Jacob about the situation during their trek over the mountains when he proudly proclaimed, "I'm a Liberty Man, true and true."

Andy also mentioned that rising tempers sometimes led to murder and arson, although the leaders on both sides were trying to keep peace among the neighbors. "One group of Tories, some said they were led by Mister Chitwood, burned McFadden's Fort," Andy said. "Lucky nobody got hurt that night."

The conversations continued nonstop, ranging over many subjects until Robert mentioned that he was at Aaron Biggerstaff's plantation a few weeks ago and had met a man named Arthur Grimes who had returned from the Nolichucky during the summer after spending a couple of years in the wilderness country. Biggerstaff, a Tory militia leader who lived near Flint Hill, was kin to Robert's wife. Robert said that Grimes impressed him and asked Jacob if, by chance, he had met the Tory.

"Met him?" Jacob exclaimed. "The scoundrel damn near killed my friend Matt and me. If my powder hadn't been damp, he would still be washing down the Nolichucky. If that river hadn't of been in flood, his bones would be dangling from a chestnut tree in 'Chucky Jack's yard. He's a sorry scoundrel...mean to the core."

Taken back by Jacob's harsh response, Robert replied, "Well, he seemed like a nice fellow to me. Captain Biggerstaff talks highly of him. I'm told he has raised a militia company to protect Tory families from rebel ruffians up on the Catawba in Burke County. Why were you shooting at him?"

"Grimes and his gang burned people out of their home, stole their food and horses, and even killed poor folk. We were ordered to capture that assassin, but he got away," Jacob said tersely.

"Don't tell me you have joined the rebels?" William demanded louder and harsher than he had intended.

"Ain't a rebel. Ain't no Tory either. I served the militia to protect folks from Indians and villains like Grimes," Jacob answered, a little more strident than he intended. "And, incidentally, its Tories like that Grimes fellow that gets muskets to the Indians. That's another reason for not joining the Tory cause."

"Most of the militia are rebel sympathizers," Robert spat back. "That's why we had to create our own Loyalist militia."

"What's wrong in wanting liberty from overseas tyrants?" Andrew angrily interjected, staring hard at his two older brothers, both of whom had married into belligerent Tory families.

Lucinda, William's wife, butted in with a shrilled voice, "Being ungrateful for the sovereign's governance is disloyal. It is treasonous talk!"

Jacob now saw why Andrew had told him that William had married a headstrong woman with a sharp tongue and a rabid Tory demeanor.

A loud slap on the table quieted everyone. The family patriarch's face was red with anger as he spoke in a low, but deliberate tone. "Enough! I've said before, and I pray I must never say it again: I will not have political fights in this house or in the presence of Mama or me. I will not stand for this family being torn apart with mean-spirited bickering. No more of it! Is that understood?"

"Yes, sir," most said in quieted unison.

Not humbled by the retort from the senior Godley, Lucinda looked up at the ceiling, rolled her eyes, and then turned to her husband. "William, it's getting late. We must get back to our house." She made no offer to help Agatha clean up from the meal.

"Jake, I meant no disrespect," Robert said. "I'm happy you are home, even with your Whig bent."

"Me too," William added.

With the first snow looming, Jacob helped Andrew and Wayne prepare the family home for winter. They finished clearing trees above Little Camp Creek for a new flax field to be planted in the spring.

George Godley was slow to heal. It was doubtful he would be able to walk again without a crutch. All said that it was a miracle he survived the tree crashing down on him. A few inches either way and his body would have been crushed beyond repair. George replied simply, "It's God's will." Jacob thought it as another irony of fate.

Some seven hundred miles to the north of Second Broad River, a British-led army of eight-thousand men set sail from New York to Savannah, Georgia. Included was an unconventional corps of seasoned American Provincial soldiers led by Patrick Ferguson, late of the Seventy-first Highlanders.

The High Command believed that the British would be welcomed in the southern colonies because of the Crown's successes in Georgia and the strong Tory sentiment that existed in much of the Carolinas. By retaking the Carolinas, the British felt that the rebellion in the North would be more easily crushed.

This new strategy would have a profound impact on the Godley family and the western Carolina frontier.

WAR GETS PERSONAL

January—June 1780

Despite traces of recent snow spotting the field, Jacob and Robert felt warm as they basked in the bright February sun. Jacob had just replaced two broken screws in his brother's rifle. He had used his father's forge to make the new parts and replace the weak ones that were beginning to crumble. "This is shabby workmanship," Jacob said of Robert's rifle as he inspected the rest of the weapon with a critical eye, replaced the flint, and made a few other adjustments.

Since Robert's home was more than two hours away, it had been a month since they last saw each other. As brothers do, they spent time talking about hunting, cleaning pelts and fighting Indians, but adhered to their father's admonishment against politics. As the afternoon wore on, Robert said, "If I'm going to get home before dark, I best be leaving now."

"I'll ride with you, at least until we get to Cane Creek," Jacob said. "It's the first pretty day we've had in near three weeks."

An hour later, as they neared the Walker plantation where Jacob would turn around, they noticed more than a dozen horses tethered in front of the colonel's home up on the hill overlooking the junction of Cane Creek and Second Broad River.

Walker began his prosperous four-hundred-acre plantation twelve years before. A long-time natural leader in the frontier region, he had been commissioned both a colonel and a judge by the royal governor, but when news came about the opening shots of the Revolution fired in Massachusetts, Walker resigned those positions to join the independence movement. After the royal government was forced out of North Carolina, Walker organized Tryon County's Committee of Safety and represented the county in the new Provincial Congress meeting in Hillsborough. Among the first orders of business for the fledgling government was the creation of several regiments to defend against the British. Appointed a captain in the independent state's first regiment, he marched north where he was rapidly promoted to colonel in the Continental Army.

An extended illness had forced Walker to resign his commission and return home just two years ago. Back in the area, he breathed new life into the sagging independence effort that was facing aggressive Tory intimidation throughout the county. As one of the more spirited political leaders in western North Carolina, he was appointed the first clerk of court of the newly created Rutherford County, a position now held by his son Felix.

Three of his sons now were serving with Washington's Continental Army. Another was with a militia unit chasing the notorious Bloody Scouts in South Carolina. Felix had been active with the militia dragoons and fighting Indians in the Nolichucky area where he first met Jacob. He came back east after his sixteen-year-old wife died during a miscarriage. The other Walker boys included William, a lieutenant in the local militia, and two preteen brothers.

When there was a gathering at the Walker home of any size, it meant something significant was brewing. "Let's see what's going on up at Walker's," Robert suggested.

Most of the men standing around the outside of the two-story house were strangers to Jacob, but Robert knew a few of them. Felix Walker yelled good naturedly to them as they rode up to the house, "Hey, Robert, you ol' Tory! What are you doing here? That your bear wrestling brother with you? Y'all joining up with us?"

Jacob winced, wishing people would forget the episode with the bear attack that occurred years ago when he first entered the Watauga region. He could not escape the reputation that all but him appreciated.

Before Robert could answer, Andrew Godley came around from the rear of the group and proudly introduced Jacob to the others present, "That's my brother Jake. He's been fighting Indians with the overmountain militia." Then with his smile fading, he coldly acknowledged his other brother, "Hello, Robert."

"Interesting company you are keeping here, Andy," Robert responded. Then turning back to Felix, he said, "I was on my way home and saw the crowd here. Just being neighborly and wanted to see what was going on. Don't mean to intrude."

As the banter was going on, Colonels Walker and Andrew Hampton walked out on the porch with a young stranger who had an express pouch strapped over his shoulder, his clothing muddy from a hard, two-day journey. Although fifteen years older than Walker, Hampton, who now commanded the county's militia, was more energetic and in much better health than the younger colonel. Hampton announced, "This fellow just brought an express from General Rutherford in Salisbury. He says that the British Army is marching on Charles Town. Things are looking bad down there. I've been ordered to raise a regiment of militia to go down and help South Carolina defend the city. Boys, if we don't stop them redcoats there, they'll be up here by summer."

The men threw a barrage of questions back at Hampton: "How bad is it?" "Charles Town can't fall, can it?" "When do we leave?" "Will we be back in time for spring planting?" "Who's going to pay us?"

Hampton waved the crescendo to quiet. "I can't answer all those questions right now. We will muster at Gilbert Town in two days. Be prepared for at least three months service. Don't expect to be back by plowing time."

The militia leader then noticed Robert and Jacob on their horses at the back of the group, "Why, Mister Robert Godley! Don't tell me you have seen the light?"

"No sir, Mister Hampton." Robert answered, refusing to recognize Hampton's militia rank, "I'm just riding by on the way home and saw all these fellows and wanted to see what's going on. I wish you all safe travel, but I stand true to my beliefs."

Andrew piped up. "Well I'm going with you, Colonel, even if my big brother is a damn Tory!"

"Papa will not approve, Andy," Robert answered sharply. "This isn't a game."

Looking at Jacob, Hampton asked, "You're Jacob Godley, aren't you?"

"Yes, sir."

"I hear you gave good service to the Seviers over in Washington County. They tell me you were brave and resourceful in the Indian campaigns there," Hampton said. "Glad you came back to help your folks. How about your sentiments? Will you go with us or stay neutral like your father?"

"Don't see it as my fight, Colonel." Jacob answered. "That Charles Town is a long way off. I don't believe in interfering with somethin' that ain't bothering me none. Besides, I'm hoping to get back to the Watauga as soon as we get the plowing done here. Now, if Andy is going off with you, it means I got twice the chores at home."

"I understand. We also need militia here at home so the friends of your Tory brothers don't try to take advantage of us being away. And since the Cherokee still pester us now and then, we could use experienced Indian fighters like you working along the frontier forts. Can you or Robert help us there?"

"If the Indians attack around here, I will stand with my neighbors," Robert answered. "I got a new farm, a house not yet finished, and two ankle biters at home. I don't believe in this rebellion, and I can't be going away when there are worse scoundrels than Indians roaming the countryside."

"Well, no personal offense, Robert, but I have to ask you to be on your way. We have Liberty Men business to discuss, and it's best such talk stay among us who are true to the cause," Hampton said in a sterner tone, ignoring Robert's innuendo about Whigs being scoundrels.

"No offense taken, sir," Robert said, lying. "Now, may I have brother Andy for a few moments for family business?"

The three brothers did not talk as they led their horses down the hill from the Walker home to the edge of the creek. Robert sat on trunk of an old chestnut tree that had fallen from a lightning strike several years before. He dropped the reins to his horse and, after Andrew sat beside him, let it wander off to graze. Jacob stood a few feet back with his horse, staying in the waning sunlight and wishing he had brought his cloak to ward off the dropping temperatures.

"Andy, all politics aside," Robert began earnestly, "you can believe what you like, and I still respect you. But going off to war is ridiculous. Mama and Papa are depending on you, and you can't help them by gallivanting down to Charles Town and maybe getting yourself killed. War is serious business; it ain't a game. Please rethink your decision."

"I've been a member of Colonel Hampton's militia for more than a year now, Robert. I believe in him and what he stands for. I will not betray him. I'm going. Nothing you can say will stop me," Andrew angrily responded, raising his voice as he talked. "Besides, I've been on Indian duty. I know what it's like to fight."

"This ain't like mixing with a handful of savages," Robert explained. "The British are going to take Charles Town back, and they will do it with thousands of the best-trained and best-equipeed soldiers in the world. They have cannon and heavy cavalry. It's a different kind of fighting. No backwoods militia can hold a candle to them."

"That's just Tory bragging. I'm no coward and resent you trying to make me one! Robert, I'm going to fight for our liberty even if you are a toady for some king who doesn't give a damn about us," Andrew retorted and turned to Jacob. "Jake, are you taking Robert's side in this?"

Jacob moved a little to escape an encroaching shadow and looked back at his two brothers. "I'm not taking sides, little brother. My druthers are for you not to go, but you are a man and have to make your own decisions. Robert is right; it will not be easy fighting a professional army. It's dangerous, even suicidal, to face other people shooting at you. I would hate to tell Mama or Papa that you got shot or, worse, got killed."

A slow rage grew in Robert after Andy called him a toady. "Look, damn it! You've no call to insult me like that. You should know better," he said harshly. Taking a more reasoning tone, Robert added, "Andy, you are not being fair to Mama and Papa. They need you."

"Well I don't see you and Will doing much to help them!" Andrew spat back.

"We help as we can, but we both have our own places and own families to look after," Robert said.

Andrew jumped up from the log and yelled at Robert. "You have plenty enough time to plunder the countryside with your Tory banditti, all doing coward's work in the dark of night. You ain't man enough to fight straight up like decent folks."

The insult hurt Robert deeply. Anger overcame reason as he hissed back to Andrew. "Do as you will! I wash my hands of you. You are no longer a brother of mine. Rest assured, I will not morn your passing if you fall in battle."

Robert angrily grabbed the reins of his horse and mounted the animal. "I'll see you later, Jacob. Try to knock some sense into this idiot's head before he goes off on a fool's errand. I've had enough of his stupid insolence."

Saying nothing to Jacob, Andy stomped back to the Walker home as Robert spurred his horse to a gallop toward his own place. Neither antagonistic sibling looked back at the other. Jacob slowly remounted and began retracing the wagon trek back home. He was the saddest he had been since hearing that Liz was dead.

In the pasture along Cathey's Creek at Gilbert Town, 143 Rutherford County Liberty Men answered the call to go to the defense of Charles Town. Each provided his own horse, rifle, powder horn, and an elated spirit of embarking on a great adventure. Only four of them had experienced a battlefield confrontation with British redcoats in the North. They had served in the Continental Army and knew the terror of massive fire from hundreds of muskets only a few paces away and the frightening charge by a wall of steel bayonets.

Jacob and fifteen-year-old Wayne were the only Godley family members present to see Andrew muster with the militia. They rode with him to the muster grounds after their parents and said their good-byes at the house, Agatha weeping as she reminded Andrew to keep his body clean, his stomach full, and a watchful eye for danger. George, although still upset that Andrew had decided to be an active participant in the war, gave the son his blessings, "Stay out of harm's way, Andrew. I pray you come home quickly, whole in body and spirit."

As an afterthought, the family patriarch advised, "And for God's sake, always think before you act!"

Looking over Andrew's musket, Jacob said, "This gun is old and its parts rusted. I wouldn't trust it in a fight, brother."

"I have to make do," Andrew replied.

Jacob reached over to the wall and picked up the rifle he had made at McCrackens. "Here, take Liz. She shoots straight and true. I don't want you killed because your gun didn't work right."

"I don't know how to thank you, Jacob," Andy replied, genuinely pleased that his brother would give him such a prized possession. "I'll take good care of it and bring it back in good condition."

On the mustering grounds, Wayne noticed two other boys his age within the militia ranks mounting their horses. He wished he could go too and experience the excitement of battle. His father flatly refused to let him go, saying, "You're too young, and the cause ain't worth dying for."

As Andrew was mounting his own horse to join his company forming up near the center of the meadow, he heard his name called and turned to see his oldest brothers, Robert and William, approaching, neither carrying a weapon. "This ain't a place for Tories," Andy said to them without emotion, yet fearing another unpleasant confrontation.

"We are here as brothers who love you, Andy," Robert said softly.

"You showed what kind of love you had when we last saw each other, Robert. I don't need that," Andy replied testily.

"I was wrong, Andy. I mean, I still don't want you to go, but regardless of what you do, I can never deny you a brother's love. I said some pretty mean things the other day. Now I beg your forgiveness," Robert said.

"We came to wish you well in this foolhardy endeavor. We don't want you hurt or killed," William added.

Andy dismounted and embraced his brothers, unable to say anything as he choked back tears. Jacob spoke to them, "This will make Mama and Papa much happier, knowing that we don't have hate among us."

Andrew turned and mounted his six-year old mare. "Thank all of you. I'll look out for myself. Y'all do the same. I'll be back after we push them redcoats into the sea and make 'em swim all the way back to England."

Jacob turned to Robert and said softly, "I appreciate you swallowing your pride and saying what you did."

"I meant it, Jake. I've been miserable over that fight we had at Walker's. I would never forgive myself if something happened to Andy and I had not made things right between us." Robert said. "Will and I had better go now. There's been more than one mean stare coming at us, and now is not the time to get in a pissing contest with all these hotheaded rebels about."

John Walker called for everyone to quiet down and addressed the militia, praising their bravery and sacrifice for such an "essential and noble cause." His remarks were short. He wished them victory and safe travel, and condemned the British to the gates of hell.

Hampton was not as verbose. He explained their order of march and let them know they would travel from sunup to sundown until they reached Charlotte Town and joined up with the other North Carolina regiments.

In company groups, the militiamen rode eastward across Cathey's Creek. Some turned and waved again to their loved ones and friends. Young boys and yapping dogs ran after the militia column that disappeared into the grey morning fog. While outwardly euphoric at the prospect of glory in battle, many were also uncertain of when or if they would return.

Andrew's return was not as jubilant as his departure. In late April, two months after haughtily riding off to the defense of Charles Town, he came home on foot, slowly plodding up the track by the river and resembling a whipped hound after sparring with a wounded bear. Barefooted, his lower legs and feet dirty and scabby from briar scratches and cuts, his shirt and breeches caked in mud and ripped in several places, he looked like a homeless vagrant. Stooped like an old man, he was emaciated, his blue eyes dull and tired. Long tresses of matted hair fell in dirty tangles around his unshaven face. He was without his rifle, knife, hat, and kit.

Jacob was plowing a field for corn, following an aged ox that was nearly blind, but still trudging along as it had done for years, following commands to keep furrows straight. Stopping at the end of a long row to wipe sweat from his face, Jacob saw, but did not recognize, the lone figure walking slowly and unevenly toward the family home. He maneuvered the ox to the grass and anchored it with the plow before approaching the stranger who was beginning to look vaguely familiar.

It had been twenty-two days since Andrew began his journey home, weathering cold rain, hostile Tories, suspicious Whigs, a pack of wild dogs, hunger, and debilitating disorders from eating rotted food scavenged along the way. Numb to his surroundings, it did not register with him that someone was approaching until he heard a voice call, "Andy! What's wrong, Andy? What's happened to you, boy?"

Looking now at Jacob, Andrew's voice cracked as he tried to put words together, "Tired...bone-tired. Help me."

Jacob led his brother to the front door and called his parents who came running along with Margaret and Josephine, his younger sisters. Wayne was up in the north pasture repairing the split-rail fence. They sat Andrew on a stump as Margaret ran to fetch a pail of water from the spring. "He don't look like he's hurt anywhere, just plumb wore out," George Godley said after running his hands quickly over his son, examining him for injuries.

Agatha took over caring for her son as she ordered Josephine to get Wayne from the field, Jacob to fetch some beef broth from the pot simmering over the cooking coals, and George to stop asking so many fool questions. "Let the poor boy rest and get his wits about him," she scolded as she ministered the open sores on Andrew's body.

After giving him two gourds of water, which he gulped down without pausing, Agatha took a rag and washed his face, arms, legs and feet. She spooned the warm broth into Andrew.

Strength returned slowly to Andrew's body and, when he realized that he was now safe, his anxiety vanished. His mother was caring for him as she always had. Thankfully, he looked up at faces of his family and tried to smile as he said weakly, "Guess war ain't what I thought it would be."

"Just rest, boy. You've got plenty of time later to tell us about it. We're just glad you are home safe," George said and watched as Andrew fell into a deep sleep that lasted more than twelve hours.

With Andrew rested, fed, and now fully alert, chores were put aside as the family listened intently to Andrew telling of the militia expedition to Charles Town. The excitement that embraced the volunteers as they left the foothills going to meet the British eroded quickly into boredom the first day after leaving Gilbert Town. Except for cold, sleet, occasional huzzahs from well-wishers along the way, and a few minor encounters with Tory partisans, the trip to South Carolina's low country was mostly uneventful. After joining other militia at Charlotte Town, they marched nine days before reaching the biggest city in the southern provinces. "There were over a thousand of us, the most people I ever saw in my life in one place," Andrew said with pride. "We looked grand even without uniforms.

"There were some skirmishes with Tory raiders along the way, but I didn't get involved in any of that. I saw Colonel Hampton and General Lillington hang two Tory spies who got caught lurking around our campsite one night. I didn't see any regular soldiers until we were just about in Charles Town. I was on picket duty when some enemy dragoons came riding by just out of rifle range. They were wearing green instead of red coats. Them dragoons are the meanest bunch in the British Army.

"Never did get to see the ocean proper, but I did see the Charles Town harbor. I bet there were a hundred boats there. The town was crowded, people living on top of each other. Wouldn't want to live in a place like that.

"Most of the time we were on the outside of town. We could see the red-coats marching back and forth too. Never got into any fight except one. That was about two or three weeks after we were down there. A lot of our boys had to dig trenches with a bunch of darkies. Ol' Hampton got our company out of that by sending us off to capture some British wagons.

"There were a dozen of us with Cap'n Jim Withrow...he lives up on Cane Creek. We ambushed the wagons. I think I shot one of their officers. They all wore red coats and the one I hit wore a white wig and had yellow fringes at the end of his shoulders. We were doing pretty good after the first volley. When we rushed in with knives and hatchets to take the wagons, another bunch of redcoats came charging down on us. They killed two of us and shot up four others.

"Cap'n Withrow told some of us who weren't hurt to set up a rearguard while he took care of the wounded and got away with the others and a couple of wagons. Us four got captured—me; Pat Pearson, who lives down south of Gilbert Town near Mountain Creek; John Latham from over on Sandy Run; and some other fellow who was from the Yadkin River area.

"I didn't get hurt, but some of the redcoats cuffed us around a bit and acted like they were going to run us through with those big pig stickers they have on their muskets. They took away everything we had and tied our hands and told us to say our prayers 'cause we would have to pay for the three men we killed. We slept on the ground with no blanket, no food, and no water.

"The next morning, they took us to see an officer. He talked real mean... accused us of doing dastardly deeds. Then he gave us three choices...go to a prison ship and rot away until the war was over, be hung for treason, or be paroled and go home. Papa, that was an easy choice. To go free, all we had to do was swear our allegiance to the king and agree not to take up arms against the Crown ever again. If I go back on my oath, it's the hangman's noose."

Looking up at Jacob and his father, he sighed. "That means no more Liberty Men work for me."

From a small leather pouch that he carried around his neck, Andrew pulled a soiled, crumpled paper, written in an elaborate scroll, that showed he was on parole under conditions that would be fatal if not followed.

"They made us give them our shoes, leggings and hats and sent us walking home barefooted. One of them smacked my behind with the flat of his sword. But what hurt the most was the way they just kept laughing at us.

"The Yadkin fellow left us that night. Can't remember his name, but he said he would rather go it alone. The rest of us were able to beg a little food along the way. Most people were afraid of what might happen to them with the redcoats roaming about. We had to beat off a pack of dogs down on the Pacolet River. Damn Tories were everywhere and we had to hide a lot. One Tory gang threatened us, but after a lot of mean talk, they honored our parole.

"I got sick eating a dead raccoon we found and thought I would die. It gave me the flux something awful. I couldn't walk for near a week."

Andrew looked over at Jacob, "I'm sorry I lost your rifle, Jake. It did shoot straight for sure. I'll try to make it up to you."

"That's all right, Andy. It's just an iron tube. I still got my Dickert, and I can always make another rifle. You're home. You're safe. That's all that counts."

Four weeks after Andrew stumbled home, word came that Charles Town had fallen, with most of its uniformed defenders thrown into the prison barges and a large number of militia paroled. The British also took the strategic southwestern outpost at Ninety Six, South Carolina, and the inland town of Camden, giving them control of the southern half of the province. New Loyalist militia units were sprouting up throughout the region to join the victorious army of the English empire. Fence-sitters, even lukewarm Liberty Men, began embracing the victors.

ON THE INDIAN LINE

June 1780

Three riders came to the Godley home in early June with news about the fall of Charles Town and word that some Indians had killed a trapper's wife and daughter near Montford's Fort. "Each family has to provide one able-bodied man to go to the Indian line," Captain Richard Singleton told the Godleys as they sat in front of their house enjoying some green onions, rhubarb, and spring water. "We need to strengthen the frontier all the way from the South Pacolet to Davidson's Fort up near Swannanoa Gap to keep those devils from crossing the mountains and causing more harm."

The senior Godley spoke respectfully, but firmly, "Andrew is on parole from the British and forbidden to bear arms. My boy Wayne is too young. I'm still crippled from being hit by a tree. Jacob serves in the Watauga militia. So we can't help you, but we'll keep a watch out along the head of the river here."

"I understand, Mister Godley," the militia commander said. "But with many of our men still down in South Carolina fighting Tories and the British, we just don't have enough fighting men near the mountains to stop those blamed Indians from killing women folk and young'uns."

Singleton then turned to Jacob. "You're Jacob Godley?"

Jacob nodded, expressionless.

"I hear you know about fighting Indians. By order of the Committee of Safety, I demand that you join us for at least three months' service," Singleton said formally. Then in a pleading tone, he said, "Jacob, we really need you."

Jacob resigned himself to his duty. "I'll go. When do you want me?"

"Now. Get your rifle and kit. You won't need a horse because it's so rugged up there; you can move faster on foot," Singleton said. "I got to gather a few more men, so report to Captain McDonald by nightfall at Fort McGaughey. You'll march with him from there to Montford Cove."

Duty along the Indian line forts was, for the most part, boring except for rare sighting of an Indian and the occasional shooting and knife fighting practice. The line consisted of a series of remote forts located between six and ten miles apart at the foot of the mountains. During his first two weeks, Jacob stood guard at the isolated Montford's Fort for a quarter of each day and kept busy at other times by patrolling the nearby mountains or helping others repair their rifles.

After several weeks of monotonous routine, he volunteered for the Rangers and went on a long, spying mission into Indian territory with two others, including Benjamin Camp whom he had met four years earlier on the Rutherford campaign against the Cherokee. They scouted between all the forts along the line and explored over the mountains for evidence of lurking Indian raiders. They searched the headwaters of Broad River, up through a vast, rugged gorge, heavily forested with hickory trees and flanked by soaring granite cliffs. They climbed a massive chimney rock near the top of one mountain that the Indians considered sacred and found a trail around the cliff to the highest waterfall any of them had ever seen. It wasn't a big stream, but it fell straight down four hundred feet.

After determining that the Broad River gorge was free of Indians, they went to Capshaw's Fort near where White Oak Creek gushes from White Oak Mountain, just south of the Green River. It was a midsize, log stockade located adjacent to a gristmill owned by William Capshaw, an outspoken Tory whose family had suffered deadly Indian attacks a few years before. The Capshaws were closely allied with their neighbor, Colonel Ambrose Mills, whose nearby plantation home overlooked Green River. The four-man garrison at the fort reported no suspicious activity and added that Mills and Essex Capshaw were down in South Carolina somewhere and had not been seen around the fort recently. The fort's defenders reported that Tory activity was increasing and they were concerned for their safety.

During the three weeks that it took to scout the mountain region between Montford's and Earle's Forts, they spent only six nights under roof. The weather had been agreeable; no recent Indian signs detected; and the pace was leisurely. Being in the Rangers was better duty than standing guard in a miserable little out-of-the-way outpost.

Should they find any signs of Indians, two would track them while the other reported to the nearest fort and a flying squad would be sent to reinforce the spies. Like Jacob, the other two Rangers were excellent scouts and well adapted to wilderness living. The three made a competent team.

They came out of the mountains by mid-July, making their way through the rolling hills bordering the Pacolet River. Jacob's patrol orders were to go to Earle's Fort on the Pacolet about five miles east of the mountains before the patrol doubled back to Montford's Fort. This was the home of Colonel John Earle, who currently commanded the frontier forts.

It was dark when they reached the vicinity of Earle's Fort, and they got on a wrong trail in the Pacolet River bottoms. Rather than stumbling around in the dark and risk missing the fort or getting shot by a nervous sentry, they decided to rest until daylight. Besides, they were tired.

Following standard practice, they hid their camp in thick of vegetation that offered natural camouflage. Another tradition that Rangers followed religiously was keeping one man awake and on guard at all times. They never allowed themselves to be lured into a false sense of security, even when close to a fort and having seen no sign of Indians. With Tories about, there was an added threat to their mission.

Jacob was on the midwatch in the early-morning hours when he heard muffled sounds of horses moving through the trees near their hidden nest in a canebrake along the river's edge. He quietly nudged his two companions awake. They awoke instantly at his touch, becoming more guarded as soon as they also heard the faint sounds of a large group trying to move stealthy through the forest. Not knowing if the mounted force of several score riders was Whig or Tory, they decided to follow along at a discreet distance. They did not believe the riders were Cherokee because of the number of horses involved. Indians were almost always on foot and in smaller numbers when making raids beyond the eastern slopes of the Blue Ridge.

Leading the mounted troops was Captain James Dunlop, a long-serving officer of the Queen's American Rangers and one of the most aggressive officers among the American Loyalists serving in the South. He had a dozen of his veteran dragoons along with fifty mounted Tory militia under the command of Colonel Ambrose Mills. They were working from Prince's Fort about seventeen miles to the south on the Tyger River and had heard that a small group of Georgia rebels, running away from the British advances west of Savannah, were camped at Earle's Ford. The day before, the Georgians had bloodied a small Tory force not too far away at Gowen's Fort.

Being from the area, Mills served as a guide and led the Loyalists about a mile upstream of Earle's Ford to cross the Pacolet at a little used and unguarded ford. He assumed that the Whigs might have pickets along the ford at the main road on Bayliss Earle's plantation. Bayliss was the brother of John Earle who lived across the small river and a little more than a mile upstream by the fort that carried his name. By crossing the river where they did between the two Earle plantations, the Loyalists had a much better chance of achieving surprise with their raid.

Dunlop sent scouts ahead on foot to find the Georgian's camp on the north side of Earle's Ford where the flat bottomland began to rise into low hills. Unlike earlier in the evening, the clouds had parted, revealing decent light from a near full moon. Dunlop's scouts saw several tents and a dozen or so figures wrapped in blankets or sailcloth lying along the edge of the wooded upslope. There were no pickets seen to provide early warning to the sleeping camp.

With information about his quarry in hand, Dunlop moved his raiders to the edge of the field and into a skirmish line. He wanted to kill or capture as many as they could before the thirty or so rebels could organize a defense. A quiet order had the dragoons draw sabers. The militia dismounted and many fixed bayonets to their muskets. They would follow the horsemen on foot and round up sleeping rebels before they realized what hit them.

With the yell of "Charge," the dragoons galloped into the camp, slashing down with their sabers any defender attempting to get to his feet. The Tory footmen ran behind the horses and used bayonets to nudge their sleepy adversaries into submission as the camp came alive to the shouts and gunfire. Those who tried to resist were shot, stabbed, or slashed. The Liberty Men, groggy from being awakened by the attackers, grabbed their rifles and ran for the forest, unsure of what was happening other than their lives were at peril.

Assuming that officers were in the tents, Dunlop and Mills rushed into the nearest tent next to the wood line as its two occupants were discarding their blankets and reaching for their boots. Faced with drawn sabers and unarmed, the young lieutenants from the Rutherford County militia raised their hands in surrender. Dunlop demanded their names. One answered simply, "Hampton."

"Damn you Hamptons to hell!" Dunlop shouted and, without further warning, thrust his saber into Noah Hampton's midsection, severing his intestines and slicing his kidney. A twist of the sword severed several arteries, killing the young officer quickly. Outraged at his friend's murder, Andrew Dunn, Hampton's tent mate, lunged at Dunlop only to receive a mortal cut from Mills's saber as the colonel shouted a warning, "Look out, Dunlop!"

"Thanks for cutting that bastard down before he got to me, Colonel Mills. Here's one less Hampton for us to contend with," Dunlop said as a barrage of rifle fire suddenly erupted from the slope above them.

Running from Hampton's tent, Dunlop saw flashes from nearly a hundred rifles shooting at them. "Where did those guns come from?" Dunlop asked no one in particular.

Mills, close beside him, responded as more flashes lit up the darkness, "There's a lot more here than our spies reported. It has to be McDowell's regiment!"

They had thought that the rebel militia commander and his main force were nowhere near the area. However, Colonels Charles McDowell and Andrew Hampton had declared Earle's Ford the rallying point for a new call-up of Whig militia. They had established their camp just before dusk, long after the arrival of the Georgians.

Alarmed at the volume of rifle fire and unsure of how many fighters they were facing, the two Loyalist officers mounted their horses quickly and rode among their men, shouting for them to remount and head for the river before the unexpected defenders could get better organized and descend upon them. With only one prisoner in tow, the Loyalists made their escape heading south across the Pacolet at Earle's Ford. They left on the ground two of their men dead and one wounded.

When the Liberty Men counted their casualties, two Georgians and four North Carolina volunteers, including the two junior officers, were dead. Nearly three dozen Liberty Men were nursing wounds, including the Georgia militia leader, Captain John Jones, who had eight saber slashes across his head and upper body.

The Loyalists did not know that McDowell and Hampton, with nearly three hundred partisans from the western counties, had encamped the evening before on the grounds of Captain Edward "Ned" Hampton's plantation that overlooked the north side of Earle's Ford. No kin to the old colonel or young Noah, Ned Hampton had more than fifty of his Spartan District cavalry also camped around his house.

It was only a few minutes from the time Jacob and his two Rangers began tracking the mounted troops until the night riders stopped and formed for battle. Jacob still had not determined who was who when the Loyalists charged into the sleeping Whig militia. The Rangers continued to maneuver closer to the action in order to identify the combatants when the shooting began. Smoke from the attacker's muskets cleared a little for Jacob to recognize that those with sabers wore uniforms, making them British. There were no uniforms among the Tory militia. Jacob took aim and fired into the galloping attackers as they went about their gristly work, hitting one who rolled off his saddle.

When more shooting erupted from the high ground overlooking the ford, they watched the Loyalist raiders quickly regroup and the footmen remount as the counterattack picked up strength. The raiders were disappearing at full gallop into the darkness when dozens of figures ran yelling down the hill. Jacob heard frantic shouts to establish a defensive line by the river.

As the three Rangers walked into the confused campsite, they carried their rifles low by one hand to show clearly that they were friendly. No one paid the trio any attention. The dimness of predawn was giving way to more light when Jacob heard a loud anguished cry among the moans of the wounded: "*Noah!*" Andrew Hampton had just found his murdered son.

Dying from his wounds, Lieutenant Dunn told the colonel and others with him what had happened. "We were still in our bedclothes and unarmed when the uniformed officer called Dunlop ran poor Noah through with his sword just because Noah said his name was Hampton. The other one, the Tory officer who cut me down, was called Mills," Dunn reported as he bled profusely.

While old colonel tried to comfort his son, Colonel McDowell, the senior officer present, ordered the South Carolina cavalrymen to give chase to the fleeing attackers. Captain Ned Hamilton already had his men saddling their horses, and would have given chase with or without orders. Scores of other volunteers joined them, many of them friends of Noah and in a rage over the sneak attack.

Captain Singleton ran up to Colonel Hampton and inquired about his son. "Noah is gone." Hampton sobbed. The young officer was the first of Hampton's fifteen children to die.

Singleton recognized Jacob's trio and asked, "What are you men doing here? Aren't you supposed to be patrolling the Indian line?"

Jacob satisfied Singleton's curiosity as he reported quickly how they happened to be at the battle scene. The captain told the Rangers that Earle's Fort was back upstream a short distance on a hill overlooking the Pacolet. Despite his grief, Hampton focused on his duties. He ordered the Rangers to inform Colonel Earle about the raid and then to alert all forts along the Indian line that British troops were in the area in force and, for the first time, had moved above the North Pacolet into Rutherford County.

"The royal bastards are now more a threat than Indians," Hampton declared.

"Make haste; keep vigilant," Singleton added. "Tell all that no quarter was given by the killers of Colonel Hampton's son. Tell them Ambrose Mills and a British officer named Dunlop were the bastards that murdered Noah."

Before Jacob took his leave, he said to Hampton, "I'm awful sorry about your boy, Colonel. Wish we could've found out who they were before they attacked."

Hampton turned to him, his eyes dry and hard, and said, "I do too, Mister Godley. Now you and your family must get off the damn fence and decide which side you will serve. All should know that I will slaughter everyone who serves with Ambrose Mills and this Dunlop character."

Jacob and his colleagues left the camp at a trot, stopping briefly to report to Colonel John Earle and reaching Fort Capshaw before Ned Hampton's avenging cavalry returned to Earle's Ford.

Galloping down the Blackstock Road, the partisan horsemen caught up with the unsuspecting trailing elements of the Loyalist raiders just short of Prince's Fort and killed eight of them before the remainder of Dunlop's force escaped to the fort's safety. Ned Hampton, who had three other brothers fighting throughout South Carolina, did not know what he would encounter should he attack the Tory fort which had fifteen-foot-high walls and was more than 150 feet across.

Now exhausted from the chase and battle, the Whig militia had no supplies and could not sustain more prolonged fighting. In addition, the main strength of Ferguson's army was in the area. After getting a small taste of revenge, Captain Hampton ordered his men to disengage and return to their camp. Making their way back to safety with their own forces, Captain Hampton's troops took with them thirty-five captured horses and a sizable amount of arms and powder abandoned by the fleeing Loyalists. They didn't make an effort to count the enemy wounded that littered the running battlefield.

Safely within Prince's Fort, Dunlop quickly organized a defense that could easily hold off five times the number of rebels chasing him. He and Mills inspected all the firing positions and powder supplies before sitting down exhausted, chagrined at suffering a surprise counterattack. Mills said to Dunlop, "That was Colonel Hampton's boy you killed this morning. I know ol' Andy. He will be seeking retribution."

A month later, in mid-August, Jacob was ordered to take an express to Colonel John Walker. Since Walker lived near the Godley home, Jacob hoped to visit his family at the same time, but when he reached Walker's place, he learned that the colonel was at Gilbert Town, another two-hour walk. Arriving at the county seat, a hamlet of one house, a small ordinary, and a couple of outbuildings, he was surprised to see several hundred militiamen, their horses clogging the pastures and nearby woodland about the Gilbert plantation. More than a few had bloody bandages and clothing. Unshaven and unkempt, all looked tired.

Crowded in an animal pen were more than fifty disheveled men huddled tightly under the watchful eyes of three dozen armed guards. Several prisoners wore filthy red coats, but most looked no different in dress than their captors. Many had bandages, dark brown with dried blood. All had a despairing look about them.

As he approached the Gilbert house, he saw Isaac Shelby, a familiar face from over the mountains, conferring with Walker and six other men, all grim faced and wearing the gorget and red sash of militia leaders. Their clothes were muddy, some torn. One had a blood-soaked shirtsleeve sticking out of a makeshift sling on his left arm.

Shelby broke into a smile when he saw Jacob approaching. "Well, if it isn't that famous bear wrestler from the Watauga! How are you, Jake? What are you doing in these parts?"

"Howdy, Major Shelby. I'm serving the Indian line and have an express for Colonel Walker," Jacob replied as he took some papers from his cowhide pouch.

"It's Colonel Shelby now," Walker said, correcting the messenger. "Let me see what you have, Mister Godley."

After handing the papers to Walker, Jacob turned to Shelby again and asked, "Where did all this army come from?"

"Some are my overmountain people. Others are Georgians with Colonel Clarke here." He pointed at the Georgia militia commander and then to James Williams. "And the rest are South Carolinians who belong to Colonel Williams here. There're some local boys too." Shelby then turned to the other officers. "This lad is one of the most famous Indian and bear fighters from the Watauga settlements, and a damn good rifle maker too! He made my trusty shooter here."

Looking at the brass ornaments on Jacob's rifle, Shelby said, "I see you are using your Dickert and not one of your own make."

"Only brought one of the McCracken rifles with me, sir. My brother lost it at Charles Town when he got caught by the British. They wouldn't let him keep it when they paroled him. Y'all getting ready to go fight the British?"

"By God's blood, boy!" Shelby exclaimed. "We've been tangling with the Royals for most the summer all over the Carolina border region. I now know almost as much about the Broad River as the Holston. It seems us militia are about the only ones having any success. Cornwallis wiped out the Continental Army at Camden a few days ago. There are only a few militia units now standing between the whole British Army and the mountains.

"We bloodied a bunch of redcoats and their Tory lackeys at Musgrove's Mill down on the Enoree River a few days ago. Killed more than sixty of 'em and left another hundred or so bleeding on the field. We captured that sorry bunch over there"—Shelby pointed to the fenced area—"and brought them back with us as prisoners. You should have seen the rest of the king's men running away like the cowards they are.

"We would have gone on to Ninety Six and run them out of there too if Colonel McDowell hadn't told us about our army getting beat all to hell at Camden. He ordered us back here. My militia's time is about up anyway, so we're heading back home, though I'm afraid we just might have to come back again soon.

"Colonel Clarke is going on to Georgia and bloody the British there. Colonel Williams and his South Carolinians are taking the prisoners east to Hillsborough and see what the powers-that-be want to do with them.

"I hear we lost a bunch of generals in the Camden fight. Colonels Hampton and McDowell are trying to block Ferguson's corps from raiding up this way. They will be falling back soon. Us Liberty Men are running mighty thin."

"So what's going to happen?" Jacob asked.

"Don't know. It sure don't look good. Stragglers are all over the place. Some are cowardly deserters. Most are just plain scared or worn out. We got to get reorganized and find a way to push the bastards back." Shelby said, adding, "But back home, Dragging Canoe and his savages are still causing trouble."

Walker handed a new express to Jacob to take to Montford's Fort, fifteen miles to the northwest. "Get this to Captain McDonald as quick as you can, Jacob. We have a real emergency on our hands here."

"I was thinking about going to see my folks on the way back," Jacob said.

"No time." Walker responded. "This is critical. The British are recruiting hundreds of Tories from all over the frontier, including here in Rutherford County. They got to be stopped before they start burning every Whig place around."

"Yes sir!" Jacob responded, and turned to Shelby saying, "Good to see you again Colonel. Tell ol' Chucky Jack and folks on the Watauga I'm doing well and looking forward to getting back there."

As Jacob turned and walked away from the house, Walker strolled along with him and said quietly, out of hearing of the other officers, "Jacob, you are going to be in a tough spot soon. Aaron Biggerstaff has organized a Tory militia company, and your brothers, Robert and William, are both with him. Are you still on the fence?"

"I don't know, sir, but I'm leaning more your way. I sure don't like what I hear about the British and some of those Tories. There's a lot that ain't right," Jacob said. "I sure don't like the idea of redcoats being here. I saw how mean they were at Earle's Ford."

"God go with you, boy. Get that express through, even if you have to walk all night."

The remaining three weeks of Jacob's tour on the frontier were uneventful. Bits and pieces of news came to the remote outposts, most of it not good. Leery of the advancing British Army, some of the local families were already abandoning their homes and moving across the mountains to a newly established refugee camp near Fort Watauga. Others were preparing hiding places nearby in remote mountain coves to protect their valuables and livestock. Jacob was worried about his family and about how they were preparing for the invasion.

He didn't wait for a formal discharge from his commander. He just informed Captain McDonald, "I figure I have served you three months as promised. Now I'm going home. Good luck to you all."

Before Jacob could begin his long walk home, McDonald had him deliver an express to Russell's Fort on the Broad River. Then Jacob was free.

Becoming a Liberty Man

4 September 1780

It was just a soft plop of a foot leaving a bed, dropping almost silently to the bare floor. To Jacob, it was the sound of alarm even though he was outside the house of a friend. He jerked awake from a dreamless sleep, unaccustomed to sleeping on a porch's plank floor. He was slower than usual getting his bearings and remembering the tragic events from the day before at the Pearson farm.

Darkness still encased the house as John Foreman pushed through the door and made his way across the porch opposite of where Jacob lay and urinated off to the side of the house. He heard Jacob stir and turned, "You awake, Jacob?"

"Yes sir," Jacob replied as he rose from the floor, still dressed as he was the day before. While he recalled the horror of burying two men killed by Tory raiders, he remembered little of spending half the night telling the story of how he arrived at the Pearson farm after ending a summer of duty as a militia Ranger protecting the frontier forts to the west.

"Take one of my horses, Jacob, and get to Colonel Hampton's place as fast as you can and tell him about what happened at the Pearsons," Foreman told him as he led him off the porch and around to the corral in the back of the house. "Use the big black; it's the best. He's called Zeus. Keep him until we get this mess over with."

They led the saddlebred over to a log shed that served as a barn and where a blanket, saddlebags, and a simple saddle were stored under a shake roof. "Haven't got the knack yet of saddling with one arm," Foreman said as he pointed to the accoutrements.

With Zeus saddled, they walked back to the front of the house where Jacob tied his bedroll atop the saddlebags. Rachel rushed out the front door as Jacob swung himself into the saddle. Tightening a shawl around her shoulders to ward off the predawn chill, she bitterly challenged Jacob, "You get those that killed my pa and brother, you hear me, Mister Godley! Don't rest 'till you track 'em down and slaughter 'em like mangy wild dogs."

"Yes'm," Jacob answered.

Foreman handed Jacob a bag of oats for the horse and quickly gave him instructions on traversing the back trails that led to the home of the county's militia commander. It would be nearly two hours away at a normal gait, but at a fast trot, Jacob could make it in less than an hour. "If Hampton isn't at home, his oldest boy Jonathon will know how to get him. Jonathon's grown, but you can recognize him by his reel foot," Foreman said.

Within the hour, it was fully light although the sun had yet peeked through the trees. Jacob splashed through Mountain Creek and abruptly halted when someone shouted, "Stop where you are, or you're a dead man for sure!"

Jacob reined in his startled horse. He was still trying to get used to the animal, thereby unable to get the rifle slung quickly from around his shoulder in order to offer resistance to the challenge. Two figures emerged from the shadows, one only fifteen feet away with a rifle pointed directly at Jacob's chest. The man talking had his rifle cradled in his arms, his right hand on the trigger guard. He looked to be in his mid-twenties, just a few years older than Jacob. Around his waist, under his knife belt, was a red sash.

"Who are you? What are you doing here sneaking around in the dark?" the man demanded again.

Jacob continued to calm Zeus as he answered, "I'm not sneaking. It's daylight already. I'm Jacob Godley, late of the Indian line Rangers. Who might you be?"

"I ask the questions! Sir, your life may quickly end if you don't answer me proper. What is your business here so early in the morning?" the man demanded briskly as he shifted the rifle to a position that it could more easily be raised and fired.

"I come from Cap'n John Foreman's place with an urgent message for Colonel Hampton," Jacob responded.

"Give the message to me and I'll get it to the colonel," the man demanded. "And stop that fidgeting around. There are two more rifles behind you. We won't hesitate to shoot."

"No disrespect, but no sir! I will not give you the message. I don't know you or who you stand for. My matter is for Colonel Hampton only," Jacob responded, leery of the circumstance that he had fallen into.

The man stated arrogantly, "I am Captain Adam Hampton of the Rutherford County militia. I'm duly authorized to receive any express for the colonel, who, by the by, is my father."

"I know this man!" someone boomed from behind Jacob. "I remember him from General Rutherford's trek to tame them Cherokees a few years back. He's one of the Godleys who live up near Brittain Church.

"Jake, I'm Jim Gray; remember me? Forgive the caution, but we're just trying to keep Tories from bothering the old colonel."

Jacob turned to look at the new voice as he tried to recognize the face of an acquaintance he had made in the Indian campaign four years ago. "Good to see you again, Jim. Tory raiders are killing and plundering not more than one-two hours away. Cap'n Foreman wants me to get the details to Colonel Hampton."

"I heard the Godley boys were riding with the Tories—Biggerstaff's bunch. Are you a Tory spy, Jacob Godley?" Adam Hampton demanded, forcing Jacob to turn and face once again the young officer in charge of the roadblock.

"I'm no spy. No Tory either. Two of my bothers are. Haven't seen them since the first of summer," Jacob answered indignantly. "I told you, Mister Hampton, I've been on militia duty at the forts all summer and just finished my time. Besides, your papa knows me. I met him back before he went to Charles Town. I also talked with him down at Earle's Ford when your brother got killed."

"I didn't see you there," Adam responded, and then looking over to Jim Gray, he asked, "Mister Gray, did you see this Godley boy down at Earle's Ford?"

"I heard that three Rangers from the Indian line came in about the time of the raid, but I was too busy chasing the king's bastards to really know," Gray responded. "But I do believe Jacob Godley to be honest."

"Well, you are showing grit, Mister Godley," Adam Hampton said. Speaking over Jacob's shoulder, he ordered, "Mister Gray, Mister McFadden. Take this Indian fighter up to the house, but keep him under the gun until the colonel recognizes him. Be forewarned, Mister Godley, it ain't safe galloping through the woods around here where people don't know you. You got Tory blood in your family, and that makes me awful suspicious, even with Jim Gray vouching for you."

There were at least twenty horses in the open field between Colonel Hampton's house and his fort. Hampton built the stockade after McFadden's Fort was burned four miles downstream by Tory raiders two years before. The colonel was sitting on a log with several men, all eating cornmeal mush from wooden platters. They looked tired, their clothes caked in dirt, their faces unshaven in days. For the past two weeks, they had been riding the Broad River basin in a dangerous game of hide and seek with Ferguson's Loyalist forces. Born in England in 1713, Hampton was the senior person in the group, both in age and rank. He rose to his feet as Jacob and his two escorts rode up to the front of the house.

Before Jacob could say anything, Hampton recognized and greeted him cheerfully, "Well Mister Godley, here you are again, showing up unexpectedly. I assume you have come to join in the defense of our country against the invading vermin?"

"Mornin', Colonel. Cap'n Foreman sent me to you," Jacob said as he dismounted from his horse.

Jacob explained in detail what had happened at the Pearson farm and the concern Foreman had of Tory bands roaming the countryside. Hampton asked, "You say this Tory gang was led by Rance Miller?"

"That's what Missus Pearson said. She said he identified himself to her before shooting her husband and stringing up her son."

"Damn!" Hampton exclaimed. "Murdering two of my neighbors and beating up on a poor defenseless woman. This Miller is more despicable than two Bloody Bill Cunninghams put together! If Miller is in these parts, that means Ferguson is probably less than a day's ride away or closer. He is bringing his army to us, and we got little to nothing to stop him with."

Hampton turned to Gray who had not dismounted. "Mister Gray, go fetch Adam. Tell him to leave a good guard on the road. We got to figure out some way to stop those British and their Royalist friends."

Turning to Jacob, Hampton draped his arm over Ranger's shoulder and led him to the log bench, "Boy, you look hungry. Come have some corn mush and hot tea. We might have some molasses to give it better flavor. Are you still patrolling the Indian line?"

"Thanks, I could use a bite, sir," Jacob answered. "I done my three months on the line and was on the way home when I happened on the Pearson place. The killers were done gone. I didn't try to track them because the women folk needed help and protection. I did cut their son down and bury him and his papa. Then it was dark by the time I got Missus Pearson and her young'uns over to Cap'n Foreman's house. He's taken them in."

"John is a good man, brave too," Hampton replied, "Lost his arm with General Washington fighting them redcoats up north. But what about you, Jacob? You can't sit on the fence anymore; you have to choose sides. You told me back last winter that the British Army was no threat to Rutherford County. Well boy, they are already here, and you are going to see a lot worse pain inflicted on our people. We can't let that happen. I need you to stay with us Liberty Men."

"I don't want to fight my brothers, Colonel."

"One of your brothers has already been fighting the British. Has the same name as me, I believe. He was with that Pearson boy down in Charles Town when they got captured and paroled. You know how bad them Royals treated those boys. Andrew could meet the same fate as poor young Pearson," Hampton reasoned. "Besides, we'll do all we can to keep you from having to fight your Tory brothers."

"Well, Colonel, I don't like what I have been hearing and seeing of late. Most of it shows me that those Tories and British ain't honorable. What they have been doing ain't right. I'll work with you, sir, if nothing more than to catch that Miller scoundrel. When do you need me?"

"Now. Colonel McDowell has taken his Catawba Valley boys back to Burke County. Shelby skedaddled across the mountains to the Holston River right after the Camden disaster, although he and Clarke bloodied the bulldog's nose at Musgrove's Mill. Colonel Graham and his South Fork boys are thin and have their hands full. The South Carolina liberty militia is scattered to hell and yonder. It's only us Rutherford County men to stand firm against invasion, and there ain't near enough of us.

"You have proved yourself a good Ranger. You will continue to be a Ranger since you already got your horse and rifle with you. That oath you took for Indian duty is still good in this fight against the Crown."

After pondering the request for a few seconds, Jacob answered, "I'll be a Ranger for you. The horse belongs to Cap'n Foreman. I only have half a horn of powder."

"There's some extra powder in the fort. Help yourself to it. That horse now belongs to the cause. Ol' John is loyal to our effort, and he won't mind," Hampton said. "Besides, with only one arm, he can't take good care of all the horses and chores he has now."

Later in the morning, a gaggle of militia leaders with a few privates crowded in a semi-circle around the old Colonel as he shared his plans. "Boys, it don't look good. There ain't enough of us to win a standup fight against Ferguson. But we've learned a lot of tricks from the Indians, so we can make him hurt.

"Captain Hampton, send two of your men east to the Little Broad near Flint Hill and find Captain Withrow and his company. Have them make haste to Bedford Hill. We'll gather our people there.

"Major Porter, see how many volunteers you can round up in the next couple of days and have them meet us on Bedford Hill. Get as much powder and provisions as you can find. Warn all Whig families to hide their animals, food, and valuables 'cause the British and their lackeys will be living off the land and taking everything they want from those who sympathize with us. Those that can't fight and are afraid to stay should be encouraged to go hide in the mountains.

"Mister Dunn, you ride to the Montford's Fort and tell the commander there of the situation. Tell him to alert the other forts along the line that they may be on their own for a long time. Tell them to store as many provisions as possible in safe hiding places away from the forts and stage their defenses as though the whole Cherokee Nation were at their front gate.

"Captain Hampton, take the rest of your troop and ride south along the Broad River down to where it meets the Second Broad and see if you can find Ferguson and his army. Put lookouts at the fords. We need to know how many regulars they got and how many militia.

"I'm taking Mister Gray from you. He knows the Green River area well," Hampton told his son, and then turned to Gray and Jacob. "Mister Gray, you and young Godley here go spy around Twitty's Ford, the fort at White Oak and Ambrose Mills's plantation. Let me know how big a force is gathering and if they are already moving north. Warn our men at the fort to be cautious around the Tories. If they got extra powder there, you take it with you. We can't have our enemies using it against us.

"Captain Singleton, take your men and set up a watch over Gilbert Town. I imagine that's where Ferguson will aim for first. Get friendly folks who live around there to be spies so they can let us know what the scoundrels are doing. Every Whig in the county should be our eyes and ears.

"Our fort here will be our headquarters for the next two days unless Ferguson gets here first. Then our rendezvous point will be Bedford Hill up near the head of Cane Creek. McDowell already has some people there now, and they can give directions for refugees wanting to go over the mountains.

"Jonathon here will coordinate getting messages to me if I have to leave in a hurry. I heard that Mills and Ferguson have put a price on my head and will be coming after me, and probably you other officers as well. Jonathon, I want you to see how much powder, lead, and recruits you can find along Mountain and Claxton creeks. If anyone asks what you are doing, whether they be friend or foe, just tell them you are doing your duty as the justice of the peace and not a part of the hostilities."

Jonathon interrupted his father. "I don't have to lie, Pa. I've been asked to marry up Tom Fleming and a young gal over near Adair's place. I'll take care of that tomorrow. Gives me a good reason for being around there."

"Good thinking," the colonel said before continuing with his orders. "Now, gentlemen, we are scattered over a mighty big area. There are probably as many Tories living in these parts as Whigs, maybe more, so don't trust nobody unless you know them real good. Don't get into any fight unless you are pushed into one and you got no place to run. There ain't no glory in being dead or crippled in a no-win pissing contest. There's more of them Royals than us. Remember, they got professional soldiers with them.

"But most important, we need more information...lots of it. So steer clear of fighting. Find out as fast as you can about their size, resources, and intentions.

"I think I know most of the local Tory leaders that are with Mills, but see if there are others besides Biggerstaff and Chitwood. I hear that Walter Gilkey may be active with the Tories again. I need to know the names of anyone living in the county that gives them help, for...and mark my words... there will be a reckoning when all this is over."

"Damn right!" one of the militia from the back of the crowd yelled out.

"Hush that cussing," Colonel Hampton reprimanded harshly. "My wife and children are right behind you and can hear you."

"My apologies, sir," the offending militiaman responded sheepishly and then turned to the colonel's wife who was standing on the porch watching the group, "and to you, ma'am, my deepest apology for a lack of manners."

Looking over his small command, Hampton continued. "We have to work like a nest of mad hornets. Move fast, sting where you can get by with it, but don't give them a chance to swat back or take any of our people. You ain't no good to the cause hanging from a tree or skewered with one of those pig stickers them regulars carry. God go with you and look over you."

Most of the men went to their horses, but a few, before leaving, walked up on the porch and extended thanks to Catherine, the Colonel's wife of thirty-two years, for fixing their breakfast. Five of her fifteen children were under sixteen years of age and still living at home, as were the older girls, all still unmarried. Jonathon's home was a half mile up the creek.

In the yard, eighteen-year-old Alexander Dunn walked up to the colonel as he stood alone and spoke quietly, "I'd druther go with Cap'n Hampton, sir. Can't you get someone else to go to Montford's? Maybe one of the old married men?"

Rather than chastising the teenage warrior whose freckled face masked a veteran with a half-year of hard campaigning across South Carolina for questioning his decision, Hampton took a fatherly attitude and wrapped his arm around the lad's shoulder as he explained, "Alex, m'boy. You've been though a lot with me. No one can ever question your bravery and sacrifice. I've given you an assignment normally reserved for officers; that's how much I trust you. We'll have plenty of chances to avenge the murder of our dear ones. Now be off with you!"

Hampton did not tell Dunn that he wanted to keep him away from being too close to the advancing enemy because the boy, still emotionally upset over his brother's murder, would be too easily tempted to take rash actions. Hatred was running deep in many of the Liberty Men who had revenge now as a greater motivator than political ideology.

Robert Godley rode at the head of the small column of Captain Aaron Biggerstaff's Tryon County Tory militia. Being on point meant that he did not have to eat dust from horses in front of him or smell their flatulence or frequent droppings. It was also the most dangerous position should they run across rebel snipers or ambushers. It was a position he preferred.

Their new orders had come during the night: move south to secure Dennard's Ford on the Broad River until met by Ferguson's corps, which should arrive any day. As the Biggerstaff company maneuvered to join Ferguson's main force, the Tory militia was also to gather intelligence and additional provisions from farmers along the way. Their orders were to request support respectfully from Loyalists, but take what they wanted from rebel sympathizers.

Godley led the band down a rutted wagon trek off the main road to South Carolina and to a small, log hovel that had no glass in the windows and only packed dirt for a floor. Standing in the doorway with her arms folded and eyes glaring at the approaching militia was an emaciated young woman wearing a filthy, threadbare, and formless shift. Her eyes were sunken, and her face looked twice as old as her actual age. It was a face gaunt and hard. "What do you want?" she demanded as Robert stopped his horse in front of her and two small, barefooted children, one of them naked and caked with mud.

"Good day to you, ma'am. We are of the loyal Tryon County militia and humbly ask your help in putting down the devil's rebellion against the true government of Great Britain and her American colonies," Robert said smiling, ignoring the squalor around him.

"Now ain't you the prim and proper one, Your Honor?" the woman snorted mockingly, "Them fancy words don't mean nothing to me. You best be on your way because we ain't got enough to feed ourselves much less fat militia men."

"We ask for little," Robert continued quietly as Biggerstaff rode to his side. "But just as these men are willing to give their lives for your safety, surely there is something you can do for them—a pone of bread, a bite of corn, or even a kind word."

The woman shooed her children into the cabin. "Protect me! Ha! Where were you two days ago when we needed protection from that other pack of damned thieves what came here? I told them the same thing I tell you—we ain't got nothing.

"They tore up my home. Took my pots, what few vittles we had, clothes and even my bed. They stole our milk cow, though she was about as dry as me. Left me and the young'uns with nothing to eat and only what we have on," she said as she tried to present some dignity, but yielded to a tear running down her cheek.

"Where is your man?" Biggerstaff quietly asked.

The woman looked over to him and cast her eyes down, "Don't know. He took off near a year ago. Left me and the babes here to fend for ourselves. He told me he was going to fight the British, but the coward is probably chasing some harlot if not drunk or somebody done him in."

"Do you mind if we look around?" Biggerstaff asked.

"No," she answered less defiantly. "Wouldn't matter if I did, you would do it anyway."

William Godley dismounted and walked briefly inside the shack. It took only a moment for him to size up the situation. Returning outside, he reported, "She said it straight. There ain't much here. The place is messed up bad. Even her shawl is ripped, nothing more than rags."

Robert and Biggerstaff looked at each other, and then turning to face the small company, Robert said, "Men, anyone with a little extra food to leave with this poor family? She and the tykes are in dire condition and their needs greater than ours. Your charity will be appreciated."

"Heartless rebels…stealing from the destitute!" Biggerstaff muttered aloud.

As the last militiaman left the area, the woman stared at them disappearing down the track before looking thankfully at a tiny pile of food in a small cracked pot left by Biggerstaff's company. There was a fist-sized hunk of cooked meat; several handfuls of oats and corn; some bread; a big turnip; a dead, unskinned rabbit; and two apples. With a little ingenuity, she could make the provisions last more than a week.

About an hour before reaching the Broad River, Biggerstaff's company stopped by a more prosperous plantation whose fifty-two-year-old owner, Peter Myers, claimed he was neutral and wanted nothing to do with either side of the conflict. "Just leave us alone; we don't bother nobody here. I'll tell you like I told them Whigs, I ain't taking sides."

"If you aren't for us," the militia captain responded emphatically, "then you are against us."

Turning to his men, he ordered the house, barn, and root cellar searched. "Stop that!" Myers yelled as the militia began their search in a less than orderly fashion.

Robert maneuvered his horse to push the farmer against a tree, preventing him from interfering with the searchers. Myers wife ran out of the house screaming, "Stop! Don't hurt him! Please, sir, don't hurt my husband."

Biggerstaff looked toward her, "We don't intend harm to anyone, ma'am, but we will stop anyone interfering with the king's business. So please...calm down...and calm your husband. You have anybody else here?"

"Our boys are done grown and gone," she answered, not volunteering the fact that two sons were with the Liberty Men militia. "We got four darkies, one in the house and the rest in the fields."

"Have you seen any armed men riding about in the last day or so," Biggerstaff asked.

"There was a party of fifteen or so by here two days ago. They stole corn and two shoats, but didn't tarry long," Myers answered.

Biggerstaff's men took six bags of oats for the horses, some freshly churned butter, and a small sack of black powder found hidden under a bed. Before leaving, Biggerstaff gave the farmer a receipt for goods taken and told him, "You are lucky I don't have you flogged for keeping contraband powder."

"I got that powder legal," the farmer protested. "I need it to protect my family from Indians or other brigands."

"Well, we are just protecting you from having the rebels confiscate it," Robert chimed in with a sinister laugh.

As the others rode away, Andrew Godley spoke to the couple, "Down the road a bit, there's a woman with two young'uns barely old enough to walk. They're in bad need of Christian charity. Rebels took what little she had, even her clothes. She has no food for the young'uns except a little that we left her. They are in a bad way, nearly starving."

"How do you expect us to feed the countryside when you men come in and steal my food?" Myers asked indignantly.

His wife spoke tartly. "Shut up, Peter Myers!" Then turning to Andrew, she said, "We will do our Christian duty, sir. I know that woman, but we haven't seen hide or hair of her in months. I heard that her husband took off some time ago, the no-good scoundrel, but I didn't realize she was so destitute."

"Thank you, ma'am," Andrew said as he turned his horse and galloped to catch up with the rest of his company.

12

VALLE TEMP

5–6 September 1780

Alexander Dunn was still fuming when he arrived at Montford's Fort. Regardless of the condescending remarks by Colonel Hampton, whom he loved like a father, Dunn believed he should be down blocking Ferguson's army from coming into Rutherford County instead of being a messenger far away from any potential action. However, over the past year, he had learned that proper soldiers obey their colonel's orders.

Montford Wilson built the stockade in the picturesque wilderness cove in the early 1770s, shortly after settling at the foot of Wildcat Mountain. However, Wilson was known to have Tory leanings and, therefore, was not trusted by Liberty Men. Over the years, the militia garrison had varied from two to more than twenty, plus the men of five families that lived close by in the cove. Over the years, Indians had attacked the post more than a dozen times, but only once had the Cherokee made a serious attempt to breach its walls. Now only six volunteers were at the fort, three had left to join Hampton, and one slipped off to enlist with the Tories. Two Rangers usually patrolled the line northward toward Davidson's Fort, which was located below the Swannanoa Gap near the headwaters of the Catawba River.

Two men were chopping firewood for the fort when Dunn arrived with news that the British were already in the county. After giving Colonel

Hampton's message to Captain James McDonald, the garrison commander, Dunn turned to walk away from the officer saying, "'Cuse me. I gotta go water the trees."

McDonald stopped him. "Use the piss bucket inside the front gate."

"Why?"

"We need your piss to make our powder. Reckon we have about sixty pounds in reserve now."

"Can you spare some powder for Colonel Hampton?" Dunn asked.

"I can let you have half of what we have; we'll hide the rest back up the mountain," McDonald told him, "If them damn king's men get up this far, Montford Wilson may try to give them the fort. We might as well make it meager pickings for them."

After Dunn relieved himself, McDonald picked up the half-filled wooden bucket and carried it to another corner of the fort where he dumped it over a smelly pile of urine-laced straw intermingled with human and animal feces. "This is our niter-bed. It'll take it about another half year before its cures proper. We've been harvesting a bed on the other side of the fort for our latest batch. We won't be beholden to nobody for powder if a fight comes our way."

"How good is the powder you are making?" Dunn asked.

"Good as anything made in the English powder factories." McDonald replied, "All it takes is about three-fourths saltpeter, some charcoal, and sulfur. We found a sulfur deposit about three miles south of here. But there ain't no saltpeter about, so we make our own with dried-up piss and dung, and that makes the explosive. Dung and piss are just as good as saltpeter, just takes longer to cure.

"My pa is our powder maker, and he is damn good at it. It's an art to know just when the nitrate is cured."

"Ain't this illegal?" Dunn asked.

"The British said it was, but they ain't in charge now, are they? I bet many folks along the frontier are making their own powder these days, but most of it ain't good enough for much 'cept making noise," McDonald said, adding, "It's getting late. Why don't you bed down here for the night and you can take powder to the colonel with my compliments in the morning."

Jacob Godley and Jim Gray walked their horses in a single file along a faint hunting trail that ran several miles west of the road that led south from Gilbert Town and across the Broad and Green Rivers. After spotting a large Tory militia patrol near Twitty's Ford on the Broad, they took a slower, more secure route along a little-used trail to make their way to Capshaw's Fort undetected. After crossing the Broad, Jacob suggested they find a place to hide their animals and continue on foot. "These woods are so thick and steep, we can move faster without the horses," he told Gray.

"I agree. There's an old trapper who has a cabin hidden back in a cove not far from here. He sells his furs to my pa, but nobody else comes near his place," Gray said. "Some say he is the wildest varmint in these hills."

After leaving the horses with the old hermit, they continued on foot, carrying a light bedroll over their shoulders and in their possibles bag some parched corn, dried apples, chestnuts, and a bit of blood pudding Jacob got at the Foreman house. It was almost dark when they waded across Green River at a place with steep banks overgrown with thick vegetation to hide their movements. By the time they reached the fort at the foot of White Oak Mountain, it was well past sundown. Rather than approach the fort at night, they decided to sleep in the woods and observe who might be there after daybreak.

They found a hidden nesting site less than three hundred paces from the fort, and the two Rangers settled in for a night of fitful sleep. At daybreak, they ate a few morsels and drank from a nearby spring before crawling to a position to spy on the fort. When they saw a figure emerge from the rustic log palisade, Gray whispered to Jacob, "Uh-oh. Trouble."

"What do you mean?"

"That's Essex Capshaw. His family owns this land, but he is a Tory through and through. Nobody trusts them Capshaws."

"When we had Indian duty here," Jacob said, "I was told he never came inside the fort."

"I know the family. They are die-hard Tories," Gray whispered, adding, "My pa does business with them, but he says they'll cheat you blind if you are not careful. They are also toadies of old man Mills."

They continued their watch as three other men walked out of the fort, one wearing a threadbare red uniform coat of the British Army. Ten minutes later two riders approached the station and talked briefly with the men there before continuing to the northeast.

"Looks like the Royals have taken over the fort," Jacob said. "I haven't seen any of our militia who are supposed to be here. They must have run away."

"Then let's get back north of the Broad," Jim whispered. "But first, let's go by the Mills's place and see if anyone is stirring there. It's a big house overlooking the Green not far from where we crossed the river last night."

The stateliest house in the frontier region, the Mills's home was a large, two-story clapboard structure with many glass windows and a wide porch running the length of the second floor over a ground-floor veranda and within the shadow of the hulking White Oak Mountain. When Mills first built his house ten years before, shortly after moving to the backwoods with his second wife, he named it Valle Temp because, he told friends, it was a temple in nature's most beautiful valley.

There were a dozen visitors sitting around a table in the front yard enjoying a meal in the warm sunshine. The most pretentious one was the British commander of Provincials, Patrick Ferguson.

Two additional uniformed men, one in the green coat of the Queen's Rangers, were also at the table. Three other men were wearing waistcoats common to country gentry, but all had a red sash around their waists, signifying them as officers. Jacob didn't know them. One was Captain Alexander Chesney, Ferguson's most trusted confidant among the militia who also served as his chief intelligence officer. A native of Ireland, Chesney had carved out a homestead eight years earlier near Grindal Shoals on the Pacolet River, a day's hard ride from Valle Temp.

The two Rangers crawled as near to the house as they dared, hiding in a dense laurel copse, close enough to see clearly, but not close enough to hear the conversation. "That old, short man with white hair is Ambrose Mills," Gray whispered to Jacob, "and the fellow on his right is his son William. I bet one of the uniforms is Ferguson. Look how they all truckle to him."

Jacob raised his rifle and took aim at Ferguson, but Gray put his hand atop the barrel and whispered, "Don't shoot. He's too far away, and besides, we are outnumbered. Remember what ol' Hampton said."

Disappointed in not taking the shot, Jacob whispered a mild protest, "I can easily get him at this distance, but you are right." He then saw three young children come running about the house and dancing around the master of the manor and his guests. Jacob felt relief that he had not taken the shot; he did not want to endanger children, including Tories.

Although they could not hear the conversation, Jacob and Jim continued to observe as the men ate a meal served on fine crockery by Mills's wife, Anna, and a cream-colored servant girl. They didn't want to leave their hiding place out of fear of being detected, so they waited patiently for several hours, hoping that the children would not bring their play near the hidden observation point or a field hand would spot them.

"Delightful meal, madam," Ferguson stated to Anna Mills as he dabbed his mouth with a linen napkin. "It is rare these days for this field soldier to have an opportunity to experience such a culinary delight served in such an elegant manner, and especially out here in the back country."

Anna curtseyed, blushed, and replied, "Why, thank you, sir. It is just a simple fare."

Ambrose turned to his wife, "Excuse us, please, madam. We must engage in war talk, which you will find most unpleasant. Take the children to the other side of the house."

Five of the six Mills children had been darting in and out among the visitors. The baby, Emily, was asleep inside. At thirty-four, William was the colonel's oldest offspring, but he was a product of an earlier marriage that ended when Ambrose's first wife, Mourning Stone, had been murdered by Indians twenty years before near Camden, South Carolina.

As the lady of the manor returned to the cookhouse out back, the officers all stood. Rather than reseating, Ferguson wasted no time in getting to business. "We should be ready to move north in mass over the next two days. My spies tell me that McDowell has run back to the Catawba to hide out in the hills. That leaves only Hampton and his banditti still in the area, but they shouldn't be any peskier than those ghastly bugs that we have had to put up with this summer."

Mills interrupted. "Those rebels might be pesky, Colonel, but they can draw blood if you are not careful. Don't underestimate them, and particularly old Hampton."

Annoyed by the interruption, Ferguson retorted, "I don't understate my adversaries, Colonel."

Ferguson continued, "The wagons, prisoners, and the rest of Major Plummer's South Carolina militia should be getting to Dennard's Ford today. Colonel Mills, you will accompany me there. Captain Chesney, you are to work with Captain Ryerson of the American volunteers and gather what forces you can with those already at Twitty's Ford. I'll send you word when we move north. You join us when we occupy Gilbert Town. Moving with a show of force on two routes should make those rebels still lingering about run for the hills. The local subjects will welcome our protection.

"I regret that we have to leave Valle Temp, Colonel," Ferguson said as he turned to face Ambrose Mills. "Again you have been a gracious host and have added a pleasant respite to the rigors of campaigning. I hope I have another opportunity to visit this peaceful abode."

As the enemy officers mounted their horses and began riding east, Jacob and Gray crawled quietly backward from their hiding place, thankful that the Mills children did not start playing around their lookout point. They did not stand up until they were well clear of the Mills home and then walked briskly another half-hour before talking in low tones. "Wonder what they were saying?" Jacob asked.

"Don't know, but I bet it was a war council. They seemed awful cocky not having no more guards around than they did," Gray answered. "We best get back and report to Hampton. Let's take a look at Twitty's Ford before we go."

There was an open field on the south side of the ford where Broad River was less than sixty feet across and usually less than a foot or so deep. The banks had been cut to allow wagons easy access to cross the river. Today, more than a hundred Tory militiamen were lolling around the meadow, taking advantage of the warm sun to clean their weapons, mend clothing and equipment, or just catch a nap. Only five red-coated uniforms were among the campers. They counted less than a dozen horses.

Staying deep in the forest shadows, the Rangers crept around the meadow's edge, stopping only to count enemy heads. They went more than a half-mile downstream before slipping down a steep bank and wading through crotch-deep water to get to the north side of the Broad. Moving back west parallel to the river on its north side, they spotted several pickets providing security for the militia camp. Bent at the waist, the Rangers crept silently, occasionally using a hand signal to alert the other to another picket or danger point.

It was late afternoon when the Rangers reached the trapper's small hut and their horses. They thanked the hermit for looking after their animals and politely refused to stay for an evening meal of squirrel stew and acorn bread. With clouds masking the moonlight after dark, Jacob and Gray dismounted and led their horses along the narrow trail, giving no thought to stopping and making camp.

Their methodical trek was interrupted by a scream of pain piercing the darkness. "Where's that coming from?" Gray whispered urgently to Jacob as they stopped their horses and brought their rifles to a ready position.

"Over yonder way," Jacob whispered, pointing through the darkness to a faint yellow glow dancing between tree silhouettes.

The Rangers hobbled their horses, checked their rifles, and crept stealthily toward the cries and glow. As they got near, they crouched and crawled to a point where they could make out the commotion. The fire illuminated the clearing where hugging a tree was a man with his shirt ripped to shreds, his arms tied by some leather straps, and his back crisscrossed with a score of bloody cuts. Three other men stood around him; one, who was wearing a uniform, held several long, slender stalks of river cane about four feet long in his hand.

Jacob thought he recognized the person tied to the tree. He motioned Gray to scout to the left as he went to the right looking to see if anyone else was close by. It took less than ten minutes for them to be satisfied there was no one else near. During their scouting, they heard the smack of the wooded whip lash across the back of the hapless victim, and with each smack, an anguished cry of pain. It was unclear if the trio was trying to get information from their captive or just whipping the poor sod out of meanness, or both.

As the two Rangers crept closer for a better view, Jacob gasped quietly when he recognized the tortured victim—it was Benjamin Camp, his fellow Ranger from Indian line duty. Gray also recognized Camp as a neighbor and close family friend.

When the uniformed soldier brought his arm back to wield another blow, Jacob threw caution to the wind, aimed his rifle, and shot the assailant in the chest, knocking him backward with a fatal wound. Before the other two Loyalists could react, Gray shot one of them in the shoulder. Abandoning his effort to retrieve a musket leaning against a tree, the other Tory panicked and fled fearfully into the dark.

After quickly reloading their rifles and making sure the wounded man was no longer a threat, Jacob cut the leather strip that held Camp to the tree. "You all right, Ben?" Jacob asked as he gently lowered his friend to the ground.

"I'll live. My old man gave me better beatings than these sum'bitches." Camp hissed, trying to mask his pain with renewed bravado. "God, you're a sight for sore eyes, Jacob."

Gray retrieved the horses as Jacob tried to ease Ben's suffering. When Gray returned, he kicked out the fire. "That fellow who ran must have some friends nearby. We got to get out of here before he brings them back."

Jacob asked his injured friend, "Can you ride, Ben?"

"I ain't a cripple yet!"

The two Rangers helped Ben on to Zeus's back and then picked up the wounded enemy, tied his hands, and draped him none too gently on his stomach across Gray's horse. They took the Tory muskets and removed parts of the firelock and triggers, keeping the flints, and scattered the dismantled musket parts far into the surrounding bushes before leading the horses to a more secure area.

It was getting light when they decided to stop by a stream, a few hundred yards out of sight from the trail that they had been traveling. Jacob figured they must have gone five miles and they needed to treat Camp's bleeding back. He also wanted to talk to the wounded Tory, whose moans signaled he was still alive but weak from the loss of blood.

Taking care of Camp first, the Rangers treated the open wounds on both injured men with a poultice of chewed sassafras leaves, wet moss, and mud from the stream bank. The Tory had a smashed shoulder bone. A ball fired by Gray had bounced out of the Tory's body, leaving a bloody mess, but causing no lethal damage.

Benjamin Camp told how he was making his way toward Colonel Hampton's place to join the Liberty Men when he was jumped by five Loyalists. Two of the enemy had left the group, taking Camp's horse and rifle, to rejoin their unit, but the other three stayed to get information about rebels in the area. Ben laughed. "I didn't tell 'em squat. How could I? I don't know anything. But those bastards didn't know that."

The wounded Tory, who looked to be in his forties, gave his name as Thomas Manning from the Fair Forest militia and serving in Major Plummer's regiment. He identified the uniformed soldier as being from New York and a veteran of fighting against Washington's Continental Army. "He's got a mean streak in him," Thomas said as he tried to hold back tears of hurt and fear. "I didn't like him beating up that boy like he did, but he was in charge."

"Where's that Fair Forest militia from and how many people in it?" Jacob asked, trying with difficulty to put kindness in his tone.

"Most of us live along the Tyger River between here and Ninety Six, 'bout a day's ride south. There's about two or three hundred of us."

"How many people does Ferguson have with him?" Gray asked.

"Don't know. There's about six hundred from South Carolina and over a hundred of the New York Provincials that I've seen. Don't know how many militia are from North Carolina."

"What about the British regulars?" Jacob asked.

"Ain't seen any other than Ferguson. The New Yorkers wear red coats, but there's some of 'em in green who say they are Rangers. They all have been fighting in the British Army for years."

"What were you doing up in these parts?" Gray asked.

"We were out looking for rebels. Been scouting for two days. We talked to a few people who didn't know anything before we ran across Mister Camp there and captured him," Manning said and then turned to Camp. "I'm real sorry they beat you. I don't favor torture. Didn't see no call for what they did to you."

"You bastard! You did nothing to stop the beating," Jacob spat disgustingly.

"Where is Ferguson going from here?" Gray asked, still maintaining a sympathetic attitude.

"I don't know. I'm just a private. Nobody tells me nothing, accept go here...go there...and I go."

"Do you know a Tory named Rance Miller? Is he around here?" Jacob interjected.

"Don't know him, but I've heard of him. He's a mean one for sure. Heard he was part of Ferguson's army."

Jacob pulled Gray aside and said quietly, "We need to get all this information to Hampton fast. Taking the wounded prisoner with us will only slow us down. Let's leave Manning here and take Ben with us. I don't think those cuts on his back are too bad. He and I can ride double a ways, and then you can take him some on your horse."

Gesturing toward Manning, Jacob added, "We'll leave that poor soul for the buzzards."

"We ain't that cruel, Jacob," Gray said. As he turned toward the wounded Tory, he spoke more loudly and in a compassionate manner, "Mister Manning, we'll take you to the road. Just go east a short ways and you will find a log house. If memory serves me, those folks have Tory leanings. Anyway, you are hurt; and they are Christians, so they'll take care of you regardless of your politics. Can you walk?"

"I think so," the wounded Tory responded quietly.

The sun was sinking behind the trees when the Rangers and injured Ben Camp arrived at Hampton's plantation. As they told the colonel what they had seen since leaving him two days before, Hampton's wife and their grown daughters, Mary and Catherine, took Camp into the house and began cleaning his back. The girls put a fresh poultice of the inner bark of a hickory tree on the cuts and wrapped his back in muslin. Jonathon looked in on Camp and offered him one of his shirts.

After receiving the detailed reports from Jacob and Gray and two other returning patrols, Colonel Hampton visited with Camp, who was lying face down on the colonel's bed. "Looks like you are mending well, Mister Camp. How's your pa doing these days?"

"He's as ornery as ever, Colonel." Camp smiled weakly. "He asked that I send you his regards and to tell you that if he wasn't so old and crippled with the rheumatiz, he'd be here."

"Two of your brothers are already with my regiment. We'll probably see them in the next couple of days when we move north. Mister Godley tells me you were on the way to join us when you got caught."

"Yes sir. Pa told me that a couple of the brothers were up here with you. We got two more with General Washington's army; but two of them, damn their souls, are siding with those blasted Tories. Heard they joined up with William Mills. Pa is madder than a wet hornet over it."

"Sorry to hear about your wayward brothers, Ben. Maybe they will see the light some day. You still want to fight with us?"

"More than ever, sir. Got me a powerful grudge to settle for what they did to me last night and for stealing my horse and rifle."

"You'll be up and around in no time. I'll see if we can find you a rifle and spare horse. If you feel like it, you can go with me tomorrow. Most likely we'll have a day's easy ride. I don't have enough troops to stop Ferguson here, but maybe we can slow him down if he tries to get into the mountains."

INVASION

7 September 1780

The southern half of Rutherford County was in turmoil. Tory militia patrols were checking every home between the Pacolet River and Gilbert Town, making inventory of friend and foe. Some Tory-leaning families gleefully informed on neighbors who were supporting openly or covertly the independence cause. Old grievances were settled, including one by a Whig who declared his Tory neighbor a rebel at heart, causing the horse of the falsely accused to be confiscated.

The Loyalists gained more than a dozen recruits from fence-sitting families who felt the British had all but crushed the rebellion. A number of self-proclaimed neutralists expressed happiness that the Whigs were getting their comeuppance. They wanted clearly to be seen on the winning side, regardless of political bent.

In Whig households, families hid valuables and themselves from the roaming Tory patrols while others stood in open, but nonviolent, defiance. More than a few had their homes ransacked, their food stocks looted, outbuildings burned, and animals driven off. Some livestock were slaughtered in the fields and left to rot.

There were several reports of beatings, one with a death occurring after fourteen-year-old Arnold Pickford, who lived near Sandy Run, tried to protect his mother from crude sexual advances by Tory raiders. He fired his fowling musket into a six-man squad from Rance Miller's company. Two Loyalists received painful wounds from shrapnel propelled by an insufficient powder charge. The two wounded men took pleasure in cutting the boy's throat after one of their comrades shot Pickford in the leg.

Targeted systematically for more plunder after the consolidation of Ferguson's brigade were plantations with family members known to be supporting Liberty Men.

Many Whig families panicked at the news of Ferguson's invasion, gathered a few meager belongings and headed north to the mountains, some in ox-driven carts, others packing a few belongings on horses or cows. Some carried only bedrolls on their back and a few morsels of food, hoping for kindness from sympathetic people along the way. Several men in the Whig militia deserted, but most held true to their commitments.

Jacob spent the day riding the back hunting trails with Jim Gray, trying to get a clearer picture of how and where the main invasion would occur. They collected interesting bits of information from each place they visited, including from a Tory sympathizer who threatened to shoot them if they did not clear his property immediately.

Large groups of Tory militia and provincial troops were massing at Twitty's and Dennard's Fords on the Broad River, well inside Rutherford County's southern border. There were already a number of Tory units patrolling in strength along the main roads north of the Broad, and some Whig supporters had felt the heavy hand of "a green-coated disciple of Satan" whose visits included threats of dire consequences if the man of the house did not pledge allegiance to the Crown. Captain James Dunlop, like Rance Miller, made no friends among the populace, nor did he care to. He wanted the rebellious backwoods peasants to fear him.

Once a Loyalist patrol spotted Jacob and Gray, but they escaped into the forest before a pursuit was properly organized.

The two Rangers rode by John Foreman's home and stopped briefly. Jacob was concerned about the safety of the Pearson family and, in particular, the teenage girl he had met a few days before. The disabled Continental Army veteran had already been visited twice by the King's men, one of them Captain Dunlop himself. Since the raid on the Pearson place, Foreman had moved most of his cattle and all but one old horse to an old Indian field, hidden deep in the woods about half a mile from his house.

Stashed in his attic behind two old trunks and under several deer hides were baskets of grain and potatoes needed to survive the coming winter; but a small amount of food stocks remained visible in the root cellar, just in case the invaders decided to plunder and take the easy pickings. The family's silver and most of the pewter were buried behind the stock shed and the site covered with a relocated haystack. A false wall off the bedroom hid two rifles and a sword, but an old fowling musket was kept in sight. Foremen knew it would be futile to openly resist the raiders and hoped that they would not consider a one-armed, old man with three women and a young boy to be a threat.

Foreman was happy to see Jacob and told him to keep Zeus as long as he was fighting the British. As they sat on Foreman's front porch, he peppered Jacob and Gray with questions about what was happening around the county. Rachel Pearson cooked some eggs and flat bread, the Rangers' first hot meal in four days. "Ferguson might have his army at Gilbert Town tomorrow," Jacob declared. "There's just too many of them for our militia to handle, more than a thousand, I suspect."

Rachel Pearson brought the men some cider, warm eggs, pieces of cold turkey shot the day before by her younger brother, and bread. Rebecca Foreman remained in the house with Rachel's mother who was still in shock over the murder of her husband and son. Rachel and her brother listened quietly to the men talk. Neither spoke until Jacob and Gray rose to leave.

"Have you seen that Rance Miller anywhere?" she blurted.

"No, but I hear he's still around," Jacob replied. "We'll find him. You take care of your mama and brother. We got to get back to Colonel Hampton and let him know what we are seeing."

"I want you to come back, Jacob Godley. Don't you go off and get yourself kilt," she whispered loudly to him as she slipped two ears of roasted corn into his saddlebag.

"Sure wouldn't want that to happen," Jacob laughed as he and Gray urged their horses into a gallop.

It was late afternoon when the two Rangers arrived back at Hampton's place, which was bustling with a frenzy of activity. Armed riders were galloping into the compound singularly and in groups. Others were leaving, speeding to the rendezvous point at Bedford Hill, sixteen miles north in the mountainous foothills. At a storage shed, two Negro men loaded a cart with sweet potatoes, sacks of grain, and baskets of corn to be hidden from Tory plunderers. Another cart was laden with apples, corn, and oats, destined to feed Hampton's troops at Bedford Hill, provided the enemy did not seize it first.

At the mill, Hampton's two young teenage sons, Benjamin and Andrew Junior, worked alongside two slaves who were rendering molasses from freshly crushed sorghum canes, all under the supervision of their oldest sister, Susannah. War or not, this work had to be done if the sweet syrup was to be preserved; molasses was a precious commodity in the backcountry. The invasion came at the height of the sorghum harvest and processing season. The Hampton family had worked through the night cooking the sorghum juice until it became thick, dark syrup. As soon as the syrup simmered to the desired consistency, the molasses was poured into two-gallon clay jugs that were then sealed with corn-cob stoppers and taken to secure hiding places in the forest. If the yellow jackets did not carry the molasses workers away, they should have the job done by nightfall, assuming no enemy forces showed up.

Hampton relayed orders to various men as he readied his horse to leave. Catherine Elizabeth, his wife of thirty-two years, stood watching from the front porch of their two-storied house with their two youngest children at her side. They observed the turmoil about their home while trying to keep a brave front, not showing apprehension of what might happen if the British Army or worse, sadistic Tories raided their place. Her senior by twenty-six years, the old colonel urged his wife to leave and take refuge north of the Catawba River, perhaps even as far as the Watauga settlements across the mountain. But Catherine would not listen to him.

"This is my home, and here is where we will remain," she stated adamantly. "I don't think that the gentlemen on the other side will make war on a poor woman and her children just because her husband is a champion for liberty. They will be less likely to burn our home if we are here. I will not abandon what we have built for so long. Surely, they are not savages like the Indians."

The colonel's five daughters of marriage age and the four youngest of their fifteen children would remain with their mother as would thirteen slaves needed to keep the plantation running. Hampton had armed the three oldest black men with shotguns. The servants pledged to protect the mistress of the house and the Hampton offspring with their lives and promised to keep meat on the table while the Hampton men were gone. Adam and John were soldiering with their father, and seventeen-year-old-year-old Michael was with a militia company somewhere in Virginia.

The oldest Hampton sibling, Jonathon, lived with his wife in a cabin about a half-mile up Mountain Creek and had agreed to stay close. With a deformed foot, Jonathon was exempt from militia duty, and although a noncombatant, he often stood guard duty at night and carried messages throughout the sprawling county for his father.

Colonel Hampton, with one rifle strapped to his back and another in his hand, ordered Jonathon to remain until all of the Whig militia had left the area and then, by the end of the week, bring any stragglers to their meeting point. The patriarch gave his wife and children instructions about where to hide, if need be, and which of the neighbors they could trust. They knew which routes to take if forced to flee the area. Once again Hampton pleaded for Catherine to take the children and go, but after three decades of marriage, he knew how stubborn his wife could be. When she got set in her way, that was it.

With a price on his head and the gallows promised by Tory leaders, there was no question that Colonel Andrew Hampton had to escape.

The colonel worried about his older daughters. Elizabeth and Susannah were comely and as sharp-tongued and stubborn as their mother. Maybe that was why they were still spinsters past twenty-five years of age. The Hampton daughters would be enticing targets for any undisciplined soldier who came plundering the countryside. The father took comfort in knowing they could not be taken easy, for he had taught the girls how to shoot and use a knife and axe, primarily to fight off Indians. They could hold their own against white savages as well, something their brothers found out the hard way. These girls were not given the instructions of social finesse common to the genteel young ladies of Charles Town; they had learned how to survive in a frontier environment.

"You take care of yourself, Andrew, and come back with victory," Catherine urged, then turned and walked back into the house before he saw her cry.

Hampton spurred his horse toward the fort where a dozen Liberty Men were making final adjustments to their saddles and personal gear. He spotted two Rangers approaching and rode toward them. There was nothing new in their reports, only confirmation of earlier intelligence and rumors that Ferguson was on his way with ten times more troops than the Liberty Men could field.

During the previous night, Captain Singleton's men had exchanged rifle fire with a party of Loyalists that had taken over the Gilbert Town area. No one was hurt, but it was obvious that the enemy was there to stay.

Hampton had received an express again this morning from Colonel Charles McDowell, urging all Whig militia to report with haste to the Bedford rendezvous. Singleton took his company ahead of the colonel on to Bedford Hill where a plan would be developed to block Ferguson from going further north and to run him back to South Carolina, out of Rutherford County.

The ingenuity and skills of the two young men before him impressed Hampton. He spoke to them more like a father than a commanding officer. "Mister Gray, Mister Godley, would you like to stay down this way and spy for us?" the colonel asked. "It will be more dangerous than what you have been doing, but we need to know Ferguson's intentions. If we know his plans, then Colonel McDowell and I can figure a way to stop him."

In his thoughts, however, was a nagging question of whether McDowell would stay and fight. Since the Earle's Ford raid, he had begun openly questioning McDowell's military competence. However, without the Burke militia, there would be no way for Hampton's small force to wage any effective defense, much less an offense against an army ten times its size. It would take much more than a few snipers and guerrilla raids to hurt Ferguson.

"Don't let yourself get caught. It won't be pleasant," Hampton cautioned. "They hang spies, you know."

Jacob and Gray dismounted to get some water as a half-dozen armed militia rode close by, spooking the Rangers' horses. Zeus reared backward and stepped on Gray's foot, cracking a bone. "Damn!" Gray yelled as he fell down, grabbing his injured foot. He tried to get up and walk, but it felt as though he had stepped on a porcupine as he crumbled again to the ground. Hampton called others to help as Jacob tried to assist his hurt friend. "Did you break a bone?" Hampton asked.

"Don't know, but it sure hurts like hell," Gray responded.

"Boys, get him back on his horse," Hampton ordered. "Mister Gray, you will ride with us till we find a safer place for you to rest that foot and get it well again."

Turning to Jacob, Hampton asked, "Will you be all right working by yourself."

"Yes sir!"

Jacob remounted and rode south to a place he could hide and observe how many of Ferguson's corps would cross the Broad and march north.

It was late in the day when Robert Godley followed Captain Biggerstaff across the Broad River to the main Loyalist camp. Along with a score of other Tryon County militia, the remainder of the company stayed behind as pickets on the north side of the river at Dennard's Ford. On the hill above the ford, Robert could see lots of activity and many uniformed soldiers. Although shallow at this point, the river had doubled in width after the Green merged with it only a quarter mile upstream. It was four times wider than the Second Broad up near his home.

The company commanders not on patrol gathered for a meeting with Ferguson at Andrew Power's home, located on the knoll overlooking the ford, on the opposite side of the river from where Biggerstaff's company was bivouacked. It was the first meeting for Godley and Biggerstaff with the legendary Scottish officer. Also present were Colonel Mills, their regimental commander, and his son William, a major and second in command.

Major Daniel Plummer and five captains represented South Carolina's Fair Forest District. Wearing the red-coated uniform of the Provincial regulars from New York was Captain Abraham DePeyster, Ferguson's number two.

More than a hundred Provincials and loyal militia already were north of the Broad River on reconnaissance missions. Captain Sam Ryerson and his brother Martin, a lieutenant, both New Jersey volunteers, were with the remainder of the Tory militia at Twitty's Ford, about eight miles upstream.

Colonel Mills introduced his officers and Sergeant Godley to Ferguson who acknowledged the newcomers to his force. In a jubilant mood, Ferguson climbed up on a stump so he could see everyone as he talked to his assembled leaders, "Gentlemen, I'm pleased you have joined us. Most of you, I understand, have had experience fighting Indians. I hear some might even have enjoyed confrontation with His Majesty's forces before seeing the light and joining in service to the Crown.

"Most of my militia have received some training in musketry, the manual of arms, and battlefield maneuvers. Since some of you Tryon County boys have not been trained, your people with horses, Colonel Mills, can keep their rifles for the time being and serve as scouts, guides, and sharpshooters.

"However, after we get to Gilbert Town and get our supply wagons up with muskets, your units will spend a few days with Captain Taylor and me to learn how to soldier with our beloved Brown Bess and bayonet."

Ferguson paused, pleased with the intense look of his subordinates. "It is my intention to subjugate Tryon and Burke Counties before we turn east to meet Lord Cornwallis, who is on the way now to Charlotte Town. Our mission is to quell the rebellion in these parts. Thanks to you loyal volunteers, we will do just that. I am not expecting a lot of armed resistance. But there are bloody rebels about, and as you well know, they can be a nuisance. If they are foolish enough to fight, then we will make quick work of them.

"Some of our people are already at Gilbert Town. I received reports today that rebels were seen lurking around nearby. They even shot at Captain Dunlop and his men but didn't hit anybody. There can't be too many of them, just local banditti.

"It is my desire to reach Gilbert Town around midnight. Dunlop's Rangers are securing the area as we speak. Colonel Mills, your lead companies will join up with them first and then patrol for three miles round Gilbert Town.

"I'm told that Hampton is already retreating northward to join McDowell. He might even take his family as refugees to the backwater region over the mountains. My spies have seen some rebel families abandoning their plantations and moving out of harm's way. Let them be if they are going peaceful. Good riddance.

"Now a few rules. No plunder unless a provincial officer is present and gives specific orders to that effect. Treat everyone with respect. Tell all the families that, for their safety, they should come and register for protection at our Gilbert Town headquarters. Those who swear loyalty to the royal government will not suffer plunder, even if at one time they may have sided with the rebellion.

"We will confiscate food supplies for men and animals only from property of known rebels. The Tryon County boys know who they are. If we need something from a Loyalist farm, always show kindness to the people and give a written a receipt for items taken. Again, none of this will be done without a uniformed provincial officer or sergeant present.

"If you are faced with armed resistance, use the force necessary to overpower it. Show no mercy until a surrender is made. Prisoners will then be treated with dignity and brought to my headquarters at Gilbert Town. Captain Taylor will be setting up a prisoner pen there. Once that is done,

Captain DePeyster will bring our existing prisoners with him when he joins us in the next day or so with the commissary wagons.

"Let me be blunt, gentlemen. I do not want to hear of any hangings, beatings, or house burnings unless authorized by me or a provincial officer. If a person is to be hanged, it will only be after a full hearing. No sham courts. Women and children will not be harmed. We need to win favor of these people and let them know that, unlike those rebel scoundrels, we operate professionally, with compassion and in accordance with law. I will harshly treat any man in this command who fails to obey these rules.

"Gentlemen, please relay my instructions to your individual commands. Any questions?"

Robert Godley raised his hand. "Colonel Ferguson, sir. If anybody shoots at us, we do shoot back, don't we?"

"Of course. I expect you to protect yourself and the corps. What I don't want is excessive independent aggression without authority. And don't go chasing after any enemy you see running away. You could be led into an ambush. That's what happened to Colonel Innes at Musgrove's Mill. Make sure we maintain unit integrity at all times. Be aggressive, but be sure of your action."

"How about old man Hampton? Are we going to hang him?" someone yelled.

"We got to catch him first," Ferguson chuckled and then turned to the South Carolina militia commander. "Major Plummer, first thing tomorrow morning, you will take some troops and go to Hampton's plantation. If he or any of his followers are in the area, arrest them, and bring them to me for justice. Colonel Mills will give you some guides to lead you. Be courteous to the Hampton women."

The Scottish officer added, "We have been taking the names of all known rebel officers and leaders. I want them apprehended. Hopefully, they will come peaceably, that is if they haven't already fled the area."

"Are we going up to the Catawba and get McDowell too?" someone asked.

"One phase at a time, gentlemen. We have with us a corps of more than one thousand men under arms. Our spies tell us that Hampton and McDowell together can't get a third of that number. Within a week or two, the Broad and Catawba basins will be pacified from the river headwaters all the way to our main army."

Ferguson paused as he looked over his men, smiled, and concluded his remarks. "Don't forget that within a day's march, we have Major Gibbs's Spartan militia looking after our flanks. So keep alert, stay ready. We will begin the advance at sundown."

Toward evening, Jacob found a perfect place to make an observation nest that gave him a clear view of the road that led from Dennard's Ford to Gilbert Town, yet hidden from anyone walking within a few feet of the site. After leaving Zeus hobbled a quarter mile back in the forest, he cut his way through a cedar and pine thicket that was covered with a massive tangle of honeysuckle vines. He carved out a tunnel within the vine clusters that took him to where he could see the road without being detected, even in daylight.

Prior to settling in, he gathered some muscadines from a wild grape vine hanging nearby. A few shakes on the vine brought a rain of the overripened, thumb-sized purple fruit crashing about him. After eating his fill of the thick-husked wild grapes, he used his bandana as an improvised sack and harvested a couple dozen more to munch through the evening.

Stalking men, he found, was no different from stalking deer or bear. All it took were patience, stealth, and keeping your mind on the task at hand. Unlike some he knew, he was not prone to fidget or let daydreams lure him away from his main purpose. His biggest worry was falling asleep in the wee hours of morning when nothing but imagination filled the void of inactivity and lulled one into a false sense of security. Tonight he willed his mind to focus on the road and nothing else.

Jacob sensed danger about an hour after sundown just before a lone rider galloped past him, heading south. *One of Ferguson's express riders, perhaps.* All was quiet for another hour; then two men on foot walked by going north, both carrying long rifles. Then, some three hours after dusk, came the hoof falls of several horses. A three-quarter moon cast an eerie grayness beyond the ebon-tree shadows, allowing some visibility within the narrow, open corridor where Jacob enjoyed a limited field of vision.

In the lead were four riders traveling two abreast, moving slowly up the road. A couple of horse lengths back, on each side of the road, were three riders in single file near the wood line. Most were just shadows to Jacob, but when the nearest off-road, mounted man passed within ten feet of his position, he recognized the features of his brother William. *This must be Biggerstaff's Tory company. Wonder where Robert is?*

More mounted militia followed the outriders, two abreast on the road. Most of the mounted men wore a tricorn, although two were bareheaded and three had round hats preferred by local planters. Some carried long rifles in their arms, but most had British-issued muskets. He thought he recognized another person, but facial features were difficult to make out in the dim light and at the distance from where he was looking.

To help keep track of the enemy, Jacob cut several lengths of honeysuckle vine and stripped them of their leaves. On one, he tied a knot for every ten mounted Loyalists he counted; another had a knot for every twenty militia footmen, and the third had a knot for every ten uniformed soldiers. He tied several leafed vines to the counting runners; the number of leaves indicated the type of troops being observed.

Several minutes behind the lead group came three other men on horseback, two of them uniformed officers. The one with the prancing horse has to be Ferguson and the short one with a fancy waistcoat and sword is surely Ambrose Mills, he thought. They were followed by another half-dozen mounted men and forty-two uniformed soldiers walking four abreast, their officers mounted in front of the column. Next came about three hundred foot militia, followed by two squads of mounted dragoons, one squad in uniform.

Jacob lost count as the footmen marched by, trying to keep in step, which was difficult with no drummer tapping cadence. The only sounds were the occasional clanking of a rifle against a knife or sword, muffled footsteps, and whispered chastisements from sergeants pushing laggards to stay alert or walk faster. Soon they were all past Jacob. There were no flags, no wagons, and no packhorses that he could see.

Other than two additional express riders, speeding down the road during the early morning hours, all remained quiet. Jacob nodded several times as the night stretched toward morning, but he willed himself to stay awake. He nibbled more on the sweet, wild fruit he had picked earlier, which caused his bowels to react abruptly. He backed out of his hiding place and walked back into the woods to relieve himself, praying that no one would pick up the foul odor he was creating. He covered his discharge with several handfuls of dirt and crawled back to continue observing the quiet darkness.

It was shortly after midnight when the Loyalist column was stopped by a harsh, whispered command, "Halt! Who goes there?"

Biggerstaff stopped his company and answered more loudly, "Highlander," the recognition password in use for this day. The sentry answered, "Fraser," the correct countersign. With his rifle cocked and at the ready, the sentry walked out from the shadows into the road to get a better look at the newcomers whom he was expecting. "Who are you?" he demanded.

"I'm Captain Aaron Biggerstaff. Major Ferguson and his corps are following."

"Wait, I'll let Captain Dunlop know you are here," the sentry said before turning and giving instructions to one of his colleagues to fetch Dunlop.

"Are we at Gilbert Town?" Biggerstaff asked.

"Ain't no town, not even a village, but it's Gilbert's place. We are so far in the backwoods now, these hill folk don't know how to wear shoes!" The sentry laughed, pleased with his analogy but not knowing he was talking to residents of the area.

Before Biggerstaff could issue an angry retort for the insult, two riders approached at a gallop. One was Dunlop, who was told that the main body of Ferguson's troops was only a few minutes behind and would be arriving shortly.

Dunlop ordered Biggerstaff to take his men on past the Gilbert house to Cathey's Creek, about a quarter mile farther up the road; relieve the picket there; and set up security around the ford. Biggerstaff would not talk to Ferguson or Mills before the next forenoon, after the commanders were satisfied with their encampment and the headquarters set up in the rustic ordinary, located in front of the Gilbert house.

RAID ON THE HAMPTONS

8 September 1780

Just before the first streaks of red glowed in the eastern sky, Jacob decided he must get word about the enemy troop movement to Hampton. He did not know where Ferguson's marchers were going, but he bet they would stop in Gilbert Town where there was an abundance of water and grass. To make sure, he left Zeus hobbled and tracked the Loyalist on foot. Walking northward through the woods and parallel to the road, he made a wide swing around a house with two excited dogs that howled his presence to the countryside.

He slipped across Holland's Creek and entered the Gilbert plantation shortly after sunup. Off to his left, Jacob spotted a picket, half-asleep and leaning against a tree about one hundred paces ahead. Jacob began circling stealthily around the plantation, avoiding other sentries. He saw more than three dozen saddled horses grazing in the meadow. A dozen or so men were moving around the Gilbert home; they looked like officers from his view-point, but he dared not get closer. A large number of men lounged within the trees beyond the house, many stretched out sleeping in the warm morning sun, resting from the night march.

Jacob slipped further back into the forest, traveled north from the biv-ouac area and waded Cathey's Creek before making his way westward, parallel to the stream. Before continuing his course several miles over a rise of land and down to Mountain Creek and the Hampton compound, he had to cross the road that led from Gilbert Town northeastward toward Flint Hill and Burke County. Ensuring no one was within sight, he scooted unseen across the road.

Instead of immediately leaving the area, Jacob crept back along the road and through the bushes toward Cathey's Creek. On the opposite side of the creek, about sixty yards away, he spotted a small group of militiamen serving as an outpost. He recognized two men talking in the middle of the road at the water's edge as his brother Robert and Robert's commander, Aaron Biggerstaff. Around his waist, Robert was wearing a striped sash indicating his rank as sergeant. A third man walked toward the two, startling Jacob. It was his younger brother Andrew. *Why is Andy here? He's a staunch supporter of the rebellion. Why now in the ranks of the enemy?* Jacob accepted, but did not understand, what he was seeing.

The Liberty Man wanted desperately to talk to his brothers but thought better of it. It was critical that he let Hampton know that Ferguson was occupying Gilbert Town in force. He also had to get back and recover his horse. Not knowing how his brothers would react, Jacob did not want to risk a confrontation at this time. It was a different atmosphere than when he last left them three months ago to serve on the Indian line.

Three hours after dawn, Major Daniel Plummer's Loyalist battalion arrived at the Hampton plantation. Captain William Lee, his deputy commander, took two companies and charged into the abandoned fort, which had already been stripped of anything useful. Captain Walter Gilkey from the Tryon County militia and Plummer trotted their horses to the main house where Catherine Hampton stood waiting on the front porch, her arms folded in front of her best dress and apron.

Plummer doffed his hat as he approached and politely wished her a good day. "I'm looking for Colonel Andrew Hampton, ma'am. Is this his home?"

She answered acidly. 'Yes, but he is not here."

"And where might he be, ma'am?"

"I don't rightly know, probably somewhere working to send you blame Tories to meet your maker."

Ignoring the barb, Plummer continued in a polite tone. "And what about your son, Jonathon. Does he live here?"

"Jonathon does not live in this house. He has a family of his own now. Why do you want him? He's crippled and not part of the militia." Concern was evident in her voice.

"And just where is his home?" Plummer patiently asked.

"Up the creek a ways."

"Ma'am, we have to search your house to make sure that no fugitives of the king's justice are here and that you do not have hidden contraband."

"Let me get my children out. They should not be subjected to your plunderer's wickedness," Catherine said bitterly. Turning, she called out, "Susannah! Bring all the children outside and take them over by the big oak."

Looking back at the Loyalist leader, Catherine pleaded. "Sir, I beg that no harm come to my children."

"Ma'am, be assured…I do not make war on women and children. As long as they behave themselves, they have nothing to fear from us," Plummer said. He turned to Gilkey. "Captain, take some men and search the house. Do not take anything other than weapons. Try not to damage the lady's property. Our issues are with Colonel Hampton, not his family."

Disappointed at the order against plundering, Gilkey dismounted, saying, "Aye, sir," and took four of his Tryon Tories with him into the house as the Hampton siblings walked out. Meanwhile, other soldiers began going through the outbuildings, the gristmill, and slave quarters. The Hampton offspring, including the grown girls, all gathered around Susannah about fifty feet from the house. Some of the young militiamen gave a few catcalls toward the young women until their commander sharply ordered them to shut up and behave like gentlemen. A sergeant and four men stood close to the siblings to ensure no mischief.

"Major!" Captain Lee, his face flushed with excitement, was yelling as he ran toward Plummer from behind the house with two of his men carrying three fowling muskets. "These goddamn niggers got shotguns! The son of a bitch armed his niggers! They ought to be hung for this," he exclaimed excitedly. "And there's hardly any grain and corn here, only a few bushels. Didn't see but one cow and three horses. They've got the rest hidden around here someplace. A whip on a nigger's back will tell us real quick where they are."

Plummer saw all the slaves now sitting in a tight huddle with a dozen muskets pointed at them. Several of the Negroes were clearly shaken with fright, but the younger men among them only stared in defiance. Catherine

Hampton's voice rose as she pleaded to the major. "Those guns are for shooting game so we can have meat on the table. My people are not fighters, sir. They are field hands and pledged to look after the children and me. We trust them with our lives. Don't hurt them, please."

Plummer inspected the weapons and ordered, after making sure they were not loaded, that the worse-looking one be placed on the porch and the other two confiscated. "Let the darkies go. We are not here to create destruction," he said in a scolding manner. "And, Captain Lee, I don't appreciate the language you are using, particularly around the ladies and children."

Gilkey emerged from the house, saying he had found no contraband or hiding rebels. Their search included the cellar, attic, and the cookhouse out back. They looked under all beds and in all cupboards. He didn't mention that they pocketed more than one hundred sixty English pounds sterling found under a false drawer in the cupboard.

Plummer sent a sergeant and ten militiamen to load the only wagon in the compound with the grain and the two bushels of potatoes found in the root cellar.

The major then ordered his officers to remount and form the battalion into a marching formation. He tipped his tricorn again to Catherine and said apologetically, "Mistress Hampton, please forgive our intrusion into your life. I regret the necessity of our actions, but since hostilities exist, we cannot permit any aid to the rebels. We must bring order back to the country and punish those who have caused all this distress. If you see your husband or son, tell them to voluntarily surrender themselves immediately if they want any sense of leniency."

Several of the dragoons rode up, leading three horses they found in the Hampton paddock. "That's a beautiful animal," Lee said as he walked to the sleek-looking, roan mare. "She's much sturdier than the nag I'm riding. Unless you object, Major, I'm taking this rebel horse for service to the Crown."

Plummer said nothing as Lee began transferring his bridle and saddle to the confiscated horse. "That's my son's horse," Catherine protested.

"It's the price he pays for being a traitor," Lee shot back sharply.

"Enough!" Plummer said, quieting the argument. "We will take the horses, ma'am. We cannot let them remain in service of rebels. Sergeant, take the extra horses with the wagon back to Gilbert Town. Mount up, Captain Lee; we have to find her son."

The major looked over to the group of field hands and yelled, "If any of you darkies want your freedom, you can go with the wagons."

The Negro men stared defiantly at Plummer. None accepted the offer.

The family matriarch remained silent, only staring at the hated Tories. Inwardly she let out a sigh of relief. Her children were unharmed. Her house was left standing and was not ransacked. Her servants were not beaten or taken away. As expected, only two shotguns, some food supplies, and animals were confiscated. She was especially appreciative that a gentleman like Plummer was in command and not the other two brutish officers who showed no empathy for her family. She had heard that Gilkey had burned out a Whig family down near the mouth of the Second Broad the year before. She did not discover the money theft until long after the soldiers had left.

Jacob used the sun to guide him westward to Mountain Creek where he would turn south and follow the stream down to the Hampton place. He had to make his report before backtracking and finding his horse, hoping that Zeus would still be there after a day's abandonment. As he approached the creek bank, he heard the soft murmur of men's voices on the other side. Jacob checked his primer and crept in the direction until he could see on the other across the creek where four men were watering their horses and resting. He recognized one as a Whig he had met in Montford Cove back during the summer—George Ledbetter, another of Hampton's company commanders.

"Ho, Cap'n Ledbetter," Jacob called out. "Jacob Godley coming in."

The men with Ledbetter crouched and readied their rifles in the direction of the voice as their leader called, "Come in slowly, Jake. Anybody with you?"

"I'm all alone." Jacob waded across the creek and downstream to where the four men waited.

"Where's your horse?" Ledbetter asked.

Jake explained his circumstances and the need to get his intelligence about Ferguson's forces to Colonel Hampton.

"The colonel is done gone north to join up with McDowell. I'm heading that way too. Had to help some folks up near Russell's Station get their animals and food stock to a safe place. We came by the Hampton place a while ago. His missus said that the old man left yesterday. We expect to be with him around sundown."

"Will you tell him what I've seen? There are hundreds of Tories at Gilbert Town and a slew of redcoats. I'm on my way to get my horse, then I can join y'all in a day or so."

Using his knotted vines to refresh his memory with more precise numbers of enemy troops, Jacob briefly outlined in more detail his observations over the past twenty-four hours.

"That's a heap of trouble we got here," Ledbetter said. "We talked to a Whig planter earlier today who saw about five hundred Tories marching toward Gilbert Town from Twitty's Ford before daybreak. They didn't have any wagons either. I'm afraid we are in for one helluva fight. Any idea where they are going from here?"

"Don't know, but if you take my report to the Colonel, I'll spy around Gilbert Town some more tomorrow and see what else I can pick up before I join you at Bedford Hill."

"You watch out, Jake. Those bastards don't take too kindly to spies," Ledbetter warned. "I'll let old Hampton know what you are doing. Stay off the main trails; those Tory scoundrels are thick as flies on a dead carcass in July."

Jacob had been following the creek south for less than an hour after leaving the Ledbetter group when he heard the whinnying of horses and the footsteps of soldiers nearby. He dropped to his knees and crawled through some thick bushes toward the sounds coming from a track running up the bottomland parallel to the creek. *The Tories must be raiding the Hampton place!*

Then he saw more than a hundred militiamen led by three officers on horseback. A half-dozen mounted redcoats were in the rear. Jacob could not recognize any of the militia who were marching through a meadow toward a cabin that faced a cornfield. He was too far away to identify the person sitting in the cabin's doorway or see the three men standing on the other side of the cabin.

Jonathon Hampton was lacing his leggings before joining several of his Whig friends to rendezvous with his father, when one of the men hollered to Jonathon, "Who's that crowd coming through your field? Friend or foe?"

Jonathon looked up. Although the troops were several hundred paces away, he recognized Walter Gilkey, and that was enough. "Clear out!" he yelled. "They're damned Tories and redcoats. Run!"

The three men turned quickly and fled into the forest as several of the Tories opened fire at a range too far away for the muskets to be effective. With the footmen running behind them, the three officers, with swords drawn, galloped up to Jonathon's cabin. The mounted dragoons spurred their horses toward Jonathon's neighbors, but were not quick enough to catch the three seasoned backwoodsmen before they disappeared into the forest. Jonathon's friends easily made their escape despite two dozen Loyalists scouring the woods for them.

Jonathon saw something else familiar; one of the approaching officers was riding his horse. He stood up and limped into the yard to greet the newcomers. Without slowing, Lee rushed his horse toward Jonathon, knocking the crippled man down as he screamed, "Stay where you are, you damned rebel!"

The horse jumped over Jonathon and danced around him, angry at his new rider's unfamiliar roughness with reins and spurs. Lee was trying to get the horse to trample Jonathon. Fortunately, the hoofs missed stomping the fallen man by only a few inches. Lee brought the horse under control and yelled, "On your feet, rebel!" His sword pointed directly at Jonathon's eyes.

More than a dozen footmen stood around them with muskets and bayonets pointed toward Jonathon as he struggled to stand erect, his deformed foot causing him to lean painfully to one side. He saw other Loyalists run around the cabin and into his outbuilding. Tenseness ran through the soldiers in front of the house as they pointed their weapons beyond Jonathon when his wife of one year and his uncle emerged from the house onto the cabin porch.

Towering over Jonathon was an aristocratic-looking militia officer dressed in a dusty, but well-tailored waistcoat and holding a sword, although not as menacingly as the young officer who had knocked him down. Still courteous in demeanor, Plummer saluted with his sword and asked, "Would you be Jonathon Hampton, a justice of the peace for the rebel government?"

"Yes, sir, I am Jonathon Hampton!" Jonathon responded without visible rancor, then turned and pointed to his family behind him. "And this is my wife, Nancy, and my uncle, Jacob Hyder."

"I am Major Daniel Plummer in service of the British Army and His Majesty, King George. It is my duty, sir, to arrest those who are aiding the rebellion against the lawful government of the American colonies, of which North Carolina is one," Plummer announced. "You, sir, are on my list as an enemy of the Crown."

As the major concluded, Captain Lee, who had dismounted, issued an order to the footmen nearest to him. "You men, let's search this house and make sure nobody else is hiding inside."

They rushed through the door, roughly pushing aside Hyder and Jonathon's wife. Both bristled but did not resist.

"Welcome, Major Plummer. Do your men have to be so rude? We offer no resistance. We have nothing to hide here." Jonathon kept his tone even and friendly.

"Who are those people running away?"

"They are neighbors who live back that away. They usually come over by here to fish the creek. I guess they got scared when they saw your army coming up. I'd run too if I didn't have this reel foot."

"Where is your father?"

"You just missed him. He left yesterday going toward Indian country. I'm sure he will be disappointed when he learns that you came a 'calling while he was gone," Jonathon said smiling.

"You are not mocking me, are you Mister Hampton?" Plummer asked sharply.

"Not in the least, sir. Merely stating fact."

A commotion could be heard from inside the cabin as Lee upended a bed and unlaced the rope support that held a straw mattress in place. Lee stomped back outside, again pushing Nancy roughly aside, while coiling the rope and laughing. "We have enough rope to hang this traitor right here and now."

Nancy screamed, "*No!*" and ran over toward Plummer before an armed militiaman blocked her way. "Please, sir, don't hang my husband."

"We'll do nothing of the sort, Captain Lee. We are not barbarians," Plummer declared. "Mister Hampton, you are under arrest and must stand trial for your crimes against the Crown."

"Sir, I have committed no crimes."

"You are acting illegally as a justice of the peace. You have performed marriages which only the Anglican Church is authorized to perform. You have given aid and comfort to those engaged in rebellion. You have preached sedition. All those, sir, are very serious crimes against the Crown."

"I will plead guilty to being a justice of the peace. But, sir, I was duly appointed to that position by Governor Caswell two, three years ago. He was the only governor in the province. There's been no British authority here that

I am aware of for five years. We are back on the edge of the wilderness, far removed from organized government. Without a justice here, there would be anarchy. Shouldn't we maintain law and order? My records are available for your inspection, sir." Well read, Jonathon had a reputation of being a smooth talker, even more persuasive than was his father or anyone else in these parts.

"And how do you plead to supporting the rebellion?"

"I will be honest, sir, and say I honor my father and his belief that we should have the right to set our own destiny without undue interference from any government that is located hundreds of miles away. But, sir, you can see that I am in no physical shape to serve in the militia. My duty, sir, is to help my fellow man."

"Damn this traitor, Major," Lee shouted. "Let's hang him now. He admits his guilt; send him to hell."

"Hear, hear!" cried some of the troops. Others yelled, "Hang him!"

"Ferguson would hang this damn mongrel as soon as he hears the name Hampton," Lee snarled.

Looking sharply at Lee, Plummer rebuked his subordinate testily. "I have said before, Captain, we do not hang without trial. Don't defy me again, sir!"

Lee's face grew red from his anger. As he started to continue his defiant protest, a thin, gray-haired, fifty-two-year-old private walked out of the ranks, put his hand on the captain's shoulder, and whispered, "Calm down, Billy. Major Plummer is right."

Plummer gave a nod of appreciation to William Lee, Senior, who had joined his son's company after Whigs in the Tyger River area confiscated both his and his son's plantations last year and kicked their families out into the winter cold with only the clothes on their back. They were forced to leave the region immediately or be beaten or hanged or both. The young Tory captain was in Georgia on militia duty, and his father was on a hunting trip when local Whigs raided their property and families. Although both Lees still boiled with bitterness, the senior Lee was more even tempered than was his hot-blooded son. The father knew when not to let anger override judgment, particularly in confronting a superior officer.

As the younger Lee brought his temper back under control, Plummer looked at Nancy Hampton, who had started sobbing softly, and to Hyder, still standing on the porch staring hard at the invaders. "You, Mister Hyder, are you a part of this rebellion?" Plummer asked.

"I am here with no weapon, offering no resistance, sir," Hyder responded, careful not to lie directly. "But my political views are the same as my nephew."

"Well, I am arresting you as well since you are associated so closely with the Hamptons. Perhaps we can sort this out with Colonel Ferguson in Gilbert Town."

Jonathon interrupted Plummer. "Excuse me, sir. We will come and appear before your Colonel Ferguson. But might I take my wife to my mother's house first and let Uncle Jacob look after my aunt? It is not Christian to leave unarmed women out here alone on the edge of Indian country with no one to defend them."

"Well, sir, if I let you do that, do you have anyone who can give security for your appearance tomorrow before Colonel Ferguson?" Plummer asked.

"I have my land," Jonathon answered.

"And mine," Hyder echoed.

"That goes without saying," Plummer responded. He turned to his officers. "Will you, Captain Lee, offer security for these men?"

Incredulous that Plummer would make such a suggestion, Lee barked back, "Hell no! I will not, sir."

"What about you, Captain Gilkey? These are your neighbors, are they not?"

"No sir!" Gilkey retorted, still remembering the embarrassment and pain of being bested in a fistfight with Jonathon's brother, Adam, during a rowdy meeting of local Tories and Whigs at Brittain Church a few years back.

"Well, Captain Gilkey, is Mister Hampton here known to be a dishonest person?" Plummer asked.

"I must say, sir, that while he might be a traitor to his country, this Hampton is regarded to be an honest man."

"Well then, Mister Hampton, I like your candor. If you promise to report to Colonel Ferguson and me tomorrow morning at Gilbert Town within two hours of sunup, I will stand your security."

Jonathon could hardly believe what he heard. Plummer's action was counter to all he had heard about cruelty of Tory officers. "Sir, thank you for your kindness. I know you are doing your duty. You can be assured I will be there."

"And you, Mister Hyder?"

"I will be with my nephew. You have my word on that, sir."

"Good. If you do not appear, I will lose my commission and maybe my head too. Then Captains Lee and Gilkey and all these fellows here will unleash a torrent of hurt on the entire Hampton family and property, and you will be hanged on the spot or, worse, be tortured without mercy and then hanged."

After confiscating Jonathon and his uncle's rifles, Plummer ordered his men to reform and began the march back to Gilbert Town. Several among the militia grumbled along the way about their faint-hearted major's refusal to hang the two rebels and, worse still, setting the rebels free on their own recognizance.

Remaining quiet in his hidden position, Jacob watched most of the proceedings without knowing what was discussed. When he saw the horse plow into Jonathon and nearly trample him, it became obvious that it was not a friendly meeting. He wanted to shoot the bastard using a horse in such a brutal way, but remained still. Jacob recognized Hampton's oldest son by his pronounced limp when he walked toward the arriving Loyalists.

Plummer's patrols scoured the area continually, preventing Jacob from slipping away without detection. Nor did he want to leave until he knew the fate of his colonel's son. He remained hidden in the brush for nearly an hour until the Loyalists departed.

After the raiders had marched away, Jacob slipped quietly around to the cabin and approached Jonathon, his wife, and his uncle, making it obvious from a distance that he was coming in peace. Jonathon gave a broad smile, welcoming Jacob. "Well, now we have a friendly face visiting our home, Nancy."

Jonathon and Jacob exchanged the highlights of their adventures of the day. When asked why he did not leave now to join his father, Jonathon exclaimed, "I gave my word, and my word is my bond. If I don't show up, it will cause serious problems for the family. Those devils are sure to burn my cabin and my parent's house as well. No telling what they would do to Nancy, Mama, and my sisters."

Nancy sobbed again when Jacob argued. "But if you do go in, they will you hang you for sure."

"Maybe, maybe not. It will give me a chance to learn more of their intentions," Jonathon mused. "But, regardless, I have to go. I am honor-bound."

Hyder, who was only eight years older than his nephew and was a long-time member of Colonel Hampton's regiment, spat on the ground. He wanted to run to the safety of the hills but knew that the old colonel, his sister, and his own wife would never forgive him if he didn't go with Jonathon. "I'll be with you, Jon. Our fate hangs together."

"Bad choice of words." Jonathon laughed, truly amused for the first time all day.

Jacob did not linger at the Hampton cabin very long. He had to find his horse before dark. He became disoriented twice before eventually making his way back through the forest to where he had spied on Ferguson's march. Zeus was still where Jacob had left him, hobbled and waiting patiently for the Ranger's return. It was already dusk, so he led Zeus through the woods, walking rather than riding so he could better see obstacles.

He avoided the roads and trails and skirted around the few farmhouses. It was after midnight when Jacob arrived in the woods near the Foreman house. He unsaddled Zeus and hobbled the horse before bedding down for the night in the edge of the forest, choosing to wait until daybreak before announcing himself to his friends.

HAMPTON'S TRIAL

9 September 1780

Rachel Pearson woke before dawn and slipped out of the main house to stir the coals that smoldered through the night in the cookhouse's open fireplace. She fanned the bank of warm ashes and added some sticks to produce a flame to heat water and last night's leftover rabbit stew. Since moving in with the Foremans, she took responsibility for the morning kitchen chores without being asked.

Picking up a wooden pail and small stool, Rachel checked to make sure the fire would last for a while and then walked to a shed to squeeze milk from her aging cow. As she placed the stool next to the cow, she heard a door close from the main house and saw the shadow of John Foreman walk over to the cookhouse for his morning tea.

The cow greeted Rachel with a nonchalant shrug and began chewing on some fresh hay that Rachel tossed in front of her. "All right, Lady Cow, time to give us a pail of milk. Else you just might become supper for our dinner table. You don't want that, do you?" Rachel said mockingly.

Unexpectedly, someone behind her asked, "Is that any way to talk to a creature providing you with the sweetness of her innards day in and day out?"

Startled by the sound, Rachel screamed as she fell off the stool, kicked over the empty milk bucket, and plopped on the shed's dirt floor.

Roaring with laughter, Jacob Godley walked closer to his bewildered new friend to help her up.

"Damn you, Jacob Godley," she shouted indignantly. "You scared the devil out of me!"

"What's going on here?" John Pearson yelled as he ran into the shed with a butcher knife in his only hand, ready to do combat with any threat to his new ward.

"Sorry, Cap'n," Jacob said as he continued chuckling, "I don't think Rachel was expecting me. I didn't mean to scare her, but you should've seen the look on her face."

"It's not funny, Jacob. You could have been one of them heathen Indians or, even worse, a damn Tory blackguard," she spat back, but with a crack of a smile coming across her face. Softening her voice, she asked, "What are you doing here? Ain't never heard of anyone come a courtin' this time of day."

"Didn't come a courtin', Missy. Got here late in the night and decided to sleep in the woods rather than disturb y'all. Your banging around woke me up," Jacob responded.

It was all Foreman could do to keep from laughing aloud at the situation, but he kept a neutral face as he said, "Come on up to the house and let's have some tea, Jacob. Let Rachel finish her milking, that is if she can keep steady on that stool. With all this commotion, that old cow may just refuse us today."

Both families crowded around the dining room table in the main house, sipping the last of the East India tea brought up from Charles Town back before the siege and fall of the city, as Jacob told of the invasion of the thousand-man Loyalist army and seeing three of his brothers in the Tory militia. He talked about the raid on the Hamptons the day before. "You should find good hiding places for your food stocks and valuables," Jacob cautioned, "'cause ol' Ferguson will be sending out his banditti to plunder the countryside."

"We've already had Tory visitors, but they ain't took nothing yet," Foreman said. "You say there's a thousand or more of them at Gilbert Town? That's a lot of mouths to feed."

"Are they going to stay around here for a while?" Rachel asked.

"Don't know, but I suspect they will go on up to the Catawba River area and raid the plantations there after they plunder everything around here," Jacob said to Rachel, and then turned to Foreman. "I'd like to use your grinder to sharpen my knives and hatchet. Can you keep Zeus for a while? "

"Of course. Anything else you need?"

"No sir. I'm going to Gilbert Town and don't want to ride a good-looking horse into that den of skunks. Those thieves might just take him. I'm going to walk up there and see my brothers. Then I'll come and get Zeus and make my way north to join up with Colonel Hampton. Hope to stop and see my folks along the way."

Rachel's mother, who had been quiet during the morning, asked Jacob as he was rising to go outside, "You see any sign of that Rance Miller?"

"No, ma'am, not yet...but I hear he's around. He's got a mean reputation, even with his own kind."

"Well, you catch him for me. You kill him!" she snarled. Then in a more motherly manner, she turned to her daughter. "Rachel, you fix this boy some food to take with him...that is if it is all right with John and Becky. He's just skin and bones."

While Rachel busied herself with preparing some corn bread and fried rabbit, Jacob honed his blades and gave his rifle a much-needed cleaning and greasing down with lard. After eating a quick meal, Jacob headed for the Loyalist encampment. Wanting to appear as a wilderness man just coming down from the high country, he left his saddlebags with Foreman, who hid them with Zeus in a small meadow surrounded by thick forest and out of sight of prying Tory eyes that monitored the roads and major trails. He also chose not to shave, leaving a three-day stubble spotting his youthful cheeks.

As the morning sun peeked over the trees, the first group of local families, some on foot, some in carts or wagons, some on horseback, began arriving at Ferguson's headquarters to seek the king's protection. Ambrose Mills, who commanded the local Tories and had lived in the region for fourteen years, sat with Ferguson's intelligence chief, Alexander Chesney, at a table just in front of the Gilbert home and across the yard from the tavern-turned-military headquarters. Mills knew personally or by reputation most of the families that appeared for protection. Many had been neutral in the conflict, but several had been espousing the rebel cause prior to the arrival of the

Loyalist army. Those who switched sides were questioned skeptically and at considerable length before Mills would believe and accept their loyalty pledge. He refused to accept one recreant Whig's word and ordered the man's arrest as a thief.

Ferguson sympathized with the Gilbert family who had to quarter some of his Loyalist officers in their home. William Gilbert was away at the time in Hillsborough serving in the province's House of Commons when Ferguson took over his plantation. Prior to his election to the legislature, Gilbert had served two years as justice of the peace and held court in his house. Although alone, Sarah Gilbert accepted the onslaught of visitors with outward poise but internal dread. She talked to the women who accompanied their husbands or fathers to the military camp. She offered them cider and shared gossip about the disruptions caused by the Loyalist invasion. Later some would accuse the Gilberts of being Tory sympathizers.

Even with troops and residents coming and going, it was not a chaotic scene. The British commander looked up from reading an express from Cornwallis and saw Major Plummer approaching with two men, one with a pronounced limp, causing Ferguson to look more carefully at Jonathon Hampton's deformed foot. Walking a few paces farther back were four militiamen carrying muskets with fixed bayonets.

Realizing that this must be the rebel justice of the peace that Plummer had mentioned the day before, Ferguson went inside his headquarters and donned his red uniform waistcoat, for what transpired next had to be of an official nature.

Plummer doffed his tricorn as he approached his superior and announced, "Colonel Ferguson, sir, permit me to present Jonathon Hampton and Jacob Hyder, who live about six miles to the west. Mister Hampton is a justice of the peace for the rebel government. He is also the son of the rebel militia commander, Colonel Andrew Hampton. Mister Hyder is a suspected rebel and is Mister Hampton's uncle. His property abuts to the Hampton place."

Each of the accused removed his hat and made a slight bow toward Ferguson as he was introduced. Ferguson, bareheaded, smiled at the two as he, in turn, bowed slightly as though the suspected rebels were visiting dignitaries. "Welcome...but I must admit that I am a bit surprised that you came this morning, Mister Hampton. With the leeway offered yesterday by Major Plummer, I expected that you would be headed toward a backwater sanctuary in the high mountains by now."

"I am pleased to meet you, Colonel Ferguson," Jonathon said as he made a deeper bow of respect. "You should not be surprised, sir. Both my uncle and I said we would appear before you today and, as men of honor, here we are, at your service, sir."

"I stand corrected, sir." Ferguson nodded again.

Hampton continued quickly, "I'm also pleased to report that Major Plummer treated my family and me with kindness and respect when he came calling yesterday, much more so than we had expected. He also kept a young, hot-blooded officer from causing mayhem at the expense of my mother and family. For that, we are most appreciative. However, I must add that the same young officer stole some of our horses, including my favorite riding horse."

Expecting something more supercilious, Ferguson was taken aback by the gracious, almost patronizing response. Yet, the commander had been warned that Jonathon was a persuasive talker who could charm a wolf's growl into a whimper. Ferguson's smile ceased as he became more formal. "We are not here to exchange pleasantries, Mister Hampton. You are charged with serious crimes, and these must be adjudicated here and now. As for your horses, consider them your donation to the king."

Ferguson turned to Colonel Mills, who was receiving another resident petitioning for protection, and asked Mills to turn those duties over to one of his officers. "I want you to join me and Major Plummer as we sit in judgment of the accused rebels."

Looking back at the tavern, Ferguson saw Captain James Dunlop leaning against the door frame. "Captain Dunlop, knowing your love of Whigs," Ferguson said sarcastically, "perhaps you would serve as the prosecutor."

"You say his name is Hampton?" Dunlop asked.

"Yes."

Ferguson handed Dunlop a document outlining the allegations against the accused. The commander then ordered additional chairs and sat at the table with Mills and Plummer facing the accused, who remained standing. "Hampton?" Dunlop mused. "I recall killing a young rebel officer named Hampton two months ago in a raid along the Pacolet." Turning to address Jonathon, Dunlop continued. "Now he wouldn't be any of your kin, would he?"

Forcing himself to keep his temper in check, Jonathon responded in a hard, but even, tone, "Yes, sir. It was my young brother Noah that you put to the sword. I heard that he was unarmed and had surrendered when you killed him."

Ferguson looked sharply at Dunlop, who only smiled wickedly. "It was at night and in the heat of battle...but it resulted in one less Hampton rebel to contend with, just as there will be one less Hampton after we hang you for spewing the same evil as your brother and father. Too bad the old man isn't here to get his just reward as well."

"Don't be too hasty, Captain," Ferguson retorted. "Make your case for hanging if you will. And you, Hampton, do you want me to find an officer to champion your defense?"

"I will not trouble you for that courtesy, sir. I feel that I can adequately defend myself, for the truth is on my side."

"Very well. Captain Dunlop, proceed."

"Your honors, long before I arrived with the advance party here in Gilbert Town, I had received several reports from reliable people loyal to His Majesty's government that the defendant, Jonathon Hampton, had violated the law by accepting a commission as a justice of the peace for the rebel government of North Carolina. These witnesses told me that Jonathon Hampton rode about the county performing a number of illegal acts, the most recent, in violation of both civil and church law, by marrying a young couple just a week ago over at the Adair plantation.

"Furthermore, other officers of the king and me received numerous reports that this Hampton aided and abetted the rebellion by carrying messages for rebel militia, encouraging citizens to take arms against the lawful forces of the king, and preaching sedition throughout the land. For these and other treasonous crimes, Jonathon Hampton deserves the hangman's noose.

"As for the fellow with him, I know little of him other than he is related to the Hamptons and rides today with Jonathon Hampton. That association alone is deserving of the most severe punishment."

While Dunlop was laying out his charges, a growing group of Tory militia and civilians from the surrounding countryside began gathering to watch the proceedings. Ferguson asked officiously, "And you, Mister Hampton. How do you plead?"

"If you please, gentlemen, first let me admit that my name is Hampton, a name that I proudly bear." Despite his deformed foot, Jonathon stood erect, appearing neither haughty nor in servitude, speaking in a clear, even voice and with no hesitation in finding the words to argue his case. "I am the oldest of fifteen children, although only fourteen now that dear Noah was murdered." Jonathon put a strong emphasis on the word *murdered*. "My father is a good man who is dedicated to the peace and well-being of his neighbors. He also believes in government that permits its citizens to have a voice in its affairs. For many years, like Colonel Mills here, he was a militia officer in service to the royal governor of North Carolina.

"When the royal governor and his entourage abandoned the province some five years ago not to return again, no government existed other than an interim one developed by citizens to fill the vacuum created by the vacating Royals. I had nothing to do with the royal governor leaving his post and responsibilities. Meanwhile, here in the west, we continued to be subjected to increasing Indian raids. In seventeen seventy-six, for example, there were murderous rampages all along our western boundaries. Just a few miles from here, homes and fields were burned. Entire families were hacked to pieces. My father was asked by the Committee of Safety to continue his service as a militia officer for the province to protect families and property from marauding Indians. I, as did most citizens, Whig and Tory, supported my father in keeping the frontier safe from the savages.

"When a new government was formed for North Carolina, it was not done at the point of a rifle. But regardless of who ran the government down east, there still existed in these parts people with criminal intent, property being bought and sold, disputes needing civil adjudication, wills needing to be probated, and marriages to be performed. There was a desperate need for a functioning legal system to keep records and order in society. Otherwise, sir, chaos would rein.

"In the absence of royal authority, after the previous justice was elected to the House of Commons—that was Mister Gilbert whose property we now stand on—it was my duty, when asked by the Committee of Safety, to serve as the principal officer of the court for this county.

"I might add, sir, that these duties were void of the politics which created this ugly war. No one suffered discrimination by me for his political sentiments. Each case was handled within its own merits according to the edicts handed down by established English law, which I have read."

Addressing Mills directly, Jonathon continued. "Colonel Mills, I recall some land transfers that your son asked me to help with back last year. There was no objection raised then to my serving as the justice of peace, and you knew full well that my appointment came from the then-sitting governor of North Carolina.

"I contend that serving as a justice of the peace is a service to all residents, regardless of the loyalties. As an officer of the law, I treated everyone honestly and with respect."

Growing impatient and angry, Dunlop shot back, "It has long been the law of the land that only the church, the Anglican Church, could sanctify a marriage here in the colonies, yet you violated that law, did you not?"

"I never acted as a representative of any church, Captain. However, there is not an Anglican Church within one hundred miles of here that I know of. The pastor of Brittain Presbyterian Church, which is located only a few miles from this site, is only here a few days each month, and most of the time he is busy with baptisms and preaching. The marriages that I performed as a duly appointed officer of the court were to ensure that spouses and children had protection of law. As a Christian, I did begin each ceremony with a prayer, requesting that the betrothed honor and obey the teachings of our Lord and that the Lord look over their fruitful life. Without someone doing this, gentlemen, we would have far too many couples living out of wedlock and our region overrun with bastard children without legal birthright. That wouldn't be right, now would it?"

"Hear, hear" could be heard from the crowd, causing Ferguson to cast a stern look at the on lookers and issue a strong rebuke, "No more comments from you spectators. If you can't shut up, I'll have you escorted away and flogged."

Ambrose Mills spoke. "I can vouch that Mister Hampton has a good reputation for being conscientious and diligent in carrying out the duties of a justice of the peace. While his father and I are bitter enemies politically, young Hampton was courteous to my family at all times when they had occasion to talk or transact business. The only ill that I've heard about him is that he is a Hampton, he speaks openly for the rebellion, and he lives with his family in what I consider to be a nest of vipers.

"Colonel Ferguson, although Jonathon Hampton serves a rebel government, I don't think his service as justice of the peace warrants hanging. This man has been diligent in his endeavors. He is well liked and respected in the community."

"That's a strong endorsement, Colonel," Ferguson responded, looking directly at Mills, and then turned and again faced Jonathon. "What about the charges that you helped your father with sedition and treason through rebellious activities? How do you plead to those charges, Mister Hampton?"

"Sir, a son must honor and obey his father. The bible says so." Jonathon continued in his unhurried and calm manor, speaking almost dispassionately as though he were in a courtroom discussing a land dispute rather than arguing for his own life. "I will not discredit my father in any way. As you can see from my reel foot, I cannot, nor have I ever served, as a militia soldier. I never rode with my father or brothers as a combatant. I never fired a shot at anyone who was in service of the Crown. In fact, sir, neither my uncle nor I carried any weapon here today nor did we have a weapon in our hands when your soldiers arrived at my house yesterday."

"And what about you, Mister Hyder?" Ferguson asked.

"I guess my sin is that I have a sister who married Colonel Hampton, and I bought property next to their plantation so I could be near her," Hyder answered in a tone that barely masked his hostility. "I just happened to be visiting Jonathon at his home when Plummer and his gang came by yesterday. I have done nothing to deserve the indignity of having to plead for my life."

"Colonel Mills, do you know anything about Jacob Hyder?"

"All I know, sir, is that he moved here from the eastern part of Tryon County a few years back and bought property next to the Hamptons. I have heard nothing about his activities with the militia, although I can't image that he isn't in league with his in-laws."

"Major Plummer, any comments?"

"I detected no animosity toward the Crown from Mister Hyder in his actions yesterday or today, sir. Can we convict a man for the sins of his father or brother-in-law?"

"Damn right we can!" Dunlop stated forcibly, strutting in front of the three senior officers and then pointing to Jonathon. "This cripple has done more to damage the king's authority than ten fighting men! He's one of the damnedest rebels in the county...a honey-tongued devil that's using his wiles to lull you into thinking he is something other than a heartless scoundrel. He should be strung up without fear or favor...and so should Hyder. They both are vile traitors.

"Gentlemen, we must send a message to every damn rebel around that we will not tolerate sedition in any form. Hanging these two criminals will do just that."

"You are wrong, my friend." Mills reacted harshly to Dunlop's summation. "I don't like the Hampton family any more than you do. I detest their rebellious adventures, but Jonathon here is not a combatant. Even though an outspoken Whig, he is known and is respected throughout the county. If you hang him, it will only strengthen the resolve of citizens, especially the neutralists, to resist our efforts to bring peace and tranquility to the frontier."

"I concur," Plummer added.

Ferguson stood up and walked away from the table, his hands clasped behind his back. After a few minutes of contemplation, Ferguson turned and addressed the defendants. "I tend to agree with Colonel Mills and Major Plummer. However, you have been serving a rebel government, and by your own words, Mister Hampton, you are sympathetic to your father's cause.

"But we are not minions of a heartless king. This war is just about over. Already most rebels and their leaders have fled the countryside. You have seen this morning that people are coming in by the score to pledge their allegiance and seek protection of the Crown. It would weigh heavy on my heart to hang you, but hang you I will unless you swear now your obedience to the king, that you will not bear arms against His Majesty's forces or agents, that you will not encourage sedition, and that you cease your service as justice of the peace for the rebel government. You do that, and I will give you parole so that you can return to your wife and family. The same goes for you too, Mister Hyder. What say you both?"

The two accused looked at each other for a moment and then turned and faced the mock court. Jonathon spoke for both of them. "You are most kind, sir. We accept your gracious offer."

Ferguson ordered Chesney to prepare the parole papers for the defendants to sign. Before taking his leave, Ferguson told Jonathon, "I also fine you five horses, including the ones that were confiscated yesterday. The two you have with you today will complete the fine."

"I'm afraid this ruling will come back and haunt you," Dunlop muttered under his breath. He then stomped away, disgusted with the command decision to spare the two men.

Jonathon and his uncle kept their heads high as they walked out of Ferguson's encampment; yet they were darting their eyes back and forth, taking in every detail they could without looking conspicuous. They had a safe pass with the fresh parole both men carried in their purses. Despite the leniency given by Ferguson, there were still many like James Dunlop and

William Lee who felt all Whigs were unrepentant rebels and the only good rebel was a dead one.

The two men walked at a slow pace until reaching Mountain Creek where they stopped and dipped their hats into the fast-flowing, clear water to quench a thirst that had been building since they first reported to Ferguson several hours earlier.

"Well, Uncle," Jonathon said with a chuckle, "looks like we've cheated death so far today."

Hyder did not laugh. He just tore up his parole and scattered the paper scraps in the water.

Into the Hornet's Nest

9 September 1780

An ox-drawn wagon containing a wizened, old man with a woman half his age and ten children, most of them dirty-faced and barefooted, creaked by Jacob's hiding place along the road. It followed two Tory militiamen escorting a drover and eight beeves confiscated from some Whig pastures. As the small caravan passed by headed toward Gilbert Town, Jacob slipped in behind the wagon as though he belonged there. He spoke to no one. After seeing the large splotches of dried blood on his patched, buckskin trousers and frayed shirt, no one wanted to talk to him. He carried his Dickert cradled in his arms and wore a dirty bandanna around his head in the fashion of veteran wilderness hunters.

When the procession crossed Holland Creek on the south side of Gilbert's plantation, a group of uniformed soldiers manning a check point eyed him suspiciously. They allowed the cattle, wagon, and others to pass with only a cursory nod. Rather than let the guards question him, Jacob took the initiative and approached them, smiling broadly as he greeted them, "Morning, good sirs. Could you be so kind as to direct me to Cap'n Biggerstaff's company?"

"Don't know him," the corporal of the guard responded, looking warily at Jacob. "Who might you be, and why do you want this Captain Biggerstaff?"

"Well, sir, I have three brothers with him. I ain't seen them in nigh on four months. Been scouting the back side of the mountains looking for Injuns. Just finished my time and was on my way home when I heard my brothers had done joined up with the British Army. How long have you folks been here?" Jacob kept the conversation low-key as he tried to act nonchalantly.

The corporal looked more closely at Jacob's rifle with its brass ornamentation and asked, "That one of them fancy Pennsylvania rifles?"

"That it is, sir. And not a truer shooting rifle in all these hills. Got a deer at two hundred paces with it just two weeks ago."

The corporal growled. "Mostly rebels use those long rifles. Had some of them shooting at me up in Pennsylvania. Are you a rebel, boy?"

"Sir, I served the militia to protect Christian folks from the heathen Injuns. As for this mess you fellows are in, I ain't seen much these days to *reebel* about. Didn't know you Englanders had come thisaway until yesterday."

"We are not British. We are American Royal Volunteers," the corporal said proudly. Turning to the militiamen who were standing around watching the confrontation, he asked, "Anybody know this Biggerstaff captain?"

One of the militiamen stepped forward. "I know of him. He's in Colonel Mills's regiment, same as me. They are camped on the other side of the Gilbert house."

"How do I know you're not a rebel spy?" the corporal demanded of Jacob.

"Now would a spy be walking up to you brave lads so boldly and with a rifle?" Jacob sounded incredulous at the suggestion. "I done been spying on Injuns all summer. Spies have to stay hidden and sneak around like a snake or else you get killed. I told you I just want to see my brothers."

Looking at the middle-aged militiaman who had spoken up about Biggerstaff, the corporal ordered, "You take this fellow and find Captain Biggerstaff. Don't let him wander off anywhere else."

Turning to a uniformed private who was two years younger than Jacob, the noncommissioned officer added, "Peterson, go with them. Don't leave this backwater man alone unless one of our officers vouches for him. If no one knows him, take him to Captain Dunlop or Captain Miller. They'll find a suitable tree for him."

The trio walked down the middle of the road, chatting as though all were long time friends. As they passed the plantation house and tavern, Jacob asked about the crowd gathered there. The mass of people blocked their view of Ferguson and his senior officers confronting Jonathon Hampton and his uncle.

"I hear they got one of the Hamptons up there, giving him a trial before they hang him," the older militiaman boasted.

Jacob asked the uniformed soldier, "Mister soldier, where do you hail from?"

"New York City…born and raised there. It's a lot more civilized than this backwater."

"You sure are a long way from home. I was born on a boat in the ocean. Lived in Pennsylvania the first ten years of my life; then Papa loaded all us kids in a big wagon and brung us here. Ain't never been to a city. Don't want to go. I like it here just fine, though it's getting a might crowded."

Jacob wanted to keep the two Tories talking in order to keep them off guard and from asking more pointed questions.

About halfway between the Gilbert house and the Cathey's Creek ford, they saw and heard a red-coated sergeant screaming obscenities while trying to get two dozen men to march and turn in line. "Never has there been such a gaggle of dunderheads as I see here today! If we have a battle, you lazy, ignorant, backwater bastards will be more dangerous than good. God, I pray that Colonel Ferguson don't put me with you militia, because you are sure to get me and yourselves killed."

"But, Sergeant, we don't plan to walk those rebels to death. We're fighters, and I got scalps to prove it," someone complained from the militia ranks.

"That's enough insolence, you dumb gollumpus! Take your rest now. When you hear my whistle, we'll march and drill until you drop or get it right. If you can't drill, you won't get the muskets and bayonets that real soldiers use," the sergeant barked.

"We got rifles. They's better shooting than those Brown Bess popguns," shouted another from the disorderly formation.

"Yes, but you can load and shoot ol' Bessie three times faster than that skinny iron, and that's the difference between life and death on the battlefield. Our muskets got a bayonet - the decider of battles. Anybody can shoot, but only a trained soldier can kill with the bayonet. You can't use either if you don't learn the drill," the sergeant screamed. "Now shut up, the lot of you. Dismissed!"

Jacob recognized Aaron Biggerstaff off to the side of the drill field where the sergeant was training the militia. "That's Captain Biggerstaff over there," he said pointing to the Tory officer. "And I see my brothers in the bunch that the loud-mouthed soldier is yelling at."

When Jacob and his escorts walked to Biggerstaff, the young redcoat doffed his tricorn and asked, "Are you Captain Biggerstaff, sir?"

"That I am, young man. Where did you find this refugee you are dragging up with you?" Biggerstaff laughed.

"Do you know this man, sir?"

"Sure do. That's Jacob Godley. His brothers are in my company." Looking more directly at Jacob and talking louder, Biggerstaff asked, "Are you here to join up, Jacob? We could use some help."

"Just got off the Injun line, Cap'n," Jacob said. "I was going home when I heard there was a big Tory army here, and y'all are part of it. Wanted to see my brothers before you marched off to war."

"The war is here, Jacob, although most of Hampton's rebels have run off to the high country."

The young escort interrupted the captain. "Excuse me, sir, but if you vouch for this man, then we'll be off. Our duty is done."

"Thanks for finding my brothers for me," Jacob said as his escort turned to return to their post.

About halfway back to their station, Captain Rance Miller and four of his dragoons stopped and questioned the two escorts. Both recognized the militia captain as the camp's provost officer, charged with maintaining security and order in the Gilbert Town area. When asked why they were away from their posts, they told Miller about taking Jacob to see his brothers. After hearing about their conversation, Miller told his squad, "We had better look in on this stranger and see what he's doing in our midst."

As the brothers approached, Jacob's first words were to his younger brother, "What in tarnation made you change convictions, Andy?"

Andrew explained how he was coerced into the Tory service. "Don't like it at all, but I get to stay with Robert and Will," he said sheepishly. "I ain't going to shoot at my friends, that's for sure."

Without mentioning his relationship with the Liberty Men, Jacob told his brothers about traveling back into the mountains looking for Indians. After hearing that the Tories had converged on Gilbert Town, he decided to come by for a visit.

The brothers joked about how easy and monotonous life was in the militia, and they thought the drills being forced on them were silly and meaningless. William indicated that they might see more interesting activity soon. "I hear we will be marching up to the Catawba Valley in a few days to clear the rebels out of Burke County. It looks like the Whigs are losing their resolve, and we can all get on with our lives pretty soon."

Happy to be together again, the brothers were talking over each other trying to cram four months of gossip into a few minutes. Jacob was careful not to discuss his joining Hampton's militia or the Pearson murders. They did not see the five men approach until the riders were upon them and dismounted. The Godley brothers ceased their talking and looked up at the provost squad stopped in front of them. Rance Miller recognized Jacob by the deer skin garments described by the road guards and walked directly to him. "I'm Captain Rance Miller, Colonel Ferguson's provost," he announced. "Tell me your names and your company."

Jacob's eyes hardened when Miller identified himself. *So that's the murdering bastard*!

Robert, in a friendly mood, spoke first. "I'm Sergeant Robert Godley, sir. These are my brothers—Will, Andy and Jake. Three of us are in Captain Biggerstaff's company. What can we do for you?"

"And which of you ain't in the militia?"

"Me," Jake answered and then explained why he was there.

"That's a pretty rifle you got there, Mister Jake Godley. Don't see many with the fancy brass on the stock. Is it a real Dickert made? Where did you get it?"

"Yes, sir, it has Dickert's mark on it. It was given to me a few years ago for fighting Injuns up on the 'Chucky River."

"Mind if I look at it?"

Jacob handed the rifle to Miller, who barely glanced at the detail on the stock before handing it over to one of his men. Miller turned swiftly and, towering a half-foot taller than Jacob, moved his face within inches of Jacob's at eye level and snarled, "Jake Godley, I arrest you as a spy! You will come with me right now."

Miller grabbed Jacob's arms to push him into the hands of two of his subordinates. Jacob reacted instinctively by dropping to the ground and kicking his legs in scissor fashion under Miller, tripping the heavier Tory officer and forcing him to fall on his face. Before anyone could react other than staring in shock, Jacob jumped on Miller's back, wrapped his left arm into a choking hold around the provost's neck, and pushed his knee into Miller's back, pulling the man's head back with the choking arm. As his arm encircled Miller's neck, Jacob pulled his hunting knife from his belt and thrust the blade's point to Miller's throat, just under the chin, causing pain to register and blood to trickle.. Miller's men began to advance toward Jacob, bringing their weapons to bear, but they stopped abruptly when the other three Godley brothers jumped in front of the provost guard with raised and cocked rifles, pointing their long guns directly at the faces of Miller's men.

Robert yelled, "Back up and uncock those guns now, or we'll blow you to kingdom come."

Miller's eyes were popping with fright as Jacob screamed into his ear. "I'm not going anywhere with the likes of you."

"What's going on, Jake?" Andrew asked nervously.

"This is the son of a bitch that hanged your friend Paddy Pearson and murdered his papa. He beat Paddy's mama senseless just a week ago and burned their house." Jacob was angry and would have plunged the knife through Miller's neck if he were not afraid that his brothers might get killed in the process.

"Take it easy, Jake," Robert pleaded, trying to make sense of what was happening.

About two hundred paces away and out of normal hearing range, Aaron Biggerstaff was talking with Major William Mills when they saw the confrontation develop. He and Mills ran to the standoff with the major shouting loudly, "Lower those guns! Stand down this instant! What's this all about?"

Glancing at his commanders but keeping his rifle pointed at provost squad, Robert answered, "They attacked my brother without cause. They are trying to kill him."

"Lower your guns immediately," Mills again ordered. "I'm Major Mills, and I am second in command of this regiment. I order all of you to stand easy...now!"

"Rest your muskets, boys," Miller croaked to his squad and then more forcibly said, "Stand down, I say!" Then the provost spoke in a softer tone to Jacob. "Boy, get that knife off my neck."

Slowly, tensions eased as the rifle and musket barrels lowered. Biggerstaff and Mills went among the group making sure all weapons were uncocked and butts placed on the ground with the barrels pointing skyward before

Biggerstaff, talking more softly, urged Jacob to release Miller. "Let him up, Jake. This ain't helping matters."

Not releasing his prisoner from a death hold, Jacob said, "Make 'em give my rifle back first."

Mills spoke to the provost guard holding Jacob's rifle. "Give me that weapon."

With eyes darting between Miller and Mills, the man released the Dickert. Mills then handed it to Robert, "Hold this, Sergeant"—Mills then looked at Jacob—"You...with the knife...back off! Let's get some order here."

Jacob released his choking grip and backed slowly away from Miller, but he kept his knife poised in his right hand, ready to slash or stab if he felt threatened.

"Explain yourself, Captain Miller," Mills ordered. "What's this fuss all about?"

Miller had met Mills earlier and knew he was the colonel's son. Hardly able to keep his anger in check, Miller tried to choose his words carefully as he reached and felt the bloody prick Jacob had caused. "Major, you know Colonel Ferguson made me provost. I have reason to believe this man is a rebel spy. I was arresting him when he assaulted me with that knife. Those other three helped the spy by pointing their weapons at my guard and threatening them with harm."

"Jacob is no spy," Biggerstaff interjected. "I know him and his family. His three brothers here serve with me. Jacob has been on the Indian line all summer, but he ain't taking sides in the rebellion."

"Why are you accusing him of spying, Miller?" Mills asked.

"By his own admission, he said he was serving the rebel militia." Miller answered testily. "Look at his dress and weapons. He came in here to spy."

"That's no proof," Mills answered. "Working the Indian line is every man's duty. It is not treason."

"Sir, I am a provincial officer. I outrank militia majors and colonels. I'm taking this rebel in!" Miller spouted angrily.

"You may be a South Carolina provincial officer, but we are in North Carolina. This is Tryon County and my father commands this county. So don't throw your arrogant weight around me, or I'll have you flogged for insubordination," Mills retorted, his voice rising and his face growing red.

Emotions became more heated as the two officers attempted to stare each other down. Mills added in a quieter, but more menacing tone, "Look around you, Captain Miller. I wouldn't try to force the issue here."

When the confrontation erupted, upwards to thirty members of the Tryon militia, including many from Biggerstaff's company, began crowding around, all with rifles or muskets held threateningly in their hands. They didn't know Miller, but they knew and liked Mills and the Godley boys.

Miller saw it would be futile to force the issue further at the moment for he could lose both the fight and his life. Abruptly, he mounted his horse while ordering his men to do likewise. "I'm going to Colonel Ferguson now! We'll see who rules here," Miller said loudly before he pointed angrily at Jacob. "That man is a damn rebel spy, and he has assaulted an officer of the king with a deadly weapon. Both are hanging offenses, and by God, I will see him hang before sundown."

The provost spurred his horse into several turns, forcing the onlookers to back away as Miller roared like a wounded bear. "And you, Major, I charge you with resisting the provost and aiding this rebel spy. You, too, Biggerstaff. And you Godleys will all face charges as well!"

The provost squad then galloped away, following their leader.

Looking first at Biggerstaff and then the Godley brothers, Mills was clearly angry. "I don't know who's right or whether or not Jacob is a spy, but nobody runs roughshod over my people. Miller's got a mean reputation of killing first and figuring out why later. That's why I run him off. But one thing is for sure; he'll be back with the redcoats and you brothers will have some tall explaining to do. I'm going now and let my father know what's happened and see if we can settle this matter quickly."

As the major left, Biggerstaff turned to Jacob. "Jake, get your skinny butt out of here right now. Don't hesitate 'cause that bastard will be back with a vengeance. He might not make the spying charge stick, but he'll have you hanged or flogged to death for pulling that knife on him. Since you ain't in our militia, I can't protect you."

Jacob, now calmed, responded quietly. "I'm mighty sorry to cause all this trouble for you and the boys, but that man killed two innocent people in cold blood just an hour away from here and burned their house. I had to bury 'em and console their womenfolk, including the mama who he bludgeoned near to death. Miller's is mean to the core, an assassin and arsonist. I ain't about to let him string me up."

"I understand, but what's done is done and can't be undone. You've brought a passel of troubles to us. Damn it, you couldn't have been any dumber by coming here than if you had jumped into a hornet's nest. Be off with you!"

The brothers also urged Jacob to leave quickly and to take messages of love to their parents. "Tell Papa we are doing fine and ain't faced any battles yet."

Jacob took his rifle and bade his brothers good-bye, saying "I really appreciate y'all standing up for me.

He walked at a brisk pace northward toward the camp's edge and waded through Cathey's Creek. After continuing on the road until out of sight of the Tory troops, Jacob slipped into woods and began trotting westerly in a loping gait that he could sustain for hours.

Now he knew what Rance Miller looked like. Although angry with himself for losing his temper and acting rashly, Jacob no longer wanted revenge just for the Pearsons. His hate was now personal. He wanted to kill Miller for his own satisfaction.

As soon as Jonathon Hampton had left the area, Ferguson, Dunlop, and a guard rode southward from Gilbert Town to inspect the Adair plantation, about three miles away, as a place for his supply wagons and reserve troops. He needed more pasture for the horses than that offered at Gilbert's. Their departure from headquarters was at the time Miller tried to arrest Jacob.

His face flush with anger, Miller grew even madder when he learned the commander was not at headquarters; only Colonel Mills, Major Plummer, and Captain Chesney were there. Miller thought Plummer to be a weak sister, and he had suspicions about Chesney because, at one time, Chesney had fought with the South Carolina rebels against Tories. Miller shouted demandingly to Ambrose Mills, "Where's Colonel Ferguson? I need him now!"

"You don't have to shout," Mills answered, a bit annoyed with Miller's disrespectful demeanor. "The colonel's gone for a while. Get off your horse and tell me what is going on to get you so torn up."

"Treason! Treason and mutiny within your command, Colonel," Miller bellowed.

"In my command? Surely you jest, sir," Mills responded with his eyebrows raised.

"I am the provost, sir! Mutiny and treason are no jesting matters. Your son and a Captain Biggerstaff and some of their militia threatened my squad and me at gunpoint, and prevented me from my lawful duty of arresting a rebel spy."

"Calm down, Miller. I see my son running toward us now. Let me hear his side of the story."

Biggerstaff arrived at the headquarters before Major Mills completed his description of the incident and then gave his own version of what occurred. Both men corroborated each other's story and accused Miller of trying to arrest Jacob without provocation, of bypassing the chain of command to confront Biggerstaff's subordinates, and of making uncalled-for threats against Biggerstaff and Major Mills. Both Tryon County officers were adamant that Miller was in the wrong, and they could provide many eyewitnesses to back them up.

"Conspiracy!" Miller yelled.

"Be quiet, Captain," Colonel Mills ordered. "Where is this Jacob Godley now?"

"I told him to go home," Biggerstaff said. "I was about to recruit him to join us, but after Captain Miller's unprovoked attack, he said he would never serve in the same army with the likes of Miller.

"Sir, I've known the Godley family for years. They are good Christian folks. Two of the older boys have long served with me. Robert married my niece. Although young Andy was caught with the rebels in Charles Town, he honored his parole and volunteered to come with us. Their father and Jacob both have stated time and again that they were staying neutral in the war, although Jacob did serve with the county militia on the Indian line this summer. The Godley family integrity is above reproach, sir."

Colonel Mills turned to Miller and said coldly, "Captain Miller, you will wait here until Colonel Ferguson returns. I am not happy at all with you riding into my command without conferring first with Major Mills or me. Had you used common courtesy, we could have resolved this issue without rancor. I do not take too kindly to you accusing my officers of criminal conduct. You have offered no credible evidence to support your claim."

It was late afternoon before Ferguson returned to Gilbert Town and, after an hour of heated arguments, made a decision in the matter. He knew Miller was rash and had a mean streak in him. He also acknowledged that he had appointed Miller the provost for the day, and any challenge of the provost was a challenge against his command. By the same token, if Ferguson sided with Miller against the officers of Tryon County, one of them the son of the commander and a close friend, it could result in losing militia and public support in a critical area. Ferguson, Chesney, and Dunlop discussed their options before rendering a decision.

"I think this is a situation where all parties acted too hastily," Ferguson announced to the officers standing before him. "For the good of the corps, Captain Miller, I ask that you drop your charges against Major Mills, Captain Biggerstaff, and those Godley boys who are in our service. Major Mills, Captain Biggerstaff, I ask that you to drop your charges against Captain Miller and his men. We have a rebellion to fight and cannot afford this bickering among ourselves. I will not permit it!

"Now, as for this so-called spy…although I haven't heard any credible evidence other than your suspicion, Captain Miller, I do think there is cause to find out for sure. Take your men and find this Jacob Godley. Bring him back to me for a proper inquiry, but temper your actions! I don't want anyone killed or beaten. You will not burn any houses or crops without my specific approval. In fact, I am sending one of the provincial officers with you as my observer. You bring your suspect back to me alive, and we can solve this issue as responsible officers."

Miller was furious, but kept his tongue in check.

Jacob made it back to the Foreman place without incident, pausing only long enough to inform Foreman and Rachel about what had happened with the encounter with Rance Miller. He saddled Zeus quickly and headed west across Mountain Creek, following an old Indian hunting path northwards to the Second Broad River basin.

A vicious thunderstorm soaked Jacob for two hours before he arrived at his home after dark. The same storm also prevented Miller's pursuit of Jacob that day.

Overjoyed with Jacob's arrival after a four-month absence, the family showered him with hugs and kisses, but his mother refused to let him in the house. "Those clothes stink to high heaven," she scolded and sent Wayne to fetch a nightshirt for his brother. "Jacob, take them dirty clothes off this instance. Wash the crud from your body and then put on the nightshirt while I fix you something decent to eat. You look like you ain't ate since you left home at the first of summer. I made you new breeches and a hunting shirt while you were away. You can put them on tomorrow."

Agatha and her daughters went to the cookhouse to prepare some vittles while Jacob sheepishly obeyed his mother. Jacob took a glob of lye soap and walked with his father and Wayne to the riverbank where he disrobed, sat in the cold water, and began scrubbing an accumulation of dirt, scabs, and blood that had caked on his body. Afterward, he shaved the stubble from his face.

Barefooted and clad only in a nightshirt, Jacob returned to the house where, under the light of a lone candle and fireplace coals, he endured a constant barrage of questions from his family. Jacob told them about the massacre at the Pearson home and his run-in with the Tory assassin responsible. He also told them of the brief meeting with his brothers at Gilbert Town and the large number of Tories and redcoats that were camped there.

George Godley tried to stop his son from talking, urging him to get some sleep, saying they could continue their discussions the next day. "I'm afraid I can't stay past daybreak, Papa," Jacob said. "I promised Colonel Hampton that I would join him for the liberty cause. I need to get information to him about the invaders.

"When I was at Gilbert's place, I heard that Hampton's son was tried by Ferguson this morning, but I don't know what happened. If that Miller was involved, I'm sure Jonathon Hampton is hanging from a tree right now. You remember him, Papa. He's got a reel foot."

"Jacob, you just got here. Don't leave us again," his mother begged.

"They know I'm a spy, Mama, so they're not going to stop looking for me. Can't quit now, even if I wanted to. I have to leave at first light. They are sure to come here looking for me, and I don't want no harm come to you. If I'm here, they'll arrest you for hiding a spy and maybe even burn down our house."

Elation vanished into anguish for the Godley parents. Their distress over the horrid news last week that Andrew had been forced into the Tory militia was mild compared to the news that Jacob had brought home. Not only were Jacob and his brothers on opposite sides of armed conflict, but also Jacob was now a man hunted by a victorious army that wanted to hang him. George got on his knees with Agatha and prayed aloud nearly an hour for the safety of their sons and a return of peace to the headwaters of Second Broad River.

Jacob didn't hear the prayers. For the first time since arriving at Montford's Fort, he slept on a real bed within a real house. Exhaustion taking over, he was in deep slumber before he could savor the rare comfort.

KING'S SERVANTS

10–11 September 1780

As the Godley family sat around the breakfast table eating corn mush and molasses and washing down the victuals with cider, Jacob, wearing his new clothes but old knee-high moccasins, talked extensively about the Loyalist forces that occupied the county. He also went into detail about his time on the Indian line and Pearson family disaster. "That Pearson girl, Rachel, is a lot like you, Mama," Jacob said. "Level-headed, saucy, headstrong, and pretty."

"Well, she won't take kindly to you if you don't take better care of yourself, Jacob," Agatha replied in a motherly way. "Your hair is longer than a girl's and full of tangles. It's a wonder a family of squirrels don't have a nest in it."

Turning to her daughter, the mother ordered, "Margaret, go get my shears. Let's trim your brother's hair before he gallivants off again to God knows where."

While his mother and sister cut his hair shorter, Jacob's youngest brother built a fire under the big iron washpot outside and filled it with water. Before the water came to a boil, Wayne threw into the pot Jacob's old clothes and some chips of lye soap to cook away a season of grease, blood, and Carolina red clay.

Once his hair was shorn, Jacob quickly said his good-byes. As he saddled Zeus to leave, his father told him, "You tell ol' Hampton for me that we don't need any more bloodshed around here."

"I'll tell him, Papa, but there's a passel of hate building all over the county. Those Liberty Men ain't about to give up now, even if the king's servants do have the upper hand. But when and where they fight, I don't know."

"Come back to us as soon as you can." Agatha told her son as she clutched his saddle. "I want to see that Rachel girl you are smitten with."

"I'll come when I can, Mama. We'll have to see about Rachel," Jacob responded.

Wayne walked with Jacob to the trail leading up over the wooded hill northwards toward Big Camp Creek and on to the more traveled trails leading to the Whig militia encampment. The younger brother again pleaded to go with him, but rather than remind Wayne of his young age, Jacob said, "You are needed here, Wayne...now more than ever. I have to go. You look after Mama, Papa, and the girls."

Less than an hour after Jacob left his family, Captain Rance Miller stood on the hilltop overlooking the Godley home. With him was a company of twenty-six men, including Captain Walter Gilkey and six area Tories. Still chafing at the humiliating assault by the Godley brothers and the stinging rebuke from Mills and Ferguson the day before, Miller was determined to capture Jacob and drag him back to headquarters for a ceremonial hanging.

From his advantage point, the provost directed Gilkey to take most of the men on foot and surround the house to prevent any escapes or surprises. After seeing the footmen get into position, Miller, with sword in hand, rode quickly to the front of the house, quietly hoping that the Godleys would physically resist him so he could exact painful vengeance upon the entire family for the sins of their sons.

Margaret was draping Jacob's wet trousers and shirt across a bush to dry when she was startled by the horses charging into the front yard. Wayne and the youngest sister were harvesting apples. Hearing the horses, George hobbled out of the house to meet the newcomers.

Suspending all pleasantries that accompany most greetings, Miller demanded loudly. "I'm looking for the outlaw and traitor Jacob Godley! He's wanted for treason and other high crimes against the king. Bring him to me now!"

"My son is not here. He's no outlaw," George answered indignantly.

"Search the house!" Miller gestured to three of his men who dismounted and rushed in through the front door, scaring Agatha, who was mending her husband's torn shirt.

"George, what's happening? Who are these people?" she screamed as she ran outside to stand beside her husband, her eyes wide with fright.

"You don't have to scare my woman like that," George begged. "I told you my son is not here."

When Wayne heard his mother scream and saw the commotion at the house, he dropped his basket of apples and ran to help his parents. Halfway there, he was tripped by Captain Gilkey who quickly seized the boy by the back of his shirt. Although dazed, Wayne grabbed a fist-size rock as he was being picked up and swung back, hitting Gilkey on the side of the head, creating a bloody abrasion. The militiaman ducked a second impact and slammed Wayne hard on the head with his fist, causing the boy to sprawl dazed across the ground.

Gilkey again picked Wayne up, this time by the hair, and half-dragged him to Miller. Agatha ran toward her son but was blocked by another militiaman before she reached Wayne. George instinctively moved to help Wayne, but his crutch was kicked out from under him, causing him to tumble face first into the dirt.

"Now listen to me!" Miller yelled. "Resisting officers of the king is a criminal offense. Assaulting His Majesty's officers is a criminal offense. Hiding or helping a rebel spy is a criminal offense. It's treason. I could have you all hanged here and now and this house burned."

Softening his tone, Miller continued in a condescending manner, "However, if you tell me where I can find Jacob Godley, I will suspend your punishment."

"We are not resisting," George said as he sat up. "We don't deserve this treatment. We have three sons in service of England now. They are with Colonel Mills and his militia."

"Those three are already in trouble for helping their traitor brother escape," Miller barked, his big, black gelding dancing around, its hooves dangerously close to the crippled Godley. "You are trying my patience! Where is Jacob Godley?"

Another Loyalist came around the house pulling Margaret by her arm and holding up Jacob's damp pants. Her body was late in maturing, and she looked younger than her thirteen years. "Wasn't that rebel wearing buck-skin?" the Tory asked as Margaret jerked free of his grip and ran crying to her mother.

"He ain't in the house or any of the outbuildings," Miller's sergeant reported as he emerged from the house.

"Mister Godley, for the last time, if you value your family and property, tell me where is Jacob," Miller hissed.

George looked at his wife and frightened children. Wayne, overshadowed by the much bigger man holding him, glared with defiant and angry eyes. "Sir, my wife and children are innocent," George cried. "Jacob did come by last night, but for only a short time. It was the first time we've seen him since summer started. He left at daybreak going toward the mountains but didn't say where. Please, don't hurt my family."

"Search the area again! See if you can pick up any tracks," Miller ordered. Looking again at George, he asked, "Did you give him a horse?"

"No, sir; we only have one old horse, and we need it for farm work."

One of the mounted men searching the perimeter of the homestead called out, "There's fresh horse tracks leading up the trail."

Miller roared as he moved his horse again to nearly trample George. "Where did he get the horse?"

"He rode in on a horse. I don't know where he got it." George's desperate plea was nearing a sob. His wife and daughters were crying uncontrollably.

Wayne screamed, "Stop it, you damn bully! Leave my papa and mama alone." He began squirming to get free, but Gilkey held him tighter.

"Muzzle that whelp!" Miller ordered. Gilkey gave Wayne a stinging slap across the face and squeezed the boys arm tighter.

A hush fell over the area as a neatly dressed, aristocratic-looking soldier rode into their mist. Unlike the militia, he was in full uniform, wearing a red waistcoat with light blue facing and with bright gold epaulettes on his shoulders. Ignoring the Godleys and militiamen, the intruder trotted his horse up next to the Tory leader and whispered in a barely audible manner, "Captain Miller, a word please."

Angry at the interruption, Miller rode with the newcomer to the side of the yard and engaged in an animated conversation for nearly ten minutes before returning. All watched the heated exchange in silence. The conversation ended with both men's faces frozen in a grim expression.

The Provincial officer walked his horse over to where George was sitting up on the ground and introduced himself as a member of the King's American Regiment. "I am Captain John Taylor, here on behalf of Colonel Patrick Ferguson, the British Army commander of this expedition. Captain Miller is correct in his pursuit of the fugitive spy Jacob Godley. He also is correct that anyone, including family, who offers assistance of any kind to any fugitive or rebel, can be punished severely. However, he also recognizes that you may not know that your son is a spy; therefore he recommends that we be lenient with you. Since you have three sons who have remained loyal to the legitimate government of the American colonies and are now serving the militia in the king's defense, I tend to agree for leniency."

George and Agatha breathed easier as Taylor continued in his refined, but obviously sarcastic, tone. "However, the lad that Captain Gilkey is holding assaulted Captain Gilkey while he was performing his duty. That is a serious crime. The lad was insubordinate and slanderous when he addressed Captain Miller. His actions cannot go unpunished. Therefore, Sergeant, you are to give him a thrashing with a rod to teach him some manners."

Agatha screamed, "*No!*" again and collapsed to her knees. "Please, no. Whip me, not my boy!"

"Fifty lashes, Sergeant," Taylor ordered, ignoring the mother's pleas.

Miller, who watched in seething silence, would have given the boy five hundred lashes and burned the house if the red-coated prig who had usurped his authority had not been along.

As Wayne's hands were tied to a tree branch, the sergeant cut a slender poplar sapling about an inch in diameter and six feet long. Another militiaman stood in front of George with his musket threatening only inches from the senior Godley's face. A second soldier's musket was aimed directly at Agatha.

Wayne suffered six stinging whacks across the back before he cried out in agony, unable to stifle any longer the pain caused by the punishing blows. Soon his shirt was shredded and bloodied from where the knotted rod bit through cloth and skin. The sergeant, used to administering corporal punishment, was impressed with how well the lad endured the beating. He was also pleased that Taylor, and not Miller, had ordered the punishment. Administering a flogging was hard, unpleasant work, but Miller would have ordered ten times the lashings.

When he was released after the punishment blows were concluded, Wayne refused his mother's help as he tried to stand erect and defiant before his adversaries. The family seethed quietly as they watched the Tories remount and ride toward the trail that Jacob had taken earlier in the day. Wayne held back tears as he silently vowed that he would get vengeance. He would remember the brutish man with the peacock feathers bouncing above his tricorn and who had badly mistreated his family. Then the pain became too much and he collapsed into his mother's arms and sobbed loudly.

The trail was narrow and rugged, hardly suited for a horse and rider. While Jacob traversed the familiar trail without problem, the posse chasing him could only move at half his speed. Crossing the ridge between Big Camp Creek and Cane Creek, one of the Tory horses tripped, broke its leg, and had to be put down.

When the patrol reached the more traveled road from Gilbert Town to Burke County, Godley's horse's hoofprints were lost in the jumble of tracks from other animals. Captain Taylor became concerned that the group was moving too far north into enemy territory without knowing just where the rebel forces were. "I suggest, Captain Miller, that we return to Gilbert Town. I would not want to venture farther without sufficient troops to ward off any attack."

Miller reluctantly agreed but couldn't resist chiding his minder. "I guess reluctance to fight is why you Provincials never put an end to Washington's Continentals up in New Jersey."

By turning south, Miller's group missed, by a few minutes, Captain James Withrow, one of the key leaders in Hampton's militia. Withrow was traveling up the Cane Creek road alone after riding the back trails for three days seeking as many volunteers as he could to join in resisting the British invasion. About half of the men serving in his militia company two weeks ago were now missing. Some, he knew, had taken their families to hide deep in the mountain forests. At least one had gone over to the Tory side. Withrow had been in militia service off and on for more than four years, fighting Cherokee on both sides of the Blue Ridge, Tories throughout the western piedmont, and British regulars in South Carolina's low country. Yet none of the previous encounters had left him feeling as depressed as he was now.

To the south and east, Tory patrols were everywhere. Residents who favored independence were in a panic.

Withrow had a 230-acre plantation on the rich Cane Creek bottoms that he had bought from his father who farmed the fertile valley along with James's brothers and sisters. James recently completed his log house, but too late to get scarce glass windowpanes shipped in from Charles Town before the British blockade and invasion curtailed trade from the port city.

His route back to the Liberty Men's camp at Bedford Hill took him close to family. Since it had been more than two weeks since he last saw them, he had sent his men on to the rendezvous point and made a detour to his home. With all the turmoil going on, he was concerned for the safety of his wife, Sydney, and their three children, the oldest only ten years of age.

As he approached his rustic house, he saw another saddled horse, its rider on foot talking with Withrow's wife under the shade of a large chestnut tree. The children played in a small stream about a hundred feet from the house. When Withrow came closer, he recognized the man as Sydney's brother Thomas Brandon, a long-serving Tory militia officer. He had last heard from Thomas more than a year ago, before the brother-in-law had fled from angry Whig neighbors and had run south to join the notorious Tory raider Robert Brown, who was terrorizing the Georgia countryside.

At one time, Brandon and Withrow were friends. Their different views led to many spirited but good-natured arguments over a jug of homemade beer. However, when Withrow espoused open support for the Liberty Men and championed independence from England, Brandon became more vocal in his opposition to the rebellion. The two men grew apart and bitter toward each other, yet Thomas and Sydney remained close. Although Sydney tolerated her husband's politics, her heart sided with the Brandon family's loyalty to the Crown.

Riding up to the house, Withrow noticed that his brother-in-law was wearing a sword. A wide, dull red sash was tied under his belt, noting his status as an officer. A musket was hanging from his saddle. It was not a good sign that a Tory militia officer would ride alone and openly this far north with all of his military accoutrements visible. It meant the enemy felt that the area was secure from Liberty Men interference.

Withrow kept his rifle in his hand as he dismounted and walked over to the pair. "What brings you to these parts, Tom? They run you out of

Georgia?" Withrow asked. Looking at his wife, he inquired, "Everything all right, Sydney?"

"Jim! It's good to see you again and all in one piece." Thomas Brandon greeted Withrow with a smile and reached to shake his hand, but was rebuffed. "I came by to see my sister, nieces, and nephew, and you too. I'm camped down at Gilbert Town with Colonel Ferguson's corps. I trust that you are not still riding with the rebels?"

"And if I am?"

"Then I hope I can persuade you to be practical and reject your losing cause before it is too late. I don't want to see my sister suffer from being branded a traitor's widow."

Withrow bristled at his brother-in-law calling him a traitor. "I see no reason to abandon my belief in North Carolina being sovereign and independent. I certainly will not betray my belief on your say or anyone else who subordinates himself to some royal arse."

"Look, Jim, I don't want you to turn against your friends, but I do beg of you to think of your family and this fine piece of land that you have carved out of the wilderness," Thomas argued passionately. "The rebel army is no more than a few isolated partisan groups like you have here with McDowell and Hampton. And they are not long for the world. I bet you they can't muster two hundred fighting men between them. We have well more than a thousand under arms at Gilbert Town alone, with more joining our militia every day, including former rebels who have seen the light.

"As we talk, the Continental Army is in shambles. Lord Cornwallis is moving toward Charlotte Town. North Carolina will fall soon, just like South Carolina has." Pausing and putting a hand on Withrow's shoulder as a friend, Brandon continued his plea, "Jim, Colonel Ferguson has authorized me to offer you and any other rebel amnesty if you will surrender voluntarily and give your allegiance to the king. There will be no repercussions for your past actions. Your land, home, and family will be protected. And you get to keep your horse and rifle."

Withrow grew angrier with each word spoken to him. Shrugging Brandon's hand from his shoulder and raising his voice in a more forceful manner, he told his wife, "Sydney, take the children and go inside right now."

"I will not!" she replied emphatically. "My brother is welcome here. He is talking sense. I will not have you pick a fight with him. Listen to him, Jim."

Withrow bristled at his wife's rejection and roared, "Damn it, woman, he is the enemy! He chose his course and now has the gall to suggest I violate everything that I hold dear...everything I believe in...everything I have fought for... have watched good men die for."

Turning to Brandon, he continued harshly. "Tom, when you come to this house as Sydney's brother and my children's uncle, you are welcome. But you are here now as an enemy of liberty...as my enemy. No servant of the king is welcome here and particularly when he comes armed. You must leave this instant. For if I still see you five minutes from now, I will kill you just as surely as I would any prowling wolf. Be gone!"

"How dare you!" Sydney screamed as her husband cocked his flintlock. "You can't threaten my brother that way. What a cruel man you are, Jim Withrow."

"Shut up, woman! I'll hear no more!" Withrow shouted, his face red with rage. Loud cries from the children, who were frightened by the loud confrontation, pierced Withrow's mind, forcing him to lower his voice.

More quieted, Withrow continued. "Woman, go look at the homes plundered at the hands of damn Tory scoundrels like Tom here. Families murdered...houses burned. You dare call me cruel! This brother of yours is part of an evil plague devouring good, God-fearing people. He's a pestilence of the worst kind that must be stopped."

Thomas Brandon fought to keep his temper in check as he said, "Jim, I am deeply sorry you feel the way you do. I hold no personal grudge against you, only for the cause you represent. I will leave now and pray all of you come out of this conflict whole." Looking over at his sister, Brandon whispered, "I love you, sister." He then reached over and kissed Sydney's cheek before turning, waving to the children and mounting his horse.

The Tory officer turned toward Withrow again and said sternly, "Within the week, Jim, we will have occupied the Catawba Valley. Any rebel not voluntarily surrendered before we march through to the Catawba will be treated as an outlaw and harshly dealt with. I will not be able to help you then, Jim, but I will do all I can to protect Sydney and the children. For their sake, I hope we do not have to meet as enemies again."

Without waiting for a response, Brandon spurred his horse to a gallop. The Withrow family watched him go down the trail, splash his horse across Cane Creek, and turn south along the narrow wagon road toward Gilbert Town.

With Brandon out of sight, Withrow turned back to his wife, still furious that she sided against him in his argument with her brother. "If you want continued protection under my house, woman, you will remember your vow to honor and obey your husband! How dare you defy me in front of others?" he bellowed.

"Don't come at me with that high and mighty attitude, Jim Withrow!" she yelled back at him with equal fury. "I married you because I loved you, but I did not take a vow to forsake my family. Since we first got married, you've been gone more than you are at home. I never know where you are, whether you are alive or dead. The fields have been fallow all season, and now we have little put aside to get us through the winter. Your duty, sir, is to take care of your family, not to be some adventuresome ne'er-do-well bent on killing and pillaging while your wife and children go wanting. I am ashamed of you!"

The children shook with fright at the increasing hostile exchange between their mother and father. Their bawling grew louder as the two youngest ran around the house and hid from the explosive dialogue. Ten-year-old Mary rushed to her arguing parents and began beating her father with her fists, shouting between sobs, "Stop it! Stop! Please stop."

James head jerked back in shock as he looked down at his distraught daughter. His eyes softened as he looked back to his wife and moaned, "Oh, Sydney. Now look what you have made me do."

Bending down to be on eye level with his eldest daughter, he picked her up gently, swallowed his pride and shame for losing his temper in the presence of the children, and said softly, "Your ma and pa ain't going to hurt each other. Sometimes we get too mad and just got to spew it out. I'm sorry our disagreement got out of hand. Forgive me, little pumpkin. I promise; I will behave."

The young mother wrapped her arms around Mary and her husband. "We love you, child. We got rid of the mad now. Let's get your brother and sister and all pray to the good Lord to forgive our transgressions. Now hush your crying. All will be well."

Mary looked up at her father and asked, "Why did you make Uncle Tom go away like that."

Sydney gave a quizzical look toward her husband, silently challenging him to answer in a reasonable manner. "Well, pumpkin," Withrow responded, "there's a war going on between grown-ups. Your uncle chose to fight for one side. I'm fighting on the other side. And we just can't get along until this war is done and over. I chose my side because I want you children to grow up in a country that doesn't have to bend to some king far, far away. You deserve a better life."

Patrick Ferguson was very pleased with the progress that his expedition was making in North Carolina. Resistance was far less than anticipated. The feared rebel militia had scattered, gone into hiding, perhaps even fled over the mountains to the backwater wilderness. More people than expected were affirming their loyalty to the Crown. *Cornwallis will be pleased with my success*, he told himself.

With minimal threats lurking, an occasional sniper or spy, Ferguson felt it time to bring his support wagons and reserve forces closer to his headquarters. It was time to put more attention toward training the new militia volunteers.

Rather than send a messenger ordering the rest of his command to move north of the Broad River, Ferguson left Gilbert Town at dusk to carry the message in person. His motive in going himself was more personal; he missed the two pleasures that he allowed himself, a washer woman and a cook, both camp followers who also doubled as his mistresses.

Ferguson liked to travel at night. It was more comfortable than riding in the hot sun; more important, it hindered the enemy from following his movements. Earlier in the summer, even night travel in the southern colonies could be sultry and uncomfortable. Now in early September, the nights were cooler and pleasant. He had four of his royal Provincials and two Tryon County Tories as escorts.

It was nearing midnight when Ferguson's party waded the Broad River at Dennard's Ford where Lieutenant Anthony Allaire, adjutant for the American Provincials, and Doctor Uzal Johnson, the chief surgeon, were waiting. After an informal greeting, Ferguson told Allaire to have all officers present at eight o'clock the next morning. Everyone would be moving that day.

Taking leave of his escorts and the two officers, Ferguson walked to his personal tent, where he awakened the two women within. Sally had been with him since he was first assigned to Ninety Six after the fall of Charles Town. A buxom redhead with a haughty demeanor toward those she felt to be inferior, she was a Loyalist refugee from Virginia, thus the nickname Virginia Sal given to her by others. The other woman who handled washing for Ferguson was Paulina or, as commonly known, Virginia Pol. Both camp followers were handsome women around thirty in age and formally listed as "aides" to the commander. While others could hire them to wash their uniforms for a fee, their personal favors were reserved only for Ferguson.

"Awww, my lovely Virginia maidens," Ferguson greeted the awaking women as he entered the tent. "I need to get a week of grime off me and then have you soothe my aching body before I call it a night."

Sally lit a candle as Paulina went outside to stoke up the fire and heat water. While he favored Sally, whose auburn hair matched his own, he enjoyed the pleasure of both women massaging his body, relaxing his muscles, and satisfying his carnal needs. They enjoyed sharing Ferguson's charms and flaunting around the camp their special relationship with him.

Because the brigade was moving much of the time, most camp followers were discouraged, but Sal and Pol had the privileges of Ferguson's wagon, and as long as they kept the Colonel happy, the other troops were happy. When the wagons stopped more than two nights in the same place, local Tory militia wives would come and cook and wash for their husbands and friends. Most wives had strong misgivings about the mistresses, but they kept their complaints to themselves.

Unmarried, Ferguson had no moral qualms of having two women on the campaign for his personal comfort, although privately the practice did not meet with favor among many of his officers who had strong religious beliefs. They politely looked the other way and were discreet in what they said to others about the situation.

Most of the troops loved Ferguson and would follow him anywhere. They believed that he deserved special treatment as a reward for the difficulties that came with command. They longed for the war to be over so that they could return to their own women. Patrick Ferguson was the leader who could bring them quick victory.

Ferguson was undressed when Paulina, carrying a bucket of hot water and washing cloths, returned inside the walled tent. The women took their time as they gently and deliberately bathed him, giving careful attention to his injured arm and array of body scars, trophies of past battles. The bath complete, they dried him, and then lay down with him sandwiched between as they began a slow massage that became more teasing, bringing him to a full arousal.

The nearest tent to Ferguson was fifty feet away, but its occupants were awake to hear the giggling and moaning. After the carnal noise subsided from the commander's tent, they too drifted back to sleep with erotic dreams emulating the luck of their commander.

The next morning Sally cooked flatbread and a freshly killed wild turkey for breakfast while Paulina shaved Ferguson and trimmed his hair. The two then helped him dress in a fresh, clean uniform, one of three that he carried on the campaign. Paulina had risen earlier and shined his boots to sparkle in the morning sun. He looked almost as polished as the dainty officers that fluttered around a garrison headquarters.

By eight o'clock, the officers were assembled to receive Ferguson's new orders. "Gentlemen, our occupation of Tryon County couldn't be smoother. The rebels have proved to be idle braggarts. They have fled to the hills and refuse to challenge us.

"I want everyone here, except for some of Major Gibbs's militia, to move up the road to Adair's plantation, about three miles south of Gilbert Town. There's plenty of forage for the animals there. I don't expect you will have any trouble, but keep alert anyway. Being cowards, these partisans can be sneaky.

"Major Gibbs, have about half of your Spartan boys patrol south of the Pacolet. Keep any roving rebel banditti in check. I also hear that Clarke's Georgia rebels could be headed this way. Bring the rest of your people to Adair's as security for our wagons and supplies. Take the prisoners on to Gilbert Town and put them in the cattle pen there. I'm leaving now for my headquarters and expect to start moving north for the Catawba region in the next day or so."

While Ferguson was holding his staff meeting, Colonels Charles McDowell and Andrew Hampton were meeting with Burke and Ruther-ford County militia officers to determine a strategy for confronting the Loyalist army. After sharing with McDowell Jacob's information about the enemy, Hampton concluded, "There is no doubt that Ferguson will be soon moving north to the Catawba Valley. He'll have to come through the South Mountains gap at the head of Cane Creek. It's a perfect place to bottle him up in a good ambuscade."

"But Colonel Hampton, your people are already telling us that Ferguson has five times the strength that we have," Charles McDowell reasoned in his typical, overcautious manner. "How can we expect to stop him, much less defeat him? Are you not inviting disaster?"

"We can lure them into a killing trap down where the valley is barely the width of the road and creek, and cause them great suffering. We have enough men to deliver devastating damage that will force Ferguson to retreat and think twice about entering our mountains," Hampton said. "That will give us enough time to get reinforcements from Shelby and Cleveland and then go on the offensive again."

Isaac Shelby was an aggressive militia commander from the west side of the mountains, more than eighty miles away, who fought with McDowell and Hampton in South Carolina during the summer. Benjamin Cleveland commanded the Wilkes County militia, forty miles to the northeast and had been battling Tories up and down the Yadkin and Catawba valleys for several years.

"I sent expresses to both of them when Ferguson started his invasion," McDowell responded. "Shelby says they can't leave their homes to the mercy of Indians who are causing trouble again. Cleveland reports that he has his hands filled with local Tories. I sense reluctance for them to get too far from home. We are on our own here."

"I don't run from battles we can win," Hampton stated emphatically. "Are we going to surrender both our counties without a fight?"

Colonel McDowell's brother, Major Joe McDowell, spoke up. "Charles, I think Colonel Hampton is right. If we can slow Ferguson up and delay his entry into Burke, we might save our people a lot of misery."

They argued through the morning, with their captains expressing eagerness to bloody Ferguson, even if they didn't have sufficient force to give him a crushing defeat. Colonel McDowell reminded the others of the massacre at the Waxhaws, near the North and South Carolina border where, earlier in the year, Banastre Tarleton's legion destroyed a Virginia regiment of Continentals commanded by Colonel Abraham Buford. "The damn redcoats have a policy of giving no quarter. I'm told that a hundred brave men or more were hacked to death after surrender. You want that to happen to our people?"

"Our people ain't Virginians. We don't give up easy." Hampton retorted. "And we are fighting Tory militia for the most part, not British regulars. But rest assured, sir, we will not forget what happened with Buford or with our people at Camden."

By late afternoon, a loose strategy was set. Hampton was frustrated with Colonel McDowell's reluctance to be more aggressive. Although McDowell refused to let his Burke militia engage in hit-and-run raids south of the mountains, he did agree that if they had intelligence of a small group of enemy troops marching up the Cane Creek road, they could set up an ambush to hurt the king's men. "Damn it, boys, don't start a fight you can't win," the colonel warned.

The commanders agreed that if the Loyalists got the better of the Whig fighters, the partisans would scatter and flee over the mountains to the Watauga settlements. In the meantime, Colonel McDowell said he would go to the Catawba Valley and urge the larger planters and cattlemen to take protection from Ferguson in an effort to prevent raids on their homes and property. "Otherwise, the bastards will plunder all the livestock and food and leave the valley with nothing to eat this winter," the senior McDowell said. "I can't have our people starving to death."

Captain Joe McDowell, a cousin who lived in the upper Catawba region called Pleasant Gardens, volunteered to travel with the colonel and convince his neighbors that, while distasteful, this was the most prudent tactic to take. With two Joes in the family, Major McDowell was called "Quaker Meadows Joe." The younger cousin, who was a physician, was nicknamed "Pleasant Gardens Joe." Both names identified where the men lived in the Catawba Valley and were used by most of the troops to distinguish between the two Joes. The colonel was more formal and always used their military titles, even in private conversations.

A sense of excitement ran through the Gilbert Town encampment on Monday, 11 September. Rumors were flying that they might soon force the rebels out of hiding.

Meeting with his principal commanders after his return from Dennard's Ford, Ferguson heard intelligence reports from Lieutenant Colonel Vezey Husbands that the rebel militia in Burke County was in disarray and refugees were seen on the roads and trails from the head of the Catawba at Davidson's Fort to some forty miles eastward beyond the mouth of John's River. Husbands reported that the McDowell brothers were abandoning their homes at Quaker Meadows just as Hampton had his place. He added that a small group of rebels was hiding out near Bedford Hill, about halfway between Gilbert Town and the Catawba at the South Mountains Gap.

After hearing how easy the pacification program was going with more people coming in to swear loyalty to the Crown, Ferguson said, "Let's just see what those rebels are doing up on Cane Creek. With two springs at that gap, that might be a base where we can send foraging parties on into the Catawba Valley."

He ordered a patrol to assemble an hour after midnight with one hundred Tory militiamen and thirty of his American Volunteers under Captain James Dunlop. The newest militia volunteers would remain behind for additional training. An exception was made for Captain Aaron Biggerstaff's company. After the fiasco a few days ago with Rance Miller, Ferguson wanted to observe firsthand how the Godley brothers would perform on a mission. Since they lived in the area, it was logical they serve as guides. Lieutenant Colonel Husbands, who frequently traveled the road, was tasked to command the Tory militia element.

Before he concluded his work for the day, Ferguson had to address the situation of Rance Miller and the suspected spy Jacob Godley. He was not happy with Captain Taylor's description of Miller's brutal visit to the Godley home. To keep the hot-headed Tory from making more mischief, he assigned Miller the responsibility of guarding the supply wagons. Captain DePeyster and Colonel Mills were told to keep a tight rein on the rogue militia officer and to not let him roam the countryside. "He's invaluable when we need fighting done," Ferguson said, "but he's a liability to winning the peace."

18

AMBUSCADE

12 September 1780

Clouds flirted around a half moon as Ferguson quickly inspected the men selected to go with him on the Cane Creek reconnaissance. Despite their open yawns, the commander was pleased with his men's appearance and readiness. The Provincials and dragoons were veterans of previous campaigns. The militia knew the local terrain, and those still carrying their long rifles served as snipers and scouts.

Each man with a musket carried thirty-six paper-enclosed cartridges of shot and powder, standard for this type of movement. The riflemen carried at least thirty balls of lead in their shot bags and a horn of powder. All had a light bedroll either draped over their shoulder or in a haversack. Most had some hard bread issued by the commissary; some had found some jerky, corn, or potatoes to supplement their diet on the two-day patrol that would be about fifteen miles up Cane Creek Road and fifteen miles back.

While most of the corps slept at two in the morning, Ferguson led the reconnaissance force, walking three abreast, up the narrow road toward Cane Creek and Bedford Hill, an eight-hour march, *if all went well*. Ferguson, Dunlop, Husbands, and ten dragoons were mounted, all others were on foot. The Godley brothers were not happy about having to leave their horses behind.

Jacob awoke with a jerk as Major Porter nudged him with his boot. He had his rifle in hand and cocked before realizing he was with friends at a Liberty Men's camp. "Enough dreaming of romping with some fair maiden, young Ranger," Porter said jokingly. "We need you to start earning all that food you been gobbling up."

"Yes sir!" Jacob responded, now wide awake and gathering his gear, though a little embarrassed that the major was reading his mind. *How did he know?*

To the east, streaks of orange peeped amidst scattered clouds. The camp already was stirring and a few fires lit. Porter motioned Jacob to follow him to a gathering of officers.

Major Joe McDowell and a militia officer that Jacob did not know were standing with Colonel Hampton, Captain Singleton, and Jim Gray around a small fire that was brewing a pot of tea. "A cheery good morning, Mister Godley," the old colonel greeted. "I got a job for you."

Jacob hoped they would offer him some tea and a piece of corn pone, but they did not. "What you need done, sir?" he asked.

"We're setting up an ambuscade down where the hills choke the road. I want you and Mister Gray to go about a mile on toward Gilbert Town and be our lookout should the Royals send anybody up this away," Hampton replied. "There's an outpost already at a place where you can see a long way down the road and spot anybody coming. If you see the enemy, stay out of sight, grab your horses, and ride like blazes to warn us.

"Captain Deveny here will have the first group for you to warn and then on up the road till you get to Major McDowell and me, where most of our rifles will be. There we will be ready to give them a proper mountain welcome when they walk into our trap."

"I hear you two boys are damn good Rangers," McDowell said as he shook their hands. "Your alertness will mean the difference between victory and defeat. There ain't many of us up here, but we can bloody them good if you can lead them to our trap. Surprise is what it takes. You boys can make that happen."

Hampton continued. "You relieve the two men on lookout. If nobody shows up today, I'll have a relief down for you about dark."

As the two young Rangers mounted for the ride to their outpost, Jacob asked Gray about his foot which Zeus had stomped a few days before. "Better now, but sore as hell," Gray answered and then asked his own question: "How you been? Heard you almost got caught."

While the horses picked their way down a rugged trail to the road by Cane Creek, Jacob summarized his adventures since they last saw each other. Once on the road, they trotted south, but ceased talking. They saw some of their militia milling around the ambush site that stretched for more than four hundred paces along the winding road through a narrow gap before the valley widened out. The little creek and road crossed more than a dozen times along the way. Dense, forest-clogged hills restricted much of the view from the road. With few exceptions, the area was mostly void of open space. It was a perfect place for the Indian-style fighting that the partisans preferred.

Had Gray not heard a horse whinny, he and Jacob would have missed the outpost. Following the sound, they spotted tracks leading up into the woods where they found two horses hobbled in a small glen, hidden only one hundred feet away from the road. They dismounted quietly and scrambled up to the ridge top. The sound of a rifle cocking behind caused them to freeze in their tracks. Turning, they saw a militia man with his weapon pointed straight at Jacob. In a low, but hostile tone, the partisan demanded, "Hold where you are. You better tell me who you are with and why you are here, or I'll blow you blame head clean off."

"Easy, friend, Colonel Hampton sent us down to relieve you. I'm Jacob Godley, and this is Jim Gray," Jacob responded. "Our sign is Walker."

The man lowered his rifle and answered with the countersign, "Colonel John. Good to see you. It's been a long night."

The other lookout chimed in. "The only movement on the road since yesterday was a refugee family leading an oxcart on the way to the high mountains."

The outpost provided a clear view of the road for nearly a quarter mile, a rarity for the twisting and tree-shrouded thoroughfare. Their horses secured, the two Rangers settled in for a long wait.

It was just before dawn when Ferguson's lead elements arrived at Fort McCaughey, about half the distance from Gilbert Town to the head of Cane Creek. There was no challenge when Aaron Biggerstaff and Robert Godley walked into the fort and shook awake the sleepy guard who abruptly realized he had guests. Furious at the lack of security, Ferguson ordered new sentries posted before giving the officer in charge of the fort and the sleeping guard a severe tongue lashing. The berated officer, one of Mills' lieutenants, was immediately demoted to private and the sleeping guard placed under arrest.

A decision between flogging and hanging the guard would be made when they returned to Gilbert Town.

A half an hour after resting at the small fort, the expedition re-formed into two groups. The lead element, commanded by Captain Dunlop, had six Provincials and twenty militia, including Lieutenant Colonel Husbands. With the county line just up the road, Burke County Tories took the point, and Biggerstaff's company returned to the large force with Ferguson.

The advanced guard marched about five minutes ahead of the main body. In addition to protection, they gave Ferguson an opportunity to check out the scattered dwellings along the valley. The dragoons were tasked with inspecting residents along the way, identifying friend and foe. While the mounted troops galloped about, the footmen continued their march at a steady, uninterrupted pace. Biggerstaff verified whether the homes along the way were friends, rebels, or fence-sitters.

At midmorning, Jacob was splashing water from a nearby spring onto his face to wash away drowsiness when he heard a soft whistle from Gray. Down the road, they saw two footmen with their muskets at the ready emerge from the south. Walking four horse lengths back were a dozen armed men with their weapons on their shoulders. Behind them were two horsemen, one wearing a green waistcoat and a black tricorn sporting a turkey feather; his gorget bright against his uniform. The other, a taller but thinner man, also had a gorget denoting his rank, but he wore a hunting shirt with a red sash draped across his chest. Both had swords dangling from their sides and muskets slung over their backs.

"I count about two dozen on foot, how about you?" Jacob said.

"That's what I see. Looks like six are redcoats. We had better git before they come closer."

Unseen by Dunlop's people, the Rangers scurried down from the wooded ridge to their horses and galloped back to the ambush site. They did not slow until they saw Captain Aaron Deveny leaning against a tree beside the road. As Gray sped on, Jacob reeled to a halt and gasped, "There's about two dozen of 'em coming. Most on foot, two on horse. Six wearing those bonny redcoats."

"That all?" Deveny asked.

"That's all we saw. Didn't see nobody behind 'em, but we didn't tarry none either."

Jacob spurred his horse and followed Gray up the narrow road.

Deveny quickly got his men into position and reconfirmed with each his orders. "We have to let 'em pass. The main killing area is up the creek, not here. We'll hit 'em only if they run back this way or if more Tories come up behind 'em. Be quiet. Be ready. And, by God, don't shoot until I do. If they charge us, shoot and then move back up the hollow to our horses. We ain't here for a stand-up fight. We are here to kill damn Tories and not get any of our people hurt."

All nodded that they understood.

The oldest man at Deveny's ambush site was a fifty-four-year-old veteran Indian fighter who had only one eye. The youngest was a barefooted, fifteen-year-old, freckled-face boy whose family lived near Puzzle Creek. The lad was a skilled hunter and understood stealth and patience while waiting for a quarry to come to him, but he had never faced an armed man before. With no doubts of his skills, he worried about doing everything right to prove his prowess as a warrior. Deveny, with his experience battling Tories and Indians, assured the boy that he would do fine. "Just do what you are told when you are told, boy."

From his position, the teenager had a clear view about seventy-five yards down the road to a bend that curved right. His anxiety grew when he saw Dunlop's two point men walking around the bend, looking warily into the trees on both sides of the road. The Loyalists were as tense as the boy and sensed that something did not feel right. Although he willed himself not to shoot, the young ambusher, following the lead of the veteran beside him, silently cocked his rife and slid his finger over the trigger, taking aim at one of the horsemen that now appeared.

Sitting on a small limb of the chestnut tree, forty-five feet above the sprawling men below, a fat crow, sated after a feast of muscadines and a field mouse carcass, watched as more men came into view on the road. From his lofty perch, he felt no threat from the intruders. He cared less about the humans and more about expelling the abundance of food that he had digested and that now bloated his bowels. Relief came when excrement spit out from under his tail feathers, gathered momentum, and fell to hit the teenaged rifleman with the force of a tossed stone, splashing a grayish-green glob into the crook of the boy's hand between the thumb and trigger finger, and bouncing spurts of smelly flux up into his eye. The suddenness and force of the unforeseen bird dropping caused a spontaneous and uncontrolled reaction by the boy, including a yelp and tightening of his finger around the trigger. The rifle shot ripped though Lieutenant Colonel Husbands's hat and flung it from his head.

Shocked by the roar, Deveny and others on the ambush line had no choice but to shoot a ragged volley as well. Several fired in near unison and without orders. Although within range, the enemy was a long way from where they should be for maximum casualties, and now the surprise was gone. One of the pilots was already knocked down screaming. A red-coated soldier fell with a ball in his head before he could unshoulder his musket. Dunlop received two balls in his leg. Two others of his command were also nicked.

"Fall back!" Husbands yelled.

"We fight!" Dunlop screamed. "Form a line to charge."

"We're too far away to rush the ambush and too few to stand," Husbands, a veteran Indian fighter, yelled. "We must move back and get a better position. You are hurt, sir."

Husbands spurred his horse and shouted to get the attention of his militia, most of whom had experienced ambushes from Indians before. They returned fire before retreating and ran for cover in the trees.

"Sergeant! Get back around the bend and set up a defensive line by that clearing we passed. When they come after us, we'll catch them in the open," Husbands yelled and then turned to the two Provincials who were acting as body guards for Dunlop. "You two...get Captain Dunlop back and stop that bleeding."

Raging mad, Dunlop hated to retreat. He hated to be pampered like an invalid. He hated being surprised. Most of all, he hated being shot. But he was a realist. He had no idea how many enemy were in front. He did know that more than a dozen rounds were fired at this group and that meant a bunch of rebels ahead. He would not be lured into a trap like Musgrove's Mill.

As they maneuvered back around the bend in the road and across the four-foot-wide creek to just past an open old Indian field, Husbands saw the best place to make his stand. He thought *to hell with the British manual of arms*, and he ordered his men behind trees and rocks where they would have a better field of fire should any rebel attackers pursue them, which would happen as sure as God made acorns. Dunlop offered no objections to Husbands's decision to fight frontier style and not in typical British formation.

In less than a minute, the Loyalist advance guard, with some of the wounded being carried or drug, had maneuvered back in good order nearly two hundred yards and taken up new fighting positions. No one else had been hit; the battlefield quieted for a few moments. Each man's weapon was loaded and cocked. Half the men had fixed bayonets, the big advantage muskets had over the long rifles.

Although Deveny was trying to keep his people back in the trees, the smell of a quick victory was too much to overcome. Seeing the king's men turn and run, Deveny's militiamen drowned out his protests with wild yells of excitement as they rushed toward the retreating Loyalists. About half had reloaded their rifles; they others had their knives and hatches in hand.

Captain Joseph White's company lay less than a hundred yards upstream of Deveny's position. Like the other Liberty Men, the sudden shooting surprised him. After the first volley, he heard shouts: "They are running!" "We got 'em boys!" "Let's go after 'em!"

White turned to the men next to him and shouted, "Damn it! Let's go help 'em. Don't shoot until to you get a target. Then make each shot count."

Twenty-nine Liberty Men chased up the road to what they expected to be easy pickings among the enemy stragglers running away from the ambush.

When the first fusillade echoed through the hills, Ferguson instinctively knew that Dunlop had triggered an ambush. He ordered his men to unshoulder their muskets, check their prime, fix bayonets, and double time toward the sound of shooting. He and his dragoons charged ahead on their horses and within a minute joined the new defensive position formed by Husbands. Relieved that there were not massive casualties, he ordered the dragoons through the open woods to a canebrake by the creek on the edge of the clearing to prepare for a counterattack. As his foot soldiers ran up, he put them in a line; backing up Dunlop's advanced guard.

Seeing Biggerstaff trotting toward him, Ferguson called out, "Captain Biggerstaff! Take your rifles up through those trees on that rise to the left and see how well your sharpshooters can pick off them rebels."

With a wave of acknowledgement, Biggerstaff signaled for his sixteen men to follow. They ran up a hill to the left of the fighting line and crossed over the crest as a volley of gunfire roared from the valley below.

White caught up with Deveny as they rounded the road bend. There was no order to the scattered Liberty Men. When they first saw Loyalists scurrying in the tree line ahead, White shouted, "There they are; give 'em hell!"

The Liberty Men rushed down the road, a few running among the trees to one side, more charging into the open field toward to what they thought would be a handful of frightened Tory militia, only to be hit by a volley of more than sixty muskets when they were about fifty yards from their quarry.

White was knocked backward, his arm shattered by a musket round. Seth Hemphill, the old veteran of the French and Indian War, took two rounds, one in the torso, the other in the head. He died quickly. Another of White's men took a round in the shoulder. Those in the open either turned and ran or quickly fell to the ground for protection as Ferguson's dragoons charged into their flank with sabers swinging. Simultaneously, with bayonets flashing, the Loyalist footmen attacked the rebels' front.

The Liberty Men in and near the trees, sobered by the reaction of their enemy and seeing friends fall in the field, ran back deeper into the forest for better protection. Others not yet to the field stopped and retreated in shock. Some shot at the dragoons before turning and running.

Robert Godley led six of his company over the hill's ridge toward the road to a point that offered a clear view of the retreating rebels. He aimed his rifle and yelled at them to stop or be killed. Several Liberty Men stopped, threw down their rifles, and raised their hands. Some kept running, trying to dodge the enemy ball.

In the meantime, Biggerstaff, with William and Andrew Godley, continued over the ridge and down into a small hollow where two twelve-year-old boys were holding a dozen horses for Deveny's company. Against orders, the boys had led the animals closer to the road so they could watch the excitement. William ran into the cluster of animals and jerked a fowler from one boy's hands. The other boy dropped the reins he was holding and ran off into the underbrush screaming, "Help me! Lord, somebody help me!" His pride of being a soldier for liberty vanished.

"Quarter," some Liberty Men down in the field yelled as the dragoons rode among them.

"Roll away from your gun, and I'll let you live, you bastard!" replied the sword-wielding dragoon sergeant who was poised to slice Deveny's head.

Both Captains White and Deveny's companies were in panic; Deveny was forced to surrender.

Biggerstaff's men, less Robert's squad, mounted the stolen horses, took the reins of others animals, and charged boldly out of the forest and down the road past the escaping and surrendering rebels. The Tory raiders raised the rifles over their heads to avoid being shot by their own people as they galloped rapidly through the astonished prisoners and on toward their friendly line. "Got a little present for you, Colonel," Andrew Godley yelled as the group halted the horses in front of Ferguson.

When the first shot reverberated down the narrow valley walls to the main ambush site several hundred yards upstream of where the fight began, Major McDowell was bewildered and demanded angrily, "What's that shooting about?"

He had ordered his men into position once he received word from Gray and Jacob that an enemy patrol was headed their way. *Something must have gone terribly wrong.* He sent Jim Withrow with the mounted reserve to find out what was happening.

As Withrow passed Deveny's initial position, he saw a scattering of militia rushing down the road ahead, disappearing around a bend. Then came the loud volley fired from the Loyalist counterattack. Withrow reined in his troop as the Liberty Men charging south suddenly stopped, turned, and, in disarray, began running back toward him. From the hollow leading up a small tributary of Cane Creek, a dozen horses, nine with riders, charged through the retreating militia and toward Ferguson's line.

"What the hell?" Withrow screamed, shocked by the suddenness of mounted men on both flanks ahead, those on the left wielding swords. On the right, he thought he recognized his neighbor Aaron Biggerstaff riding one of the horses. Withrow had his men dismount and form a skirmish line among the trees as he maneuvered to better see the battlefield and repel the enemy attack should it advance farther. Ahead of them, a number of Liberty Men began moving south along the road and field with hands high and empty. The captives, surrounded by soldiers with bayonets, were prodded quickly to the Loyalist line. Other Tory riflemen were taking forward skirmish positions to stop any further rebel advancement.

Withrow noticed a red-coated body in the road and a Tory militiaman lying near him, clutching a bloody wound in his side. "This is one big mess,"

Withrow grumbled to himself before remounting and heading back to report to McDowell and Hampton. He did not see the barefooted teenager sitting beside the road, his rifle across his lap, his head lowered between his knees, bawling like a baby.

Meeting McDowell, Hampton, and a dozen other riders coming toward him, Withrow summed his report quickly. "It's a disaster!"

Hampton sent Jacob and Gray forward to observe the enemy and to give early warning if the enemy decided to continue their advance toward the Liberty Men's main positions. As new defense lines were organized, the militia commanders rethought their situation.

The Loyalist officers held a quick conference as the prisoners were herded to a collection point nearby. "There's a planter's cabin about a mile or so back," Ferguson said. "It offers a better defensive position than this place. Leave the wounded prisoners who can't walk here. Let's move everybody else back and regroup." Turning to Biggerstaff, he said, "Use your company to escort the prisoners. Kill any prisoner that tries to escape or doesn't move fast enough."

"I won't go on a stretcher," Dunlop cried out, trying to sit up, as others wrapped bandages around the two wounds on his leg. "Just give me a boost up on my horse."

Robert forced the prisoners to a fast walk after making them discard their shoes, knives, and anything else they were carrying. Recognizing Deveny, Robert told Ferguson that the rebel officer was an acquaintance who lived near Gilbert Town.

Ferguson asked, "What's your name, rebel?"

"I'm Captain Aaron Deveny, sir, of the Rutherford County militia."

"How many more of your people are up the road?"

"Maybe five hundred, maybe more." Deveny lied without hesitation. "They were all waiting for you, but somebody got an itchy finger and messed up the ambuscade. Otherwise, all of you would be trying to weasel your way into glory by now."

Dunlop called out again to Ferguson, "Kill that bastard! The coward murdered my men."

Ferguson ignored his wounded captain. After Deveny was led away, Dunlop asked, "How many men did we lose?"

"It looks like we left one or two men on the field. You are our only serious wounded here. We wounded three rebels, maybe killed a couple more. Someone said he saw a rebel with a hole in his head. I counted seventeen prisoners and twelve horses. One was a pack animal with a powder barrel. To get caught off-guard, I say we have we done exceptionally well… so far," Ferguson said.

Hampton and McDowell moved through the woods to the edge of the field so that they could better see what the other side was doing. They watched a number of dragoons moving about and riflemen scurrying along the tree line. "They must have two hundred or more people over there!" McDowell said.

"Could be, but we can maneuver around and smash them on their blind side and then skedaddle back into the hills before they know what hit them," Hampton offered.

"I don't think so. We've already lost more than a dozen men. I can't risk any more. My brother gave orders for us to get back to the Catawba after the ambuscade, and that's what we should do. I suggest you head for Turkey Cove. I'll take my people to Quaker Meadows, and then we'll all rendezvous over the mountains at Fort Watauga in a couple of days."

"I don't like running while we still have fight in us," Hampton insisted, getting testy.

"I can't tell you what to do, Colonel, but I'm leaving with my Burke County boys," Major McDowell said, equally as strident. "You and I have been in enough scraps this summer to prove our bravery, but I must agree with my brother. We don't know what Ferguson has out there, but we barely have a hundred people between us here now, and Ferguson's got more than a thousand coming this way."

Hampton and Major McDowell watched from a safe distance as Ferguson's force made a deliberate withdrawal back toward Gilbert Town. A twelve-man rearguard of Tory militia with fixed bayonets walked backward, ready for any action that the partisans might spring on them.

"Ferguson now knows we are no pushover," McDowell said with pride. "This gives us a good opportunity to reposition ourselves before he returns."

Hampton again argued to send snipers to harass Ferguson, but McDowell vetoed the use of Burke troops, which Hampton had no control over. Not having enough men to launch further offensive action, Hampton reluctantly agreed to withdraw from the area, but not before ordering his Rangers to follow Ferguson at a discreet distance and monitor the Loyalist's actions. William Walker, a lieutenant about Jacob's age and the son of Colonel John Walker, was in charge of the Ranger patrol because, like Jacob, he knew the Cane Creek valley like the palm of his hand. "You are just to keep an eye on them," Hampton warned. "Let us know if they change their minds about retreating. Don't get yourself in a fight or caught 'cause there won't be nobody to help you."

After a half-hour's march, Ferguson stopped his men at the log home of Samuel Andrews, an outspoken Whig who farmed several hundred acres along Cane Creek just north of Jim Withrow's place. Andrews had built his house on a rise so that he could see most of his property from his front door. With open fields on all sides and a rock wall around the house, Ferguson had a small fortress.

Andrews, like many of his Whig neighbors, had fled into the South Mountains, leaving his frail, but strong-willed, wife to tend to the place. She stared with hatred as the Loyalists commandeered her home and moved Captain Dunlop to the only bed. She told Ferguson, "You ain't welcome here, General, but my Christian duty is to give shelter to them poor boys that's done shot up. If'n I was a man, I'd of been out there fighting you too, damn it."

Ferguson brushed the woman aside. "Woman, take your leave and go to a neighbor's house. We'll be gone by morning."

Stomping out of the house, she recognized Aaron Biggerstaff who lived only three miles to the east. "I should a'knowed it was worm dung like you coming and taking advantage of a poor old woman while her man is away. Have you no shame, Mister Biggerstaff?"

"Sorry, ma'am, but there's a war going on. Your husband's rebel friends ambushed us and shot up some good men," Biggerstaff replied unapologetically. "I didn't see Sam there."

The exhausted Loyalists had had only a few hours' rest the night before; however, there was enough enthusiasm for those not on guard to chase down and capture every chicken and goose in the farmyard and prepare a hot meal for the evening. Corn, dried beans, and apples were in abundance in the cellar along with eight earthen jugs of freshly made muscadine wine.

Ferguson called Andrew Godley over to him and asked his name. "Are you one of those lads that gave Captain Miller trouble the other day?"

"He was trying to give us trouble, sir."

"Well, you did good today, son. Capturing those horses showed pluck. I liked the way you lads brought the battle trophies to me. Now, I want you to take an express back to Colonel Mills and Captain DePeyster at Gilbert Town. On the way, stop by Fort McGaughey and tell the sergeant in charge to bring all his men here on the double to give us a hand. Tell him to move with all haste."

Ferguson gave Andrew a note that he had hastily penciled:

Reb atk repulsed at head of Cane Ck. 1 pvt dead. Dunlop & 1 pvt wounded. Cap 17 rebels, 12 horses & powder. Rebs lost 1 or more dead, 3 wd. Make John Walker's place a forward hq and hospital. Ensure strong defense around house. Get Corps ready to move. Returning soon as men rested. PF

Without hearing any threat, Andrew knew that Ferguson would also be keeping an eye on his two older brothers until he returned. "I'll get the express through; you can believe that, Colonel." Andrew's sympathies for the Liberty Men seem to have evaporated as he felt a closer kinship with those whom he had just shared danger.

"Take the best rebel horse. Go at a gallop and tell Captain DePeyster not to tarry." Ferguson ordered.

Andrew mounted a feisty sorrel, looked over at his brother William, and yelled happily, "See you tomorrow, Will." Then with a loud "whoop-whoop," he spurred the horse forward.

As the camp settled down, Ferguson began talking to the prisoners individually to find out more about the rebel band that assaulted him today. He learned that the rebels were much fewer than what Deveny told him, less than half that number, but could have caused serious damage had they been able to trap the Loyalists in the narrow gap ahead. He also learned that McDowell and Hampton would now probably head over the mountains to join up with another nemesis, Isaac Shelby.

One of the more defiant prisoners proudly told the British officer that he was from the Holston River area. "Any more of you backwater people in this rebellion?" Ferguson asked.

"Ain't nobody across those hills going to bow to no king. No sir! A bunch of us are fighting this side of the mountains and more is coming," the prisoner answered defiantly.

By midday, the Liberty Men had evacuated the Bedford Hill area, heading north away from the invaders. McDowell took most of his Burke County militia and followed the road along Silver Creek to his family's plantation at Quaker Meadows along the Catawba River. Hampton took the remaining militia on the track by Muddy Creek and northward across the Catawba River. As the hills became higher, the Rutherford County boys followed the North Fork of the Catawba toward Turkey Cove and the foot of the first high wall of the Blue Ridge. It was nearly midnight and twenty-one miles without a break before Hampton stopped to rest, although nearly half the mounted men had already fallen asleep in the saddle.

With only an hour of sleep, Ferguson was up before midnight to welcome the Tory reinforcements from Fort McCaughey. He ordered Husbands and Biggerstaff to take the wounded to Walker's plantation, a home that Biggerstaff had visited several times before. "Reinforcements and a surgeon will meet you at Walker's place. Take the prisoners who are not wounded on to Gilbert Town. Keep alert and on guard at all times," Ferguson warned before climbing into his saddle to return at a trot with a two-man escort to Gilbert Town.

He didn't hear the grumbles of tired soldiers being rousted out of their sleep for another long-night march.

Jacob heard the Loyalists breaking camp and quietly woke Billy Walker and the other sleeping Rangers.

WOMEN'S WOES
13 September 1780

His old bones ached from another night of sleeping on the ground, but James Chitwood suffered silently in the early twilight as he rode to take charge of his neighbor's home. A Tory militia captain for many years, he had the unpleasant task of telling his neighbor Elizabeth Walker that he was commandeering her house. It was a dreaded chore.

Elizabeth Walker watched with apprehension as the mounted militia rode up the hill to her house. For the past week, Tories had been coming by almost every day looking for her husband and grown sons. More often than not, they stole livestock, grain, and anything else that suited their fancy. There was little left to steal. Now this bunch led by her neighbor. *The gall of that man!*

At twelve years of age, George Walker was acting as man of the house. Following the example of his older brothers who were away fighting, he took an old shotgun down from wall pegs and made ready to take on the intruders. His bravado was dampened when his mother made him put the fowler back, saying, "There's way too many of them. You show that gun, and you will get all of us killed."

George wanted to overrule her, but as his brothers learned before him, no one disobeyed Mother Walker. She walked out onto the front porch, her arms folded and eyes cold as Chitwood approached. George and his nine-year-old brother Jake stood by her, trying to look defiant and protective of their mother, but their eyes betrayed fear of the armed men before them. A middle-aged house servant, Sadie, looked on from inside the door, much more frightened than her mistress was.

"Morning, Mistress Walker," Chitwood called out cheerfully and nodded to the sons, "Lads."

"Mister Chitwood," she responded icily, "you don't need an army to come calling."

"Sorry, ma'am," he said, as he dismounted. "There's been a fight up at the head of Cane Creek, and lads on both sides are hurt. They'll be here by midmorning. Colonel Ferguson requests your house for their care."

"Are you throwing me out of my own home, Jim Chitwood?"

"No, ma'am," Chitwood replied, trying not to look boastful or ashamed. "But we will be quartering the wounded here, maybe some officers as well. Don't know how many for sure, but at least six, I imagine. You and the boys can make a sleeping place in the cellar." What was understood, but left unsaid, was that they were held hostage to thwart Whig reprisals.

"The cellar will be preferable to sharing rooms with the likes of your Tory friends."

Elizabeth was relieved that they would not be burning her house, at least not yet, but she was both angry and frightened at being forced to remain there amidst mortal enemies. She resented even more the news that she and Sadie would have to cook and clean after the king's men.

The brigade surgeon, Doctor Uzal Johnson, and Lieutenant Anthony Allaire, adjutant for the American Volunteers, arrived at Gilbert Town about the same time as Ferguson returned from Cane Creek. The doctor was sent on to Walker's place with another company of militia and some more Provincials. Allaire organized his writing material for Ferguson to dictate a quick report to General Cornwallis, whose advance on Charlotte Town was moving much slower than anticipated; partisan harassment on British supply wagons and express riders was taking a toll on the British Army.

While Allaire was preparing the reports, Ferguson assembled the other senior officers to discuss new strategies. "Cane Creek shows that the rebels don't have the discipline to stage a decent ambuscade. They are disorganized and not good in follow-up," Ferguson reported.

"But they drew blood, sir," DePeyster interjected. "That means they still got some fight left in them."

"Yes, they still have some sting, but it's like a mosquito—a damn nuisance that can be smashed easily. If they run back across the mountains, then we shouldn't have any more problems from them. If they stay in the area, we will crush them for good. Our spies are searching the countryside for them as we speak."

Ambrose Mills spoke, "We are getting more and more people declaring support for the king. I saw at least twenty Whigs yesterday denounce their stance for the rebellion."

"More likely they're getting protection fever. But that's here on this side of the mountains," Ferguson responded. "I got disturbing news about the backwater country last night from one of the prisoners who fought with Shelby. He says a good number of his neighbors are still east of the mountains with the rebels. I don't intend on taking us across the mountains unless ordered, but we've got to put a stop to that nonsense."

Pausing and thinking for a moment, Ferguson then asked, "Don't we have a prisoner who claims kin to Shelby, a fellow we captured down near Musgrove's Mill?"

"Yes sir. I think his name is Phillips…Sam Phillips," DePeyster said.

"Get him up here."

Turning to Allaire who was writing across the room at Gilbert's Tavern, Ferguson said, "When you finish writing those expresses, I have another for you to pen, Mister Allaire."

While his adjutant completed the reports, Ferguson sipped hot tea and nibbled on fresh, molasses cookies baked by the wife of a local Tory. After signing his express to the general, Ferguson returned to his dictation. "Take this letter for Isaac Shelby, Mister Allaire. My dear Colonel Shelby, or should I just say sir?"

He pondered his own question, but rather than resolve the issue, continued with his dictation. "It is my honor to report that His Majesty's forces have quelled the rebellion in South Carolina. The rebel army and most of its militia are destroyed. Lord Cornwallis is now bringing North Carolina under protection of the Crown.

"Tryon County is fully under my control and its rebels eradicated. Citizens are flocking to pledge their loyalty to the king. Within the week, the Crown will have no more interference in the Catawba Valley.

"In order to secure peace within this province, I insist that you and your neighbors cease all rebellious activities. Unless such acts of treason stop immediately, I will have no choice but to march my army across the mountains and lay waste to the countryside with fire and sword and hang all rebel leaders.

"I have the honor to be Patrick Ferguson, commander of the Provincial Forces in service of his Royal Highness, King George the third."

The adjutant scribbled furiously, trying to keep up with his commander's dictation. Allaire would then make a formal copy with salutations, comments, and closings adhering to correct protocol, grammar, and style. "Got all of that, Lieutenant?" Ferguson asked.

"Yes sir."

"Now, bring me that prisoner."

Samuel Phillips had broken his arm when knocked unconscious by a fall off his horse while Shelby's militia was riding north after the battle at Musgrove's Mill a month ago. When he didn't quickly revive, he was left at a friendly planter's home to recover. Two days later, Phillips regained his senses and, a week later, was captured by Tory militia, who first threatened to hang him, but instead, turned him over to Ferguson in hopes he could be traded for captured friends. Small in stature, barefooted, his linen shirt in tatters, his skin caked in dirt, and hair resembling a wild hawk's nest, Phillips did not look like a warrior. A burly guard pushed him into the room before Ferguson. "Colonel, here's prisoner Phillips."

Ferguson eyed the prisoner for a full two minutes. Phillips became more anxious by the second and began to fidget. His eyes darted around the room, looking for danger and possible ways to escape. Until now he had been treated fairly and fed as well as his captors. Now he began to worry whether or not he would live to see another sunrise. Looking hard at the prisoner, Ferguson asked, "Are you the same Samuel Phillips that murdered some of my men at Musgrove's Mill?"

"I was there, sir, a soldier fightin' for liberty," Phillips answered nervously. "If my shootin' was true, I'm sure some of your boys got to see their maker. But I didn't murder nobody! All my fightin' was fair and square."

"Is it true that you are related to the rebel leader Shelby?"

"That is true, sir; me and the colonel are second cousins. We only live about two miles apart up on Beaver Dam Bottoms."

"If I set you free, will you take a message to him without delay? Can you make it over the mountains in the next three or four days?"

Phillips's eyes brightened. He stood a little straighter. He could hardly believe his good fortune. "Yes sir! I can walk fifty miles a day blindfolded when I have to. I'll be honored to take your express."

"And will you swear never to take up arms against His Majesty's government again?"

"I will do that, sir, but please don't make me fight my kin and neighbors. Just couldn't do that to them, sir. Wouldn't be right."

"Very well. Lieutenant Allaire here will draw up your parole papers. It is important that you get my express to Isaac Shelby as quick as you can. But remember, if we catch you engaged in any rebellious acts against the king, or if you fail to deliver this message, you will be hanged on the spot without trial. Is that understood?"

"Done seen all the fightin' I care to see, Colonel, sir. You can be certain for sure I'll get your express through. Do I get a horse? It'll get me there faster."

"Your freedom is all that I am empowered to give you, Phillips. God gave you feet and legs. I suggest you put them to good use and be gone as soon as the lieutenant completes your parole papers that will also serve as your safe passage."

Staying in the trees at a discreet distance, Jacob and William Walker followed Ferguson's Cane Creek survivors. Both men had excellent night vision, and the moans of the wounded made it relatively easy to keep up with the enemy until daylight provided better visibility. With two wounded men on stretchers, the Loyalist procession traveled much slower than a normal march.

Since the two Rangers could walk through the dense, hilly forest faster, they left their horses with another Ranger, who was told to take the animals to a glen that Jacob described on Big Camp Creek, about four miles from where they were and a mile north of the Godley home. If they didn't rendezvous within three days, he was to rejoin the retreating militia. William ordered two other Rangers, including Jim Gray, to scout the Flint Hill area and report back directly to Hampton.

William and Jacob made a wide skirt around McCaughey's Fort and Brittain Church. They nearly missed seeing the column turn onto the lane leading up to Walker's home. "Damn them bastards!" William swore in a harsh whisper when he saw where they were going.

"Easy, Billy, let's find a place where we can see better."

"That's my house they are going to! My mother's there."

The area around the Walker home was alive with men chopping trees, dragging leafy limbs and logs to form a defensive barrier about seventy-five yards out from the house. The Rangers saw the stretchers being carried into the house.

"Do you see my mother or little brothers?" William asked.

"No, but I bet there's two hundred Tories over there. Too far away to make out who's who."

After pausing for several minutes, Jacob continued. "Look, they're marching the prisoners on toward Gilbert Town, but not the wounded. Looks like my brothers may be guarding them. Can you tell?"

"Could that be Robert holding a rope around one of our people? Can't tell from here. Wait, that's Aaron Biggerstaff up in front. I'd recognize his fame anywhere."

After the prisoners and their guard moved out of sight, William said, "Jacob, I got to find out about my mother and brothers. Pa will skin me alive if I don't."

"Where is Colonel Walker?" Jacob asked.

"He, Felix, and Felix's wife left about the time Ferguson came to the county. I think they went to the Watauga settlement where Felix used to live. Mother wouldn't go with them. She refused to leave the house to damn Tories."

"So how are you going to get closer without being caught?"

"I'll circle round to the back side and see if I can get to the spring-house. There's cover there. Somebody's always going for butter, cider, or fresh water…mother, Sadie, one of the boys. I'll be real careful," William said. Remembering that he was the officer in charge, he told Jacob, "You follow those prisoners on to Gilbert Town and see what you can learn. We'll meet at that hill up across the river from your house. If you ain't there by morning, I'll head back to the horses."

"You be careful, Billy. Hope Rance Miller ain't over there."

"From what you said, I don't want to meet up with him. You'll be dead for sure if he spots you. Take care, Jake."

William Walker knew every animal trail and fold in the earth within two miles of his home. He had no trouble eluding detection during the hour it took for him to make his way to the family spring house, a roofed, rock structure built into the side of the hill adjacent to a laurel thicket not more than thirty yards from the main house. It was big enough to store large quantities of perishable foodstuff during the hot summers. The Tories were building their fortification on the other side of the house, out of sight and well below the spring area.

Captain Biggerstaff walked at the head of his prisoner guard. His small company had been augmented by another dozen Tories to help control the twelve captives whose numbers had been reduced by two who stayed at Walker's for medical care and three who had managed to escape during the night.

Aaron Deveny was the last man in the single line of shoeless prisoners. His arms were bound behind him, and a noose was draped loosely around his neck. Biggerstaff told the prisoners that if anyone tried to escape, Deveny would be hanged on the spot.

As the column marched by a log house set back from the road about halfway between the river and Gilbert Town, a woman with four small children tagging along and a baby in her arms ran out toward the group yelling, "Is that my Cap'n Deveny with you?"

Upon hearing his wife's shout, Deveny made an effort to go toward her, shouting, "Here, Sara!"

Robert Godley jerked the rope, forcing Deveny to fall backward to the ground. "Stay still, damn it!"

"Stop treating my husband that way," the hysterical woman screamed, running toward her fallen husband, the baby still clutched to her bosom. "He ain't no animal. Untie him this instant!"

Two guards rushed toward her and used their weapons to block the woman from getting within ten feet of her husband. "Go back, Sara. Protect the chil'un. I'm all right," Deveny told his wife.

Biggerstaff stopped the march and ran back to restore order. "Mistress Deveny, please calm yourself! Your husband is safe, but he is our prisoner."

The twenty-four-year-old woman, with tears streaking down her face and her hair in strings dangling from under her mobcap, shouted, "How dare you, Mister Biggerstaff! You know my husband's a good man. Just 'cause you are a Tory bully, you got no right to treat him worse than a dog. Turn him loose this instant; we need him here with the chil'uns and me!"

"Can't do it, ma'am," Biggerstaff said softly, feeling sorry for the woman he had met over the years at gatherings in Brittain Meeting House. "He tried to kill us up on Cane Creek yesterday, he and the rest of his rebel band. But we got the best of them, and I'm to deliver all these prisoners to Colonel Ferguson at Gilbert Town…and deliver them I will."

"But do you have to have that rope on his neck? It ain't right him being led around like a cow?" Sara screeched.

Robert helped Deveny back to his feet and said softly, "Your woman is making too much fuss, Deveny. Can't you make her stop that screeching?"

Deveny shook his head. "Hell, Mister Godley, I can't control her even when things are peaceable."

Biggerstaff turned to his men. "Y'all get moving." Then turning back to Deveny's wife, he said, "Look, ma'am, Colonel Ferguson is the only one who can release your husband. He's at Gilbert Town, and that's where we are going now. Stop your bawling. We're not going to hurt your husband as long as these prisoners behave themselves."

As the guards and prisoners marched on, Sara handed her baby to her seven-year-old, picked up the two-year-old toddler, plopped him on her hip, and herded the children a half mile to a neighbor's cabin. Heeding her tearful plea, the neighbors agreed to watch the four oldest children while Sara took the baby and chased after her husband.

She did not slow down or speak to a gaunt-looking man in rags rushing by her, headed toward the mountains and asking if she had any shoes to spare.

Jacob caught sight of the prisoner entourage just before it reached Cathey's Creek on the north side of Gilbert Town. Lurking back in the underbrush to avoid detection, he was puzzled by a distraught woman carrying a baby and chasing after the group. She was crying loudly. Must be a prisoner's wife, he thought.

Remembering his last venture into the enemy's lair and the altercation with Rance Miller, Jacob stayed well outside Gilbert Town. He made himself comfortable in a laurel cluster where he could watch the road at the creek ford, yet not be seen by those passing by.

It was midday when Biggerstaff marched his charges in past the headquarters and toward the cattle pen where prisoners were kept wallowing in filth created by livestock and humans. Ferguson was startled by the woman running behind the group, crying and begging loudly, "Please let my Aaron go! Please!"

Biggerstaff turned the prisoners over to Captain Walter Gilkey, who was officer of the guard, saying, "They are yours now, and good riddance."

He turned as Sara Deveny ran up to the two officers, shrieking. "You can't make him stay in with that slop! Please turn my husband loose."

From within the prison compound, Deveny, embarrassed by his wife's continued ruckus, pleaded, "Sara! I'm not hurt! Stop making a damn fool of yourself."

When Deveny tried to walk to the split rail fence, three guards raised and cocked their flintlocks. They pointed the muskets directly at Deveny, forcing him to back up. Gilkey was taken aback by the woman's outburst and yelled to her, "Shut that wailing, wench! You're making enough noise to wake the dead. Calm down!"

"This here's Aaron Deveny's wife," Biggerstaff told Gilkey. "He's the rebel officer over there that we caught yesterday, the one with the noose over his head. They live up the road from here toward the river. Been listening to her screamin' for the last hour. She ain't let up one bit, but she's your problem now." Biggerstaff turned and walked away quickly, escaping Sara's curses that questioned his parentage.

"Woman, I won't tell you again, shut up! I can't help you," Gilkey bellowed.

"Well, if you can't help, who can?" she demanded.

"Only Colonel Ferguson can say what we do with these prisoners. I keep them here or shoot them if they try to escape. Now get away from me!"

Gilkey motioned to two guards who had been snickering at the officers being berated, "Get this woman out of here!"

"Where do I find this Colonel Ferguson?" she cried.

One of the guards pointed to the tavern and the slender, red-headed figure standing in the door, wearing a blue-checked shirt with the sleeves rolled up and gnawing on another molasses cookie. "That's him over there, ma'am."

Sara turned and stomped over to Ferguson. Although amused at first by the confrontation at the prisoner pen, his smile changed to a frown as the crying woman came squarely in front of him and demanded between sobs,

"Mister Colonel Ferguson, sir, let my Aaron go. Me and the chil'uns need him bad."

"Ma'am, your man would not be where he is had he not shot my soldiers. He is a rebel, an enemy of the king. Yesterday he caused the death of one of my men and wounded a senior officer. And you want me to turn him loose? I think not," Ferguson said not too kindly. "Now, please, ma'am, quit your bellowing."

His blunt words caused her to wail more. Now her baby, who had been silent since her mother first ran from their house, began to bawl. Instinctively, Sara pulled her right teat out from her dress and plopped it into the baby's mouth, quieting the child while she continued her crying, "I don't know nothing about this awful fighting, sir. I just know I got hungry chil'uns at home and they're in bad need of their pa. How can you be so cruel? Please...I beg you...let my husband go."

Annoyed, Ferguson abruptly turned and walked back into his headquarters and slammed the door. Sara was shocked at the rejection and fell to the ground crying even louder, the baby still suckling, contented. Everyone around the Gilbert house and tavern watched the woman as she sat in the dirt in front of Ferguson's headquarters, wailing loudly and babbling incoherently.

For another fifteen minutes, the woeful crying penetrated the walls of the tavern-turned-headquarters as Ferguson tried to converse with his officers. Exasperated, he stood and exclaimed, "This has to stop! I can't hear myself think." The commander paused and paced the floor before continuing to talk aloud, mostly to himself. "It just wouldn't look right if I had a woman with a suckling baby flogged or thrown forcibly out of camp. Damn it all to hell!"

He jerked open the door and stomped outside, yelling, "Captain Gilkey! Bring this wretched woman's husband to me...now."

Sara Deveny looked up; she stopped yowling abruptly, but her tears continued to flow. Everyone in the camp watched as Gilkey and two guards escorted at a trot Aaron Deveny to Ferguson. Sara pushed herself up without help of others, the baby still at her breast. "You letting him go, sir?" she asked between sobs.

Ferguson ignored her and looked sternly at her husband. "Are you an officer in the rebel militia that made the cowardly attack on my people yesterday?" Although he had interviewed Deveny just after the battle, Ferguson's actions now were more for show and to vent his own anger.

"Aye, sir. Captain Aaron Deveny of Colonel Hampton's regiment."

"How old are your children, Captain?"

"We got five of them, sir. The oldest is seven; the babe is not six months yet."

"You know that I could have you hanged for that ambuscade you pulled up on Cane Creek, don't you? That was an uncivilized breach in the conduct of war."

"Aye, sir."

"You also know I could have your woman flogged for this unladylike conduct in disturbing this camp, don't you?"

"Aye, sir. But I beg you don't punish my Sara. She is a good woman with a heavy burden," Deveny pleaded, and as an afterthought, he added, "and just a mite bit high-strung."

"You should have thought of your family before running off on those foolish adventures with Hampton," Ferguson snapped. Then in a quieter, but stern voice, the commander added as he looked hard at Sara Deveny, "If I let you go home to take care of your family, will you forsake this damned rebellion, swear unwavering allegiance to your king and never take arms against the Crown again? Because if you violate that promise, this woman's tears will soften the soil for your grave beneath a hangman's tree."

"Aye sir, I promise not to take arms against the Crown and I'll take good care of my family, sir."

Turning back to Allaire, Ferguson said, "Draw up a parole for this man." Then turning and looking directly at Deveny's crying wife, he added, "But only if this woman hushes up her damn caterwauling this instant and gets out of my sight and hearing!"

Sara Deveny tried to reach for Ferguson's arm, which he jerked away. She sobbed, "Oh, thank you, sir, thank you. My man ain't going to run off to fight no more." She took her apron hem and blew running mucus into it.

A few minutes later, Deveny received his parole papers and surrendered his red sash and officer's gorget. He took his wife by the elbow to lead her from the Loyalist camp, but first she turned back toward Ferguson, curtsied, and said with a wide, angelic smile, "Thank you for your kindness, good sir."

As she walked away with Deveny, she looked up at her husband, her voice getting shriller, and berated him for causing so much trouble. She loudly warned him to never again leave his family. Ferguson shook his head as he turned to go back into the headquarters. "I think that poor sod would be much better off staying a prisoner. God, I'd rather see ten men dead than one squalling woman!"

For the next week, the story spread throughout the Loyalist ranks about the fearless and iron-willed Ferguson backing down before a teary-eyed woman. It was one of those rare moments of levity enjoyed at the expense of their commander.

From his hiding place, Jacob recognized Deveny and his wife as they waded through Cathey's Creek. He followed the couple away from Gilbert Town before showing himself and calling out, "Cap'n Deveny, a word please."

Deveny and Sara turned. Recognizing Jacob, Deveny asked bewildered, "What are you doing down here?"

Before Jacob could answer, Sara intervened tersely. "Is this one of your Liberty Men friends? You are crazy talking to him! Do you want to get hung for breaking your parole even before we get home?"

"Shut up, woman!" Deveny snapped sharply, causing his wife to step back, her mouth pursed closed. "You've made enough racket for one day. I ain't violating parole by talking to a neighbor."

"What's going on, Cap'n?" Jacob asked, motioning the Devenys into the trees bordering the road and out of sight of any traveler.

Deveny quickly explained his situation and added, "I took parole to take care of my family. Tell Colonel Hampton I gave my word, so I can't be joining him back."

"What's Ferguson going to do now?" Jacob asked.

"Looks like he's getting ready to take most of his army on up to the Catawba. He's got spies looking for Hampton and McDowell now. He says our folks will pay dearly for what we did at Cane Creek.

"Also, tell the colonel that we winged Dunlop real good…two shots in the leg. He'll be laid up for a while. Some of our boys got shot at the Cane Creek fight, and two are being held at the Walker place. Johnny Criswell and Pete Branks should survive. I saw Captain White fall in the battle.

"By the by, I heard one of the guards say that Ferguson sent a message to Colonel Shelby saying he'll go over the mountains and burn all their homes and hang the leaders if they didn't quit the rebellion."

Jacob absorbed the information before asking, "What happened at the ambuscade? What went wrong?"

"Somebody shot too soon, long before the Tories got into the killing area. Don't know who or why, but it was one of my men, probably the boy. Once that first shot went, everybody jumped in. I couldn't believe it happened at the time, but it did."

"Thanks. I'll pass this on to ol' Hampton," Jacob said, then turned to Sara, and added, "Sorry to have bothered you, ma'am. You can be proud of Cap'n Deveny; he was mighty brave in battle yesterday."

"Pshaw!" Sara spit out venomously. "He got himself caught and damn near kilt, makin' me a widow and our babes orphans. Just git away from us! We are through with this miserable war."

William Walker lay on his belly for more than an hour in the bushes just seven feet from the springhouse. When his brother George came to get a bucket of water for the working Tories, William caught his attention. "Psst, George!"

The boy turned to see who had called him, but William whispered loudly, "Don't look, George; it's me, Billy. Go inside the springhouse and tell me what's going on."

George ducked inside the springhouse before looking back at the bush where his brother was hiding. He asked in a near whisper, "Billy, how did you get here?"

"Not important. How're Mother and little Jake?"

"They're all doing good. Mister Chitwood's in charge of the Tories. They're making us sleep down in the cellar...Mother, Sadie, little Jake, and me. He says we have to stay there so that Whigs don't come and burn the house down now that it's a Tory fort."

"After you take the water bucket back, have Mother tell the Tories she is sending you and little Jake up to the back pasture to get the cow for milking."

"The Tories took all our cows last week," George complained.

"They don't know if we have others or not. Make them think we do. When y'all get out of sight of the house, sneak over to the backside of this hill, then follow that little branch down to the river. Go on to the other side of the river, but stay hid and make your way upstream to the mouth of Camp Creek. Be careful that you ain't seen crossing the river or road. Do you remember our favorite fishing hole up there? That's where I'll find you.

"Tell Mother and Sadie that after you and Jake leave the house, they should come out to the springhouse like they getting some butter. I'll sneak them off when the Tories ain't looking. We're going to the Godley place."

"They's Tories!" George gasped.

"Jacob Godley works with me. He's a Liberty Man true. When I get there with Mother, we'll all head over the mountains to join Pa and Felix."

A half hour later, William saw his two brothers playfully meander toward the back pasture. No Loyalist seemed to notice them. Shortly after the boys disappeared over the crest, Elizabeth Walker and Sadie walked out from the house toward him. They carried an empty basket and an earthen crock jar. From his hidden position, William told his mother and Sadie to wander on into the woods as if they were looking for roots, and he would lead them to safety.

Sadie said no, that she would go back to the house; otherwise, the Tories would know too soon that everybody was missing. Her mistress would have more time to escape if, when asked, Sadie told the Tories that the mother was not feeling well and was lying down and that the boys had gone to fetch a cow. "But what if they try to hurt you for letting us leave?" Elizabeth asked.

Sadie just laughed. "Ma'am, to those rascallions, I'm just a dumb darkie wench who don't know nothin'. I'll take care of the house while you are away, Miz Lizbeth, don't you worry. You and them boys leave. It ain't right how they's treating you."

"God bless you, Sadie. You are always family to us."

"Wait till I take some cider to that guard over by the porch and get him looking away," Sadie said as she retrieved a jug of freshly made cider from the cool water.

When William saw Sadie distract the guard, he motioned his mother farther into the woods. They walked along the same route that William had sent his brothers and joined them before sundown. It was dark when they reached the hill across the river from the Godley house.

After sundown, Jacob watched his home for more than an hour, making sure no Loyalists were lurking about. Satisfied that it was safe, he first waded across the river and wasn't surprised to see William lead his mother and brothers from their hiding place. "Hello, ma'am. Pleased you got away," Jacob said. "Let's go on over to my house. We can spend the night there and leave at first light."

As he approached the house, which was lit by a single candle in the big room, Jacob yelled out, "Hello in the house. It's me, Jacob. I'm coming in with friends."

Wayne had a fowler in his hand as he opened the door cautiously for his brother and the Walkers. Agatha and George Godley were surprised to see Jacob back so soon and shocked that the Walkers were with him. They hustled the visitors in, with Agatha making Elizabeth Walker as comfortable as possible. "It ain't safe for you here, Jacob," his father warned. "Right after you left the other day, Rance Miller and his banditti come a looking for you. They threatened to hang us and burn down the house if we didn't tell where you were. Wayne got a terrible flogging…they beat him right in front of us. They warned that we would all be hung if we helped you again."

Shocked at how badly his family was treated, Jacob swore. "Bastards! I'll kill that son of a mangy whore!"

"Jacob!" his mother scolded sharply, "You know that language and tone is never permitted in this house!"

"Sorry, Mama, but I didn't know about Miller coming here. It's my fault. Sorry you got a whipping, Wayne," Jacob said remorsefully.

"Didn't hurt much," Wayne said, lying. "You should've seen that bloody head I gave old man Gilkey when he tried to drag me around. Clobbered him good, I did."

"They had Tories come by a few times since, but because your brothers are in their militia, they haven't bothered us none. I'm real scared for the little ones, Jacob, scared for all of us," George Godley added.

Jacob explained their current situation. "The Tories took over the Walker place and were making Miz Walker and the boys live in the cellar. Billy helped them escape; now we got to get them over the mountains to safety. Can we spend the night here?"

"It's not safe here, too dangerous for everybody," the senior Godley said. Turning to his wife, he said, "Agatha, find some traveling garments for Mistress Walker and the boys, something to keep the chill and damp off. It's already cold in the high country."

George Godley turned back to Elizabeth. "Ma'am, you know you are welcome here. But for your protection and that of our children, it's best you move on quickly, lest the likes of that Miller brute comes a callin' again. We'll fix you some food to take with you."

"Thank you, but you shouldn't risk your lives for me. I am indebted to all of you," Elizabeth said sincerely. "Mister Godley, you have always been a good neighbor. I hate to ask more of you, but our Sadie chose to stay behind to mislead the Tories as where we might be. Could you look in on her for me? She didn't have to make that sacrifice, but she insisted."

"Don't worry. We'll look after her."

Jacob's young sisters brought in a leftover stew that was simmering on the coals in the cookhouse. It had remnants of rabbit, fish, dove, assorted grains, potato peels, and corn but was warm, tasty, and filling. The Walkers didn't complain as they spooned the pot's contents; they had not eaten since morning. An hour later and after good wishes from all around, the Walkers and Jacob slipped out of the house into the darkness. The two younger boys were each carrying a bundle of sailcloth and linsey-woolsey blankets tied to their back. William and Jacob both had sacks of food - corn, turnips, oats, dried apples, and jerky.

After retrieving their horses in the nearby glen, Elizabeth rode double behind William. William's brothers doubled behind Jacob and the other Ranger. With Rance Miller looking for him, Jacob decided they should travel only at night until after they were well north of the Catawba River.

CATAWBA VALLEY

14—17 September 1780

The tongue lashing was severe, colorful, and quite public. Never, in his sixty-one years, had the old patriarch received such a barrage of verbal abuse as that which Patrick Ferguson heaped upon James Chitwood after learning that the Walker woman and her boys had escaped the day before. The Tory officer bit his lip as he listened in raging silence until Ferguson's anger eased.

"I do not shirk my responsibilities, sir!" Chitwood answered icily after his commander demanded to know how the escape had occurred. "May I remind the colonel that my charge was to prepare defenses from an outside attack? Your Provincial officers took charge of the house and its contents before the Walkers went missing."

No officer at the plantation escaped Ferguson's wrath that morning except the wounded Dunlop, and all breathed easier when the irate Highlander finally mounted his horse in disgust and continued his march northward toward the Catawba Valley with three hundred Tories and thirty of his Provincial regulars. DePeyster and Allaire followed that evening with the remainder of the Provincials and two hundred more militia, leaving Chitwood's company as the primary defense for the Walker home. Doctor Johnson remained behind to take care of the wounded, but he fell ill with fever and was bedridden for nearly a week.

Working from Gilbert Town, Colonel Mills took charge of the county's security and had patrols foraging the countryside and seeking signs of rebel activity. Rance Miller and his company became a reserve force to call on in case of serious trouble.

As he neared the site of the ambush two days earlier, Ferguson met with two spies from Burke County. They reported that McDowell was at his Quaker Meadows home the day before, but many of his militia had retreated across the Blue Ridge. One spy said he had tracked Hampton's small regiment to Turkey Cove and heard from settlers there that the rebels had gone over the mountains toward the Watauga.

The news pleased Ferguson. There would be no better coup than capturing McDowell at home. After a few hours rest, he continued before midnight his march to Quaker Meadows, fording the Catawba River under a bright moon. Ferguson's scouts, mostly from Vezey Husbands's Burke militia and now working on their home grounds, fanned out in advance of the main force, looking for partisan activities. Many were disappointed when they found none. Shortly after sunrise, the scouts searched the vast Quaker Meadows cattle fields and nearby woodlands before Ferguson led his troops to Charles McDowell's home on the north side of the meadows. The half-dozen steers grazing in the pasture were a tenth of the actual herd owned by the McDowell family. Most of the others had been driven up Johns River and hidden in remote mountain coves.

Ferguson remained mounted as Husbands banged loudly on the door of the McDowell house. Margaret O'Neill McDowell, a striking woman of sixty-three years with her silver hair tied tightly into a bun under her mobcap, opened the door and in a thick Scots–Irish brogue, demanded, "Ye don't have to beat the door down! What do ye want?"

"A good day to you, ma'am. I'm Vezey Husbands of the loyal Burke militia," Husbands smiled as he introduced himself and then turned to face Ferguson. "May I present Colonel Patrick Ferguson of the British Army?"

"Englanders!" She shouted the word as a curse. "I've no use for such swine. Leave my house and property!"

"Madam"—Ferguson spoke with firm authority and no hint of friendliness—"We are here for Charles McDowell. I am told this is his place. We seek him and his brother Joseph on charges of treason and rebellion. Step aside so that my men can search."

Standing stiffly in the doorway with her hands firmly on her hips, the McDowell matron resisted defiantly. "Ye've no right to burst into me home like this. Charles is me son. He lives here, but he left yesterday. Other than servant help, I'm all alone. I demand ye leave this instance."

"Captain Grimes, take your men and search the house from top to bottom for rebels and contraband," Ferguson ordered.

Grimes led his men through the door, pushing the ninety-eight-pound matriarch aside as though she was broom sage. "Not so brutish, Captain!" Ferguson cautioned and then spoke again to the woman. "Now, madam, where did Charles McDowell go?"

"How should I know?" she spat back. "I've seen little of him since this war started."

Maintaining her composure, the fiery Margaret McDowell continued her caustic retort, "Had ye approached as gentlemen, I would have invited ye into my house out of common courtesy, English or not. But ye Englanders always have to lord it over us common folk, and particularly me, a poor old lady with no means to defend herself. Typical of your lot."

Ferguson chuckled. "My dear lady, no sword could compete with a tongue as sharp as yours. My apologies if you feel we are abusing your sensibilities, but your sons chose to make war against the rightful ruler of this wilderness land. They must be brought to justice and account for their crimes."

"Poppycock!" she retorted.

Grimes and his men emerged from the house. "Nobody here except a servant woman, sir," he reported. "And we found two fowling guns and a hunting knife."

Speaking to Husbands, Ferguson said, "Keep a company here in case McDowell comes back. I want no harm to come to this lady or this house; is that understood? Take what livestock and other commodities that we can use."

Before Husband could say, "Yes, sir," Ferguson was turning his horse to ride away with most of his entourage. The Burke Loyalist commander said nothing as he watched Grimes's men reenter the house to help themselves to men's clothing, blankets, and a silver-capped walking cane.

"Damn thieves! Bring back those things this instance!" McDowell's mother protested shrilly. "That's me dear departed husband's cane and those clothes belong to me son."

"Hush that mouth, woman," Grimes ordered loudly and with a wicked smile. "When I find Charles McDowell, I will kill him immediately and without mercy. But when I catch your other son Joe, I'll let you watch him get down on bended knees and pray for his life before he falls to my blade. Then I'll burn this house down around you."

"Easy, Captain," Husbands intervened. "We are not animals, ma'am, but your family has caused far too much harm to the law-abiding families of this region. Sitting here in this big manor house, you have been blinded to the evils of the scoundrels you have spawned. I suggest you calm yourself and pray that they surrender to the benevolent Colonel Ferguson."

"It will be ye Tories begging for mercy when me boys get through with the likes of ye."

On the other side of the expansive meadows, another Tory militia company ransacked Major Joe McDowell's home. Twelve years younger than Charles, he had built his house for a new bride so that he could be his own master and get away from the shadow of his brother and mother.

Across the first high ridges, Hampton's troops trudged along the banks of the Toe River, following it upstream though a remote, narrow mountain valley, heading for Roaring Creek and then following it up the steep Brice's Trace across Yellow Mountain Gap, the highest obstacle along their route. In another day and a half, they should be at Fort Watauga. Most of his followers wanted to stay back and engage in hit-and-run raids against the king's men. Hampton's pride wished the same, but his duty compelled him to cajole and plead with his men to hold together. "Men, if we stayed back and nipped at their heels, they would kick us around like stray dogs. There's just too many of them. We got to get some help and build up a stronger army so we can return and skin those bastards alive."

He had less than half the volunteers that had answered muster three months before. Some had fallen to wounds or illness. Others had been captured. Some surrendered after Ferguson invaded the county. Others simply faded into the countryside without a by-your-leave. Still a handful, including Jacob, remained behind to harass the enemy and gather intelligence on their activities.

At least twice a day, the old colonel was asked if Shelby and Sevier's mountain men would join them to expel the British expedition. Many had fought with Isaac Shelby in upper South Carolina during July and August and admired the audaciousness of the dashing twenty-nine-year-old leader from the Holston River country. They were with him when he and Hampton forced a superior number of Tories to surrender Fort Thicketty without a shot. Some who had fought the overhill Cherokees also knew John Sevier, the Washington County militia commander. Like Shelby, Sevier had followed his father as his county's military commander. The exploits by the two overmountain officers were legendary.

There were a couple dozen of Burke County boys with the column. They were chagrined that their colonel had refused them permission to stay behind and fight. They agreed with Hampton that Charles McDowell was a likable man, but just too timid when it came to locking horns with the enemy.

All along the Catawba Valley, dozens of planters and stockmen followed Charles McDowell's advice and went to the advancing Loyalists requesting protection of the Crown. Most, like the old Indian fighter John Carson, one of the largest landholders in the Pleasant Gardens area, were reluctant to engage in the ruse, but agreed with McDowell that they must preserve the herds if the residents were to survive the winter. They also wanted to protect their own homes and necks. Being married to McDowell's cousin, Carson went along with the colonel's plan.

Others in the valley, however, refused adamantly to be subservient to the Crown for any reason or to lie for their own protection. They thought it cowardly, and unpatriotic. Instead, they drove their cattle, sheep, and hogs into hiding deep within the mysterious coves along Buck, Mackey, and Curtis creeks where bears and wolves were more a threat than the invading humans. As much wool, flax, grain, molasses, dried fruit, beans, and other commodities as could be saved within a few days were packed away into isolated caves and huts where Ferguson's plundering troops could not find them.

Word spread among neighbors that true believers of liberty did not think too kindly of anyone who collaborated with the enemy, regardless of their motives. "Tory rot" was one of the kinder characterizations given to those who took protection from the invaders.

Although he missed capturing the McDowell brothers, Ferguson was elated with the success he was having on this expedition. He marveled at the beauty of the wide Pleasant Gardens area with its soaring mountains and hundreds of acres of flat bottomland choked with lush grasses and tall corn. It made him homesick for the hills of his native Scotland.

The number of people seeking Crown protection exceeded expectation. However, Ferguson's sixth sense warned him that things were too easy, that many of those now expressing support for the Crown were doing so only to protect their property and stock. To find out just how true these converts to the king were, he rode with Major Plummer's regiment and several Provincials up the valley to observe for himself.

On Ferguson's third day in the upper Catawba Valley, John Carson was riding with a Tory patrol when they came upon a large cattle herd grazing along a five-acre canebrake near the river. Carson knew the owners of the cattle were Tories but said nothing. When asked, he replied that he "guessed" they were on the property of a Whig partisan. Ferguson turned his men free for a frenzy of slaughter, which provided prime beef dinners for all his troops and a hefty supply of smoked jerky. Some steers were taken back on the hoof, but far more animals were killed and their carcasses left to rot.

The cattle were, in fact, owned by three Tory militiamen who were back at Ferguson's forward camp performing picket duty that day. They were already upset that they were not selected to guide Ferguson's raiders through their home valley, but not nearly as much as they were when they saw the sides of beef and cattle hides draped across horsebacks and stacked high in carts being brought back to the camp. They asked where the beeves were found and were shocked to learn that it was their own cattle butchered and not some rebel's herd that had been appropriated.

Clearly upset, Joseph Brown, Harold Dement, and Stephen Johnstone left their picket posts, marched furiously to Ferguson and Plummer, and demanded to know why their animals had been slaughtered and who was going to pay for their loss. So great was Dement's anger that he left the Loyalist ranks and went home in disgust, declaring that he would never fight for people who stole from their own troops.

Ferguson, embarrassed at having been deceived, apologized and ordered the arrest of Carson who had the good sense not to return to the camp with the Loyalists. Instead, he fled to a remote cave to wait until the situation quieted.

A four-year veteran of Indian duty with the Whig militia by his nineteenth birthday, Josiah Brandon was pleased that he had not been drafted to help block Ferguson's invasion into the Catawba Valley. Other than a three-month, mounted cavalry jaunt chasing Bloody Bill Cunningham down in South Carolina, most all of his militia service had been on the Indian line. He now wanted to stay at home and protect his mother at the small plot of land that they farmed on the banks of the Catawba between Pleasant Gardens and Davidson's Fort.

Josiah's father, Thomas Brandon, had left the county two years before to fight with the Tories in Florida and Georgia. His departure was speeded by neighboring Liberty Men's threat of a tar and feather party for which the senior Brandon was to be the featured guest. He was accused of leading Tory raids against families that were actively supporting the independence movement.

Josiah was ashamed that his father had been ostracized from the community and had abandoned his family. His mother, however, would not speak badly of her estranged husband, but neither did she speak well of him. Theirs was a marriage of convenience in which romance was rarely evident.

While serving as a guide for Ferguson's patrols into the upper regions of the Catawba, Thomas Brandon took pleasure in confronting his former neighbors and denouncing them publicly as rebel sympathizers. That condemnation led to the Whig families losing their livestock and what little food or other commodities they had stored in their modest log homes. Looms were smashed, forges wrecked, and all weapons confiscated, including rusted fowling guns. At one place, Tory militiamen used an old man's grinding wheel to sharpen their own knives, bayonets, and sabers before smashing the stone wheel against the rock platform that served as the family forge. The man who instigated the tar-and-feather party for Brandon was left standing naked as his family's clothes, home, and outbuildings were burned.

With no significant resistance in the valley, Brandon was granted a furlough to visit his family. When he walked through the door of the two-room cabin, his wife, Elizabeth, merely looked up and said matter of factually as though he had left that morning, "So, you decided to come home." There was no emotional greeting by either of them.

After supper that evening, father and son walked out beyond the corncrib. Josiah declined the offer of tobacco from a small, leather pouch his father used to feed a clay pipe. Thomas bent down and, taking two flints, created a small fire in some crushed, dried twigs. As one wooden splinter blazed, Thomas lit the pipe, puffed a few times, and then said to his son,

"Josiah, I know we haven't been close these past few years, but I hope you understand why my duty has kept me away."

"I understand, Father," Josiah answered awkwardly. He did not understand, but he did not want to pick a fight either.

"I accepted a commission from the royal governor to serve back in the early seventies. Working with some of the very people we are fighting now, we fought diligently to make the country safe from murdering Indians. I made a vow to serve my country and king. Just because some hotheaded neighbors wanted to turn against the legitimate government, I could not in good consciousness join them or violate that oath. It was against every principle that I hold dear.

"Then they started making threats against the family. I could handle personal threats, but I could not stand the thought of them burning our home or putting you and your mother in harm's way. That's why I left.

"Now this ill-conceived rebellion is falling apart. Order is restored in Georgia and South Carolina, and soon North Carolina will be back in line. McDowell and his cowards chose to run rather than fight us. They tried to ambush us down near where your Uncle Jim and Aunt Sydney live on Cane Creek. But the rebel cowards ran there, just like they did at Camden.

"Did you know your Uncle Jim was an officer in the rebel militia? I saw him last week and tried to talk some sense into him. Didn't work, but for your aunt and cousins' sake, I was able to keep the local Tories from plundering his place.

"I understand that you have been a part of the local Whig militia as well."

Josiah responded without looking directly at his father, "Just about all my time has been working out of Davidson's Fort against the Cherokee. When Colonel McDowell went down to Charles Town to keep it out of British hands, he wouldn't let me go with him. He said I might run into you, and he didn't want a boy having to shoot his pa. So he kept me here at the fort." He said nothing of the three months he spent chasing Tory raiders.

"Makes sense," Thomas answered. "But, m' boy, times are changing, and when the new order comes back permanently to this valley, there's going to be a reckoning...a hard reckoning with all those who aided in the rebellion. Not just the fighters, but those who supported them and their families. That includes you and your mother."

Taken aback by the threat, Josiah blurted. "I'll kill anybody that tries to hurt Mother!"

"I know you will try, but if you are outnumbered, there is little that you can do. Besides, most of it will be legal, like confiscation of land and forced settlement elsewhere."

"But this is your land, and you are fighting with the Tories; won't that give us protection?"

"You have been serving the rebels for past two years, Josiah," his father said sternly. "And you are recognized as the man of this house by local folk. Your mother has been none too kind to the Tory families here about. I've heard some mean rumors."

"So what do you want me to do?"

"I want you to join my company; be of service to the king."

"I can't go against my friends. That ain't right," Josiah protested.

"Look, McDowell and Hampton and all their rebels have fled across the mountains with their tails tucked between their legs. Ain't no more fight left in 'em. A lot of young men like you have seen the light and returned to the bosom of the Crown. More are coming over every day. There's no rebel left here to fight. You come with us, and then we can better protect your mother and our property."

"And if I don't?"

"Then I can't help if you are arrested and punished, maybe even hanged, for supporting this damned rebellion."

They argued for another hour before turning in for the night. "Let me pray about it till morning," Josiah said as he bade his father a good night.

The next morning, Josiah reluctantly agreed to join the Loyalists. "It is a son's duty to honor his father," he told his protesting mother.

After several days of traversing the length of the Catawba Valley, Ferguson decided to pull his forces back southward. He had made the king's presence felt by the residents. The plunder that he had sent back to Gilbert Town included several hundred cattle; dozens of horses; and numerous cart loads of grain, hides, and other supplies taken from the few rebel plantations that had anything of value to plunder. Satisfied that no organized armed resistance existed in Burke County, Ferguson began to worry that he was getting too far from Cornwallis. The general's orders gave Ferguson considerable latitude to quell the rebellion, but also stated that he was to stay close enough to reinforce the British Army or be reinforced if need be.

As Ferguson was beginning his plunder of the Catawba valley, Andrew Hampton led remnants of his bedraggled regiment and some refugee families into the frontier fort alongside the Watauga River in the early afternoon of Sunday, 17 September. A few hours later, Colonel McDowell and what remained of his command joined Hampton. Shortly before dark, Jacob Godley and the Walkers arrived, exhausted and hungry, at the fort that now served as a refugee center for those crossing the mountains to escape advancing British forces.

After getting Elizabeth Walker and her younger sons settled in with the Proctor family, William Walker and Jacob went looking for Colonel Hampton to report their observations since the Cane Creek skirmish. The young Rangers were thanked for their diligence and dismissed. William then began looking for his father while Jacob decided to go on to the McCracken home for the night.

Jacob had a tearful reunion with his adopted family. Stuffed with a meaty hunter's stew and freshly baked apple pie, Jacob stayed up deep into the night telling about the British invasion of North Carolina and his brushes with the notorious Rance Miller.

Colonels Hampton and McDowell were welcomed warmly by John Sevier and Isaac Shelby, the militia commanders for Washington and adjacent Sullivan Counties. The two overmountain officers had been at a horse race earlier in the day when they heard that the refugee militia had arrived at the fort. Hampton told Sevier that he hoped they could rest for a few days, recruit some more fighters, and then head back with renewed strength and spirit to take on Ferguson, but they needed support from the overmountain militia. He urged the two local colonels to join him and McDowell with as many mountaineers as they could spare. Sevier said he was more concerned about Dragging Canoe and his Chickamaugans who were threatening new raids along the frontier. He just didn't know how many men that he could muster to go fight east of the mountains.

Shelby suggested everyone rest and they have another war council at noon the next day. He then returned nineteen miles northward to his home overlooking Beaver Creek, a tributary of the Holston River. Until a year before, this area was part of Virginia. Now, with the border agreed to by provincial leadership, it was called Sullivan County, North Carolina.

Just short of thirty years old, Isaac was unmarried and still lived with his parents. They had settled in the Beaver Dam Bottoms eight years ago after Evan Shelby had some disastrous business deals that caused them to lose the family's expansive holdings in Maryland. The Shelbys began a lucrative fur trade with the Indians and built a large fort on the hill overlooking the bottoms near their house. As the most powerful political family in the area, Evan served as the county colonel until earlier this year when he relinquished the militia command to his son. Isaac, popular with his neighbors, had proved his military skills time and again in scraps with Indians, as an explorer in the Kentucky wilderness, and as a supplier for the Continental Army. His fame grew after going across the mountains and joining McDowell's forces, leading a bloodless victory at Fort Thicketty and causing a deadly rout of Loyalist troops at Musgrove's Mill. Those who rode with him didn't have to exaggerate when they returned home to tell stories of hard charging raids and vicious fights in South Carolina's up country.

It was already dark when Isaac arrived at his father's home, Sapling Grove, to find Samuel Phillips sitting on the front stoop waiting, plum tuckered out after walking barefooted 122 miles over difficult mountain trails and with little sleep or food. Phillips had refused to go inside because he was filthy and his clothes tattered. Sharp rocks and tangled briars had left his bare feet and lower legs covered in oozing sores and bloody scabs.

Evan Shelby, the sixty-one-year-old family patriarch from whom Isaac had acquired the traits of leadership, tenacity, and organizational skills, was sitting along with several friends listening to Phillips tell of his exploits in the fight against the British when Isaac rode to a stop in front of the group.

After handing the reins of his lathered horse over to a stable boy with instructions to walk the animal, cool him down, and give him a good rubdown, Isaac turned to walk toward the house when he saw Phillips waiting for him.

"Sam!" Shelby called out happily surprised. "Good to see you, cousin. I thought we left you for dead down in South Carolina."

"Just a bad bump on the head, Isaac," Phillips answered. "Got captured though and ol' Ferguson held me for a spell."

"Did you escape? You look like you've been through hell. Do you need food, water?"

"No sir. Your folks took good care of me already and gave me some vittles," Phillips said as he reached inside his pouch to retrieve Ferguson's letter. "Ferguson himself turned me loose. He wanted me to bring you this here letter."

"Well let's get in by the candlelight and see what it says."

"I done read it so I could tell you what he says in case I lost it. Almost lost it coming across the Catawba. The letter is mean-spirited, Isaac. He says he's going to come over here and waste our places with fire and sword. He says he will hang you and all the other leaders."

"That son of a poxed whore!" Shelby exclaimed angrily. "Let me read this for myself. Come on in, and if the old colonel hasn't drunk it all, we should have a jug of whiskey about. We both could use a drink now."

"Calm down, Isaac," the senior Shelby said in a soothing tone. "I already gave Sam a snort, but I'll join you two in another. Looks like this Ferguson fellow has done thrown down the gauntlet for you to pick up."

Samuel Phillips did not follow them in for a drink. With his mission now complete, he just leaned back against the house and for the first time in four days entered into a deep, untroubled sleep.

ACCEPTING THE GAUNTLET

18–24 September 1780

Unable to sleep and still in his nightshirt, Isaac Shelby stumbled through the darkness into the parlor. He fanned the coals that were banked in the fireplace so that there would be enough flame to light a candle, then two more. In the corner of the room, he heard the steady snores of Sam Phillips, who had not stirred since Isaac and his father picked the man up a few hours earlier, carried him inside, and placed him on a bear rug. Phillips was worn out and needed rest.

Isaac reread Ferguson's letter, opened the stationery desk, pulled out a sheet of paper, sharpened a quill with his small pen knife, and began writing a letter to Colonel William Campbell, who lived in Virginia's upper Holston River Valley, thirty-five miles to the north. After a sleepless night of mulling through all options, Isaac reached the decision that it was essential that an armed force go back over the mountains to stop Ferguson. But since they had to leave the wilderness counties some protection against Indian raids, they needed more troops for a successful expedition. Campbell's Virginians could be the solution.

Without consulting with McDowell, Hampton, or Sevier, he explained the situation in a brief letter and urged Campbell to join forces with them. By the time he finished writing and brushing away the pounce used to dry the ink on the paper, it was getting light outside. His mother and her servant were already preparing breakfast in the cookhouse out back. Isaac returned to his bedroom, dressed quickly, and then rousted Moses, his nineteen-year-old brother, from his slumber. He explained the urgency of the situation to Moses and the necessity of getting the express to Campbell as quickly as possible. Moses was small in stature and the best horseman in the bottoms, making him the logical choice to deliver the express.

After gulping a quick breakfast, the young captain saddled the family's fastest animal and began the long dash up the Holston's valley to Campbell's Aspenvale home. For Moses, it was a happy diversion from doing chores around the plantation.

As his young brother galloped north, Isaac rode south for another meeting with the militia colonels to inform them of the dramatic change of events. His anger at the threatening letter from Ferguson intensified with each hour.

There was much happiness in the McCracken home. Jacob was feted as a long-lost son who finally made his way home. Anna mothered over him as she would a twelve-year-old rather than the young man that he now was. She kept pushing food to him at the breakfast table until he was stuffed with eggs, roasted venison, blackberry jam, and buttered wheat bread. The McCracken siblings all wanted to hear more of Jacob's exploits against the horrid king's men who they heard were pillaging, raping, and killing on the other side of the mountains.

Jacob enjoyed the adulation and again being with his adopted family, but he remembered his duty to report to his colonel, although somewhat belated. Matthew rode with him to the fort crowded with refugee families and militia units trying to reorganize. After chastising the young Ranger for wasting half the day, Captain Singleton ordered Jacob to report to John Carter's plantation where Hampton and McDowell were staying. Carter, whose home was the nicest in the region, was one of the area's original settlers and had extensive landholdings along the Watauga. He had commanded the militia that successfully defended the Watauga against devastating Indian raids in the early 1770s. Too old now for soldiering, he was still revered by the residents for his wisdom and guidance.

Hampton, McDowell, Sevier, and Carter were sitting under a tall maple tree talking when Jacob arrived, a bit uneasy about reporting late. Jacob recognized Sevier immediately and called to him, "Hello, Major; good to see you again."

"Welcome home, Jake. I've heard good things about you from Colonel Hampton. Are you still dancing around with she-bears?"

"Dancing with bears?" McDowell asked, puzzled.

"Killing three Indians in one morning weren't enough for this boy, Colonel." Sevier laughed. "Young Jake had to go off and wrestle with a she bear to get more excitement, and him not yet old enough to shave."

"Major, please, it ain't funny," Jacob protested, his freshly shaved face turning rosy with embarrassment.

Chuckling, Hampton interrupted. "It's Colonel Sevier now, Mister Godley. He got promoted since you lived over here. We can hear about your youthful exploits later; first tell these gentlemen what you saw firsthand about Ferguson's army."

After Jacob gave a succinct report, Hampton said to him, "Since you know the Watauga so well, Jacob, I want you to stay close and serve as my messenger."

"Yes sir."

As Jacob went to secure his horse, Isaac Shelby galloped into the yard. He dismounted with a leap and threw his reins to Jacob, whom he did not recognize, with a brisk, "Take care of my horse, boy! Rub him down good."

Shelby rushed to the other colonels, and without the usual pleasantries of greeting, he blurted, "I have new intelligence that gives more credence to Colonel Hampton's wish to go back across the mountains and confront Ferguson.

"When I got home last night, there was an express from Ferguson himself, saying he would be coming over these mountains to lay waste to our land with fire and sword, and that he would hang all of us. My cousin, who was captured at Musgrove's Mill, said Ferguson himself wrote the letter. My man Sam Phillips said he was paroled with specific orders to get it to me as quickly as possible. He walked barefooted all the way from Gilbert Town with little sleep or food. So, gentlemen, do we wait for Ferguson to come here, or do we go get him first?"

Sevier responded first. "That is disturbing news, but we don't have enough fighters to go on an offensive over the mountains and still defend our homes against the Indians at the same time."

"I know. That's why I took it upon myself to send an express this morning to Colonel Bill Campbell asking him to bring some Virginians down to join us. If we get several hundred riflemen from him, then we can leave enough of our people here to keep Dragging Canoe back in his lair."

Like Shelby, Sevier knew Campbell well. The three had been on numerous Indian campaigns together since first serving as lieutenants in Dunmore's War and as captains in the 1776 campaign against the Cherokee Nation. Campbell was a brave fighter, a skilled tactician, and well liked by all who knew him as a friend.

"Do you think he will join with us?" McDowell asked.

"How can he refuse?" Shelby responded. "If we don't stop Ferguson, then there's nothing to keep them damn redcoats from marching right on up the Holston and New Rivers to the lead mines at Chiswell."

"Then we need to start getting ready," McDowell said. "Our men and horses have taken a beating the last couple of weeks. Let everyone rest today. But tomorrow we need to make sure all harnesses and saddles are in good condition and all rifles in working order."

Pausing to reflect a moment, McDowell continued. "Gentlemen, I still don't think we have enough firepower to face Ferguson's army. I can alert Colonel Cleveland to have the Wilkes and Surry County militia to unite with us, but I don't know if he will respond. He has been having a lot of trouble himself with the local Tories. They have a mean bunch of them up along the Yadkin River."

Hampton interjected, "I've got sixty, maybe seventy men fit to fight that's with us here. When we get back to Rutherford County, we will probably pick up at least that many more. The question is, when and where are we going to face the bastards?"

Although McDowell was thought to be timid about battle, he was respected for his organizational skills. As a former supply officer for the Continental Army, Shelby readily saw McDowell's talent and followed his lead in contingency and supply planning.

By midafternoon, it was decided to call a muster of the Sullivan and Washington Counties militia to determine who would stay and who would go across the mountains with an expeditionary force. Shelby would coordinate with Campbell whenever the Virginians joined them. Sevier and Shelby offered to get local supplies needed for the offensive. As soon as they knew what Campbell would do, McDowell said he would send an order for Cleveland's militia regiment to join the expedition.

In the meantime, McDowell sent a small group of veteran scouts back to the Catawba area to spy on Ferguson's activities. Hampton began getting the refugee militia back into fighting order.

After Shelby began his return home, Sevier told Jacob to ask Amos and Matt McCracken to inspect all rifles at Fort Watauga and to make any necessary repairs of the militia weapons. Although most of the refugee riflemen were resting from their flight over the mountains, the commanders ordered them to give their weapons and equipment a thorough cleaning before day's end.

McDowell stated that each man should have a full horn of powder and at least forty balls in their shot bags, preferably sixty. "We need to get back into fighting condition before there's a lot of lolling around," he added.

William Campbell greeted Moses Shelby warmly when the young captain arrived after a hard, six-hour ride from Sapling Grove. "I got this express for you from my brother, Colonel. He says it's right important."

Campbell read the document twice; asked Moses a couple of questions, which the messenger could not answer fully; and then stood looking down the river valley for twenty minutes while Shelby ate some apples to sate his hunger. In his mid-thirties but beginning to bald, Campbell had an imposing look. Frowning, he said to Moses, "We have a dire situation on our hands, young Captain. You ride back and tell your brother that nothing would give me more pleasure than hanging British hides on every tree around. Ordinarily, I would bring our regiment to join him in crossing the mountains, but I just don't see it possible at this time. We have intelligence that Cornwallis has his sights on coming up through Flour Gap to capture Virginia and particularly the lead mines. I will need every man to defend the commonwealth. As much as I would like to, I just can't send my troops down to chase Ferguson."

Moses repeated the message and requested the loan of a fresh horse to rush back to his brother with Campbell's reply.

Isaac and his father talked about contingencies long after sundown. The old colonel told Isaac that if half the Sullivan County militia could stay behind, it should be adequate to hold back any Indian raids. "The Cherokee are splintered and have nowhere near the strength they had four years ago. I will take command of what militia that don't go with you, son." Evan said. "You know, I can understand the savages wanting to kick us of out of here, but it's the worst kind of evil for a white man to threaten to burn us out. Damn that Ferguson and his Tories to hell!"

They talked as father and son, as mentor and student, and as equally competent warriors. They agreed to call a general muster of the Holston-area militia within the next couple of days.

It was well after dark when they decided to go to bed but were distracted by the sounds of a rider approaching. They had not expected Moses back until sometime the next day. The young captain rushed in with the devastating news from Campbell that the Virginians would not be coming. After again repeating Campbell's reasons for rejecting Isaac's request, Evan sent Moses to bed, an order that did not take much urging since he was exhausted and saddle-sore from riding more than seventy miles in one day.

"Damn!" Isaac swore to the darkness as he and his father mulled through their options. "McDowell's and Hampton's regiments are worn thin. Many of their men have been campaigning against the British without stop since the redcoats attacked Charles Town. A bunch more are in hiding with their families. Between them, I bet they can't put two, three hundred men in the field. We must have reinforcements if we are to stop Ferguson."

The old colonel put his hand on his son's shoulder, "There's more than one way to tease a bear out of tree, boy."

"What do you mean?" Isaac asked.

"Tomorrow we send a new letter back to Campbell with a stronger argument that compels him to reconsider. Include a copy of exactly what Ferguson wrote you. Tell him about the pathetic plight of the families run out of their homes by Ferguson and the need to escort them back. Then write another letter just like the first to his cousin, Colonel Arthur Campbell. Urge Arthur to convince Bill that their survival is dependent on stopping Ferguson first.

"I fought alongside the Campbells many times when we were part of Virginia. They are not men with faint hearts. If we make them think this through, we just might convince them to see it our way," Evan stated.

"I'll do that now," Isaac said groggily.

"No, in the morning. You are dead tired, boy, and you need a fresh brain to make your case. While you are writing, I'll get Moses and another express rider saddled and ready to go as soon as the ink is dry. Right now, we need sleep. Go to bed."

Like his cousin and brother-in-law, Arthur Campbell had built a reputation as a brave and resourceful Indian fighter as well as one connected to political leadership in Richmond. Back during the French and Indian War, when he was only fifteen, his Ranger unit had been attacked by the Wyandotte Indians near Lake Erie. Young Arthur had been wounded and held captive for three years, during which time he earned the respect of the Indians. The chief adopted him before he escaped and made his way more than two hundred miles through the wilderness to safety at a British outpost.

After returning home from studies at Walnut Academy in Lexington, he married his cousin, William Campbell's sister. His leadership and political connections helped him to rise quickly through the ranks to command the county militia and then be appointed by the governor as the senior military officer of the county. Nicknamed "Long Jaw" because of his snappish repartee, Arthur often was highly respected even though he was known to be highly opinionated.

On Tuesday afternoon, 19 September, the two riders carrying letters from Isaac Shelby split at the junction of the lane leading to Aspenvale; the one with the strongest horse rode seven miles farther to the spacious mansion at Royal Oak, the home of Arthur Campbell. Arthur quickly grasped the urgency of Shelby's argument, and while the messenger ate and rested, Arthur rode immediately to William's home to discuss the matter.

Both Campbells were aggressive, politically astute, and not afraid of adversity. The state's first written statement threatening armed resistance against British authority, the Fincastle Resolutions of 20 January 1775 contained thirteen signatures, including William Campbell, Arthur Campbell, and Evan Shelby. William's political capital was further strengthened through his wife's family; she was the sister of the fiery orator and antifederalist, Patrick Henry, who was the commonwealth's first governor after the country's declaration of independence. The Campbell clan also owned a huge chunk of southwestern Virginia, and little happened without at least the family's tacit approval.

When Arthur dismounted at Aspenvale, William Campbell greeted him cheerfully, "Well, Cousin, looks like Isaac Shelby doesn't give in easy. Did he call on you as well to plead his cause?"

"His cause is just," Arthur responded as he climbed up the steps to accept William's hand. "I just got back yesterday from Richmond where Tom Jefferson and I had a long talk about the situation in the Carolinas. The governor told me that we have to stop the redcoats before they get to Virginia; we can't wait until they get to the border. So far, the state has been spared the ravages of war, but our fragile economy might not survive if the British bring havoc here.

"He's having a hard time rebuilding state troops after that idiot Gates and the coward Buford wasted good men in South Carolina. Washington is stepping up his demands for even more men from Virginia, and we don't have them."

"I've given this further thought too, Arthur, and now believe Isaac Shelby is right. He's got a good head on his shoulders, just like old Evan.

"If Ferguson gets control of the Watauga and Holston valleys in North Carolina, he'll just pick us all off piecemeal and bring destruction right on up here. You and I both will then be targets for his gallows." William paused a moment. "But we still can't strip the county bare of our militia. There is just too much Indian threat lurking about and Tories waiting to come out from under the woodpile."

"Let's have a militia muster at Abingdon on Friday. That gives us three days to get ready and determine who we will keep behind for Indian duty. I've been ailing lately, so I will stay with them. You take the others and join Shelby to give this Ferguson character his comeuppance."

Reflecting further, Arthur added with disgust, "I can't imagine a true Scotsman fighting for England! Damned if I will give in to them."

The news from Campbell reached an assemblage of field officers at Fort Watauga late Wednesday, 20 September. With a big grin on his dirt- and sweat-streaked face, Moses Shelby arrived at the gathering exhausted. He had changed horses at Sapling Grove but did not tarry at his home. Despite hunger and tiredness, he rode on to report to his brother: "The Virginians are calling out their militia and will cross Sycamore Shoals of the Watauga River by the twenty-fifth."

McDowell immediately dispatched an express to Colonel Benjamin Cleveland directing him to bring all the troops he could from Wilkes and

Surry Counties to meet the new mountain brigade at Quaker Meadows no later than the 30 September.

Sevier and Shelby began in greater earnest preparing for two conflicts: an offensive against Ferguson and securing their area from Indian raids. Sevier's father agreed to resume his colonel duties for home defense in John's absence, just as Isaac's father had.

Lacking any official government backing, there was no money for supplies. Sevier went to the county's entry taker who said he had no authority to release the nearly thirteen thousand dollars that he had collected from the sale of state land. Sevier and Shelby pledged their wealth against the loan of the government money and said that they would go to the provincial legislature to get approval as soon as the emergency was over. Reluctantly, John Adair relented. "What the hell. If the redcoats come, they'll take the specie, and we won't have anything anyway. But if you prevail with victory, I trust the country will forgive my conduct. Best that it goes for liberty."

The commanders determined that each man should have at least a pound of powder, enough for nearly one hundred shots. Each rifleman carried about a half pound to a pound in his powder horn.

Sevier called on Mary McKeehan Patton, who had the largest powder-making operation in the region. An avid opponent of English rule, she provided five hundred pounds of quality powder, depleting her inventory. Mary had learned to make powder from her father in Pennsylvania. After the war started, she and her husband John sold their mill, moved to the mountainous Watauga region, and built a new powder mill near a sulfur deposit and bat caves that they found about four miles southeast of Fort Watauga. The bat guano was rich in nitrates.

Two days later, a pack train carrying lead arrived from Chiswell, and most of the men molded more than the minimum number of fifty balls that each needed to carry in his shot bag. Every militiaman also had to carry at least three or four extra flints for their weapons and fire building.

The McCrackens contributed eight spare rifle barrels and other parts that would be taken on a packhorse, led by Matt McCracken, now designated the expedition's chief armorer. His father was too ill to go on the campaign, and Jacob refused to serve as a gunsmith except in emergency. "I'm a Ranger," he told his colonel.

The encampment was jubilant with news about the Virginia militia joining them. The reinforcements meant that Rutherford and Burke men would now be able to get revenge for the suffering caused to their kin and neighbors by the king's plunderers.

Jacob had mixed feelings. He did not want to leave the peaceful surroundings of the Watauga settlement, but he wanted to see his mother and father again. He hated the thought of confronting his Tory brothers in battle, yet was anxious to get Rance Miller in his sights. He had several wrongs to settle with that man.

Refugee families were to remain behind until it was safe for them to return to their homes. However, several wives demanded they be allowed to march along with their husbands to help with cooking and mending clothes. The colonels rejected the women's requests, yet they knew some wives would tag along anyway.

The regimental commanders agreed with a movement plan conceived by McDowell before he returned to the Catawba Valley to secure the Quaker Meadows and determine the disposition of the royal invaders. If the Loyalists were gone from the Catawba region, McDowell would gather what hidden beef and grain that he could find to feed the new brigade that was growing in strength and renewed vigor. If the Loyalists were still occupying the area, McDowell would send expresses to Cleveland and the overmountain contingent naming another rendezvous point. Leaving Major Joe McDowell in charge of the Burke regiment, the colonel took ten men with him back to Quaker Meadows.

The night after Charles McDowell left Fort Watauga, Jacob had messenger duty and sat near Colonels Hampton and Shelby as the two commanders enjoyed the evening air and reminisced about the campaign they had against the British in South Carolina. Hampton said to the younger officer, "Isaac, you made a good impression during those months. I just wish all our officers had half the gumption that you have for battle."

"Kind of you to say so, Colonel." Shelby did not feel like commenting further on the statement and sensed that the old warrior had more on his mind.

"I don't like to talk ill of anyone," Hampton continued, "but I am concerned for our success if Charles McDowell leads this expedition."

Hiding his elation that Hampton felt the same as he did, Shelby merely asked, "And why do you say that?"

"Don't get me wrong, he's a good man…patriotic and dedicated to the cause as anybody. He's a good thinker and politician. He cares about his people. But I have concerns for his fighting ability. For example, that night back at Earle's Ford when my son was killed, he didn't post pickets like he should have. He assured me the camp was safe. But that damn Dunlop came in with Mills and a bunch of Tory banditti and murdered my Noah in his bedclothes." Hampton sighed bitterly, looked off to the darkened mountain ridges and added as an afterthought, "I can never forgive him for that."

Shelby stood. "I share your concerns. You know in all that time I rode with Colonel McDowell this summer, he never was out front on any attack. He didn't hold any of us back when we wanted to venture out against the king's men, but he never led us into the fight."

"Let's call it a night. This is something we need to ponder more," Hampton said as he bade his young friend good night.

Noticing Jacob watching the two officers, Hampton told him to get some sleep and added, "Mister Godley, you mustn't repeat what you heard tonight. It's just soldier talk."

Back across the mountains, the last of Ferguson's raiders marched south through the narrow South Mountain gap at the head of Cane Creek and returned to Rutherford County. In their wake, many Whig-owned livestock herds were decimated, and much of the Catawba Valley's grain was stolen or burned, except that which had been hidden or belonged to Tory families that gave allegiance to England.

"A smashing success!" Ferguson exclaimed to his officers. He was more subdued in the formal report to Cornwallis. His mission was being accomplished with little adversity. Protection fever was rampant as more residents flocked to declare their allegiance to the Crown, although some of them could not hide the hostility in their eyes. So pleased with success in the western regions, Ferguson ordered his militia commanders to give those volunteers who had not been home in more than month a few days off to visit their families. Satisfied that he had brought peace and stability to the mountain frontier, Ferguson relaxed.

Near the end of the day, Ferguson received an express informing him that a Loyalist force had defeated six hundred rebels under Colonel Elijah Clarke at Augusta, Georgia. Fifty rebels were killed in action, many more captured. Afterward, twenty-seven Liberty Men were hanged. Ferguson was warned to be on the lookout for Clarke, who was heading for the Carolina mountains with a large number of refugees.

Overmountain Trek

25–30 September 1780

The fields around Fort Watauga were crowded with citizen-soldiers in various manner of dress except military uniform. Children ran about laughing and animals grazed seemingly unconcerned with the commotion around them as adults busied themselves with goodbyes and looked after last-minute details for a long campaign. A carnival atmosphere prevailed as they awaited the arrival of the Virginia militia before embarking on a quest not only to take back Rutherford and Burke Counties but also to deliver a punishing, if not a fatal, blow to Ferguson's army.

Amid the jubilant atmosphere, wives and mothers tried to hide their anxieties as they watched husbands and sons prepare once again to march towards harm's way. Most of the backwoods warriors had already sharpened their knives and hatchets to a razor's edge. Footmen rechecked their haversacks or blanket rolls, discarding anything but necessity. Barefooted frontiersmen searched about for shoes of any kind and wished they could borrow a horse to carry them on the long journey ahead.

A small herd of cattle was gathered to feed the troops during the march ahead so that no time would be wasted on hunting.

Since arriving back in the Watauga region, Jacob had forged eight new butcher and patch knives and had traded seven for needed supplies, including a new canteen to replace the leaky one he had used all summer, a second powder horn full of the black powder, a decent waterproof tarp to protect him from the elements, and a bag to carry oats for Zeus.

Late Monday afternoon, gunfire erupted near the river's Sycamore Shoals on the back side of the fort, causing people to run toward the sounds. The roar of more flintlocks and echoing "huzzahs" announced the arrival of William Campbell's militia from Virginia, two hundred strong and most of the men mounted.

"We got our brigade!" Shelby shouted happily as he clapped Hampton on the back.

A short time later, another two hundred Virginian militiamen arrived, these led by Arthur Campbell who would stay behind to organize defenses against Indian raids.

Since they hosted the gathering of the county regiments for the campaign, Lieutenant Colonel John Sevier's small regiment had the honor of leading the first day's march. More than a thousand men, seven hundred horses, and two score cattle were ready to start the long trek over the mountains to confront the British.

As they lined up to begin the journey, Sevier called on a local pastor, Reverend Samuel Doak, to render God's blessings on their endeavor. The Presbyterian minister stood upon a tree stump as though it was a pulpit. Most of the people at the assemblage could see and hear him pray, his booming voice calling for the Lord's intervention in striking down the "heathen British" just as he had aided Gideon to lead successfully a small party of Israelites in destroying the larger army of Midianites.

Soon, many of the men grew restless as the oration seemed to ramble on more like a long-winded sermon rather than a prayer. Using a reference to a biblical message from the book of Judges, Doak concluded, "Oh, God of Battle, arise in Thy might. Avenge the slaughter of Thy people. Confound those who plot for our destruction. Crown this mighty effort with victory, and smite those who exalt themselves against liberty and justice and truth. Help us as righteous soldiers to wield the sword of the Lord and Gideon. Amen.

"My friends, let the tyrants hear your battle cry!" Doak paused, looked over the restless gathering, raised his arms upward, and shouted with a final inspiration, "The Sword of the Lord and of Gideon!"

The mountain men echoed loudly and enthusiastically, "The Sword of the Lord and of Gideon!"

Sevier gave the order and the brigade began snaking its way, men two abreast, along the Watauga and then turned southerly, following a road up Gap Creek and across to the Doe River basin toward the first of two high alpine gaps in the Appalachian Mountains that needed to be crossed.

On the day that the mountain men began their journey, General Cornwallis was more than 120 miles to the southeast, leading his four-thousand-man army into Charlotte Town. He was several weeks behind schedule. The British commander rode in a carriage with Josiah Martin, the royal governor of North Carolina who had fled the province under duress five years earlier. Contrary to their expectations, the British were not welcomed in Charlotte Town.

For days, determined partisan fighters had slowed the British advance with guerilla raids and ambushes against supply wagons, patrols, and foraging parties. Snipers picked off sentries, officers, and couriers, shattering morale of the British troops. A deliberate disinformation campaign confused the British intelligence effort. In addition, too many redcoats became ill with fever, including the general's most effective fighting commander, Banastre Tarleton.

Cornwallis's advanced guard, a troop of Tarleton's Legion, pranced arrogantly into the heart of the crossroads village where a small band of rebel fighters under William Davie surprised them with blistering gunfire, causing some casualties and forcing the British to maneuver their forces before the partisans slunk quickly off into the nearby forest. It was not a pleasing reception for His Majesty's envoys.

Rain began during the midafternoon on the mountain brigade's first day of travel. When the early drizzle turned into a heavy downpour, Sevier stopped the column after advancing twenty miles and ordered his men to get shelter the best they could. The powder kegs were put under a large rock shelf to stay dry. The drovers slaughtered three steers and gave each man a chunk of meat to take back to his camp where fires sprouted for warmth and cooking.

The rain stopped early the next morning; the air was noticeably colder. Some of the cattle had wandered off in the night. While some militia went to round up the wayward animals, a few other men took advantage of a local settler's forge to reshoe their horses. The delay frustrated the colonels who held a called meeting. "Look, if we are going to get to Ferguson, we have to move a lot faster than we are doing," Shelby cajoled. "We have to leave the cattle; they are slowing us down. Our men on foot have to keep up with the horses."

The colonels agreed. The order went out to butcher several more steers and parcel out the raw meat for cooking at the next campsite. It was noon before the column began moving again. The well-defined trail was steep and narrow, not wide enough for two men abreast. Some of the mounted riflemen offered footmen a ride on their horses to help conserve the walking men's energy.

As they came within several hundred feet of the nearly-mile-high gap between Yellow and Roan mountains, they sloshed into an unseasonably early snow that was shoe-top deep. Crossing over the ridge line, a fiercely bitter wind blasted into them, causing the men to bundle in blankets or wool coats or anything that could provide some sense of warmth. Many just suffered through the discomfort.

The wind also blew away the blue haze that usually masked the Carolina mountains during warm summer months, making visibility across to the far peaks of the snow-covered Black Mountain range crystal clear and the ridges stark against the blue sky. Jacob did not take much notice of the scenery or that some of the trees were holding on to their last color. He was miserably cold and not happy to be stuck in the middle of the caravan. Although he enjoyed the company of Lieutenant William Walker, to whom he continued to be assigned, Jacob preferred solo Ranger duties, scouting alone, far removed from officers giving orders, horses farting, and hapless footmen trudging through muck. However, he took pride in being part of a true army that now could do some pushing instead of being pushed.

After starting down the steep slopes of Bright's Trace and clearing the snow line, the troops halted again and made camp along Roaring Creek. Fires were built for warmth and to cook the beef slaughtered earlier in the day. They had traveled only seven grueling miles that day.

The next morning, Sevier discovered that two of his men, James Crawford and Samuel Chambers, were not present for headcount. They had disappeared without telling anyone. While a handful of men dropped out because of sickness or a turned ankle, all had asked permission to lag behind. It was not a good omen to have desertion on the first few days out, particularly with no more adversity than a little snow, cold, and wind.

Shelby's regiment took over the lead as the militia continued its march down Roaring Creek to the Toe River and then down the river valley nearly twenty miles to the mouth of Grassy Creek.

When the overmountain men began arriving at Cathey's station on 28 September, some sixty miles as-a-bird-flies to the east, Major Joseph Winston, leading a hundred Surry County Whig militia, joined up with Colonel Benjamin Cleveland's 250 Wilkes County boys at the Tory Oak on the Yadkin River, a landmark made infamous as the execution site for several notorious Tory agitators. From here, it was a seventy-mile trek before joining with the mountain brigade at McDowell's place on Quaker Meadows. Only about half had horses, but all had weapons in reliable operating condition, mostly rifles but some muskets and fowling guns. All were itching for a fight.

Unaware of the creation of the rebel's mountain brigade, Ferguson decided to move his command to south of the Broad River because his horses were overgrazing the meadows around Gilbert Town, and the local grain was fast-consumed. He also wanted to be in a better position to intercept the rebel leader Elijah Clarke, who was fleeing from Georgia.

Captain Dunlop, recovering from wounds suffered at Cane Creek, and Doctor Johnson, recovering from his long illness, moved by wagon further to the southeast of the main body and found shelter in the Tory homes. Captain Biggerstaff and the Godley brothers were assigned as the rearguard to screen Ferguson's progress from any partisan mischief that may occur from the north. The brigade's movements were casual, as it was blissfully ignorant of the gathering storm coming from the mountains.

On Friday, 29 September, the mountain colonels decided to split into two groups and take different trails across the last high ridges and on to Quaker Meadows. This would make it easier for the horses to find edible grass along the steep, twisting trails. It was doubtful that either trail could support the appetites of seven hundred horses. Also, by dividing, they could traverse the difficult trails faster and not be strung out from hither to yonder as they had been on Yellow Mountain.

The shortest route had the most difficult path. It would take the second group a longer distance to reach Quaker Meadows, but travel was easier. Major Joe McDowell and some of the Burke militia led Sevier and Shelby's regiments over McKinney Gap and down into North Cove where they would camp overnight before proceeding across Linville and Silver mountains the next day to Charles McDowell's plantation.

Hampton took the lead of the second element with his Rutherford County boys and the Burke volunteers from the upper Catawba Valley under "Pleasant Gardens" Joe McDowell. Campbell's Virginians followed along. They crossed over the mountain at Gillespie Gap without incident and snaked down a steep, narrow, twisting trail along Armstrong Creek and past the modest cabin of Henry Gillespie, the first white settler in Turkey Cove.

Hampton and Campbell's group made camp a couple miles farther on in the meadows of William Wofford, a wealthy stockman from South Carolina who at one time owned the most prominent ironworks in the Spartan District. Hampton had doubts about the loyalties of both men. Gillespie was an avowed neutralist and refused to take sides. Wofford claimed many times he had strong independence feelings, but he took protection from Ferguson just two weeks earlier and escaped the Tory plundering. Both men were kept under guard until the militia moved on the next day after helping themselves to Wofford's food storage.

The Wilkes and Surry contingent made more than twenty miles their first day out and camped at Fort Crider, about halfway from their homes to Quaker Meadows. The next morning, Colonel Cleveland's younger brother Larkin led advance scouts toward Lovelady Ford on the Catawba where they were ambushed by Tory partisans. Larkin suffered a severe wound in the thigh and became the first casualty from hostile action in the Liberty's Men new offensive. Upon hearing the shots, Colonel Cleveland rushed reinforcements forward to attack the ambushers, but their prey had sneaked back into the forest and escaped. Lieutenant Larkin was carried by stretcher on to Quaker Meadows where Colonel McDowell's mother took him in and nursed him back to health after the militia continued to move on toward Ferguson.

The three militia groups converged in the late day at Quaker Meadows, swelling the little army to nearly fifteen hundred fighting men. Colonel Charles McDowell had steers slaughtered and cooked for an evening meal. His brother Joe offered dry fence rails for fires. Neighbors pulled hundreds of ears of corn from mountain caches. Scouts patrolled more than five miles out but found no evidence of enemy forces; Ferguson had abandoned the area.

As the men enjoyed the repast after the arduous trek over the mountains, local Whigs distributed some whiskey jugs; not enough for drunken reveling, but enough to elevate a partying spirit.

Jacob did not share in the festivities. He, William Walker, and Jim Gray left Quaker Meadows before dusk for a long patrol to the head of Cane Creek and Bedford Hill. Colonel Hampton told them that he did not want to suffer the same fate that Ferguson experienced by walking into an ambush. The Rangers' orders were to search the area thoroughly.

It was on this evening that an angry split developed in the congeniality of the commanders. The six colonels, along with Majors McDowell and Winston, gathered in Colonel McDowell's home for an evening meal of beef, roasted goose, sweet corn, potatoes, cooked onions, and apple pie, all prepared by McDowell's mother and servants. A generous supply of scuppernong wine washed down the food. The wine had been hidden from Tory plundering.

Afterward, as several officers puffed pipes in the parlor and sipped the last drop from a jug of excellent plum brandy that appeared from some secret hiding place, McDowell informed the others that no help would be coming from other militia units to the east. Referring to express exchanges with partisan leaders in the piedmont, McDowell said, "They are all trying to stop Cornwallis at Charlotte Town and can't send us any help. William Lee Davidson has been promoted to general, replacing Rutherford as commander of the Salisbury District. I report to Davidson now and am still in charge of the western region. It is my opinion that we should do all we can to hinder Ferguson from reinforcing Cornwallis."

"Hinder, hell!" bellowed Cleveland, a hefty, 250-pound man feeling the impact of excessive wine. "We need to crush that fartleberry and scatter his innards for the buzzards to feed on!"

"Your vulgarity is uncalled for, Colonel," McDowell scolded.

"You are not going soft on us, are you, Charles?" Hampton asked, purposefully using his familiar name rather than rank.

"You know me better than that, Colonel Hampton." McDowell bristled. "I'm looking at the total situation. Need I remind you that we are going after an army that's bigger than us and has highly trained regulars with it? We just can't run blindly into them and hope to win a fight."

"I didn't bring my people over the mountains on a hope to win," Shelby said sharply, irked at McDowell's cautious suggestions. "We came here to drive Ferguson out of the state. You don't seem to be as aggressive as you were back in Watauga when Ferguson was still occupying this valley."

"I resent your implication, sir!" McDowell retorted stiffly. "I am as determined as anybody to see Ferguson driven out; but as a commander, I have to think of the men's welfare, commissary needs, enemy strength, and the disposition of other friendly forces rather than just the bravado of vengeful combat."

"Who put you in command? We are equals here," Shelby shot back.

Hampton calmed the atmosphere as he said slowly, "Now, boys, let's just simmer down. We still have ol' Pattie and his Tories a day's ride from here at Gilbert Town, hardly five miles from my home and family. I'm leaving with my troops at daybreak. If we can catch him, we will fight him, with or without the others. We ain't running from him no more."

"Daybreak?" McDowell made the statement a question. "We don't know for sure where Ferguson is. The men are tired. Shouldn't we rest here for another day while our spies find him?"

"I already have my best Rangers on the way to Rutherford County. My son's calvary troop is checking the Indian line forts. They gave up that feast out on the meadow to find out how many Royals are lurking about the Cane Creek area. They are scouting the region as we speak now," Hampton stated.

Campbell, who had remained quiet while the North Carolinians squabbled, declared firmly, "My Virginians and I came to fight. We will be with you, Colonel Hampton."

Sevier and Shelby wasted no time in joining in with saying in unison, "Hear, hear." Cleveland looked over at Major Winston who nodded with a slight smile, "Us Wilkes and Surry County boys will be marching at sunup with ol' Hampton here! Is Burke dropping out?"

"Of course not!" McDowell replied, embarrassed at being outmaneuvered.

Colonel McDowell felt relieved when his mother walked into the parlor interrupting the conversation and announced, "It's getting past ye bed time, boys. Quiet down now, and let poor Master Larkin get his rest. Ye seem to forget he got shot today and could lose his leg."

The men all stood as Hampton said to the McDowell matriarch, "Madam, never have I had a more scrumptious meal from such a gracious host. Thank you for your warm hospitality."

The others also expressed appreciation for supper, but all declined the opportunity to sleep in the McDowell manor. "When I'm campaigning, I always sleep with my men," Sevier said.

Colonel McDowell turned to his brother and said reluctantly, "Alert the captains. We will be on the march at sunup."

When the mountain men first arrived at Quaker Meadows, Ferguson was forty-two miles to the south at James Stepp's plantation, not too far from Colonel Ambrose Mills's home on Green River. Ferguson had scattered his units over a wide area so as not to overgraze local fields. Most of the mature grain in the area had long been threshed.

The brigade's supply wagons, prisoners, and Ferguson's female companions were sent eight miles to the east at Dennard's Ford just below the confluence of the Broad and Green rivers. Dunlop went farther south of the Pacolet River to convalesce in the home of a friendly Tory family.

Captain DePeyster interrupted his commander's conversation with Mills and Plummer. "Colonel! Hate to interrupt, but I have some disturbing news."

"What?"

"Those two men over there," DePeyster said, pointing toward two backwoodsmen who looked tired and unkempt, "they say they escaped from a rebel army that is coming from the backwater region over the mountains and are bent on fighting us."

Ferguson looked over at the men and motioned them forward. "Come here!" he shouted. "Where are you from and what do you know?"

Looking apprehensive at the well-dressed officers around them, James Crawford walked over to the commander with Samuel Chambers, a boy of seventeen, following sheepishly along.

"How do you know all this information?" Ferguson demanded.

"Well, sir, we live up near the Nolichucky River and got drafted by the Washington County militia; that's Colonel Sevier's regiment. He and Colonel Shelby from Sullivan County and a bunch of Virginians have joined up with Colonels McDowell and Hampton and their refugees. They say they're coming over here to chase you out of North Carolina, sir. There's got near about two thousand of them and over half on horseback."

"Who is leading the Virginians?"

"One of the Campbell clan from just north of the border. Colonel Sevier says he is one helluva mean Injun fighter."

"And why are you telling me all this?"

"This ain't our war, sir. It's not like you are coming over the mountains attacking us. I mean I don't need to get in any fight over what happens on this side of the Blue Ridge. Besides, I never have felt good about this rebellion anyway. Always believed we should be true to the king. Young Sam here agrees with me."

"Are they all militia? Do they have any Continentals or cannons with them?"

"All militia. No cannon. No wagons."

"When did you leave the rebels?"

"I believe it was 'bout four days ago. We left 'em on Yellow Mountain. Been walking ever since."

"I appreciate you bringing this information to me. You men did a brave and correct thing." Ferguson's expression changed to a hard stare as he added sternly, "Be forewarned; if I find that you are deceiving me in any way, I will hang you instantly."

The two mountain men were escorted away, disappointed that they had received no reward but, instead, pressed into service for the British. Ferguson told DePeyster, "Keep a close eye on those two. I never trust deserters, no matter whose side they serve. But I can't ignore them either.

"Recall all militia who are on furlough. Get some more spies patrolling northward. Find the whereabouts of this backwater mob now. I must know just how many fighting people they have. I want all provincial and militia officers, except those already at Dennard's Ford, to meet with me here at daybreak. Have the troops ready to move as soon as that meeting concludes."

Before he turned in for the night, Ferguson wrote a quick report to Cornwallis, apprising him of his latest intelligence about a large rebel force coming from the northwestern mountains and another rebel group coming up from Georgia. He added that he would begin moving eastward to be closer to the main British Army at Charlotte Town. In closing, Ferguson hinted that he would welcome reinforcements, but did not put any urgency in the report that would not be dispatched until the next morning.

THE CHASE

1–4 October 1780

In the early morning on the first day of October, the two armies began stirring at the same time, although still forty miles apart. The mountain brigade continued its march south, now more alert than ever for enemy activity. Andrew Hampton's small regiment took the lead, moving the Liberty Men back toward Rutherford County. Charles McDowell hardly spoke to him as the county regiments formed to push forward the chase of Ferguson.

Before Ferguson began his dawn officer's conference, two riders came galloping into his headquarters near Green River and identified themselves as Burke Tories who had stayed behind to spy on rebel activity. They had ridden all night after observing the gathering at Quaker Meadows.

"I'm John McFall, sir," the oldest of the riders reported excitedly to Ferguson. "Them rebels got over a thousand horses! Maybe two thousand men. My brother and me saw them real good at McDowell's station on Quaker Meadows. That ol' rogue Ben Cleveland from up Wilkes County way was there. He's the one that's been hanging loyal folks and burning their places all up and down the Yadkin. He brought a bunch of rebels with him.

"My cousin talked to some overmountain boys when they came in yesterday. She said they had a slew of Virginians with them, all boasting that they are going to rid the world of the devil's disciples. I guess they mean us, sir."

After asking a few more questions, Ferguson thanked McFall and praised him for his work that verified what the two deserters had reported the day before. He had heard of Cleveland but did not know much about him and even less of the Virginia commander.

Throughout the day, spies continued bringing word that the populace was stirring over news that a rebel army was advancing from the mountains. Put out by these rumors, Ferguson sat down and wrote a proclamation that he ordered be read throughout the countryside:

Tryon County, October 1, 1780.

Unless you wish to be eaten up by an inundation of barbarians, who have begun by murdering an unarmed son before the aged father, and afterwards lopped off his arms, and who by their shocking cruelties and irregularities, give the best proof of their cowardice and want of discipline; I say, if you wish to be pinioned, robbed, and murdered, and see your wives and daughters, in four days, abused by the dregs of mankind—in short, if you wish or deserve to live and bear the name of men, grasp your arms in a moment and run to camp.

The backwater men have crossed the mountains; McDowell, Hampton, Shelby, and Cleveland are at their head, so that you know what you have to depend upon. If you choose to be pissed upon forever and ever by a set of mongrels, say so at once, and let your women turn their backs upon you, and look out for real men to protect them.

PAT. FERGUSON

In his officer's meeting of the day, Ferguson reviewed his situation. "Gentlemen, there's upwards to two thousand backwater rebels coming from the north. They are led by McDowell, Hampton, and Shelby. We've been up against them all summer. Shelby is probably the craftiest one in the bunch. Like the Indians that they live amongst, these barbarians have little discipline when it comes to the battlefield tactics. Still, they got a bite to them.

"There's a bunch of Georgia rebels coming up from the south under Clarke. They got hurt bad by our lads in Augusta, so we don't know what shape they are in.

"As soon as this meeting is over, I'm going to Dennard's Ford. Drop hints to folks who live about that we are heading south to Ninety Six to join with Colonel Cruger. This might pull those rebels off our trail until we know more about them." Ferguson turned to his local Tory commander. "Colonel Mills, have a few of your Tryon County boys go to their homes and tell their families that they are heading south and don't know when they will be back. As far as our troops are concerned, we are going to Ninety Six."

Mills interrupted, "But sir, we can handle rebel militia. We kicked them all across South Carolina and out of Tryon and Burke Counties. I don't like running from them."

"We are not running, Colonel. I'm taking us eastward, closer to Lord Cornwallis. His orders direct us to protect his western flank, so this is a precaution in case those rebels from the mountains turn east directly toward Charlotte Town instead of trying to come after us. Since we are nearly a hundred miles from Charlotte Town now, we have to move that way."

By late Sunday afternoon, a heavy rain began with an unrelenting ferociousness shortly before the mountain men reached their stopping point near the heads of Cane and Silver Creeks, forcing the men to work hastily as they built makeshift shelters to keep bodies, weapons, and powder dry. Each regiment staked out its area, dug water-clogged latrines, hobbled their horses, and tried to find enough fatwood to start cooking fires. The temperature turned bitter as night descended, and the rain continued to pound.

It rained steadily during the night, soaking most as they fought unsuccessfully to stay warm and dry under leaky tarps and lean-tos. Those who had them were thankful for the bulky and itchy, lanolin-rich wool blankets or coats they had thought to bring along; otherwise, there would have been hundreds of cases of hypothermia. Still many shivered uncontrollably.

The deluge continued after daybreak Monday morning when Colonel McDowell sent runners to each county commander stating that they would not march that day until the men were able to dry out their clothes, powder, and equipment. He called for a command meeting of the colonels at a nearby abandoned cabin that belonged to an uncle of one of his militiamen. Each commander brought with him an officer as an aide and a horseman to serve as a messenger. For his runner, Hampton picked Jacob, who had hoped to slip down to his parents' home that day.

The rain eased shortly after dawn but resumed with renewed vigor an hour later. It continued until afternoon, ceasing long before a weak sun emerged late in the day. The runners huddled on the leeward side of the cabin where they listened to the acrimonious arguments among their leaders.

By the time that all colonels arrived at the cabin, McDowell had a fire going in the fireplace with a pot of sassafras and mint tea brewing. He began the meeting by asking sarcastically, "Do any of you gentlemen question my decision to wait until the rain ends and we get body and material dry before continuing on? Or would you prefer we churn up the road with our horses, making it difficult, if not impossible, for the last half of the column to slosh through arse-deep mud? Or that we meet the enemy with damp powder?"

"It's the right decision," Campbell responded. "Powder must be dry, but our boys are used to fighting in all kinds of weather."

"Thank you, Colonel Campbell," McDowell said. "Now, the real reason for this meeting. Gentlemen, we cannot achieve victory if there is dissension in command. I cannot be effective if we don't work together and my decisions are being constantly questioned or circumvented."

"We are all equals here," Hampton said. "Most of us believe bold action is the only way we are going to win. We don't have time to ponder. This expedition's leader must be battle-proven, someone willing to fight without hesitation."

Stung by the rebuke, McDowell responded icily, "By law, I *am* the senior colonel!"

Isaac Shelby spoke up. "With all due respect, Colonel McDowell, you are a fine man and a true patriot. But the fact is, sir, you don't have the gumption needed to win. I served under you for three months this summer. But I never saw you in the heat of action. You did a good job of keeping the horses fed and the camps clean and spies running about, but you weren't with Hampton and me when we took Fort Thicketty. You didn't come with Williams, Clarke, and me when we gave the Tory bastards a sound thrashing at Musgrove's Mill. You were not at Glendale Springs."

"So, Colonel Shelby, are you suggesting that we make you the overall commander?" McDowell asked indignantly.

"No sir! Quite frankly, I may be a bit too rash," Shelby replied with false modesty. "I'm the youngest colonel here in age. Chucky Jack is only a lieutenant colonel, and he ain't much older than me. Ben over there is as bold as they come, but he's like me and jumps sometimes before he thinks. And

Colonel Hampton, God bless him, is older than dirt. That leaves Colonel Campbell as the most logical choice."

"Now wait a minute, Isaac," Campbell interjected. "My commission is from Virginia. I have no authority over North Carolina troops."

"You have whatever authority we grant you, sir! You have proved yourself to be a fighting leader who gets results. You have, by far, the largest single regiment here. You came the furthest," Shelby argued.

"Back when we all were lieutenants, Jack and I fought with you in Dunmore's War; and we worked together chasing Cherokee renegades up and down the Nolichucky and Holston rivers these past four years. You and Colonel Cleveland fought together to put down the Tories along the New River. Besides, since you are the only outsider, we won't have a pissing contest as to which North Carolina county is in charge. I believe most folks will accept you better than anyone else."

McDowell suffered through the arguments in a silent rage. He did not have a single ally present other than his brother who did not have a voice in the discussion. He had never been so embarrassed in his life. Yet, as a pragmatic man, he just could not think of how to solve the dilemma without creating irreconcilable friction.

Before he could retort, Hampton interjected bluntly. "My age should not be a factor, young Mister Shelby! Sure, I'm old enough to be everybody's pa here, maybe even your grandpa. But I can hold my own in the saddle with anybody on this venture. Can't see as far as I used to, but I still can shoot and hit a deer at a hundred paces. I still got half my teeth. I hear what I need to. And by God, I can out arm wrestle any one of you young bucks, except maybe ol' Roundabout here."

Hampton looked over at the huge-bodied Cleveland who enjoyed the nickname given by his troops and continued, "and I ain't about to arm-wrestle him 'cause he's half ox, half bear, and meaner than a riled-up rattlesnake!"

The messengers outside were startled by the roar of laughter that erupted in the cabin after more than an hour of rancor and hostile shouts. Cleveland, who took the brunt of the verbal jab, had the loudest guffaw. Even McDowell came out of his depression some, cracked a smile, and chuckled as the uncomfortable tenseness that gripped the group eased.

As the laugher died, Hampton continued emphatically. "I am at an age where I don't need the glory. All I want is to get those damn Royals out of my county, and I'll ride with the devil as a private if it'll give us victory. I'm comfortable with any of you as long as you will take us to the fight."

"There is one thing certain," McDowell interjected. "We will not defeat Ferguson unless we all work together. We have a full brigade here, but all independent regiments with five colonels. We have no orders from the powers that be. We got this far on our own, nobody but us directing us. I doubt if the provincial assembly even knows we are on the warpath even though I sent them an express a few days ago.

"For the good of the cause and even though I am the *legitimate* senior officer, I will accede to your wishes and step aside. But we need a general. General Davidson has his hands full with Cornwallis. Rutherford, if alive, is still in a British prison, and Gates is in Hillsboro."

"Why don't we write General Gates and have him send us a general, maybe old Dan Morgan? In the meantime, we can continue rotating the officer-of-the-day position," Shelby said. "I suggest we elect the next day's officer of the day each evening. Two-thirds of us have to agree on whoever is selected. Can we all accept that?"

With agreement around the table, Shelby then said, "I nominate Colonel Campbell as tomorrow's officer of the day. He hasn't had his turn yet, anyway."

"I second your choice, Isaac," Hampton said. "Here, here," echoed around the table.

"Any objections?" Shelby asked.

No one said anything, so Shelby spoke up again. "Colonel Campbell, will you command us for the next day?"

Before Campbell replied, Cleveland stated, "But before we go into battle, I think it best that we all have a war council and agree on the tactics to be used. I ain't following nobody blindly into a fight."

There was no dry paper with them with which to write the letter. Hampton said, "One of my captains, Jim Withrow, has a place nearby on Cane Creek. He may have good writing paper there. First thing in the morning, ahead of the brigade movement, a couple of us should go there or the nearest house where we can find paper and ink, and draft a letter."

"All of us colonels should sign it," Cleveland said. "Don't you agree, Colonel McDowell? Maybe as the district's senior officer, you could take it to General Gates or the governor to emphasize the urgency of our request."

Reluctantly, McDowell agreed to the letter, but was quietly pleased with the face-saving excuse offered for him not continuing with the expedition. It would be embarrassing to his men seeing him inferior to the other colonels. "As promptly as I can, I'll get a general officer here to lead us to victory," he said. "My brother Joe will command the Burke militia while I'm gone."

Rumors were rampant throughout the camp about dissension among the commanders. The Burke County troops were visibly agitated over their colonel's rejection; the McDowells were popular throughout the county. Some openly threatened to quit and go back home.

Sensing unrest among the troops, the next morning the colonels called the full brigade together before lining up for their march. Colonel McDowell, using a firm, authoritative tone, told the Liberty Men that he was going to get a general to lead them, and until then, the brigade's acting commander would be elected daily from the remaining colonels. Loud grumbling was heard from the Burke regiment until Benjamin Cleveland stood up on a fallen tree trunk and roared, "Listen up, me brave fellows! The enemy is at hand, and we must be up and at 'em."

A robust, uncouth frontiersman, Cleveland had a way of inspiring people with his raucous demeanor. "Every man jack of ye is needed for this righteous cause. When all is done, ye can make yer children quite proud that ye were among the conquerors of Ferguson and his wretched followers. Now if any want to shrink away from this coming battle and glory, ye can back out now and leave. Ye have a few minutes to consider."

Smiling, Major Joe McDowell jumped on the log next to Cleveland and, looking directly at a group of Burke men, announced, "I'm going forward to lick Ferguson. What kind of story will those who back out now have to tell the folks at home after you leave your braver comrades to do all the fighting? Are we going to let the king's thieves rule our lives?"

Shelby leaped on to the log, grabbed hold of Cleveland's shoulder to steady himself, and shouted, "You heard the offer. Those who don't want to go with the rest of us take three steps to the rear."

No one moved. Then several began shouting "Huzzah!" The cheer grew into a crescendo as more than fourteen hundred voices joined in, lustily shouting their commitment to free their country. Jacob cheered along, proud to be part of such a gallant group.

As the brigade organized for its march, Shelby and Hampton rode ahead with a contingent of Rangers, including Jacob, and Captain Withrow's company as the advance guard. While the letter requesting a general was being penned at Withrow's home, the Rangers rode ahead to scout the route to Gilbert Town and to see if any Tory militia might still be around. The mountain brigade resumed its southern trek down the Cane Creek road shortly before noon, but they did not get far.

The road braided with the creek as it twisted through the narrow South Mountains gap. It was still flooded in places and not near dry enough to take the heavy tromping of such a large number of horses and infantry. It was bad enough for the lead elements, but the trailing regiments found themselves mired ankle-deep in the sticky clay that caked heavily around the legs of beast and man, making each step more difficult that the previous one. Several of the footmen lost their shoes; most took their shoes off and sloshed barefooted in the muck.

After only five miles, Campbell called a halt at the base of Marlin Knob; they had to give the road another day to dry. As the new camp was being established, the colonels rode ahead for nearly a mile to Withrow's place so all could sign their names to the letter requesting a general. That done, McDowell and one escort left the group immediately to carry the letter to General Horatio Gates who was at the provincial capital in Hillsborough some 150 miles to the east.

As the Rangers patrolled southward, William Walker found his family home in shambles; however, Sadie was unharmed and getting the house back in order. He learned from the family servant that Ferguson had pulled all his people back to South Carolina. Nothing was left to eat at the place except for what Sadie and her husband could scrounge from the forest and neighbors. The Liberty Men who had been wounded at Cane Creek two weeks before were given their parole and left at Walker's to heal.

The Rangers rode on to Gilbert Town and found the place deserted of Loyalists. Sarah Gilbert told them that she had heard that Ferguson was headed south toward Ninety Six. After scouting the area and talking to a few more residents to confirm that Loyalists had indeed abandoned this part of Rutherford County, the Rangers galloped back north to report their findings.

On their way, Jacob detoured to check on his parents and young siblings. He and Walker were warmly greeted by the senior Godley, who reported no additional harassment from the Loyalists. Wayne, whose back still had not fully healed from the beating he took, again asked Jacob if he could join up with the Liberty Men, but the older brother said no, Wayne needed to stay and take care of their parents and young sisters. "Four boys off fighting is enough for this family," their mother stated emphatically as Wayne pouted over the rejection.

"I got more reason than anybody to pay them Tories back for the pain they brought us," the teenager declared as he stomped out of the house.

While the Rangers were on their reconnaissance, Colonel McDowell was making his way east along the southern slope of Flint Hill when he ran into a camp of some South Carolina Whig militia who were looking for the mountain men. Colonel William Hill and Lieutenant Colonel Edward Lacey had nearly three hundred men, mostly remnants from Thomas Sumter's command, still licking their wounds after being mauled badly by Banastre Tarleton's Legion at Fishing Creek more than a month earlier. Most of Sumter's force was killed, wounded, or captured in that raid and the rest scattered by the daring early morning attack.

With the South Carolinians were Colonel William Graham and about sixty men from the Lincoln County militia, the county between Rutherford and Charlotte Town. The day before, they were joined by another South Carolinian, Colonel James Williams, who had put together an ad hoc regiment of about one hundred men, mostly refugees from South Carolina who were staying with North Carolina friends or relatives after being driven from their homes by the British. General Davidson had encouraged the demoralized militia units to move to the western area and support McDowell's request for help in fighting Ferguson, but Davidson's instructions were sketchy at best.

After exchanging pleasantries and explaining his mission to get a general officer for the mountain brigade, it became obvious to McDowell that this new camp was not unified. Williams and Hill hated each other; the animosity between the two was caused by a feud that went back before the war when a business deal between the two soured. They also clashed rudely several times when serving in Sumter's brigade until Williams, a five-year veteran officer in the South Carolina militia, was able to create a separate command and seek action against the enemy elsewhere.

Unlike the differences in the mountain commanders, Hill's and Williams's lack of respect included open animosity and distrust of each other.

Each refused to be subordinate to the other. The rancor disgusted McDowell who told them that getting a general to come to the west should solve any problem of command. He rose abruptly and continued his journey. After McDowell had left, Williams sent an express to Shelby, with whom he had served at Musgrove's Mill, to let the mountain colonel know he was nearby with reinforcements.

William Walker and Jacob Godley were mud splattered when they reported at dusk to Colonels Hampton and Campbell at the Marlin Knob camp. Their news meant there would be no battle for the next day or so. Ferguson was moving away from them; just how far, no one knew. All indications, Walker reported, were that the Loyalists were headed south toward the British stronghold at Ninety Six.

The next morning, as Ferguson was making his way eastward on the north side of Broad River and his wagons followed a parallel course south of the river, the mountain brigade marched into Gilbert Town and set up camp where, only a few days before, Ferguson had his headquarters.

Patrols were dispatched to try to locate Ferguson's army. Jacob piloted a Wilkes County squad toward Twitty's Ford on the Broad River.

Sergeant Robert Godley was not happy to be marching away from the fight where he knew he had the upper hand, but he was pleased that Colonel Mills had assigned his company to the rearguard and a mission to confuse the enemy. His company was preparing to abandon an ambush site when they saw three riders nearing Twitty's Ford. Robert motioned Will and Andy to set their sights on the approaching trio.

Andy was the first to recognize Jacob's distinctive high moccasin boots. "That's Jake!"

"Damn!" Robert said, "Shoot to the right."

Instead of waiting until the targets got closer, the three brothers squeezed their triggers while the riders were still two hundred yards' distance. They aimed away from the man who looked like their brother.

Before the Whig patrol heard the Tory rifle shot, John Martin was falling from his horse, his head bleeding from where his right ear had been. Instinctively, Jacob and the other Liberty Man turned their horses into the trees for protection. When they saw six armed riders galloping toward them from the ambush site and the smoke from more rifles fired from the trees ahead, the two Whigs spurred their horses to quickly escape from the area and elude capture, hoping that their friend was all right.

Biggerstaff was furious at the Godley brothers for shooting before the enemy was within effective range. "What's the matter with you, Sergeant?" he shouted. "Why didn't you wait till they got closer?"

Robert did not reply, but Will bragged smugly. "I hit the man I aimed for."

Without waiting for further explanation, Biggerstaff spurred his horse down the road to join the rest of his company that was inspecting the rebel body. Believing Martin to be dead, they took his rifle and horse. They would catch up with Ferguson the next day.

Martin, however, recovered consciousness shortly after the Tories left him and was able to walk six miles back to camp where he was declared unfit for further duty.

After returning to Gilbert Town, Jacob went to John Foreman's place to visit for an hour with Rachel Pearson, but most of the time was spent answering Foreman's questions about the expedition against Ferguson. Jacob was away from camp when his fifteen-year-old brother Wayne visited Colonel Hampton and begged to join the Liberty Men.

At first Hampton rejected Wayne's request to join his regiment because he was too young and did not have a horse. The boy insisted that he was sixteen, an excellent shot, and could outrun most horses. The old colonel, who wanted to get back visiting with his wife and daughters who had walked to Gilbert Town from Mountain Creek, liked the boy's spunk and assigned Wayne to George Ledbetter's company with orders for the forty-year-old captain to keep the boy out of harm's way as much as possible.

The best news for the Liberty Men that day was the arrival of two small units of reinforcements, including Major William Candler with thirty Georgians, part of Colonel Elijah Clarke's command. Clarke, Candler told the mountain colonels, was escorting refugees from the Augusta area to sanctuary far away from the king's men.

Arriving from neighboring Lincoln County was Major William Chronicle and twenty of his neighbors who lived along the South Fork of the Catawba. All were experienced fighters.

At the same time as the reinforcements arrived in Gilbert Town, some thirty miles to the east, in the South Fork area, Abram Collins and Peter

Quinn were hiding in a forest well north of the route they had intended to take to deliver Ferguson's message about the advancing rebels to General Cornwallis. Initially, they had traveled fast toward Charlotte Town and stopped at Alexander Henry's plantation near Kings Creek to refresh their horses and share in some hot food. Both knew Henry's reputation as an outspoken Whig partisan. While they ate, drank cool cider, and enjoyed Henry's warm hospitality, both bragged about their support of the liberty cause and said were on their way to join up in the fight against the British at Charlotte Town.

Henry's son thought the messengers were too verbose in their claims and went to a nearby tavern to ask if anyone knew either of the men. Someone spat out, "Liberty Men, hell! Those two scoundrels are stinking Tories through and through. They've been fighting for the Brits since before Charles Town fell."

A posse of a dozen Liberty Men quickly formed and an enthusiastic search began. The chasers nearly caught the Tory messengers before losing their trail after the two abandoned a lame horse, splashed on foot up a creek, and slithered through a massive canebrake for nearly two miles before hiding in a deep forest, refusing to travel further during daylight. Not being told the urgency of Ferguson's express, the Tories went out of their way northward before heading east, making only about ten miles before finding another hideaway to elude the rebels searching for them. They were lost much of the time, but if caught, they knew it would be certain death.

Ferguson's troops camped the night of 4 October at Jesse Tate's plantation overlooking the Broad River near the mouth of Buffalo Creek. Tate was not there; instead, he was off somewhere with the rebel militia. One of the visitors in Ferguson's camp was John West, a spry old man who claimed to be 101 and a Crown supporter. Toothless and talkative, he walked with the slow gait of a centenarian whose life was about worn out. He confabbed with the senior officers on into the night, amused them by dancing a jig, and boasted of exploits against the Indians nearly fifty years earlier when he and his family had carved out their homestead in the midst of an uncharted wilderness. As the evening lengthened, West excused himself to return to his home about two miles northward. He refused offers of an escort, saying with some indignation, "I'm perfectly capable of taking myself home, thank you."

SHIFT IN STRATEGY

5–6 October 1780

Daybreak on Thursday morning found old man West plodding steadily northward to find his grandson who was serving in Graham's Lincoln County militia. West stopped briefly from time to time, as he put it, "to rest my bones" and to sip water from a stream or munch on wetted cornbread from his wallet. Despite his age, he was determined to tell the Liberty Men about Ferguson. He had walked nearly fifteen miles, taking one short, painful step after another before stumbling into the partisan camp shortly before dusk.

Graham was enjoying supper with the South Carolina colonels when the old man was brought to him. Graham knew West to be trustworthy and, despite his age, still mentally bright. The colonels were surprised when West told them that Ferguson was moving toward Charlotte Town. Earlier in the day, Williams had received an express from Shelby that indicated Ferguson was headed toward Ninety Six and that the mountain men were in pursuit.

"We need to get this intelligence to the mountain men. Where are they now?" Graham asked.

"They were at Gilbert Town this morning," Williams answered. "I imagine that now they are at the Green River or beyond. With a third of their people on foot and tired, they can't move too fast."

Since he was in the best physical condition and had campaigned with Hampton earlier in the spring near Charles Town, Lacey became the logical messenger. Only a senior officer could persuade the mountain brigade to shift course.

One of the Lincoln County militia who was a frequent visitor to the western regions of Rutherford County volunteered to go as Lacey's pilot. Lacey used Hill's horse because it was a good night traveler.

Jacob had been on the advance guard that secured McDaniel's Ford on the Green River late in the afternoon of 5 October, an hour or so before the arrival of the Liberty brigade. He did not learn about Wayne joining the militia until nearly dusk when he spotted his younger brother carrying a pail of water up to his company's camp. Jacob protested to Hampton, urging him to send Wayne back home, but the old colonel said the teenager was fit to fight and they needed every man they could get.

"I can't let you smash those Royals without me getting my licks in for that beating they gave me," Wayne insisted to Jacob. "You will not deny me that, brother."

"You got a horse?"

"No, I'm with the footmen…Cap'n Ledbetter's company. By the by, we got a man there who's got three brothers with the Tories like us."

"Who's that?"

"See that older fellow over there making the fire. He's Preston Goforth. Lives down on the eastern end of the county."

Wayne introduced Jacob to Goforth. Jacob had seen the man a few times along the trek from over the mountains, but had never talked to him nor was he aware of Goforth having brothers serving the enemy like the Camps and Godleys. Goforth told Jacob and Wayne that there were hard feelings within his family over the rebellion, but even though his brothers would not talk to him, he did not know how he would react if he saw one in his rifle sights. Wayne and Jacob had the same doubts about confronting their Tory brothers.

After asking Ledbetter to look after Wayne, Jacob felt better about his brother's chances of survival but cautioned the youngster to stay with an experienced fighter.

At the colonel's meeting that evening, Shelby vented his frustration over the lack of progress in their march. Placing his hands on his hips, he declared, "We got to make some changes if we are going to take Ferguson before he reaches reinforcements. We are going way too slow. We've got more lame horses and sick men than you can shake a stick at. Hell, I saw one horse that's blind. A dozen more horses look like they can't go another day. The flux is rampant among the men; so is fever. More men than I can count got the piles. The foot soldiers are dog tired and dropping out with twisted ankles, blisters, sore feet, and all kinds of ailments. I bet a hundred or more don't even have shoes."

"What do you propose?" Sevier asked.

"We pick only those men and horses that are strong enough for two days' hard riding and use them to go chase down Ferguson before he joins British regulars. The rest can follow along as best they can when they can," Shelby said.

Campbell looked at his fellow commanders. "Any objections?"

Hampton pondered the idea aloud. "I don't like cutting our strength like that; it will hurt our chances to overpower the Royals. Yet, Isaac is right. If we don't go faster, them snakes will slither away. I say we ride the sons of bitches down and chop off their heads while we can."

Orders went out for the captains to personally select only men with no infirmities, who were physically fit for hard riding, carried a trusty rifle, and had a strong horse to go with the reformed attack force. Those without a horse or whose horse was not strong enough could follow on foot, if able, but the mounted troops would not wait for them.

Jacob heard one of Captain Singleton's men cry because he would be left behind, suffering a painful boil on his rear, making it impossible for him to sit in the saddle. Earlier in the day, one of Withrow's men had to put his horse down when it broke a leg after stepping in a hole. He was visibly disappointed but found a horse from another Whig who was having second thoughts about going into battle.

In the Wilkes County regiment, Captain William Lenoir, who led a company of foot Rangers, was determined not be left out. He saw a soldier whose breeches were bloody from protruding hemorrhoids and talked him into letting Lenoir take his horse. Colonel Cleveland approved the trade, but told Lenoir that he would have to go as a private and not as an officer.

Through the evening footmen, desperate to be on the attack, walked from campfire to campfire trying to beg or borrow a horse. Nearly 125 animals were rejected as unfit to continue. There were a few slackers, not many, among the militia who feigned illness and let others use their animals. Men with painful hemorrhoids, rheumatism, jaundice, or other ailments reluctantly gave up their mounts for the cause. Preston Goforth's cousin loaned him a horse because the cousin's abscessed teeth had become too painful for him to bear.

During the early morning hours, three young Virginians had picket duty on the Gilbert Town road just outside the Whig camp. The largest, a burly nineteen-year-old, stepped out in front of two charging horses that came down the road out of the darkness toward him and bellowed, "Stop or I'll shoot your arse dead!"

Lacey and his companion pulled tight on their reins as the horses slid to within a whisker of slamming into the sentry. "Who are you, and what do you want here?" the picket yelled again.

"I'm Lieutenant Colonel Edward Lacey, Chester District, South Carolina militia. Is this the Liberty Men's mountain brigade?"

"What's the password?"

"I don't know."

"You a Tory or Liberty Man?"

"I am fighting for liberty, young soldier. Now if you please, take me to your commander. I have very important news for him," Lacey said.

Within a minute, Lieutenant Robert Edmonston came running up the steep hill telling the sentry, "Hush up that yelling; you are waking up the camp." Turning to Lacey, Edmonston asked, "Now, who are you, sir, and what is your purpose here?"

Lacey again identified himself and said he had vital information about Ferguson. Edmonston also was leery. "I have to blindfold you before taking you to the camp."

Another guard was sent running ahead to wake up the commanders as Edmonston led Lacey's horse slowly down the road to the river ford; Lacey's escort stayed with the pickets. They waded across the river and stopped in front of several senior officers standing around a fire being stoked back to life.

When Campbell asked who his commander was, Lacey answered, "Colonel Thomas Sumter, sir, but he's down east somewhere. We are independent now. General Davidson from Salisbury sent us up this way to help you people. We've got about four hundred men, counting some North Carolina militia. But the most important news is that we now know where Ferguson is."

Andrew Hampton, who was standing in the background, asked, "Don't I know you?"

"We met near Charles Town back in the spring, Colonel Hampton. Our two regiments shared a campsite," Lacey replied.

The colonels listened as Lacey explained that Ferguson was already twenty to thirty miles east, headed toward Charlotte Town. He gave as many of the details as he could remember from West's report. "They were still at Jesse Tate's place near Buffalo Creek this morning."

Campbell turned to Hampton. "What's the best way to get to Charlotte Town from here?"

Hampton thought and then stated, "Let's take the ridge road south of the Broad to Saunders's cow pens. That's about twenty miles east. It's a good easy road, no rivers or big creeks to cross. We can make better time than going north of Broad River. From the cow pens, we head northeast and cross the Broad at Tate's Ferry or Cherokee Ford. That's where we are most likely to find the Royals."

"Aren't those cow pens just up the way from Thicketty Fort?" Shelby asked.

"Sure thing, Isaac. We stopped over there one day last summer, remember?"

Lacey interrupted. "I know exactly where it is. It's about a ten-hour march south of our camp. I'll go back, gather our people and meet you there by nightfall."

Lacey remounted and rode back up the hill to get his guide and disappear into the darkness. Once it became light, they were able to urge their horses from a trot to a gallop for the last part of their eighteen-mile ride to Flint Hill where they would coordinate the meeting between the South Carolinians and Lincoln County militia with the mountain brigade.

Jacob and the Rangers left before daybreak to scout the road to the cow pens, a major landmark for drovers to rest their stock when taking them to markets. At the Green River camp, units were reformed, some regiments losing only a few horsemen, others nearly a fourth. Lenoir counted heads as the reorganized brigade rode by up Sandy Plains Road away from the Green River. He reported 710 mounted men were on hoof, about half the men who had set up camp the night before. He did not count the Rangers and cavalry troop that went on ahead of the main body or the nearly four score footmen who, on their own volition, followed behind at a fast walk, determined to be in on any fight that may come. Included in the latter group was Wayne Godley.

Colonel Hampton rode at the head of a combined Burke–Rutherford regiment.

Major Joseph Herndon of Cleveland's regiment took charge of the remaining foot militia. He dismissed more than 160 men and boys as unfit for service and reformed those remaining into provisional companies. By midmorning, the main body of the brigade's footmen began walking toward the cow pens to support those on horseback.

After a day of rest, Ferguson had his command preparing to move before daybreak on Friday, 6 October.

The units were forming for the march when two of Ambrose Mill's neighbors arrived with disturbing news. They told Ferguson that they rode all night after learning more about the mountain men during the course of giving apples to the rebels when they arrived on Green River. They reported talk among the rebels about going toward Ninety Six, but they also learned that some reinforcements had arrived from Georgia and South Carolina. They estimated the enemy force to be several thousand, about half on foot. They were unaware of the Liberty Men's shift in strategy.

Ferguson wrote a hasty express to Cornwallis:

My Lord,

A doubt does not remain with regard to intelligence I previously sent your Lordship. The rebels are since joined by Clarke and Sumter, a course that makes them an object of some consequence. Happily, their leaders are obliged to feed their followers with such hopes and so to flatter them with accounts of our weakness and fear that, if necessary, I should hope for success against them myself; but numbers compared, that must be doubtful.

I am on my march towards you, by a road leading from Cherokee Ford, north to Kings Mountain. Three or four hundred good soldiers, part dragoons, would finish this business. Something must be done soon. This is their last push in this quarter, etc.

Pat. Ferguson

As with previous messengers, Whig partisans forced the express rider to take a slower, more circuitous route, and it would take two full days to complete a journey of less than forty miles.

Meanwhile, Abram Collins and Peter Quinn, carrying Ferguson's earlier express about an approaching rebel army, had almost reached the Catawba River by dawn but were still afraid they would be seen in the daylight, found a remote place in the forest in which to hide until dark. Hopefully by the morrow, they prayed, they would reach the British headquarters.

After crossing Buffalo Creek, Ferguson's brigade stopped for a midday rest at Peter Quinn's plantation, six miles west of Kings Mountain, a high, jagged peak sticking up uncharacteristically from the low, rolling countryside. Stretching several miles southwesterly from its pinnacle was a long, low ridge that completed the mountain. The old Cherokee Path, now a wagon road, went through a gap in the ridge. Ferguson was told about an elongated open glen running along the top of one of the hills near the road that would make an excellent camp site.

A number of Tories lived in the area and had flocked to Quinn's place to welcome the Loyalist army. They brought fresh eggs, fried turkey, rabbit, squirrel, and other foodstuffs, which the Godley brothers happily ate for their midday dinner. At past stops, others had beaten them to the local hen nests, causing eggs to be long gone before they got any.

Among the Tory visitors at the campsite was a crippled man, Joseph Kerr, who was born with one leg shorter than the other. He blended in with the visitors and carefully disguised the fact that he was a spy. Everyone at Quinn's place seemed in a jovial mood, and the Loyalist soldiers freely shared information about the brigade's intentions—some rumor, some factual—with anyone who would listen.

After Ferguson's brigade resumed its march, Kerr retrieved his horse and headed south toward the cow pens with the latest intelligence on Ferguson's intentions.

Weary from riding all night, Lacey arrived back at the Flint Hill camp about two hours after dawn that Friday morning. Within thirty minutes of Lacey briefing his fellow commanders on the situation, the South Carolinians and Lincoln County militia broke camp and were heading toward the cow pens.

The advance guard, including Rangers and Captain Adam Hampton's cavalry troop, arrived at the cow pens around noon. Jacob and Walker joined Adam at the door of the station owner's house. Hiram Saunders, a wealthy Tory, was in his nightshirt when he opened his door to Adam's loud pounding. "I'm a sick man. What do you want?" Saunders demanded.

"Just the use of your station for a while," Adam responded. "Some of my friends will need to refresh their horses here, if we may?"

"Ain't nobody here but me and a few darkies taking care of the stock," Saunders said without any hint of hospitality. "I take it you are rebel partisans up to no good."

"We are Liberty Men, sir, true and true. It'll be best that you stay in your house. Where is your family?"

"They are in Charles Town, safe from you plundering rebels."

Leaving Lieutenant Walker in charge of guarding the Saunders home and making sure no strangers came around, Adam took one of his troopers and galloped back up the Green River road to report their findings to the approaching brigade.

The mounted Liberty Men arrived at the cow pens in the midafternoon. Seeing the plump cattle, Campbell ordered enough steers slaughtered so that the men could cook their fill of beef. The brigade quickly stripped a large cornfield of its remaining produce and chopped rail fences into firewood. Within minutes, six dozen fires were blazing with meat sizzling and corn roasting to feed the tired soldiers who had traveled with no rest or food since dawn.

Over the next two hours, the footmen, who, on their own initiative had followed the horses out from McDaniel's Ford, began straggling in, exhausted. When the march started, it was a sunny morning, but the sky gradually turned gray and ominous by late afternoon.

As he strolled into the area, Wayne saw Jacob snoozing under a tree and went to him. Jacob awoke with a start but was not surprised that his determined brother had come ahead on foot. Jacob retrieved some meat and corn that was warming by his group's fire and shared it with Wayne who, after a few bites to sate his appetite, said he was bushed and dropped into a deep sleep. The young brother's stamina was impressive and made Jacob proud.

It was an hour before sundown when the contingent from Flint Hill rode into camp, welcomed by loud huzzahs from the mountain men and some rifle shots until the senior officers ordered no more shooting. A few minutes earlier, the spy Joseph Kerr had arrived from the Loyalist camp and reported what he had learned about Ferguson's intentions.

Lacey, Williams, Hill, and Graham joined the gathering of senior officers on the lawn in front of the Saunders home. As they walked up, Shelby wrapped his arms around Williams, greeting him as a long-lost brother. The two had shared one of the few Whig militia victories of the year at Musgrove's Mill. The affectionate greeting appalled Hill, who expressed disgust with a loud "Harrumph!"

Saunders, now dressed, sat alone on his veranda, glaring with contempt at the invaders. Nearby, two guards lazed on the front steps gnawing on some ribs. The officers had taken a table and ten chairs from the house and sat under an enormous willow oak, well out of range of Saunders's hearing.

Speaking primarily to the newcomers, Campbell led off. "Gentlemen, we have a whole passel of colonels here, but no general. Colonel McDowell has gone to Hillsborough to get Gates to appoint one for us. In the meantime, we satisfy the needs of command each evening by the regimental commanders electing the next day's officer of the day. That's my status on this day. Can you South Carolina boys live with that?"

"Well, you are in South Carolina now," Hill stated in a pompous manner. "I think either Colonel Lacey or I should take over since we represent Colonel Sumter, the ranking militia officer in this province."

"And why not Colonel Williams?" Shelby asked.

"He has no authority here," Hill declared.

Williams interjected with a humorless smile. "Colonel Hill, as you might surmise, doesn't like me. The feeling is mutual. But, gentlemen, if you are going after Ferguson, my regiment and I will follow whoever the majority says should command. We came to fight."

Lacey spoke up. "This issue doesn't deter us from going with you to catch and kill the king's men. We have much to avenge."

Campbell took over the meeting. "Just before you South Carolinians came in, a spy reported that Ferguson was headed toward King's Mountain. He says that it's about twenty miles northeast of here. He thinks they will camp there along the Cherokee Path that cuts through the ridge."

"I know that area well," Graham said. "My home is near the mountain."

Chronicle, one of the three majors present, the other two were Joseph Winston and Joe McDowell, added, "Sir, I've hunted all over that mountain. It ain't much compared to what you blue mountain boys are used too, but it does stick up over the rest of the land. Many of my South Fork boys live near or have relatives in the area."

"That's good to know, Major," Campbell said. "We'll use your people as our pilots tomorrow. "

Lacey also volunteered his men who lived in the vicinity of King's Mountain to serve as guides.

"The big question is will Pattie stay there or will he move on to Charlotte Town in the morning?" Campbell asked.

"What about Tory militia around here?" Williams asked, indicating the area around Saunders's station.

Hampton responded. "A Tory officer named Gibbs has a plantation about eight or ten miles southeast of here. We've heard he has several hundred militia with him. We got heavy guards up just in case they come this way. Our patrols are looking to see if any of the rascals are roaming about."

"I don't want to fight in a sideshow here," Campbell stated. "Now that we have Ferguson's scent, and we shan't be led astray."

Cleveland, unusually quiet until now, spoke, "That means we need to leave here as soon as the men are rested a wee bit and go catch the royal laddies while they're napping. Let's go as soon as it's dark."

"As always, Ben, you are right," Campbell said. He turned to the newly arrived colonels. "Gentlemen, you've had a hard march already today. I suggest you do as we did this morning, reform your regiments with only the strongest horses and men with good rifles. That way we can move fast without hindrance. Any footmen who want to come along will have to keep up. They are on their own; we don't wait for them."

"We'll lose half our men," protested Hill. "Can we afford to reduce our strength that much against a foe like Ferguson?"

Williams turned and chided Hill. "Don't you want to catch those bastards?"

"Gentlemen, please!" Campbell begged, making no attempt to hide his annoyance at the two bickering officers.

After studying the darkening clouds in the sky, Campbell added, "Looks like we might have a good rain coming. It will hide our movement from Tory spies, but it will slow us down. I suggest you have your men ready to move out at dark."

Hill spoke up. "Sir, a wound that I got in battle a few weeks ago is acting up again from that long ride today. I'm afraid I don't have the strength to continue on the campaign. I beg to be relieved to convalesce. Lieutenant Colonel Hawthorne will take my command."

No one objected.

Jacob had taken some fat from a steer's carcass and was putting a protective coat of grease on his and Wayne's weapons when the South Carolina militia arrived. He did not join in the rumpus created by many of the excited mountain men until he noticed a familiar face among the newcomers, the Catawba Indian who had saved his life four years ago. Jacob jumped up and shouted, "George Bluebird!"

The Indian's head jerked up and looked around for the voice that called his name. He saw Jacob waving and running toward him. At first he was puzzled and then recognized the running figure as his young companion on the 1776 Rutherford campaign against the Cherokee. He was embarrassed by the show of emotion from Jacob, who threw his arms around Bluebird while yelling, "Damn, you are a sight for sore eyes. I never got a chance to thank you proper for saving my hide back over the mountains. Now you are here. What regiment?"

"I'm riding with Colonel Lacey. The Tories burned most of us Catawbans out of our homes, so Chief New River and some of us joined Sumter's militia. Tarleton whupped us good down on Fishing Creek. The few of us who survived are scattered from hell to yonder. I lit out with Lacey. But what about you?" Bluebird then chucked. "You're still so skinny that you won't make a decent meal for a bear."

Jacob invited Bluebird over to the Rangers' fire and introduced the Indian as the man who taught him to be a Ranger. Pointing over to Wayne, Jacob said, "That scrawny runt sleeping over there is my baby brother, Wayne. I've been trying to get him to go home, but he won't go."

"He looks just like you did when we tore up those Cherokee towns back in seventy-six."

The other Rangers laughed as Jacob said, "Come now, George, I didn't look that bad, did I?"

"Yep, and even worse after you got through dancing with that she-bear!"

The guffaws became louder, Jacob blushed, Wayne slept on, and the Rangers begged for more information about the encounter with the bear. Their laughter turned to awe when Bluebird described how Jacob killed three Cherokee warriors that same day as his encounter with a bear.

The shadows were getting long when Ferguson first stood along the northern tip of a narrow, bald, oblong spur stretching down from the craggy King's pinnacle about five miles northeast. The ridge was about two hundred feet higher than the rolling piedmont that surrounded it. Open for more than a thousand feet along its narrow crest, it looked to Ferguson like a natural defensive position.

Below the northwest corner of the ridge, there was a fairly level area in the open forest that was easily accessible from the road for the eighteen supply wagons. Being on the hill's leeward side with an approaching storm, it offered a protected campsite for the Loyalist brigade. Several bold springs bubbled on both sides of the ridge. "We'll camp here," Ferguson declared. "Only God can remove me from this mountain unless I want to go."

Shelters were quickly erected as the clouds darkened. Most of the Tory militia had no tents, including the Godley brothers who found a place to build a lean-to of fresh-cut saplings and the tarps that the three shared. They were able to get to the commissary wagon before all the day's rations were parceled out.

Selected for early picket duty, the brothers were pleased that, for once, they would get a night of uninterrupted sleep. Major William Mills told them that the rebels were at least a day's march away, if that close. Captain Biggerstaff warned them to stay alert, "There's always the risk of some deranged partisan slipping in to do harm."

For his command tents, Ferguson chose a flat, wide place atop of the ridge where he could look down on his army below; however, his location was at the mercy of wind and driving rain.

Except for this ridge top, the hills around were covered with towering chestnut, tulip poplar, and oak trees. There was little undergrowth except around the springs and streams, making movement and camping easy. Horsemen could ride through the mature forest without much hindrance. Most of the slopes leading to the top were not difficult to traverse, but there were scattered patches of extremely steep, rough terrain, blocked by rocks and ravines.

The Loyalists had scouts out along the roads to the south, north, and west. A day's ride south was Major Zacharias Gibbs and his Spartan militia, gathering up furloughed Tory militiamen and providing protection on the southern and western areas of the Broad River. Cornwallis was within a day's ride to the east. Ferguson felt fairly secure. Besides, as he had often said, *"What can backwater militia do against a trained army?"* He decided to wait until the next day to determine whether to wait for reinforcements there or travel on eastward to be nearer Cornwallis. His rational thinking helped him ease his mind, permitting him to escape the rigors of command and enjoy a relaxing body rub from his two Virginia camp followers.

When the gray skies morphed into darkness, the reinforced mountain brigade now numbered around one thousand mounted Liberty Men. The horsemen turned their campfires and excess beef over to the footmen staying behind. Every man in the main force was on horseback and in reasonably good health and good spirits. Chronicle's South Fork boys had gone ahead to find a safe place to cross the Broad River and ensure that no enemy ambushes would surprise them. The Georgians were assigned to Colonel Williams's ad hoc regiment.

While most of the men traveled with their home unit, many, including Jacob and Bluebird found themselves riding with strangers. They felt the first splatter of rain as Campbell gave the command to move out. Some heard faintly the old clock in Hiram Saunders's parlor chime eight.

As did most of the veterans, Jacob wrapped his rifle in sailcloth to protect it from the rain, but kept his hand close to the trigger guard so he could get to the weapon quickly if he had to. Tied atop his saddle was his linsey-woolsey coat, readily available should the rain became heavier or colder. Keeping powder dry and rifle ready for action took priority over body comfort.

Bluebird rode next to Jacob, renewing a bond that comes from men who had shared danger in times past. Jacob told the Catawba Indian about his three brothers serving in the Tory militia. He described the scoundrel Rance Miller who had his brother Wayne flogged and nearly had Jacob arrested when he was visiting Ferguson's camp at Gilbert Town. As the rain increased in tempo during the evening, he talked about Rachel Pearson and the tragedy Miller had brought to her family. "I ain't never had a hate like I do for that son of a bitch," Jacob said bitterly.

"Well, we'll just have to kill him," Bluebird replied unemotionally.

Walking along behind the mounted warriors were more than seventy militiamen, including the barefooted Wayne Godley, seemingly oblivious to the cold rain or muddy trail they were slogging through. The footmen represented nearly every county in the brigade, yet they had no designated leader. Like Wayne, most did not care in which regiment he fought as long as he could bloody the enemy.

It was not just the rain that soaked every Liberty Man to the skin; discomfort also came from the chilling wind that whipped the big tree boughs above like wisps of slender wheat stalks. The riders hunkered under whatever protection they had with them. Jacob was better off than most. Despite the rain, his heavy wool coat, which also served as a sleeping robe, protected him from the wind and kept his body heat inside.

After the first hour into their journey, Jacob and the others fell quiet, wrapped up in their own inner thoughts and trying to ignore the storm about them. Many, like Jacob who was riding in the middle of the pack, drifted into snatches of sleep, letting their horses follow the one in front, unaware that sometime before midnight their guide made a wrong turn and led them miles up a wrong trail, getting Campbell's division lost from the other half of the brigade.

Prelude to a fight
7 October 1780

Long before daylight, word passed down the water soaked line of horsemen that Colonel Campbell's column was lost. They had gotten off on the wrong trail in the darkness. By the time Campbell's frantic pilots could determine their location, they had circled around and were only five miles from the cow pens. Although they sped up their march after finding the right way and made extra efforts to keep from losing stragglers, they were not able to sneak across the Broad River under cover of darkness.

Jacob was soaked to the skin and miserable this Saturday morning. It had rained all night, sometimes hard, but mostly a steady drenching. In addition to his group straying off course, he was annoyed by having to look for wayward militiamen who, in the wet darkness, had failed to keep in touch with the horse in front of them and wandered off lost in the forest. Most were found, but only after hollering and thrashing about by both those lost and those searching.

Their biggest fear was an ambush or heavy defenses at the Broad River crossing. During the night, some South Fork boys slipped across the river and scouted both Tate's Ferry and Cherokee Ford. One of the Whig scouts was a character named Enoch Gilmore, a practical jokester with a gift for gab and who knew the countryside like the back of his hand. As Jacob rode up to the river's edge at Cherokee Ford in the early morning light, he heard Gilmore singing in a loud voice from the other side the bawdy song "Bonny Lynn," the signal that the muddy Broad could be crossed safely. No Loyalist troops were about. Still unknown was that Ferguson's camp was less than twelve miles away at Kings Mountain.

The Broad at Cherokee Ford was more than three times the width of where the Liberty Men had crossed it nearly forty miles upstream at Twitty's Ford. After a night of rain, the water level had risen, making the normal shallow wade a hazardous waist-deep ordeal for those on foot, yet the brigade made it to the north side without mishap.

Three miles farther, a halt was called for the men to rest their animals. A few had a little food in their saddlebags or wallet. Jacob's traveling feast was a roasted ear of corn and some charred beef from the day before. He and others fed their horses some raw corn that they had pulled from the fields around the cow pens..

There was no letting up in the rain, and noting the miserable condition of men and beasts, some colonels suggested that they extend the halt. Shelby adamantly objected, stating, "I've gone too far to quit now! We are continuing on, even if I have to follow Ferguson into Cornwallis's tent!"

When Shelby yelled for his men to remount, the other officers echoed the command. Rain or not, the mountain brigade was moving again, determined to catch its nemesis.

The foot soldiers did not get lost like Campbell's division had and were able to stay on the main road, with most of them arriving at Cherokee Ford before the last horses of the mounted brigade splashed ashore on the northeast side of the Broad River. The lucky ones were able to hitch a ride behind mounted horsemen; others grabbed a saddle, rein, or horse's tail to steady themselves in the current. Despite the heavy current, all successfully crossed the river.

Wayne Godley was among the fifty or so walking militia that still had the stamina to keep up the grueling pace on the muddy road. More than a dozen footmen dropped out with exhaustion. At least another dozen more quit just because they wanted to get out of the rain. The footmen straggled out over a mile, but still they plodded on with no designated officer leading them, each determined to be in on any fight.

Soaked and cold, the Tory Godley brothers crawled out from under their lean-to to greet the day after a near-sleepless night. For ten hours, the rain had been nonstop, though at times it seemed to be tapering.

Unlike most of the militia under Ferguson, Biggerstaff's company kept their long rifles. In case of a fight, they would serve as skirmishers and snipers. But now, their concern was keeping their flintlocks and powder dry, a difficult task in this weather. They had made special sailcloth sleeves to protect the weapons, but it did not keep the dampness out.

"I wonder if Jake is as miserable as us," Andy asked his brothers as he dried his weapon.

"He probably found some tree hollow to curl up in and is as snug as a bug," Robert said with a chuckle. "I doubt if his rebel friends will march in weather like this. Ain't fit for ducks, much less man. Bet we don't move our camp either."

At the command tent on the ridge top above them, Ferguson conferred with his officers. "We'll stay here another day," the commander declared. "Hopefully, this rain will move on, and we can dry out before day's end. The rebels can't travel in these conditions, but just in case, Colonel Mills, I want mounted patrols out at least five miles in all directions." Looking at Plummer, he said, "Major, get several foraging parties ready to go out as soon as the rain lets up. The rebel plantations north of here should be ripe for plunder. We need more grain for the horses."

After his officer's conference, Ferguson had Allaire write out a repeat of the express that he had sent to Cornwallis the day before. He entrusted the delivery of the new express to John Ponder, a fourteen-year-old Tory who had proved to be a trustworthy messenger over the past week. The rain became little more than a drizzle when the boy left the Loyalist camp. Since his home was only a couple miles west of the mountain, Ponder decided to detour to tell his parents he was going to see the famous British general in Charlotte Town. With a strong horse and hard riding, he could still visit his folks and then make the thirty miles to the British lines by nightfall.

Eight miles southeast of Saunders's cow pens, Major Zachariah Gibbs and many of his Spartan District Tories relaxed at his spacious plantation. He was pleased when spies reported back to him at midmorning that hundreds of rebels were still camped at Saunders's cow pens. "They have heavy pickets out, so we couldn't get too close, but there could be more than a thousand of them. Lots of cook fires are going. They're just lazing around, but it don't look like they are going to move until after this rain stops."

"Good job. Get to a fire and dry off. We'll keep watch on them," Gibbs said. "As soon as the rain stops, I'll send an express to Ferguson and let him know the situation. There's no sense for us to march until we know what the rebels are going to do."

Moving up the ridge road between Buffalo and Kings Creeks about four miles from the river, the Liberty Men's lead scouts stopped at Solomon Beason's house where two Tory patrollers had taken refuge from the rain. The Lincoln County scouts took all three without a fight. Beason, a man whose loyalty depended upon which side had the greatest strength at hand, readily identified his two guests as enemy militia and indicated that Ferguson's camp was eight miles farther up the road, just east of Kings Creek. Refusing to talk at first, the prisoners quickly changed their mind when Cleveland threatened them with hanging. Knowing that the enemy was near, the two captives were forced to ride at the head of the column. In case of ambush, they would be the first to die.

As the Liberty Men continued their advance, the lead element spotted Enoch Gilmer's horse about 150 yards ahead, tied to a gate in front of a modest Tory home. Colonel Campbell, with twenty partisans, rushed to the house, burst through the front door, and found Gilmer sitting calmly at a table enjoying hot biscuits and tea with the two spinster sisters who lived there.

"We got you, you damn rascal!" Campbell yelled as he approached Gilmer with a drawn pistol and jerked the man to his feet.

"I'm a true king's man, by God," Gilmer exclaimed boastfully as he steadied himself, "and not ashamed to admit it."

It was all the partisans could do to keep a straight face as Gilmer played his dramatic role with the skill of a seasoned thespian.

Grabbing a rope with a noose from his sergeant and draping it over Gilmer's neck, Campbell snarled, "I've chased you enough. We'll hang your murderous hide to that arch on the front gate."

Major Chronicle interceded, pleading sincerely to Campbell. "I beg that you not hang him here, sir. His ghost will haunt these poor ladies now and forever. Let's take him to the woods out of their sight. He can meet his maker there. It's the Christian thing to do."

In tears, the two women cowered in the corner of their great room as the muddied rebels marched the prisoner out of the house, leading him with the noose dangling around his neck. Once in the trees and out of sight of the house, the Liberty Men burst into laughing as Gilmer told how he had won entrance to the home by claiming to be a loyal Tory looking to join Ferguson's corps. "They were overjoyed to find a kindred soul. And with me looking like a wet hound dog, they took pity and invited me in, gave me some vittles, and told me that just last night before the rain began, they took eggs and chickens to Ferguson's camp. He's just off the Cherokee Path near the ridge top. There's a campsite there used by a lot by hunters."

"Hey, that's our old camp, ain't it, Major Chronicle?" Captain John Mattocks interrupted.

"Sure is," Chronicle responded. "Colonel Campbell, we know that mountain from top to bottom. We hunted on it last winter."

Before moving on, Campbell, as he had done after visiting the previous Tory homes, ordered two guards to keep the occupants from sneaking off to warn Ferguson that the Liberty Men were near.

Another mile up the road, some of Chronicle's advanced scouts sneaked up on a potential ambush site and discovered three Tories manning an outpost. Engrossed in trying to get a fire started so they could dry out, the three were taken without a struggle. When the main column arrived, the captives were standing in the road, their arms tied behind them. It took little effort to get the prisoners to confirm the location of Ferguson's camp. However, the captured Loyalists did not know the defensive layout because they had been at the outpost since dusk the night before.

Some more Rangers, including Jacob and Bluebird, galloped ahead to reinforce the Lincoln County scouts in the advance party. They had just crossed a small stream, about one and a half miles west of the ridge line, when Jacob saw a trotting horse carrying a youthful rider. The Rangers maneuvered their horses skillfully to trap the rider who had a musket strapped to his back and was unable to use it.

"Whoa there!" Jacob demanded as he grabbed the reins of the boy's horse. "Where are you going in such a damn hurry?"

"I'm Johnny Ponder. I'm just going to see my folks, sir," the frightened boy responded. "They live up this branch a ways."

Bluebird recognized the express pouch slung around the boy's neck and shouted, "That's a king's purse! Give it to me!"

"No sir!" Ponder, drawing courage from his sense of self importance, stated adamantly. "That's official business and of no concern to you. The Lord General Cornwallis will be mad if anyone messes with his express."

Jacob drew his butcher knife and thrust it menacingly toward the boy's neck. "But he won't care if his scrawny messenger is skinned alive, now, will he?"

They took Ponder back to Campbell, who read Ferguson's express. "It looks like ol' Pattie is worried, boys," the Virginian said. "He's asking Cornwallis to send him reinforcements."

As they were questioning Ponder on the layout of the camp, Campbell shared the dispatch with the other senior officers. The youngster succumbed to fear and confirmed the previous intelligence as he provided more details about the Loyalists positions.

Feeling like near-drowned puppies, Abram Collins and Peter Quinn were hungry, filthy, wet, and cold as they approached the British sentries on the outskirts of Charlotte Town, their difficult journey thankfully over. They identified themselves as Ferguson's messengers. The skeptical private on guard called his sergeant who, in turn, called his lieutenant who escorted the disheveled messengers to British Army headquarters where the adjutant demanded the express. The weary Tory messengers were fed and given hot tea while the adjutant took the express to the general.

Cornwallis was discussing logistical details with his commissary officers when the adjutant interrupted. "You may want to read this now, your Lordship," the adjutant stated. "It's from Ferguson."

After reading the message twice, Cornwallis looked puzzled. "This express is five days old! Why did it take so long to get here?"

"The two Tory militiamen bringing it reported that they were waylaid by a band of rebels and forced to abandon their horses. They were chased through the wilderness for several days before they got free of their pursuers. They became lost, but finally managed to find their way here."

"Damn militia! You can't trust them with anything critical." Cornwallis snorted. "What's done is done. Ask Lieutenant Colonel Tarleton to report to me now."

Thirty minutes later, Tarleton, who had been sleeping in a commandeered home, appeared before his commander. After being bedridden for almost a week with fever, he was weak and pallid.

"How do you feel?" the general asked his most resourceful dragoon.

"Still on the puny side, sir, but on the mend."

"Ferguson may have gotten himself in a bit of trouble," Cornwallis said as he handed the express to Tarleton who read it carefully. "I want you to take your legion and give Ferguson some support."

"Sir, I have not recovered sufficiently to take to the saddle. I should be better tomorrow, but if a relief force is needed today, I suggest you send one of the foot battalions," Tarleton responded. "This express doesn't indicate any sense of urgency."

"Have your legion ready to go by morning. Ferguson may be overcautious, but this is something we cannot ignore," Cornwallis said before adding jokingly, "Now back to bed with you. I can't have my best fighting officer all sickly, can I?"

When the rain stopped completely at noon, Ferguson assembled his corps along the open spine of the ridge. It was just barely level and long enough to permit limited small-unit drills. Before going to the top, the Godley brothers draped their wet blankets and coats across some bushes to dry as did most of the other militia. They moaned at the idea of having to go through what they considered to be senseless drills when they should be out looking for the rebels.

The army's needs were much more than practicing the manual of arms. Weapons had to be dried, cleaned, greased, and checked to ensure proper working order. Damp cartridges were laid out to dry. Sergeants inspected their troops and every piece of equipment to insure that mud and grime was cleaned from weapons, uniforms, belts, blades, and straps. With the open, high meadow away from the dripping trees, the task of maintaining combat readiness was more pleasant for the soldiers than working under the wet forest canopy.

As the senior Loyalist officers walked along the ridge line, DePeyster asked about putting up breastworks or an abatis, just in case. Ferguson scoffed, "That won't be necessary. If the backwater boys are anywhere near, we would know about it. After that overnight rain, I doubt if they are even up and about yet, much less traveling. But should they come, all the rebels in hell can't force us from this hill."

The militia officers remained quiet, but Ambrose Mills had his doubts. "These backwoodsmen are used to fighting Indian style in all kinds of weather. I wouldn't underestimate them, sir."

"I don't underestimate them, Colonel Mills, and I certainly don't fear them. We have the high ground and a well-trained cadre. It's been proved time and again that undisciplined militia can't hold a candle to trained soldiers on the battlefield."

As young Ponder was being questioned by the rebel colonels, another squad of Rangers brought forward two partisans whom Ferguson had paroled within the past two hours. John Jones had been captured at the Cane Creek skirmish, and George Watkins was taken near his home on the Pacolet River. Both were intercepted by the mountain brigade scouts just after the freed Whigs crossed Kings Creek, about a mile west of Ferguson's camp. Ecstatic, the parolees reported that most of the Loyalists were on top of the ridge drilling or drying clothing and equipment. The main camp was in a forested area on the northeastern side, just down from the crest near the road. The wagons and tents were there, but most of the people were on top of the ridge.

"Oh, by the way," Watkins said, "when I left, Ferguson was not wearing his uniform. He had on a blue-and-white-checked hunting shirt. Guess he didn't want to get that pretty red coat of his all wet and dirty."

When thanked for their keen observations, both men said they wanted to come along with the brigade. "We got some issues to settle," Jones said.

"Didn't you take a loyalty oath to the king?" Hampton asked.

"Yes, sir," Jones snickered, "but I was fibbing."

Hampton also laughed. "We don't have any extra rifles, but tag along, and if someone falls, you take their weapon."

"Aye, sir, that we will," Watkins answered.

Campbell called a quick meeting for all the key leaders to develop a battle plan. At the same time, Colonel Graham received a message from his wife who lived nearby and was due to give birth at any time. She said she urgently needed her husband at home, so Graham requested and was granted emergency leave. Major Chronicle was asked to take command of the Lincoln County militia because Campbell felt Chronicle would be more effective than the fifty-three-year-old Lieutenant Colonel Frederick Hambright. A ferocious fighter, Hambright's English was so bad when he became excited that few could understand the old German.

Since he was intimately familiar with the terrain around Ferguson's camp, Chronicle took a stick and drew a rough map in the soft clay road showing the way through the gap between the hills, the campsite, and the ridge top where most of the king's men were located. After tossing around several ideas, a bold tactic was agreed to that was fitting for men more accustomed to unconventional fighting rather than the rigid European formality of war favored by the British.

Campbell summarized the plan. "We'll surround the hilltop and hit them from all sides at the same time. Pattie will not expect that. They have no defenses up there other than being on high ground.

"I propose we divide into two divisions and each division into four elements. I'll take a division and go around to the south and east side of the ridge. Colonel Hampton, your Rutherford and Burke regiment will lead the way for my group and go up the east side of the ridge. Capture the campsite and wagons on the east before hitting the hilltop. Colonel Sevier, your Watauga and Chucky boys should be between my Virginians and Hampton and hit the southeastern part of the hill. Isaac, you and your Holston River gang will be on my left hitting the southwestern corner. My Virginias will come up the south slope.

"Colonel Cleveland will lead the second division up the road on the left, putting his Wilkes County boys in just north of Shelby. Then the South Carolina regiments under Lacey and Williams and the Lincoln County regiment up on the northern tip. Major Winston will swing his Surry County boys north of the road and come in from the far northeast. We will then have the bastards encircled and can tighten the noose till we squeeze them dead."

As he gave his instructions, Campbell drew arrows in the dirt showing the general direction where each unit would travel in its approach toward the enemy. "When we cross Kings Creek, each division will peel off the road. About a half-mile out from the ridge, all but the senior commanders should dismount and hobble their horses. Each regiment will form into two skirmish lines. Put your best knife fighters out front to sneak up on the pickets and cut their throats before they have a chance to give alarm. The pickets should be about two or three hundred yards from the ridge top.

"Remember, surprise gives us the edge, so don't shoot unless they are shooting at you. I will start the attack with yelling and shooting when we are ready to charge the top. Each of you will follow instantly in your area. Don't stop for the pickets. Rush through 'em. We got to hit 'em hard. Hit 'em fast. Keep 'em confused. Don't give 'em a chance to organize. If we surprise them and not waver, then victory will be ours.

"You will be on your own after we leave here. Everybody has to be his own general. There's good cover until we are just about at them. Remember, there's not much more of them than of us, so there's no reason to let 'em get the upper hand. Any questions?"

"This is one bodacious plan! But by God, it will work," Shelby exclaimed before looking up at the sun beginning to peek through the clouds. "Now there's a good omen. The good Lord is shining down on us."

Hampton smiled as he added, "Hell is sure to receive a bountiful crop of Royals this day."

Campbell continued his orders, "Inspire your officers and men. Have them double-check flints and prime in their rifles. Remind them that the Tories have green leaves in their hats, so our lads should all have white paper or cloth patches pinned to theirs. We don't want to be shooting our own people."

Campbell then turned and put his hand on Chronicle's shoulder, "Major, give each regiment a pilot who knows this area good to lead us into our attack positions."

Addressing all the officers, Campbell concluded, saying, "We will move out in twenty minutes. After we cross Kings Creek, there will be no talking and no stopping. Quietly dismount when you are about a half-mile from the enemy. Remember, surprise and quickness are essential for us to carry the day. Godspeed, my friends."

26

DEVIL'S CAULDRON

7 October 1780

With the rain gone, Robert and William Godley stretched across a rock outcrop on the crest of the ridge and basked in the warmth of the emerging afternoon sun. The drills, now completed, had been short, more like makework to keep idle warriors busy. Captain Biggerstaff walked over to them and began speaking formally. "Sergeant Godley, have the company ready to ride an hour before sundown. We have to patrol the roads for signs of rebels roaming about."

"Sure beats the hell out of standing picket duty," William said, smiling now that they had relief from dull camp life. "I guess I better round up Andy…" His sentence was interrupted by a shot that echoed through the trees on the southeast of the ridge.

"That picket's got a itchy finger," Robert said aloud, but mostly to himself.

In quick succession, the sound of two more shots cracked through the trees.

When the third shot sounded, Ferguson raced for his mount and yelled to the drummer to beat a call to arms. Still wearing his hunting shirt, Ferguson galloped southward; he had no time to properly don his uniform coat that was in his sleeping tent. Loyalists rushed to the pyramids of muskets along the ridge and grabbed the first weapon they could reach. Most were still buckling their equipment belts, carrying cartridge boxes and bayonets, as they ran to their screaming sergeants. With no prepared defensive strategy, officers and sergeants rushed their men to the sound of shooting as they fast considered options for meeting the unexpected threat. There was no time to form the corps in parade fashion.

After sending a sergeant down into the forest to determine what the shooting was about, DePeyster leaped on his horse and herded a mix of provincials and militia southward along the ridge to form skirmish lines facing the direction of the gunfire. Before galloping to the sound of shooting, Ferguson ordered Mills to put his riflemen on the northwestern side of the hill to watch the Cherokee Path located a little more than one hundred yards below. Biggerstaff herded his company away from the shooting and ordered them into positions just below the crest where they had a clear field of fire through the trees toward the road. Thinking he would miss the action on the other end of the ridge, William cursed aloud. "Damn it, them redcoats always get all the fun."

As the Provincials were quickly fixing their bayonets and forming their battle lines on the southern quarter of the hill's spine, some of Plummer's better-trained militia veterans intermingled with the uniformed veterans, their muskets ready for action. Above the din, Ferguson's famous silver whistle was heard piping directions as the militia officers, many of them confused with the suddenness of the situation, tried to get their commands together. The whistle signals added to the chaos; many mountain Tories were still unsure what each blast meant.

The first shot of the battle came from a picket in front of Shelby's advance. Many of the scattered sentries were silenced by knives, but one alert Tory saw two frontiersmen creeping through the woods, and fired at them before turning to run back toward the hilltop. Surprise gone, an overmountain fighter took aim, shot, and killed the sentry before he had gone twenty yards. A second picket shot at the rebel shooter but missed. He, too, met a quick fate. The majority of Shelby's men rushed on toward the enemy, unperturbed by the shooting.

Just around the hill on Shelby's right, Campbell was leading his men up the heavily wooded southern slope toward the crest when the first shot echoed through the trees. Leading his Virginians on foot, Campbell had doffed his coat, rolled up his shirt sleeves and opened his collar. He wielded a huge claymore, a double-sided broad sword carried by his ancestors against English armies in battles past. When he saw red uniforms through the trees, he shouted to his men and pointed toward the enemy. "There they are, my brave lads; shout like hell and fight like the devil!"

The overmountain men yelled loudly as they walked purposely through the forest toward the hilltop, pausing only to shoot when they saw a clear target and to reload their rifle. Some could reload while on the move; others were not as skilled and had to pause behind a tree, breaking the even flow of the skirmish line.

Remembering the same bloodcurdling sounds from past encounters, Captain DePeyster screamed, "It's those damned yelling boys again!"

Lieutenant Allaire hastily formed a mix of Provincials and militiamen into a double line when he heard and then saw the lead skirmishers of Campbell's regiment advancing steadily through the trees up the southeastern slope toward Allaire's position. The Provincial officer calmly shouted his command "Prime and load!" and the phalanx of sixty men, formed into two ranks, made a quarter turn as they brought their muskets to the priming position.

"Handle cartridge!" In unison, each man retrieved a cartridge from the ammunition box on his belt and held the end of the cartridge containing the ball in his right hand. Using his teeth, he ripped off a paper end and calmly spat it out.

Although sporadic rebel balls were now heard flying overhead and one man in the center of the first rank fell from a hit in his mouth, the Loyalists pulled their hammers back to a half-cock on the command of "Prime." Quickly, each placed a small amount of powder in the priming plan and closed the frizzen.

The Loyalist line held its basic formation as the jagged lines of mountain men became more visible and advanced steadily forward.

"About!"

As though on the parade field and seemingly oblivious to the growing chaos of flying balls around them, each Loyalist soldier dropped the butt of his musket to the ground and poured the remaining powder in the cartridge into the barrel, followed by the ball and wadded paper.

The veterans of previous battles calmly and swiftly followed through on succeeding commands: "Draw Ramrods!" and "Ram down the Cartridge!"

When Allaire yelled, "Present," fifty-nine muskets were locked into fifty-nine shoulders, their hammers pulled back, and the barrels pointing toward the attackers who fired as they emerged from the trees about sixty yards downslope. As the first rank kneeled and aimed, Allaire's detachment took its first hard look at the enemy coming toward them.

Before Campbell's ragged line reached fifty yards of the Loyalist formation, three more Loyalists fell. Allaire shouted, "Fire!" and twenty-six muskets spit out ball, flame and smoke in unison, decimating the first ranks of attackers. The opening fusillade killed Lieutenant Robert Edmonston and Ensign John Beattie and wounded several others. It stopped the Virginia line.

As partisans fell and staggered from the first onslaught of Loyalist fire, Allaire's second rank fired. The ad hoc company immediately leveled its muskets on Allaire's orders and charged into the Liberty Men with bayonets glistening at belly level. Having no defense against the rushing steel blades, the Virginians, who had not reloaded their rifles, turned, and ran back down the slopes, deeper into the forest. Allaire rode back and forth in the midst of his troops, swinging his sword and slashing out at any rebel he could reach. Seeing the wall of steel come toward them, the Virginians were terrified. Campbell and other officers ran among them, unable to stop and turn the Liberty Men back into the fight until a shrill whistle was heard and the Loyalists halted their charge and returned to the crest of the ridge.

Ferguson watched the charge with satisfaction. *Just as the rebel cowards ran before the bayonets at Camden, here they do as well.* From his right—on the southwest—where there had been the first sporadic shooting, a barrage of rifle fire was heard from another group of partisans—Shelby's men—as they emerged from the trees.

The shrill of Ferguson's whistle alerted his officers to the new danger.

Simultaneous with Allaire's counterattack, Captain Ryerson formed a protective line and, after preliminary musket fire, sent a phalanx of bayonets down toward Shelby's regiment. Like the Virginians, the Holston River men retreated hastily back down the hill into wooded cover, but not before a sharpshooter fatally unhorsed Ryerson, one of Ferguson's best officers.

As he began planning his next move, Ferguson was startled by sounds of battle behind him, from the north and west sides of the ridge. Shooting could be heard elsewhere to the east as well. The scope of the assault, much wider and more intense than expected, surprised him. Spread out to meet the growing threat, the Tory militia, for the most part, became a hodgepodge of makeshift fighting teams, with unit cohesion all but lost in the growing confusion. As one threat was neutralized, another developed elsewhere, causing Ferguson to quickly assign officers new sectors to defend with whatever troops that were close at hand. The hectic fluidity of the battle gave him no time make sense of the multiple enemy attacks. The constant shifting of troops to new hot spots made it more difficult to formulate a workable defense. He had yet to fathom that he was being surrounded.

When the bayonets were recalled from the short-lived charges, Campbell and Shelby quickly got their men back under control, and with rifles reloaded, they returned to the offensive, this time moving and shooting more deliberately. Shelby told his regiment, "Next time they charge with those pig stickers, get behind a tree and let 'em run right past you. Hack 'em with your ax or shoot 'em in the back!"

As skirmishers on the far-right flank of Campbell and Sevier's sectors, Jacob and four other Rangers led the Rutherford and Burke troops on a wide swing around to the eastern slopes of the ridge. The Rangers had replaced their hats with bandanas tied tightly around their heads like many other frontiersmen who knew that hats had a terrible habit of snagging on tree limbs and bushes. Jacob saw no pickets as he came in sight of Ferguson's tents and wagons, about sixty yards below the ridge line. The Loyalists were unprepared for an attack from the rear.

The Rutherford–Burke Liberty Men were maneuvering into position for their assault when they heard the first three shots from Shelby's sector. In the camp, teamsters and a few Tories on service details stood still and stared in the direction of the shooting, wondering what was happening. They had yet to see Hampton's Liberty Men approach.

Hearing the yells and shooting by Campbell's troops and then Sevier's, Hampton ordered his men to attack, catching the teamsters, commissary workers, prisoner guards, and other support personnel in the base camp unawares. Some Loyalists tried to resist and were shot. Others ran. The teamsters dropped to their knees, raised their arms, and begged, "Don't shoot! Don't shoot! We ain't soldiers."

Freed Whig prisoners of war picked up enemy dropped muskets and cartridge boxes and joined the fray.

Several of the Loyalists sprinted to the crest to join Ferguson's fighting units. Others fled into the forest, away from the battle. Many were shot down, including a woman called Virginia Sal. Another woman, Paulina, was found cowering under a wagon.

Charging into the base camp, Hampton's horse stumbled and fell, breaking its leg and sending the old colonel sprawling. Major McDowell, Jacob, and several others rushed to his side. "I'm all right," Hampton protested, brushing them aside; "I just got the wind knocked out of me."

He grabbed McDowell's shirt. "Major, you get our people up into that fight! My old bones can't keep up as good as I use to. I'll keep some men here to hold the wagons."

As McDowell turned to resume battle, Hampton yelled, "Show 'em the devil, boys!"

Biggerstaff's sharpshooters could see rebels about one hundred yards away, merging from the forest near the bottom of the hill's steepest slope on the northwestern corner on the ridge. Andrew, who reluctantly had joined the Tories, told Robert that he could not shoot the Liberty Men. Robert told him to shoot close to them and at least scare them. The Tory riflemen's first salvo caught Major Chronicle just as he raised his hat and yelled, "Face the hill, my brave lads!" Chronicle and William Rabb, who was advancing at Chronicle's side, were killed instantly. Three other South Fork men were wounded. Lieutenant Colonel Hambright immediately regrouped his partisans and led a second assault up the slope.

Inwardly, Ferguson nearly panicked when he saw rebels in his base camp below, yet his outward actions were displays of cool leadership. *Too much is happening to fast,* the seasoned officer thought. Despite his extensive combat experience in Europe and America, he had never witnessed such a chaotic situation. His training helped him focus on priorities such as regaining control of his supply wagons before his command ran out of ammunition. Ferguson quickly formed a provisional company from militiamen nearest to him and ordered Major Plummer to lead them and retake the supply wagons.

Seeing a counterattack forming, the handful of Whig militia guarding the captured camp area with Hampton used the wagons as redoubts and fired into Plummer's counterattack and slowed the Loyalist push. The partisan colonel knew he did not have the strength to withstand a sustained assault by more than three dozen Loyalists advancing toward them, but held his ground as he sent a runner to McDowell for help. He was much relieved when the Surry County troops came charging out of the trees from the northeast and hit Plummer's open flank. Additional help came from McDowell who broke off his assault on the hilltop and sent troops to help Hampton repel the Loyalist counterattack.

After leaving the Indian path to circle around the ridge on his approach to the battlefield, Major Joseph Winston's guide had led the Surry militia up a wrong hill north of Ferguson's position. When they heard shooting to their south, they quickly realized their mistake and ran through the forest to the sounds of battle. Their advance warriors opened fire as soon as they saw the Tories charging toward the wagons and Hampton's men. With devastating rifle fire, Winston's troops killed or wounded a third of Plummer's men, stopping the Loyalists attack cold. The king's men were then driven back up the ridge, licking their wounds. Plummer's retreat sealed the Loyalists' last avenue of escape. Ferguson's corps was now fully encircled.

The defenders faced many frustrations. No sooner had they forced back one attacking group than a multitude of threats emerged from behind them and on their flanks. Except for a few rocks along the crest and a couple of fallen trees, there was little protection from the mountain brigade's deadly rifles, many shooting well beyond musket range.

The Loyalists found many of their cartridges still damp from the heavy morning rain, making misfires far too common. After the first few minutes of battle, they didn't wait for orders; they shot as fast as they could reload their muskets, often more than two shots a minute. Some of the Tory militia armed with muskets had fewer cartridges than were normally issued when entering a battle and quickly ran out of ammunition.

The bayonet charge, second in terror only to a mass, heavy-cavalry charge, proved less effective on steep, wooded slopes around Kings Mountain. Usually, this tactic was decisive on an open battlefield with no obstructions to keep the deadly steel spears from moving as a massive spiked wall, cutting down everything in its front. At Kings Mountain, the forest forced the king's infantry to break apart its bayonet formations as men skirted around trees, rocks, and uneven ground. After the first two charges, the Liberty Men became adept at countering the deadly bayonet attacks. Hiding behind trees and letting the redcoats run past them, they hacked the enemy in the back and then shot Loyalists when they began returning to the hilltop. Snipers worked from the flanks to eliminate the enemy officers and sergeants. With Loyalist leadership being depleted, the unfavorable terrain, and the unconventional style of fighting by the rebels, bayonets became less effective in forging control of the battlefield.

Ferguson did not know how shallow each of the partisan's scattered lines was. Nor was he aware that the rebel army had no reserve. Had he known, he could have, in the first half of the battle, massed his forces and easily punched through the attackers. Ferguson believed there were far more rebels than actually existed. Protected by the trees, the Liberty Men kept up a blistering rain of ball from all sides of the ridge, causing the Loyalists to falter time and again, weaker each time they reorganized. He desperately tried to counter each onslaught, but after the first thirty-five minutes of action, he found it difficult to mass sufficient firepower in any one direction. To bolster pockets of defenders, he continually moved squads of dragoons from one hot spot to another.

The Loyalists had difficulty shooting down over the curve of the crest without unduly exposing themselves; many of their shots went high over the attackers. When they did get exposed enough to see their enemy through the smoke, they were targeted by the backwoods sharpshooters.

The partisans, particularly the seasoned hunters, were patient in their shooting. Just as they had hunted deer, most propped their rifle against a tree as a steady platform and waited for a Loyalist head to appear over the crest. The mountain men were used to shooting in hill country and easily adjusted to elevation changes when aiming their rifles. This was ideal ground for their style of fighting. The attackers had an abundance of protection within the forest while the defenders had little to hide behind and were caught in deadly crossfire.

Jacob was shooting sparingly, only one round ever four to five minutes and only at targets he could clearly identify through breaks in the thick, acrid smoke that shrouded the battlefield, making visibility difficult at best. Many of the partisans just shot into the billowing clouds of sulfur and nitrate without concern as to whether or not they hit an enemy. When there was an occasional clearing in the haze, Jacob would pick off an officer on horseback, a sergeant directing troops, or a Tory sniper. Once, looking over in

Sevier's sector, he saw a redcoat aiming at a mountain man who was looking in another direction. The Liberty Man never knew Jacob had saved his life.

Gradually, the attacking Liberty Men wore the defenders down with deadly fire from all sides of the ridge. Campbell's division of overmountain men began pushing the Loyalists back northward along the ridge top and into compact groups, bunching them into even easier targets for the partisan sharpshooters. When a Tory militia fighter ran out of ammunition, he usually threw up his hands and called for quarters, but the blood lust among the Liberty Men was high. Many requests for mercy went unheeded. Some were answered with a shouted "Tarleton's quarters," in reference to rumors from earlier in the summer that Tarleton's Legion had slaughtered a large number of Virginia troops after they had surrendered in a battle at the Waxhaws. Little compassion was exhibited toward those serving the Crown.

During the early stages of fighting, William Godley became separated from his brothers and was running to help fill in a weak defensive position when a ball shattered his kneecap. He lay in pain for nearly fifteen minutes while the battle raged around him; then his comrades retreated past him. As the mountain men advanced, William raised his arm in surrender. His plea for mercy was ignored by a buckskin-clad frontiersman who smashed the butt of his rifle into the side of William's head, knocking him into a daze. As he struggled to sit up again, another rebel slashed William across the back of his neck with a tomahawk, severing his spinal cord and causing a speedy death.

As with most of the riflemen, Jacob moved steadily from tree to tree, inching his way toward the crest of the smoke-clogged ridge. His face was streaked with carbon from the burnt powder, his eyes stung from the smoke, his thoughts only on the task at hand, the threats he could see. He shot whenever he could make out a target and verify that it was not one of his brothers. Standing behind a tree each time after shooting, he calmly poured a new measure of powder into the barrel and put a ball down the barrel which he followed with a greased patch. As though he were at muster training, Jacob calmly used his ramrod to push the projectile and packing to the base of the barrel. He replaced the rammer into the ramrod pipes below the barrel, once remembering a hapless volunteer who, in his excitement, failed to secure the rod and then, after moving to another location, was unable to tamp his charge when reloading his weapon.

Nearer to the crest, the trees thinned. Although there was less cover from enemy fire, the volume of fire from the defenders also became less intense. Jacob made his way through the smoke to a small rock formation about midway along the edge of the crest. He watched as partisans swooped down on wounded Loyalists, many with hands up in surrender, begging for mercy, only to be stabbed, clubbed, hacked, or shot at close range. Not all the Loyalists gave up so easily. Some of the Tories caused bloody causalities among the Liberty Men as they bravely fought back in scattered hand-to-hand melees. To Jacob, it was a devil's cauldron.

Advancing amid the carnage, Jacob recognized Aaron Biggerstaff lying on the ground clutching his midsection. Bending down on his knee, Jacob asked the Tory captain, "How bad are you hurt, Mister Biggerstaff?"

"Bad. Gut shot," Biggerstaff gasped as he gradually brought Jacob into focus. "Are you the one who done me in?"

"Don't think so," Jacob replied. "Where are my brothers?"

"Robert is on the other side of this rock. He's down too. Don't know about the others."

Jacob stood and looked around the rock. Amid the litter of bodies, some squirming in pain, some still, he saw Robert trying to sit up, blood flowing from holes in his chest and right arm. Rushing to his brother, Jacob was grateful that Robert was still alive. He pulled Robert to a more protected location out of the flow of combatants. "You'll be all right," Jacob said, not convinced of his own words.

Although confused for a moment, Robert recognized his brother. "Guess Papa was right about this war after all," he managed to say with a slight smile. Then grimacing from his wounds, Robert desperately asked, "Andy was near me; do you see him?"

Jacob cut strips of Robert's shirt, which he put over the bleeding wounds. "Let me see if I can find him. You be still. Plug the bleeding with this cloth."

It took less than a minute for Jacob to find Andrew who was face down about fifteen yards away. Andrew had jumped up when he saw Robert fall and was running to his brother's side when a ball slammed through his throat, cutting his jugular vein and smashing his larynx. He had bled to death quickly, unable to call out to his oldest brother.

Jacob screamed, "Andy!" and lifted his blood-drenched sibling into his arms. Oblivious to the battle din around him, Jacob dragged Andy's body over next to Robert. "He's dead!" Jacob sobbed to his eldest brother.

No longer rebel and Loyalist, they were brothers clinging to each other, stupefied with grief. "This is all my fault," Robert cried in anguish. "Andy didn't want to come, but I made him. Forgive me, dear God. Please forgive me."

"It's fate, brother. It's nobody's fault. He'd gone back home if he really wanted to."

"Andy ain't no coward. He's a man of his word," Robert whispered, his strength draining.

Two Rangers who had been advancing with Jacob directed other Liberty Men away, protecting the Godley brothers from further harm. Jacob had no sense of the protectors as he looked after his brothers.

Robert grabbed Jacob's sleeve and shouted, "Will? Where's Will?"

Jacob searched the bodies near him and did not see his other Tory brother. "He's not here. Maybe he's still fighting somewhere."

"At least Wayne is safe at home," Robert continued.

"I think he's safe, but not at home," Jacob replied. "He joined our militia last week, but he didn't have a horse. We left the footmen behind yesterday so those of us on horseback could catch up with y'all before you reached Cornwallis. Thank God he doesn't have to see this horror."

Wayne and a gaggle of footmen heard the first sounds of battle before they crossed Kings Creek. In groups of two or three and sometimes as solitary fighters, the footmen increased their loping pace to join in the fighting. Wayne arrived behind Cleveland's regiment, which was now moving onto the crest. Without pausing, he ran up the slope and neared the top only to be knocked back by a single two-third's-inch-diameter musket ball crashing into his forehead, killing him before his body sprawled backward on the ground, before he celebrated his sixteenth birthday, before he had a chance to fire a single shot and experience the exhilaration of battle.

On the other side of the ridge from Wayne, Preston Goforth was with the Rutherford troops and saw a Tory aim his musket at him. He fired at the adversary before he too fell dead, not knowing whether he hit his target or not.

Several Loyalist officers tried to raise white cloths in surrender only to have them knocked down by Ferguson. "We fight, m'lads, for God and king! Use your bayonets and make them bleed. Fight on! Fight on!"

Noting that the rebels had taken the southern third of the ridge and were continuing to press hard with increasing ferocity, DePeyster pleaded with his commander that the situation was futile. "The rebels are using us like a turkey shoot. We must stop this slaughter now, sir."

"We haven't lost yet. I will not give up!" Ferguson snapped. He already had several horses shot out from under him, and his shirtsleeve was bloodied from a flesh wound that went untended. He raced back and forth, setting the example of courage as he cajoled his fighters to be more aggressive in countering the rebels. "Form a new line. Give them another taste of steel!"

James Withrow somehow had gotten his company in the wrong column back when the mountain brigade approached Kings Mountain. Instead of the division with his Rutherford regiment, he went into battle with Cleveland's division. There were many similar mix-ups throughout the hastily formed attack. After the shooting started, however, it did not matter. It became a close and personal battle within dozens of clusters around the hill.

When the enemy was identified, Withrow's riflemen formed a skirmish line and steadily made their way up the western slope toward the ridge top. As the attack picked up momentum, he ran to keep up with his men who were flush with adrenalin and felt victory at hand. He was running past fallen defenders—some wounded, some dead—when a wounded Loyalist called out to him, "Jim! Jim Withrow! Help me, please."

Captain Tom Brandon[1], Withrow's Tory brother-in-law, was lying in a pool of his own blood, doubled over in pain, shot twice in the body. "Call your friends for help, I've got a fight to win," Withrow scoffed and rushed past his wife's fallen brother.

Colonel Ambrose Mills saw his son fall and gathered remnants of his regiment into a protective circle around the young major who was still breathing, but in considerable pain. Mills had no intention of leaving his son to the whims of frontier barbarians.

With the circle of rebels getting tighter and the defender's casualties mounting at an alarming rate, DePeyster again urged Ferguson to raise the white flag. Again the commander refused. DePeyster pleaded. "Sir, we are beat! At least see if you can get some of us out. We'll try to follow you."

---

1   There were two Thomas Brandons in the Kings Mountain battle. Col. Thomas Brandon of the South Carolina Whig Militia fought as a captain under Col. James Williams.

Although Ferguson knew the situation was hopeless, he could not admit it. "Get a horse, follow me!" he yelled to those around him. "We'll break through their lines on the northeast; that's where they are the weakest."

DePeyster formed a double line of about thirty men with bayonets to fire a volley and charge into the Lincoln County sector as the senior officers on horseback began galloping toward the rebel lines with sabers swinging. Ferguson's distinctive blue-and-white hunting shirt made him the most recognizable target on the hill. He charged down the slope through a clearing in the grey smoke, his bloody left arm swinging his saber, his reins in his mouth as his useless right arm flapped by his side. Within seconds, eight balls slammed into Patrick Ferguson's body, knocking him from the saddle. One foot became entangled in the stirrup, and he was dragged another fifty yards before two Loyalists stopped the frightened and badly wounded horse.

Lieutenant Colonel Husbands and Major Plummer rode with Ferguson on the desperate attempt to escape. Both were quickly shot out of their saddles, Husbands killed instantly and Plummer seriously wounded. Both of their horses were slain. The attempt to escape by a small group of Loyalists failed almost as quickly as it was launched.

"Enough," DePeyster shouted after seeing Ferguson fall. Feeling helpless, he tied a white handkerchief to his sword and raised it high, yelling again, "Stop shooting. It's over. We beg quarters."

Shelby shouted back, "If you want quarters, put your guns down on the ground now!"

Two hundred feet away, but out of sight of the accepted surrender, Colonel James Williams led his South Carolinians into another melee before suffering the devastating blow of a musket ball into his mid torso. His men were stunned, then angered at their commander being shot. With hardly a pause, and despite the frantic calls to cease fire, the South Carolinians renewed their attack with greater vengeance, ignoring cries for mercy and surrender from their overwhelmed adversaries. They blindly kept killing or maiming any Loyalist within their reach.

Stopping the killing frenzy was no easy task for the partisan commanders. Officers and sergeants had to grab some of the shooters to make them quit. John Sevier stood in front of his own son's rifle barrel, forcing the sixteen-year-old to stop shooting into a huddle of prisoners. James Sevier was in a rage because he thought he had seen his father fall in battle, only to learn later that it was his uncle who had been mortally wounded.

Gaining some order within the chaos, the victors forced the Loyalists to lay down all weapons and remove belts and hats. Loyalist officers surrendered their swords to any partisan officer they could find, most of whom had no swords or were not even familiar with the formal surrender customs of more civilized warfare. The rank-and-file prisoners were segregated into a different area from their officers. Both groups were moved into tight clusters with guards posted around them. Most of the captives were numb and in shock from the ferocious fight they had just survived and lost.

Although demoralized, many, like Rance Miller, were both angry and scared. No longer the arrogant terrorist, Miller quickly and discreetly discarded his sword, gorget and red sash that indicated his officer status. He threw away his distinctive feathered tricorn and hoped that he could hide among the privates until finding an opportunity to slip away without being identified. There was a high price on his head.

To many, the battle seemed to last only seconds; to others, if felt like an eternity. Uzal Johnson, the Provincials' surgeon from New Jersey, recorded the first shot at three o'clock in the afternoon. After the last shot was sounded, he looked again at his pocket watch and recorded that only sixty-one minutes had elapsed. His work had just begun.

27
BITTERSWEET VICTORY
7 October 1780

Jacob paid no heed to the change in the battle's tempo. He stayed with his two brothers, one needing comfort, the other beyond pain. Captain Withrow saw Jacob and called to him, asking, "Where's Colonel Hampton? Are these our men?"

Jacob looked up. "These are my brothers, Robert and Andy. They were Tories with Aaron Biggerstaff. He's near-dead on the other side of the rock. Don't know where the colonel is."

Withrow knelt beside Jacob, placed his hand on the Ranger's shoulder, and said softly, "Sorry, but it's my sad duty to tell you that William is dead as well. I passed his body on the other side of the hill."

Robert moaned and whispered desperately, "I need to see him. Help me."

"Robert, you are not in any shape to move at all. I'll get somebody to bring William to you and Jacob," Withrow said.

Now that the enemy was conquered decisively, Withrow replaced animosity with compassion. He walked around the rock to his Tory neighbor Aaron Biggerstaff and tried to comfort him. Biggerstaff nodded and said weakly, "Guess we won't get to sit out with a jug by the creek and tell war stories in our old age, Jim."

"Sure we will, Aaron. You just got a little nick."

"I'm kilt, Jim. Gut wounds are lingering death," Biggerstaff moaned.

"I've got to look after my men now, but I'll be back shortly," Withrow said as he started to stand up. "By the by, William Godley is dead. I saw his body a while ago. His brother Andy is gone too, and Robert is in a bad way."

Tears formed in Biggerstaff's eyes as he whispered, "Such good, brave lads. I failed them so."

Withrow saw Jim Gray and William Walker inspecting the dead and wounded, looking for people they knew. The captain told them about the Godley tragedy and asked them to carry William Godley's body over to where Jacob and his two brothers were. Walker knew all the Godley family, but Gray knew only Jacob. They readily agreed and recruited George Bluebird to help them carry the body.

Men on both sides were exhausted after the intense fight. The mountain brigade had traveled more than forty miles in thirty-six hours without sleep and much of the time in the rain, but somehow they kept functioning. While some collapsed into a stupor, others recognized much more work had to be done. The wounded had to be cared for, prisoners guarded, rifles cleaned, enemy weapons and powder collected, the dead buried, wounded horses euthanized. Dozens of men replenished their powder and ammunition by recovering unused cartridges, picking up spent balls, and prying lead from trees.

Since the long rifles were not fitted for bayonets, the prisoner guards slung their own hunting weapons over their shoulders and used confiscated British muskets mounted with sharp bayonets to maintain order. With their anger still high, guards were not hesitant to poke any captive Loyalist who looked like he was trying to escape or even sass a guard, and some guards ignored their own officers by stabbing their captives just out of spite.

Colonel Campbell assigned details from the various regiments the grim task of sorting the human litter of battle and moving the wounded to a field hospital set up at the tent camp where Tory and Whig physicians, mostly self-taught wilderness healers, worked side by side to staunch open wounds and do what patchwork that they could. Loyalist physician Uzal Johnson took charge of surgery; he had more experience than the frontier doctors who had little or no formal medical training. All were now allies in the healing campaign.

Some Liberty Men refused to help a redcoat or Tory; however, most believed that since the fighting was over, it was their Christian duty to assist any man found suffering. Contrasting examples of hatred and compassion were numerous throughout the battlefield.

Searchers first thought Wayne Godley's body was that of a Tory, but Withrow, who was looking for one of his missing men, recognized the barefooted Godley boy. "Go fetch Colonel Hampton. Tell him it's important," he instructed one of his privates.

Hampton, his clothes muddy and rumpled, was using an improvised walking stick as he limped slowly to where Jacob sat with his three brothers. With an audible grunt, the old colonel plopped down on a rock; the fall from his horse an hour earlier hurt more than he cared to admit. Jacob watched and listened to Robert rasping from a punctured lung. At first, the Ranger didn't acknowledge Hampton when the colonel began talking softly, "Jacob, I'm terribly sorry about your brothers. This is a painful loss for your family."

"Thank you, sir," Jacob mumbled but wished silently that people would leave him alone in his grief.

"I am afraid there is more bad news," Hampton continued. "It's your other brother...the lad who joined us just a week ago and walked all the way here from Green River. A ball caught him in the forehead. He died facing the enemy, a brave young soldier of liberty."

Jacob turned to face his commander, shaking his head in disbelief and crying, "No! Not Wayne! This is too much, too much. How do I tell Mama and Papa?"

Two of Withrow's men brought Wayne's slender body and laid it gently beside his brothers. Robert turned his bleary eyes to look briefly at his baby brother and then breathed his last breath.

Despite shouted huzzahs and boastful jubilation after the battle, it was a bittersweet victory for some. The Godleys weren't the only family tragedies that day.

Preston Goforth and all three of his Tory brothers died in that battle. Three Edmonston brothers from Campbell's Virginia militia were killed. Joseph Henry from Lincoln County's South Fork area had two brothers, John and Moses, shot dead. Joseph was wounded. Daniel and Joseph Williams watched their father, Colonel James Williams, fall with fatal wounds near the end of the battle. Enoch Berry from the Burke County Whigs saw his father fall and his brother carried from the field wounded. Colonel John Sevier's brother Robert was mortally wounded and died before he could return home.

Nor were the Godleys the only family with split loyalties at Kings Mountain. In addition to the four Goforths, there were five divided Camp brothers, also from Rutherford County, with three fighting for the Whigs and two for the Tories. None of the Camps was hurt. Four Logan brothers from Lincoln County were split equally in their loyalties. John Logan, a Tory, suffered a severe leg wound and was left on the battlefield.

Remembering his brother-in-law, Captain Withrow made his way back to where he last saw Thomas Brandon lying in pain. Someone had propped the wounded Tory against a tree, his lower torso soaked in blood. He was not taken to the makeshift hospital; only those with a chance of survival were carried there. Bending over to see how bad Brandon was hurt, Withrow consoled him. "Sorry I couldn't help earlier, Tom. But I had my duty first."

"I'm dead anyway, Jim, or will be before sunup," the gravely wounded Tory said. "Will you tell my sister and wife that I love them? I know I haven't done for them like I should, but I was right in my cause. Ask my wife to forgive me for making Josiah come with me."

"Josiah is here?" Withrow asked in dismay.

"Yes. I just pray that he's not hurt. Will you find him for me, Jim?"

Withrow did not ask why his nephew had joined the enemy. When he last saw Josiah earlier in the year, the boy was in McDowell's regiment, serving on the Indian line. Rather than searching the scores of bodies scattered about, he first went to where the prisoners were clustered in a tight group. Withrow did not know the captain of the guard, one of the overmountain men, but told him about the situation. "If he's here, you can take him to his pa. But you are responsible for getting him back," the guard officer said.

Josiah was deeply depressed, scared, and on the verge of tears. He had not seen his father among the prisoners and was afraid some of his Whig neighbors with whom he had served in the militia would recognize him and cause him harm. Already he had seen dozens of instances of vengeful meanness where Liberty Men clubbed, stoned and, in one case, stabbed their Tory neighbors from home. He jerked his head up when he heard his named called several times. Dreading the worse, he stood up and was relieved to see his uncle standing next to several guards.

Josiah slowly made his way through defeated Loyalists, keeping his head down, unable to look Withrow in the eye. Surprisingly, his uncle did not rebuke him for joining the king's forces; instead, Withrow spoke softly.

"Josiah, your papa is in a bad way. He's gut-shot and dying. He wants to see you. If you promise not to try to escape, I'll take you to him."

"I promise," Josiah said.

As they walked to where his father lay bleeding, Josiah explained why he came to be on the wrong side at Kings Mountain. Withrow hardly listened; no reason justified his nephew switching loyalties.

The price for the one-hour melee was 244 Loyalists dead, including Ferguson, the only British soldier in the battle. Wounded were 163 of the king's men. Another 668 were captured. Only a handful of Loyalists escaped the mountain. The Liberty Men suffered twenty-eight killed and sixty-four wounded. It was a complete victory for the mountain brigade, far greater than that imagined before the fight.

After the wounded were collected, prisoners worked until dark taking their dead comrades to a central place for mass burial. The mountain men collected their dead in a separate location. Other Liberty Men systematically dispatched horses wounded beyond repair, some crying more for the horse than a human carcass next to it. When it became dark, most grisly tasks were suspended until morning. Some efforts continued through the night to comfort the wounded, although there was little with which to provide relief from pain or anguish.

Some of the victors wanted Ferguson's body paraded around as a trophy. Many ripped his clothing apart, taking shreds of his shirt and breeches, buttons, and even his silver whistles as souvenirs. Desecration of their commander's body horrified Loyalist officers who begged their captors to show respect for the dead. Ferguson's body was carried to a point by a small stream where, at Lieutenant Allaire's insistence, Virginia Sal was laid next to him. The bodies were entombed under rocks stacked several feet deep.

When men from both sides walked by Ferguson's grave site that evening and the next morning, many tossed another stone on the tomb in salute. Several of the rebels, however, showed their disdain by urinating on the grave.

Among the partisan officers, there was still the nagging fear of Tarleton's Legion showing up and causing havoc, even reversing the battle's outcome. They were too close to the British Army to become lax in vigilance.

Word spread around the ridge about the Godley and Goforth brothers. Those who knew Jacob tried to console him. Sevier and Shelby both came by with brief words of condolence. Colonel Campbell, whose regiment suffered the most casualties, took a moment to remind Jacob that grieving would have to come later; there were other critical matters at hand.

Once, an officer who did not know Jacob tried to push him to help clean up the battlefield. Only the intervention of friends kept Jacob from taking the officer's head with his belt ax. Hampton saw the situation and scooted the insensitive officer to the other side of the ridge.

Bluebird was with Jacob when his young friend calmly took his patch knife and cut locks of hair from each of his brothers. A small square of cloth was cut from each of the victim's shirts and meticulously folded around the tresses of each brother. These Jacob would give to his mother so she would have a memento of her sons.

Jacob looked over at the Indian. "See that little rise over yonder, about three hundred paces or so?"

Bluebird nodded.

"That's where I'm going to bury my brothers. I don't want 'em thrown in a pile with all those other Tory bastards. We've been split apart as a family far too long. In death, we need to be together. Mama would want that. Can you help me carry them over there?"

"Jacob, you go on over and mark off where you want to bury 'em. I'll get some of the fellows to bring your brothers along," Bluebird said gently.

When the bodies were brought to him, Jacob did not pause from his task of loosening the damp soil with his belt ax and scooping the dirt aside with his hands. He nodded his gratitude to those who brought the bodies and his brothers' rifles to the burial site. Bluebird went to the British wagons and found a pick and two spades that he took after staring down the sergeant in charge of keeping the wagons from being looted. Speaking firmly with unmistakable determination, Bluebird said, "I need these tools to bury four brave men, and if you try to stop me, you will be the fifth to eat dirt."

They made one massive hole four feet deep, six-feet-by-six-feet square. Jacob did most of the digging and chopping through buried roots, but let his friends spell him a couple of times. Bluebird ripped down a Loyalist tent and used the canvas for the floor of the grave. Jacob gently placed the bodies side by side, with the two bigger ones, Robert and William, on the outside, and then folded the makeshift shroud over the corpses.

There were no words, no prayers, no tears; just a silent good-bye. With the burial done, Jacob sat next to the grave, leaned back against a large poplar tree, and drifted into a fitful sleep filled with vivid dreams of his brothers dying over and over again. The most disturbing part of the nightmares that haunted him for days to come was the nagging question, *Why not me?*

Preposterous Victory

8–12 October 1780

Jacob awoke in a fog of bewilderment. It took several moments for him to orient himself in the dull grey of predawn before the horror of his brothers' violent deaths swept over him. Someone had put his sleeping robe over him to ward off the chill. When he saw the fresh dirt of his brothers' grave, he tried to stifle a wail, but then gave into the grief for a few minutes. A canteen appeared before his face, and he looked up to see George Bluebird and William Walker standing above him. They had cleaned his rifle and retrieved his horse.

"You ready to go back to work?" Walker asked gently.

Jacob nodded and looked up at the hill above where men were already scurrying about moving bodies. Whiffing around him was the stench of death with a mixture of burnt powder, vomit, feces, and blood. The air echoed with moans from the wounded.

Prisoners under heavy guard carried their dead colleagues to a pile on the south end of the ridge. Another group of prisoners used sticks and rocks to scoop out dirt for a shallow mass grave.

Walking up the hill, Jacob recognized among the Tories something familiar about a big man lifting a body – *Rance Miller!* With that realization, Jacob erupted into an uncontrollable rage and rushed Miller, swinging his rifle butt to smash the terrorist's head. In his peripheral vision, Miller saw the attack coming just in time to deflect much of the force, but not enough to keep from being knocked down and suffering a bloody mouth. Walker, Bluebird, and two guards grabbed Jacob and pulled him back before he could swing the weapon again, while other guards quickly herded prisoners away from the altercation.

"What's going on here?" Colonel Campbell roared as he ran over to where Jacob was being restrained. Captain Singleton, Hampton's number two since Major Porter was wounded in yesterday's battle, followed him. Furious, Campbell demanded of Jacob, "Why are you disobeying my orders against harming prisoners?"

"That's Rance Miller there…the murdering son of Satan…hiding like a coward with the privates," Jacob screamed.

Turning to Singleton, Campbell asked about Jacob, "Is this one of your men?"

"Yes sir!"

"Then get him under control. He's not the only one who lost kin on this battlefield. If he doesn't behave, have him flogged in front of the prisoners."

Campbell turned and stomped off before Singleton could mutter, "Yes, sir."

As other guards were now hustling Miller away, Singleton tried to hold in his own anger. He was not as close to Jacob as was the colonel; but though he felt sympathy for the Ranger's staggering family loss, they were part of a militia unit and duty came first. "Do you have your senses about you now, *Private* Godley?" he snarled.

Jacob felt the emotional energy drain from his body as he replied, "I'm all right, Cap'n. But that was the bastard who had my brother flogged in front of my mama and papa. He hung poor Patrick Pearson just a month ago, murdered his papa, beat his mama, and burned their house. Why is he still alive?"

"He'll have to be tried by law first," Singleton said. "Then we'll hang him. I'll talk to Colonel Hampton about it."

Turning to Walker, Singleton said, "Lieutenant, get your Rangers together, including this hothead"—he pushed his finger toward Jacob— "and go out to where we crossed Kings Creek yesterday and set up a guard post until we get everybody away from here. As soon as the bodies get buried, we're heading back to the hills before the real British Army gets here."

Walking to where the colonels were gathered, Singleton passed Jim Gray bandaging the leg of a wounded Tory and called to him. "Leave that scum be, Mister Gray. We've more important chores this day. You are needed for a picket with your Ranger friends."

Gray looked up to the captain and said defiantly, "This Tory is my neighbor. He's a good Christian man, honest in his conviction. He deserves a helping hand, and I'm giving it to him."

Singleton only grunted and stomped away.

The dominant worry among the commanders this morning was Banastre Tarleton coming with his legion to avenge the mauling given to Ferguson's command. While the Liberty Men were not lacking in bravery, the battle had depleted much personal energy as well as powder and ball. It would be difficult, if not impossible, to withstand a determined attack by a smaller unit of professional soldiers.

The sun was barely up when the first of nearby residents began arriving at the mountain. They had heard the massive shooting and seen the smoke rising from the ridge during the late afternoon before, but many feared venturing into the battle site at night. Some came by foot, others on horseback, a few by carts. One woman, around forty years old but looking much older, was standing on an ox-drawn sledge. She stopped as she reached Jacob's post and asked, "Excuse me, sir. Have you seen my husband? His name is Preston Goforth."

"I've met him once, ma'am," Jacob answered, "but I ain't seen him since we left the cow pens."

"We live just aways over yonder," she said, pointing to the northwest. "I have a fearful feeling he might be shot here. Where would the other soldiers be?"

Jacob pointed her up toward the ridge and wished her good fortune in finding her husband. He learned later that all the Goforth brothers had perished in the battle.

By midmorning, the captives were lined up and flanked by mounted guards on each side with orders to shoot anyone trying to escape. Before marching from the battlefield, each prisoner was required to carry a captured musket, minus the flint. The stronger ones carried two of the ten-pound weapons. More than twelve hundred muskets and rifles were confiscated after the fight. All prisoners, including officers, were forced to leave their shoes, which were quickly picked through by the Liberty Men, some who were barefooted and others with footwear falling apart from the long, rugged trek to Kings Mountain. For the first time, several of the poorer partisans enjoyed the luxury of professionally made shoes.

Colonel Shelby took charge of the prisoner detail while Campbell kept his regiment behind to bury the dead Liberty Men. The wounded Tories who couldn't walk were left on the battlefield to be cared for by people who lived nearby, if they were so inclined. Most would be taken in by local residents before day's end.

Some of the more seriously wounded Liberty Men were also abandoned after the victims chose to stay behind rather than ride in a bouncy wagon or be draped on a horse. Although not expected to live, Colonel Williams was carried on a stretcher fitted between two horses. Several of his men walked next to him and tried to comfort him. Williams died several hours after leaving Kings Mountain.

Two dozen wounded partisans who were unable to ride a horse were packed into four captured wagons, layered with a foot of hay and leaves to ease the jolting trip back to mountains. Confiscated powder, bayonets, grain, and the officers' baggage were crammed into three other wagons. The remaining wagons were rolled across campfires and burned with tentage and other material not taken by the Liberty Men.

In Charlotte Town that Sunday morning and oblivious to the disaster thirty-three miles to the west, Tarleton again informed Cornwallis that he had not recovered enough to take to the field. The general still felt that Ferguson could handle twice his number of rebel militia, and did not worry too much about his western flank. The issue could wait another day; he had enough other problems with the local partisans. After attending church services conducted by an Anglican priest, Lord Cornwallis wrote home: *This is a pleasant village, but a damnable hornet's nest of rebellion.*

The victorious army marched only twelve miles before making camp on the northeastern side of Broad River, near the mouth of Buffalo Creek. They met the brigade's remaining footmen who had marched up from cow pens after a day of rest and stuffing themselves on Saunders's beef. The footmen who were not in the fight took over guard duties, giving the battle veterans a much-needed rest. Foragers searching nearby found a large patch of sweet potatoes with enough tubers to feed most of the army and its prisoners that evening. There was scarcely anything else to eat.

After his detachment arrived in camp that evening, William Walker reported to Colonel Hampton that Jacob was determined to kill Rance Miller. The threat, he emphasized, was not idle. Hampton walked over to the Rangers' campfire where Jacob was chewing on a half-cooked yam. "Mister Godley, I need you to do something for me."

"Whatever you want, Colonel," Jacob answered nonchalantly.

"When you get through eating, I want you and Lieutenant Walker to ride on to my place tonight and tell my son Jonathon to gather enough food-stuffs to feed all our boys and prisoners. We should be either at Gilbert's or Walker's place in the next couple of days.

"Let everyone know that Ferguson and his Tories have paid dearly for the harm they caused our county." Then speaking much softer, Hampton added, "And Jacob, stop letting this hate eat you up. Go see your folks and let them know about your brothers. Stay with them as long as you like."

"Thank you for your kindness, Colonel," Jacob said without standing up, "but what about Rance Miller? He's got to pay for his sinful ways. I have to see to that."

"Believe me, he will pay," Hampton said firmly. "But he will be handled in a proper way as will the other brigands."

As Jacob prepared to leave, he confided in George Bluebird his disappointment over being sent away. Bluebird promised that he would keep an eye on Miller and make sure he did not escape.

Jacob and Walker left camp in the dark and rode four hours up the narrow road before stopping for a few hours sleep. They were up before dawn the next day and arrived at Hampton's plantation by midafternoon; their news was received ecstatically. Along the way, they told everyone they passed—Whig and Tory—about the magnificent victory. Only Jacob could not bring himself to be jubilant.

It was dark when Jacob arrived at his family's home, burdened with guilt and dreading the task ahead. He entered the front yard and yelled his arrival so those inside would not suspect an enemy, "It's me, Jacob. I'm home."

His father opened the door and was silhouetted by the candles glowing on the table behind them. Crowding next to him was his mother. His two sisters, excited that one of their big brothers had returned, ran to the door in their night shifts.

"Welcome home, son," George Godley called out, "Praise Lord, we are so happy to see you again."

Jacob choked at the sight of his family. A crushing force that he could not explain prevented him from taking another step or speaking. He just looked at them in the half-light, his voice not functioning, his lips quivering, his eyes watering.

"What's wrong, Jacob?" his mother asked as she moved toward her son, a deep worry clouding her face.

Looking at the dried blood caked on Jacob's clothes, sensing her son's mood and praying that he did not bring unwelcome news, she demanded, "Who died?"

Jacob choked back the tears swelling in his eyes and mumbled, "Brother."

"Which one?" George demanded, anxious but fearing what his son might say.

"All," Jacob whispered.

"All?" his father asked incredulously, "Robert? William? Andrew?"

"Yes, Papa, and Wayne too."

Agatha Godley collapsed to the ground, her fist jammed into her mouth trying to muffle a scream that pierced the evening quiet. Her husband staggered back against the wall of their house, dumfounded, as the two girls rushed to console their mother. Jacob still could not move.

"How?" George muttered.

"We had a big battle at a place called Kings Mountain, two...three days' ride from here. I thought Wayne was left behind with the footmen. But he somehow kept up with the horses.

"It was a complete victory for liberty, Papa. A near massacre too. All the king's men that weren't killed or wounded were taken prisoner. I found Andy and Robert lying with Aaron Biggerstaff. Mister Biggerstaff was gut-shot, but still alive when I left him. Some friends brought William and Wayne to me. Robert was the only one still alive when I got there, but he died soon after. He told me to tell you he loved you all and was awful sorry he took the boys to war."

Jacob bent down to help his mother up. He and his sisters led Agatha, still numb from shock, back into the house. Although death was common on the frontier, losing four sons at one time was difficult to bear. However, she quickly composed herself and asked Jacob, "Have Robert's and William's wives been told?"

"No ma'am."

"Then we will go to them first thing in the morning. Poor dears."

After he had refused anything to eat, his mother and sisters went to bed for a sleepless night. Jacob sat on a bench, staring at the lone candle flame as he told his father, "Papa, I didn't shoot them. I made sure every shot I took was aimed at somebody I didn't know. But the place was covered in smoke so thick you could hardly see the man to your side. Men were falling and yelling and crying and killing. It was awful. The noise was so loud you could hear it for miles. We surrounded 'em and kept shooting. Even after they gave up, some of our boys just kept on killing. It was terrible...terrible."

Jacob was now sobbing. "I know I didn't shoot my brothers, but I killed them just the same. I shouldn't have gone with the militia. I should've made Wayne stay home."

"Stop blaming yourself, boy. It's God's will, not yours." George placed his arm around his son's shoulder and tried to console him. "Get yourself together. You need to be strong for Mama...and for me."

Jacob told how he had wrapped his brothers in sailcloth before digging and marking a single grave separate from the mass graves. George said they would take the wagon and go get his dead sons as soon as it was safe to travel. He wanted to bring them home for a more proper burial.

The next morning, the family loaded into a wagon and took the distressing news to the young widows of Robert and William. After telling his sisters-in-law about their husbands deaths, Jacob left his parents with them and rode on to inform Mary Biggerstaff about her husband. When asked how serious the Tory captain was hurt, Jacob answered straightforward, "He was gut shot, ma'am. But he was alive when I left. People living in the area are helping the wounded what can't travel."

Both knew that a belly wound was nearly always fatal. Biggerstaff's sister Martha, who was staying at the home to help Mary with the children, asked Jacob sarcastically, "Did you shoot my brother?"

"No ma'am. I always liked Mister Biggerstaff. I wouldn't shoot him any more than my own brothers, even if we were enemies."

"And what about my husband?" Martha asked.

"I saw him with the prisoners. He didn't look hurt."

"It took a lot of grit for you to come here, Jacob," Mary said. "I hate the news. I hate your rebel cause. But, still, I appreciate you caring enough to come and tell us."

Three days after the battle, rumors began spreading among Whig families in Charlotte Town that Ferguson had been badly beaten. When the rumors first reached Cornwallis, he dismissed them as preposterous. But he was worried; no word had been received from Ferguson since the belated express brought in the past Saturday.

Tarleton, now up from his sickbed, put together a battalion of light infantry, his legion, and a three-pounder canon and began marching to reinforce Ferguson. When the British relief column reached the rain-swollen Catawba River at Smith's Ford, about fifteen miles southwest of Charlotte Town, Tarleton met two Tory militiamen who, though still in shock, had just swum their horses across the river. They told an incredulous story that everyone in Ferguson's army had been killed, wounded, or captured. The two militiamen had escaped only because they were out foraging at the time of the attack.

Finding the news hard to believe, Tarleton demanded greater details. The older of the militiamen said, "When we heard the shooting, we were nearly a mile east of the mountain. Three in my party stayed with the wagon, and three of us rode back. We tied our horses and sneaked through the trees the last quarter mile and saw rebels swarming all over the mountain like ants on a melon. The shooting stopped shortly after we got there. Those rebels were treating our people awful.

"We stayed hid and then saw one of our men crawling away from the fight, a fellow from the backcountry. He was crying and bleeding in the head. We patched him up and helped him get away. He said Colonel Ferguson was dead, shot off his horse while leading attacks against the rebel devils. Some of our field officers are also down. I heard Husbands and Plummer and Cap'n Ryerson. The rebels caught the camp by surprise and completely surrounded our corps before we knew it."

"How many rebels were there?" Tarleton asked.

"Had to be two, three thousand at least," the Tory militiaman guessed. "They were everywhere. All the South Fork area is in a panic. People are downright scared of these mountain demons, and they got a right to be.

"Most of the foraging parties went back to help the wounded that were left behind. Some went home to protect their families. We come to tell you."

After writing a detailed express to Cornwallis, Tarleton ferried his battalion across the river to give protection to refugees and gather more intelligence about a rebel army large enough to defeat one of the most talented British officers in America. He had trouble believing that Ferguson's command was totally wiped out.

Although victorious in battle, the mountain brigade commanders were far from elated. They were plagued with a lack of food for horses and men, the dying wounded, escaping prisoners, constant protests of mistreatment from the captured officers, and a nagging fear that the British Army would swoop down on them at any moment. In addition, special efforts had to be made to keep their own men from slipping away and going home.

Rance Miller glared at George Bluebird. He did not know who the Indian was and nobody else could tell him. Each time Miller edged toward a weak spot in the prisoner guard, Bluebird was there, his black eyes piercing into Miller's soul. *I have offended him somewhere, but where?* Miller asked himself.

Unlike many of the guards who were overtly hostile to the Loyalist prisoners, Bluebird said nothing; he just stared at one man. Even the guard officers could not understand what this Indian was up to. Most did not know him at all; he never seemed to have any other duty. Although Bluebird did not bother or threaten anyone, friend and foe felt uneasy around him.

Escapes were commonplace; several a night. Many were successful, but one hapless prisoner ducked out of the march and hid in a hollow tree, only to be found by a South Carolina Liberty Man and hacked to death, despite cries for mercy.

With threats of severe punishment, Colonel Campbell issued stern orders for his men to stop the senseless harassing and killing unless a prisoner did something overt, like attack a guard or try to escape, and then only enough force to control the situation could be used. "Damn it, we are not animals. Act like the Christian you are!" he roared to a guard detail.

On Wednesday, four days after the battle, a Whig militiaman, recently paroled by the British in South Carolina, stumbled onto the brigade's march and reported that he saw eleven Whigs executed by the king's men at Ninety Six for no reason other than they fought for freedom. He did not say that all the condemned also had violated paroles by rejoining the rebellion. The news of the hangings further infuriated the Liberty Men. Demands for retribution and vengeance on the prisoners became more vociferous.

The commanders had already received dozens of allegations of murder, arson, beatings, and thievery against specific individuals among the captives. Many of those charges were aimed at Rance Miller. Now with news of the Ninety Six atrocities against prisoners who fought for independence, the mood among the partisans became uglier, their demands for revenge more formidable.

After they arrived at John Walker's plantation on the evening of 11 October, the field officers met and agreed to ease the tension by holding a formal trial for those prisoners accused of the most serious crimes. If they failed to act quickly, their highly emotional army could easily become a mob and massacre many, if not most, of the prisoners. Several of the North Carolina senior officers who were magistrates declared that they could legally hold criminal trials but that no prisoner should be punished unless the culprits were proved in a trial to be guilty of a crime. In the Walker home was a North Carolina law book to guide them.

Early the next morning, all prisoners were paraded and segregated by counties, so that the Liberty Men could more easily identify their Tory neighbors suspected of serious crimes. More than fifty, including Rance Miller and most of the Tory militia officers, were indicted and marched to an isolated cattle pen where they were tied and were forced to huddle under watchful eyes of more-attentive guards.

Not being from the Carolinas, the Provincial officers were spared. As commander of what was left of Ferguson's corps, Captain DePeyster vehemently protested to Colonel Campbell. "Sir, this is a flagrant violation of the rules of war. I must protest as strongly as I can and urge you to stop this insane harassment of men whose only crime has been to fight honorably for a cause in which they believe and for the country they love. What you are doing, sir, is illegal and most improper."

Campbell sighed and picked up the copy of the North Carolina statutes. "It says here, Captain DePeyster, that in this province any two magistrates can convene a court. We have more than six magistrates among our officer corps, and they have lawfully ordered that people who are suspected of crimes against the citizens of this province be held accountable. We are not trying anyone for being a king's soldier or for fighting against us.

"You and your New York officers will observe the proceedings, but you cannot interfere with the administration of justice as lawfully established by the North Carolina House of Commons. I might add, sir, these are basically the same laws that govern criminal conduct in England."

As the late-afternoon sun dropped toward the distant, high mountain peaks, Andrew Hampton awarded himself the luxury of basking in its warm glow and letting his mind wander away from the heavy responsibilities that had burdened him over the past six weeks. His thoughts were interrupted by Benjamin Camp and his two brothers who served in Hampton's regiment. "Excuse us, Colonel, sir. We've been wondering what will happen to our brothers out with the Tories? They ain't going to be hung, are they?"

"Prisoners that don't dance with the rope will be taken north and the powers that be will decide what to do with them," Hampton said. "As for your brothers, don't worry about 'em being tried. They're not criminals, just misguided souls."

"Well, sir, can we take our brothers home with us? We'll keep them locked up in one of the outbuildings at our place till the war is over. Pa would surely appreciate it, knowing that they were safe and all."

Hampton thought for a few minutes. After looking over at Campbell who made a slight nod of agreement, the Rutherford commander said, "Well, we can't feed all the mouths we have here now. Go ahead and take your foolish brothers and make your own prison." And then with a chuckle, he added, "If I know your pa, those two probably will wish that they had stayed under our gun and marched all the way to hell and back."

Bluebird watched Miller carefully as the Tory was shuttled roughly along with the other accused. Miller kept starring at Bluebird, and with his options running short, his apprehension grew. The gloating rebels made no secret that there would be a big trial the next day or so and vengeance would come at the end of a rope for all convicted. Most—captor and prisoner—thought the trial was no more than a ruse to justify a mass hanging.

Shortly after dark, Jacob arrived at the Walker plantation. He brought from home a sack of fried chicken, boiled eggs, cooked potatoes, and pickled squash to share with Bluebird. They went to a quiet spot to eat and share news of what had transpired over the past two days.

Miller saw his two nemeses walk off into the nearby trees and realized that if he was to escape the hangman's noose or assassination, he had to make his move that night. For some time he had been gradually loosening the rough rope that bound his hands until at last he could free himself. He looked around and saw many of the guards relaxed and talking among themselves in the festive atmosphere created by news of the trial.

After darkness descended, Miller lay down in the muddy corral and crawled slowly on his stomach over to a little drainage ditch. Inching along slowly, he made his way under a rail fence and down toward a small ravine. Twice he came so close to a guard that he could reach out and touch him. Instead of being alert as they would be later in the evening, these guards were jovial and talking among themselves or throwing taunts to a gaggle of prisoners in their charge. Miller's strong ally that evening were clouds blocking the moon, limiting visibility.

It took nearly an hour for Miller to work his way three hundred feet away from the fence. Not seeing anyone close in the darkness, Miller stood and, resisting the urge to run, casually walked past a camp of Surry County militia and on down the hill to a small stream that flowed through the nearby woods toward the river. He had only a vague idea as to where he was.

VENGEANCE

13–14 October 1780

Jacob waited until the militia from the Watauga settlements took over guard duty at midnight when his friend Matt McCracken was assigned to the special prisoners. He and Bluebird talked McCracken into letting them sneak in to find Rance Miller; but despite deceptive efforts by the other prisoners, they soon found that the Tory miscreant was missing.

An alarm was raised, and Colonel Sevier ran to the area upset both that an important prisoner had escaped on his watch and that Jacob had been let into the compound. "You sure you haven't already done away with him, Jake?" Sevier asked accusingly.

"I ain't done nothing to him...yet," Jake protested. "But why are we waiting? We need to go after him now."

"And how do you propose to track him in the dark?"

Jacob was furious. There seemed to be no sense of urgency on the part of the guard commander. "Miller ain't the cause of killings and burnings on your side of the mountains," Jacob spouted accusingly, "but he's a bloody assassin here, damn it!"

"Watch your tongue, boy!" Sevier warned. "I'm sure old Hampton will let you in on the chase come daylight; that is, if he doesn't have you flogged for this foolish stunt by you and your Indian friend."

Bluebird pulled Jacob away and said softly, "Let's go get some sleep."

"How can I sleep with that bastard loose?"

"Easy. Lay your head down. Close your eyes," Bluebird answered half jokingly. "We'll need all our strength to catch him tomorrow. He can track him easy. Couldn't you tell that?"

"What do you mean, George?"

"Have you let your mad cloud your eyes, boy? Did I waste my time teaching you how to see things?" Bluebird scolded. "The man is missing three toes on his right foot. We'll leave at first light and track him down. Now get some rest."

Before the first hint of dawn, Jacob and Bluebird scouted the perimeter of the prisoner compound and quickly spotted in the dew-covered, matted weeds where someone had recently crawled. Within minutes, they found the faint track of a man's foot with missing toes. "Got him!" the Indian said quietly. "Bet he went to that branch down the hill and then to the river."

Mounting their horses, they rode toward the shallow river, following crushed grass stems and broken twigs, signs of someone moving in a hurry. Seeing disturbed dirt and vegetation on the far bank, Bluebird did not bother to dismount. "He's making this too easy," he told Jake.

Sevier reported the missing prisoner at the field officers' morning meeting held on the front porch of the Walker home, which now served as a hospital for wounded Liberty Men. He said that Jacob and Bluebird were probably in pursuit.

Hampton said, "Let the Godley boy and that Indian get their revenge on Miller and be done with it. We need to move the prisoners over to Biggerstaff's place today; I can't spare any more men to chase just one sorry Tory.

"We got to get on with the trial before Tarleton comes this way. Most of my men are already at Biggerstaff's setting up a bivouac area. That's Tory country, so Ferguson hadn't plundered much over there. Grass is plentiful enough for the horses, at least for several days. My lads have confiscated a good supply of grain, beef, beans, corn, and apples from the turncoats who kissed Ferguson's behind when he was this way."

"Colonel Hampton is right," Campbell said. "Let's move the prisoners who will face the tribunal first and get them settled, and then later today, we'll take the rest of the Royals to a separate pen at this Biggerstaff place. Will we have enough witnesses to testify in the trials tomorrow?"

McDowell and Hampton reported there were many witnesses within their ranks, and people living nearby were coming forward with damning accusations.

By early afternoon, the mountain brigade and its prisoners had relocated five miles to the plantation overlooking Robertson Creek. Aaron Biggerstaff's two-storied log home with its distinctive red-clay chimneys was taken over as the Liberty Men's new headquarters. Biggerstaff's wife Mary, her eight children, all fewer than fifteen years of age, and Aaron's sister Martha were forced to move out of the house and crowded into a small cabin normally used by field hands. Martha's husband, John Morgan, was among those captured in the battle. She was allowed to give him some food. Most of the Liberty Men learned quickly that Mary was the wife of a Tory officer left badly wounded at Kings Mountain. Some treated her with sympathetic respect; others went out of their way to be rude.

All during that Friday, women, children, and old men came into the area looking for fathers, sons, brothers, and neighbors in both armies. From time to time, the air pierced with shrieks of happiness when sons or husbands were found alive; and occasional mournful wails filled the encampment as women learned that someone dear was left dead or severely wounded at Kings Mountain. Junior officers and sergeants tried to keep order as civilians wandered about the camp asking questions, offering meager rations, or just gawking at the largest gathering of men the county had ever seen at one place. Some even threw rocks at the Loyalist prisoners and had to be chased from the area.

While some Liberty Men tried to console recent Tory widows, others only gloated. When Lucinda Godley demanded to know from a Whig partisan if he had been the cause of her William falling, he boasted, "Wish I was the one what sent your husband straight to hell to burn eternally. And if I had my way, every Tory here would be buzzard bait with him."

Horrified and frightened by the animosity toward her, Lucinda turned and ran without stopping two miles back to her house where her parents and neighbors were gathering to mourn.

About twenty miles south, along Green River, Anna Mills was knitting on the veranda at Valle Temp when word came of the tragedy at Kings Mountain. She gave a sigh of relief when she learned that her husband,

Ambrose, had not been hurt but had been captured. A quiet prayer was offered for her stepson, left on the field bleeding, unable to travel. With news that the prisoners were near Gilbert Town, she made preparations to find her husband.

By late Friday afternoon, Jacob and Bluebird were confident that they were near their quarry. "He's slowing down, getting tired, more careless," the Indian said.

They passed many signs to show they were on course—a nest that Miller had made of leaves, a field where he had dug some potatoes, and a stream where he had disturbed sand by kneeling to drink water. After studying Miller's pattern of movement early in the chase, they gained quickly on the fugitive by predicting his route several hundred yards in advance and galloping ahead. They were right most of the time, and when they did misguess, they lost little time in picking up the fugitive's trail again.

Miller was frantic. His sole mission was to survive, get back to South Carolina, and be among people loyal to the Crown. Only then would he feel safe. Once he had crossed the river in the dark after escaping from the camp area, he believed that the rebels would not bother to follow. But he couldn't be sure.

Cut and bleeding, his bare feet hurt as he thrashed about using the sun to guide him southward. At times, he walked an animal trail, but more often he forced his way cross-country. He was unsuccessful in finding a horse to steal. By midday, Miller collapsed, made a nest in some bushes, and slept for nearly three hours. Afterward, he cursed himself for taking such a long nap and renewed his determination to add more distance between him and the rebels. Six days of forced marching with little food and constant abuse by his captors left him with little strength; only adrenalin kept him going.

Late in the day, Miller began to relax; his escape appeared to be successful. His dream was startled when two horses bolted through the brush from the backside of a pine thicket to block his way. Someone yelled in a harsh voice, "Stop or you're dead right now!"

Shock and exhaustion caused Miller to sag as he recognized the Indian who had been spying on him since his capture and *that crazy Godley boy.* He said nothing, just leered at his captors, heaved deep breaths, and silently prayed for a weapon of any kind. After a long pause, he spat at Jacob and said defiantly, "You got me. So kill me and get done with it."

Jacob slid off his horse, his rifle trained on Miller, his anger barely under control, his hatred even more bitter. "Killing you now is too easy. If I shoot you, know that it'll be in your bollocks. Maybe I'll cut your doodle off. Or hack off your nose. But I'm keeping you alive for the hangman's noose. And by the time I drag your sorry arse back to Colonel Hampton, you will wish I had killed you outright," Jacob said in a slow, menacing tone.

Bluebird dismounted, and taking a section of rawhide that was dangling from his saddle, he walked toward Miller and grabbed an arm to tie the fugitive's hands behind his back. Jacob also moved closer, his rifle coming less than an arm's length from Miller's face.

Instincts that had kept Miller alive over the years took over. With the sudden savagery of a trapped bobcat, he twisted free of Bluebird and grabbed Jacob's rifle barrel, pushing the weapon down and outward from his head and pulling it forward simultaneously. The sudden tug on the rifle caused Jacob's finger to jerk the trigger. The gun roared; its ball slammed into Bluebird and knocked the Indian against a tree.

Miller ignored the heat of the barrel and tried to pull the weapon free of Jacob. Having wrestled with bigger men most of his life, Jacob understood leverage by instinct. After a half-second of resisting Miller's strong pull, he suddenly turned the rifle loose, causing Miller to fall backward, off balance. Jacob leaped at the bigger man, drawing his butcher knife from his belt while in midair. Jacob's momentum was enough to knock the undernourished Tory to the ground, and before Miller could develop a counter move, Jacob drove his foot-long blade in between Miller's fourth and fifth rib, puncturing the lungs and severing the internal thoracic artery. Jacob twisted the knife to cause more damage, then withdrew it swiftly and plunged it several more times, twice hitting Miller's heart.

His rage was so fierce and consuming that Jacob never knew exactly when Miller stopped resisting or how many times he had stabbed the Tory. Exhaustion and Miller's stillness slowly brought Jacob back to his senses. Realizing that Miller was dead, he looked over with dread at his friend who lay nearby clutching his side, blood seeping between his fingers. Bluebird was alive but hurting.

Jacob rushed to the wounded man, sobbing that he was sorry for causing his friend to be shot. He cut Bluebird's hunting shirt clear of the wound.

Jacob was relieved to see that the projectile had gone through the Indian's side and had not lodged in the body. A large splotch of black powder burn covered the skin where the entry wound was made. They spoke few words as Jacob turned Bluebird over and took strips of cloth to block the bleeding. That done, he told the Indian, "Hold this! It will stop the leaking while I get a better bandage for you. That ball went clean through you. There ain't a lot of blood spilling out, so you just might live after all."

It was dark by the time Jacob had completed a poultice by chewing the leaves of wild geranium—Jacob knew it as rockweed—and tamped the damp astringent into both holes. He packed mud on top of the chewed leaves and then tightly wrapped strips of cloth around Bluebird's body. The bandaging came from Jacob's linen shirt that he wore under his heavier hunting smock

Other than to say that Miller was dead, they talked little about the situation until Jacob was through nursing his friend. Once Bluebird was patched, a fire built, the horses secured, and water retrieved from the nearby stream, Jacob began trying to determine just where they were. The enormity of the day hit him like being slammed with a fence rail. He was worn out physically and emotionally. Sleep came quickly.

They woke before the sun rose on Saturday. After Jacob made a new poultice and changed the bandage on Bluebird's wound, the two discussed what to do with Miller's blood-drenched body.

"He's two damn big and messy for me to throw over a horse," Jacob said, "and it ain't fair on the horse to have to drag that heavy carcass such a long way. But Mistress Pearson wants to see him dead, and I promised her I'd make it happen."

"Cut his head off," Bluebird suggested. "It'll show everybody that we didn't let the bastard get away."

Jacob had never mutilated a body before, and though he had a passionate hate for Miller, he found the task of removing the head emotionally difficult. With his knife and belt ax, he severed the head and wrapped the hideous trophy with the dead man's shirt.

Helping the shirtless Bluebird up on his mount, Jacob saw that new bloodstains had worked through the Indian's bandages. Leaving Miller's body for the buzzards, they moved westward through the forest for more than an hour before finding the road from Gilbert Town to South Carolina. Another half hour after turning north on the road, Jacob began to recognize landmarks; he was only a mile or so from John Foreman's place.

"I'm taking you to some friends who can care for you," Jacob told Bluebird. "You don't need to ride any more than necessary if you are going to get those holes healed up."

Everyone in the Foreman house ran out to help Bluebird off his horse and inside to a bed. The women busied themselves with cleaning his torso, making a new poultice, and tying new bandages around the wounds. As Rebecca Foreman and Mary Pearson worked to make Bluebird comfortable, Jacob led John Foreman back outside where the one-armed veteran peppered him with many questions about the battle at Kings Mountain. Rachel joined them about the time Jacob mentioned the deaths of his brothers. She gasped and tightly grabbed Jacob's arm, as much for her own support as to comfort her friend.

When Foreman got around to asking how Bluebird got shot, Jacob told him.

Looking down at Rachel, Jacob said, "The man who killed your papa and brother is dead. I got his head tied in that shirt on the back of my saddle."

"Let me get Mama," Rachel said unemotionally before turning and running into the house.

Foreman just looked at Jacob and said nothing until Rachel and her mother came back out to them. "You say you killed that son of Satan?" the Pearson matriarch asked harshly, her eyes burning with fury.

"Yes'um. I brung his head to you like you asked me to."

"Let me see him."

Jacob untied Miller's shirt from the saddle and put it on the ground. He pulled the bloodstained cloth back from the head, revealing Miller's dark eyes still open, staring sightless at them. Rachel stepped back as though the Tory raider had come back alive. Her mother looked unmoving for a long minute and then spat into the dead eyes. She turned, but before stomping back into the house, ordered tersely, "Get that ugly thing out of my sight! Let the wolves choke on it, but get it out of my sight. Now!"

Jacob quickly bundled the head back into the shirt, tied it to his saddle, and walked his horse out behind a shed. He took no joy in what he had done, but was content that he had fulfilled a promise.

Foreman put his arm around Jacob's shoulder and led him back into the house. They ate a midday dinner in silence, except for a long prayer from Foreman who thanked God for delivering the cause of liberty a decisive victory and for keeping Jacob safe. He asked God to look after Jacob's brothers in the hereafter and his parents here on earth. He prayed for Bluebird's recovery and the safe journey of the Liberty Men back to their homes. Raising his eyes to the ceiling and lowering his voice a little, Foreman concluded, "And thank you, Lord, thank you for ridding our world of the devil's disciple, Rance Miller. We take great comfort that he now resides with the demons of hell. Amen."

After the meal, Rachel begged Jacob to stay longer, but he reluctantly said that he had to report Miller's death to Colonel Hampton; it would be almost dark by the time he rejoined the brigade. He also needed to be with his folks because they had not had a proper time to grieve as a family. He looked at her a little differently than at any other time in their short acquaintance. "I…I'll be back. I've got to bring Zeus back to Cap'n Foreman," Jacob stuttered. "And I…I guess I want to see you again too."

As he rode northward, depression set in on Jacob as he reflected remorsefully on the past eight weeks, the loss of his brothers, the Pearson tragedy, and the vengeance he had wreaked on Miller. Now shocked at the hatred he had experienced, Jacob felt guilt stack on top of guilt with each step his horse took until he stopped near a vine-clogged gulley, dismounted, and untied from the saddle the shirt holding Miller's head.

The skies billowed with impending rain and turned darker, matching his mood. He did not want to look again at the results of his macabre work. Instead, he heaved the bundle as far as he could, remounted, and rode on at a gallop, praying to distance himself as much as possible from the ghost of Rance Miller and pain of the past week.

TOO UGLY A SIGHT

14 October 1780

One week to the day after the gory battle thirty-three miles to the southeast, Mary Biggerstaff's dining table was set up under the towering shade trees in front of her house. Frontier justice would be served in the open-air makeshift court. There were chairs for the three colonels who served as judges. A book containing the laws of the province was open to the criminal statutes. To the side of the table were three split-logged benches placed on two-foot-high sections of tree trunks, seats for the officers who made up the jury.

An area was roped off for the accused who were marched out in groups of ten and guarded by carefully selected Liberty Men with bayonet-fitted muskets captured in the battle.

Nearly half of the mountain brigade was assigned to guard those prisoners not on trial. Since first mention of the trials, an ugly mood had been growing among the captives. The guards were cautioned to be extra alert; even though the prisoners had no weapons, six hundred or so angry men, all experienced warriors, could cause a lot of trouble. No breach of conduct would be tolerated. There would be no leniency for any prisoner attempting mischief of any kind.

As the ranking Tory officer, Ambrose Mills was the first to appear before the tribunal. Andrew Hampton served as prosecutor. The Whig colonel told the jurors that although Mills had been a respectable citizen in the past, he became a rogue when Americans decided on a course for independence and kicked the British out of the Carolinas. Looking directly at Mills as he spoke, Hampton laid out the nature of charges:

"First, in the summer of seventeen seventy-six, this Tory was arrested for leading an insurrection against the new government of North Carolina and jailed in Salisbury. Three months later, Mister Mills swore allegiance to the new government and was released from his chains on condition that he abides by his oath. But soon after his release, he was back to his dastardly ways and recruiting hundreds of Tories to cause mayhem on innocent, God-fearing families of this county, thereby violating a sacred oath. He was arrested again but escaped again.

"Second, Ambrose Mills conspired with the Cherokee Indians, who are British allies, to swoop down on white families within this county. Women and children were butchered; houses and crops were burned.

"Third, Ambrose Mills led a sneaky raid just this past July when he and a Captain Dunlop stabbed to death my son Noah and Lieutenant Andrew Dunn, while both were still in their bed-clothes, unable to defend themselves. Young Dunn gave me a dying declaration. They were not given the honor of defending themselves. It was murder, pure and simple. Cut down in the prime of their life, they were.

"Fourth, Ambrose Mills failed as a commander to prevent troops under his command from plundering the countryside here in Rutherford County. Scoundrels under his command stole food, including livestock from citizens who had little to start with. They beat innocents, including women and children, and in several occasions caused the murder of men who loved liberty.

"And fifth, Ambrose Mills was directly responsible for the brutal death of Captain Benjamin Merrill of the Rowan County Militia in seventeen seventy-one by giving the man to then-Governor Tryon who had poor Merrill hanged, drawn and quartered and his head impaled on a pole. Captain Merrill's brother is a Liberty Man with us today. I call on him to testify."

Murmurs of anger washed through the several hundred militiamen crowded around the trial area, forcing Colonel Cleveland to bellow, "Quiet down, the lot of ye. This is serious business."

After William Merrill told in horrid detail about his brother's brutal demise following the uprising in Alamance and Rowan Counties, long before the first shot of the revolution was fired in Massachusetts, Mills was permitted to address the court, but he was not permitted to cross-examine witnesses.

The fifty-eight-year-old Tory leader was not a tall or imposing man. Despite the exhausting marches, lack of adequate food and water, constant harassment from his captors, and a seven-day, grey stubble on his chin, Mills maintained a calm aristocratic demeanor. He tried to brush the dirt and mud from his torn waist coat and breeches but was not successful. Nor was he able to smooth out the stringy, thin, grey hair that dangled unkempt from his head.

Slowly with tired eyes, he looked at each juror and then at the judges. Clearing his throat, he spoke in a deliberate, yet respectful, tone, "Gentlemen. As victors, it is within your power to do your will upon my comrades and me. We are at your mercy.

"My militia, what's left of us, and I are here today as soldiers unfortunate in the outcome of last week's terrible conflict. I would have preferred to leave this earth in the glory of battle for a just cause rather than going through this charade of being accused a common criminal. I resent those implications made here today."

Mills paused, stood a little straighter, and said defiantly, "I am guilty of being a soldier and of doing an officer's duty. I am guilty of being loyal to my king and serving him to restore lawful order to this country. I stand proud of my service which has been honorable on all accounts and for which the Loyalist officers here today can attest. I have no apologies to extend to you or my maker for the conduct of my life."

Mills paused to gather his thoughts. He looked over at his wife, Anna, and gave her a slight, but quick, smile before continuing. "As to the charge of violating an oath, it was an oath taken to an illegal government. Shortly after that oath was given for my parole, several misdeeds were heaped upon my family and me by Whig leaders of this county and province. By their own actions, those officers representing the province of North Carolina nullified that promise, not I.

"As to the charges of abetting Indian raids, I adamantly deny the allegations. First of all, I was in custody in Salisbury during much of the time in question. My own property was subject to Indian raids, just as yours. Since settling in this area, I have frequently participated with my neighbors, Whig and Tory alike, in defensive actions against the Indians in the Green and

Pacolet River areas. I do have some Cherokee friends, and it was them who helped our local militia capture and punish the renegades who raided homes here in Tryon County.

"By the way, my dear first wife was brutally murdered by Indians, so I have no love for them.

"As to the charges of murdering Colonel Hampton's son and his friend, I am sorry for the Colonel's loss, but this unfortunate act was done in the heat of combat. Those two, young officers bravely resisted our efforts to capture them. We had no choice in our actions. Each of you would have done likewise if you were in that same situation.

"I might add that I championed the release of Colonel Hampton's son Jonathon, who stood before Colonel Ferguson just a month ago accused of numerous treasonous acts. If not for my actions, Jonathon Hampton would not be alive to witness this tribunal today."

The judges and jurors all looked over at Jonathon who stood and said clearly, "He tells the truth as it relates to my arrest and trial by the invaders. Had Colonel Mills not spoken in my behalf, I would surely have been hanged."

Mills bowed slightly to Jonathon before turning to face the jurors again. "To the charge that I sanctioned men under my command to harm innocent people or to steal from families, that simply is not true. As does your army, we had to live off the land, and to do so, we plundered the crops and livestock of rebel participants. My orders to my militia has been firm that they must at all times conduct themselves as gentlemen and be fair with friend and foe alike. You have produced no witness to testify to the contrary.

"As for the death of Captain Merrill, yes, I recall arresting him. It was my duty under the commission that I and some of this tribunal had at that time. Captain Merrill was aiding the so-called Regulators in armed defiance of the lawful government. Since it was my duty, I surrendered him to the governor. I had nothing to do with Captain Merrill's subsequent trial nor of his execution.

"Gentlemen, if you choose to hang me, it is only because I am a soldier with the misfortune of serving the losing side in a battle against you. These criminal charges are a sham. They are preposterous and unfounded."

Cleveland asked if anyone else had anything to add. When no one said anything, Ol' Roundabout turned to the jurors. "What's the verdict?"

Without leaving their benches, the twelve officers huddled for less than a minute, and then Major Jonathon Tipton stood and said formally, "We find the criminal Ambrose Mills guilty on all counts."

"Stand to Colonel Mills," Cleveland ordered. "A jury of twelve men, all citizens true, finds ye guilty of five heinous crimes against the people of North Carolina. Ye are ordered hung by yer neck until dead. And I don't think God will have mercy on yer soul."

A woman's shrieked, "No, dear God, *no!*"

Clutching her baby, Anna Mills pushed through the crowd and ran to her husband, her face in shock, tears flowing down her cheeks. Three guards jumped to block her, but Colonel Hampton intervened. "Is that your mistress and baby?" he asked Mills.

"Yes sir."

"Then she can sit with you if she promises to keep quiet and behaves herself."

Mills bowed. "Thank you for that kindness, sir."

His hands bound, Mills was led to another heavily guarded area set aside for condemned prisoners. Anna, who had left her home by carriage the afternoon before had in her arms their daughter Milly, just ten months old. She left her other children with servants and friends. After the verdict, she sat stunned for the remainder of the day and held her husband's hand. Anna was oblivious to the proceedings going on around her and found it difficult to comprehend that this crowd was going to kill her children's father. Nor could she fully comprehend the instructions Ambrose calmly gave her for managing their plantation and raising a fatherless family.

Tried next was Captain James Chitwood, whose home was a few miles south of the Biggerstaff place. At sixty-one, he was the oldest Tory in Ferguson's brigade.

"This man was a cowardly night raider in Rutherford County for more than a year before Ferguson invaded us," Hampton charged. "He forced at gunpoint Mistress John Walker and her two young sons to cower in the cellar of their home until her son serving with me, Lieutenant William Walker, was able to rescue her and his brothers.

"In addition, he led the Tories that burned McFadden's Fort on Mountain Creek last year. Fortunately no one was killed, but that arson put the whole region at risk from murdering Indians.

"In the dead of night, he led his Tory banditti in raiding homes of Whig planters in the area. He caused honest men to be beaten in front of their wives and children, and at least one died from these vicious attacks. Women were abused. Small children were flogged until blood flowed from their backs. Food stocks were destroyed or stolen. Several of my regiment who suffered at Chitwood's hands are here today, and I call upon them now to testify."

Within fifteen minutes, three privates spoke briefly of the humiliation and hardships that they, their families, and their neighbors suffered from what they called Chitwood's unmerciful raids. Walker testified to the treatment of his mother and his young brothers.

After the incriminating testimony, Chitwood rose and, following the example of Colonel Mills, did not humble himself before the tribunal, nor did he berate them. He said straightforward, "I burned no fort. I had no part whatsoever in that raid at McFadden's. I did not indiscriminately raid homes of innocent people.

"It is true, that on orders of Colonel Ferguson, I confiscated the Walker home to be a hospital to treat wounded men from the fight at Cane Creek. I might add that some of those wounded included several rebels who had ambushed our patrol. But if Elizabeth Walker was here today, she would tell you that I never treated her, her sons or her servants in any way other than with respect.

"It is true that militia under my command did whip two of those men who just testified. What the blackguards didn't say is our action came because they had burned out a half dozen defenseless families here in Tryon County; families whose only offense was having Tory leanings. Incidentally, in one of those raids by the rebels, a little innocent boy, the son of a Tory advocate, was killed when his head was smashed against a tree.

"Colonel Hampton didn't tell you that I complained several times to him and to Colonel Walker that those scoundrels were terrorizing the countryside, but your colonels refused to do anything to stop or punish their renegade friends. We had no choice but to act in self-defense against such senseless barbarism.

"Gentlemen, I am no criminal. I have violated no laws. I am just a citizen doing a soldier's duty for God, king, and my fellow man."

The jury rendered a quick verdict; the sentence was death.

Three other Rutherford County Tory officers, Captain Walter Gilkey and Lieutenants John Biddy and Thomas Lafferty, were also tried in trials that lasted less than fifteen minutes each. All three were convicted of assault, plunder, and arson.

When Captain Arthur Grimes was called forward, Colonel John Sevier took over the prosecutor's role. He identified Grimes as an assassin, a horse thief, a house burner, and a notorious highwayman who created terror throughout the Watauga and Nolichucky region for nearly a year. "I hanged two of his gang last year, and his bones would be rotting on the banks of the Nolichucky today if he hadn't escaped a posse that broke up his band of brigands."

Major Joe McDowell described Grimes as "the meanest Tory that every roamed through Burke County. No man is more deserving of the noose than he." McDowell called off a dozen names who were victims of Grimes's treachery, "...including my own brother and mother."

When he stood before the judges table, Grimes snarled at Cleveland. "I have nothing but contempt for you treasonous vermin. You rebels will all burn in hell for what you are doing this day."

Grimes reacted to his death sentence by spitting in Sevier's face.

John McFall was accused of using a switch to beat the nine-year-old son of a Whig supporter. Major Joe McDowell argued that although what McFall did was a criminal offense, perhaps a flogging would be a more appropriate punishment. Cleveland, one of the judges, roared in protest. "That coward beat Martin Davenport's son while Martin was serving the cause of freedom in my command. No one who abuses children of our brave soldiers deserves to live."

McDowell was more successful in arguing for John's brother, Arthur of Turkey Cove. At twenty-nine, Arthur McFall had gained an enviable reputation as an Indian fighter and hunter. "Unlike his brother, Arthur doesn't have a mean bone in his body," Major McDowell testified. "He's a good man and has rendered valuable service to our region by protecting the frontier... that is, up until the time he took up with the Tories. Since he got shot in the arm last in week's battle, I believe he has suffered enough for joining the enemy ranks."

Arthur was spared the noose, but not his brother.

There were not many South Carolina Tories among the accused. Two of them, Augustine Hobbs and Lieutenant Robert Wilson, were both charged with abetting Bloody Bill Cunningham and Rance Miller in their brutal raids along the Carolina border. Both were sentenced to die.

Instead of condemning the two deserters from Yellow Mountain, Colonel Sevier defended James Crawford and Samuel Chambers. Sevier said he had known Crawford as a friend and neighbor for many years; their families were close. "We hunted together and fought Indians together. I will not be comfortable going home having my friend hung.

"As for young Chambers, the boy is only seventeen. He's still gullible to the leanings of his elders and shouldn't be held responsible for being led astray. He just did not know better.

"Both these lads are remorseful for leaving us on the mountain and going over to Ferguson. They will have to live with that shame for the rest of their lives. That is far greater punishment than a quick death by rope. I say let them live."

Angry at Sevier's plea for leniency, Andrew Hampton argued to convict and hang the two for desertion and treason, but a split jury that included overmountain officers from the Watauga settlements, gave into Sevier's request.

The trials continued until dusk. In all, thirty-two Tories were sentenced to die by hanging, and twenty-one were acquitted, including three former Whig officers who were captured while fighting for the Tories. The three had been serving with the Liberty Men only weeks before the battle, and one had been an officer with Shelby at the Musgrove's Mill battle. The three accused argued successfully that they had been coerced under threat of hanging to switch sides. Their Tory neighbors, who were also captured at Kings Mountain, testified that the men were forced under duress to join the Loyalist ranks. Each of the accused pledged to rejoin the Liberty Men and resume fighting for independence. Renouncing the Crown, the Whig officers were released from captivity that day.

Meanwhile in Charlotte Town, the confidence that General Cornwallis enjoyed when he first entered the area had vanished. With the loss of Ferguson's thousand men, the British Army's entire western flank protection was destroyed. Fever had nearly a fifth of his regular troops in Charlotte Town unfit for duty. Raids by Frances Marion's irregulars in South Carolina frequently disrupted his supply lines. But most of all, the constant harassment by piedmont partisan guerrillas made the British Army's stay in North Carolina untenable.

As the trials of the Loyalists captives were under way seventy-five miles to the west, Lord Cornwallis recalled Tarleton from his mission to Kings Mountain. The general ordered his command to pack up. The once-victorious British Army of the southern colonies began a retreat seventy miles southward to Wynnsborough, South Carolina, where it could regroup in winter quarters.

Jacob arrived at Biggerstaff's as dusk descended. The area was lit by the flickering of several hundred torches held by partisans crowded around the tribunal and condemned prisoners. He dismounted and forced his way toward the center of the crowd where he saw Ambrose Mills, James Chitwood, and Walter Gilkey—their hands tied behind their backs—boosted up on to three saddleless horses.

Captain Abraham DePeyster again protested loudly to the Whig colonels that such actions were barbaric, uncivilized, and criminal. The Loyalist officer begged the victors to wait at least until they could make rational decisions without the emotionally charged atmosphere of vengeance. "You have won, for God's sake," DePeyster argued passionately. "You've already killed Colonel Ferguson and hundreds of other good men. You have wiped out an entire corps. Isn't that revenge enough? For the love of God, have you no mercy?"

"Captain DePeyster!" Campbell responded sharply, "Your objections are noted. Now get back to your position."

Anna Mills was restrained by guards as the horses carrying her husband and his two officers were led to a large oak tree with massive limbs springing in all directions. Three ropes with loops in the end were tied to the lowest limb, about fourteen feet off the ground. As the horses were positioned and ropes slipped over the heads of the condemned, a guard pleaded sympathetically to Anna, "Ma'am, you shouldn't watch. It's too ugly a sight."

Anna refused the advice and kept looking at her husband, and he at her. Campbell asked Mills if he had any last words. Mills raised his head, looked directly at his executioners, and replied loudly, "God save the king and bless those who serve him."

Getting a nod from Campbell, William Merrill, satisfied at avenging his brother's death, slapped the rump of the horse carrying Mills. At the same instance, Chitwood and Gilkey were also unhorsed. The three bodies swung gently, their limbs twitching for a few moments until all was still. There were a few "huzzahs" from the crowd, but mostly all watched soberly.

Lieutenant Allaire later wrote in his diary: "*They died like Romans.*"

Released by the guards and still clutching her baby to her bosom, Anna walked over to the tree and stood near her husband, not turning away from a face distorted in death.

Told that their father would not die that night, James Chitwood's two distraught daughters had been led away from the scene before the hanging. However, they soon learned that they had been lied to and ran back wild-eyed and yelling, almost knocking Jacob down as they rushed by him toward their father's corpse. Several men grabbed the hysterical daughters and carried the young women, screaming and kicking, away from the execution area.

The next three to hang were Grimes, Wilson, and Lafferty. Then three more - McFall, Biddy and Hobbs. With each trio swinging from the horses, there were fewer huzzahs. Jacob was numbed by the mass executions. This killing was much different than that done in the heat of combat. Most of his fellow warriors, although no strangers to witnessing death, shared his feelings but said nothing.

As the horses returned to pick the next three men scheduled to hang, a twelve-year-old boy from Burke County ran past the guards and wrapped his arms tightly around his condemned brother, Isaac Baldwin, and cried loudly for all to spare his only brother. The brothers fell to the ground as the boy sobbed continually and screamed, "Oh Lord, please don't take my brother! He's all Mama and me got."

Some of the onlookers were amused by the scene, others saddened. Several arms tried to pull the wailing boy from Baldwin, who had been condemned for raiding homes and stealing food, furnishings, and clothing from the occupants and, in one case, beating a Whig supporter and leaving him naked, tied to a tree. No one noticed that the youngster had a pocketknife in his clinched fist. The boy lay on top of Baldwin, wiggling and thrashing around to keep guards from getting a firm grip to pull him away. Guards and spectators were falling over each other trying to separate the pair. While both brothers yelled about their love for family, the guards could not see the boy slice through the ropes that bound the prisoner.

Confusion reigned as Baldwin and his brother continued to roll about, causing more Liberty Men to trip and fall. Torches waving about by the excited partisans gave an uneven and distorted light above the crowd but cast not a glimmer on the senior Baldwin, who took advantage of the chaos of sprawling bodies to crawl through the legs of men crowding around him. After advancing twenty feet through a mass of legs, Baldwin stood up and walked nonchalantly through the darkness to the outer reaches of the crowd as Liberty Men continued jostling each other and straining to see what was happening in the center of the din. They paid no attention to a man walking among them as though he belonged there. Baldwin quickly reached the forest edge and disappeared before anyone realized he had escaped.

Some wanted to hang the boy in his brother's stead. As they argued over the younger Baldwin's fate, three more condemned men were hoisted on horseback amid a growing chant among the Liberty Men, "Enough! Enough!"

A much smaller number yelled, "Hang 'em all!"

Caught up in the emotions, Colonel Isaac Shelby halted the proceedings by charging his horse to the front of the gallows tree and waving his sword, he shouted, "Stop it! No more! There's been enough killing for one night."

Amid the scattered vocal protest from the troops, the colonels quickly conferred. All but Cleveland agreed to end the executions. "We've made our point," Campbell told the crowd. "I've seen enough killing this past week to satisfy a lifetime. No more executions. Let's get everybody rested so we can get on to the Catawba in the morning. We still have Tarleton and the British Army to worry about."

The bodies were left swinging as the reprieved prisoners, their sentences annulled, were escorted back to join the rest of their colleagues. As the partisans drifted away, Jacob overheard Captain Paddy Carr, a Georgian who hated Tories with a passion, say loudly, "I wish to God that every tree in the forest should bear fruit like that!"

Anna Mills was sitting on the ground under her husband's body, not ten feet from Carr. She paid the remark no heed. Nor did she react as the first sprinkles of rain fell on her. Martha Biggerstaff went to Anna and urged her to come into the cabin with her family. Anna refused to budge, but did let Martha take the baby as she continued her night-long vigil beneath her husband's body.

Jacob finally got Hampton's attention and reported that he had caught Miller, but had to kill him in a scuffle that left Bluebird wounded. "You did good, Mister Godley," the old colonel said, obviously weary from such a tiring day. "Best you get some sleep. We're marching north tomorrow, and it looks like rain is coming to make it a harder day."

Looking up at the nine bodies swaying from the tree, Jacob shook his head sadly. "That ain't right, Colonel. Mister Chitwood was a good man, my papa's friend. He ate at our table. We just can't go on killing, can we?"

Taking a more fatherly tone, Hampton replied, "War makes for a lot of unpleasant things, lad, and getting blood on your hands is just one of them. But it's necessary to get rid of the tyranny that the Crown has heaped upon us. Now, let's get ready to travel."

"I ain't going, sir," Jacob said bluntly.

"And why not?" Hampton bristled.

"I'm done fighting. Ain't got no hate in me no more."

Hampton could have Jacob flogged for refusing an order. The old man stared up at the nine corpses again and, for a long time, reflected on the past few weeks. Gradually, he turned his gaze back to Jacob.

"Son, don't confuse hate with duty."

AFTERWORD

Heavy rain came before dawn on the day following the hangings. Fearing that the British Army was on their heels, the mountain brigade had their prisoners up before light and marching north. The mood among prisoners and victors seemed to match the dismal weather. A cold, hard rain was unrelenting most of the day. It was after sunset when they forded the fast-rising Catawba River, twenty miles north of the hanging tree at Briggerstaff's. During the forced march, approximately one hundred prisoners, fearful of more hangings, took advantage of the storm and escaped into the wet forest. Little effort was made to recapture them. It was more than a week before the victors of Kings Mountain learned that the dreaded British Legion had gone back south instead of chasing them.

Three months after the Kings Mountain battle, many of the same Liberty Men again answered the call to arms and joined General Daniel Morgan at Saunders's cow pens to make history once more. Here, for the first time, a predominantly militia force, coupled with some Continental units, met and soundly defeated a similar-sized corps from the British Army led by Banastre Tarleton. The American citizen-soldiers stood toe-to-toe on an open battlefield against the regulars; their abilities enhanced with more than a touch of frontier ingenuity and bravado.

When Cornwallis began marching his army north again in the spring of 1781, he encountered more determined partisans sniping at his columns in numerous raids and ambushes that did much to destroy British supplies and troop morale. At Guilford Courthouse, a combined force of militia—including many Kings Mountain veterans—and Continental troops under General Nathanael Greene inflicted heavy casualties on the redcoats in a battle Cornwallis called a victory, but as reported by an opposition member in the British Parliament, "Another such victory would ruin the British Army."

By the time the British Army arrived at Yorktown in Virginia, they were worn out, undermanned and dispirited. Cornwallis found himself trapped and surrendered there to a combined army of Continentals, French regulars, and American militia.

✺

William Campbell, praised throughout the new nation for his leadership at Kings Mountain, was a hero again in fighting the British at Guilford Courthouse. He was promoted to general and led the Virginia Militia in the battle at Yorktown. Shortly after the British surrender, Campbell died at the age of thirty-six before he could return home.

Shortly after Kings Mountain, Isaac Shelby moved to the Kentucky wilderness where he became that state's first governor. In his later years, he tried to discredit Campbell's leadership at Kings Mountain, but numerous witnesses who fought there refuted the allegations.

John Sevier saw additional action in 1781 against Indians and Tories in South Carolina. He was instrumental in creating the state of Tennessee and became its first governor.

In 1781 Charles McDowell led western North Carolina militia across the state to help drive Cornwallis out of Wilmington, but the British general had left for Yorktown before McDowell arrived. Shortly afterwards, some of McDowell's officers filed fifteen charges against him that included giving preferential treatment to Tories, illegal confiscation of lands, and taking troops away from the frontier, thereby leaving the forts inadequately manned to resist Indian raids should they have occurred. A court-martial found McDowell guilty on eight counts and relieved him of command. However, the state's political leadership not only over-turned the findings, they also promoted Charles McDowell to gen-eral and commander of a newly created military district for the western frontier.

Joe "Quaker Meadows" McDowell succeeded his brother as the colonel for the Burke County militia and led a regiment at the Battle of Cowpens. Unlike his federalist brother, Joe voted against adopting the United States Constitution at a state convention because it did not then contain the Bill of Rights. After service in the state legislature, he served several terms in the U.S. Congress.

Joseph Winston, the Surry County commander at Kings Mountain, led his troops again at Guilford Courthouse. He also served honorably in the state legislature and the U.S. Congress.

Benjamin Cleveland, Ol' Roundabout, had some business reverses after the war, lost his plantation, and moved to western South Carolina. Despite not having a formal education, he became a highly respected judge and grew to be nearly four hundred pounds before dying at the age of sixty-nine. Jesse Franklin, Cleveland's adjutant at Kings Mountain, went on to serve as a U.S. congressman, U.S. senator, and North Carolina governor.

After the war, William Walker moved to Tennessee and lived to be eighty years old. His brother Felix and father remained in Rutherford County and continued their prominence in political affairs.

Jim Gray rose to the rank of captain and spent another year in active service, helping to drive the Loyalists militia from South Carolina. His grave overlooks McDaniel's Ford (now called Alexander's Ford), the last overnight camping place of the overmountain men on their way to Kings Mountain.

James Withrow served a term as Rutherford County sheriff and several terms in the state legislature. He eventually left his wife and started another farm nearby at the foot of Flint Hill, now called Cherry Mountain.

Josiah Brandon and several other Whig militiamen who found them-selves fighting for the Loyalists at Kings Mountain returned to the ranks of the Liberty Men several weeks after the battle, and served the independence cause honorably for the remainder of the war. Josiah later married, became a preacher, and sired fifteen children.

Andrew Hampton continued to command his troops for another year before resigning his commission to serve three years as sheriff of Rutherford County. He lived to be ninety-two. For many years, Hampton's son Jonathon was prominent in county politics, serving as a justice of the peace, sheriff, and state legislator. Ironically, Jonathon's great-granddaughter married the great-grandson of the Tory Major William Mills.

William Mills recovered from his wounds at Kings Mountain but hid for a time in Indian territory west of White Oak Mountain. His property, as was that of most Tory militiamen, was confiscated by the courts but was later returned to him. After the war, he returned to Rutherford County in the area that became Polk County and where each succeeding generation of Mills has produced notable and respected citizens.

According to family legend, William Merrill, whose damning testimony sealed the fate of Colonel Ambrose Mills, was rousted from his home in February 1781 by night riders reportedly led by William Mills. He was bound and forcibly taken to the infamous hanging tree at Biggerstaff's where he was executed.

A few days after the battle, Aaron Biggerstaff died from wounds suffered at Kings Mountain.

Several weeks after his escape at Biggerstaff's, Isaac Baldwin, whose younger brother saved him from the hangman's noose, was killed in a shoot-out with a Whig militia patrol near the South Mountains.

Major Dan Plummer recovered from the wounds he received at Kings Mountain and later had his property confiscated by the South Carolina government. He and his family were forced to flee with the British to Florida where he died in 1799.

Most of the Provincial and Tory militia officers who served under Ferguson and survived the battle found themselves unwelcome in the new nation. Many relocated to Nova Scotia. Doctor Uzal Johnson, however, returned to New York and lived out his life as a prominent physician. Alexander Chesney fled to Ireland.

Because of wounds received at Cane Creek, the Loyalist Ranger Captain James Dunlop was not with Ferguson at Kings Mountain. After his wounds had healed, he returned to action, leading Loyalists in raids against those championing independence in South Carolina. In March 1781, Dunlop was wounded and captured after a fierce battle that saw thirty-four Tories killed at Beattie's Mill on Little River near Ninety Six. He was taken to Gilbert Town, about one hundred miles north, where the Gilbert home had become a military hospital. During the night, Liberty Men, believed to be friends of

Noah Hampton, broke into Dunlop's bedroom and killed him. The other Loyalist prisoners with him were not harmed. He is buried near the house.

Had Jacob Godley been a real person, I imagine that he would have married Rachel Pearson and settled into the quiet life of a reclusive farmer and gunsmith. Other than returning to Kings Mountain with his father to recover the bodies of his brothers, he would never again travel more than twenty miles from his home.

"Here less than a thousand men, inspired by the urge of freedom, defeated a superior force entrenched in this strategic position. This small band of patriots turned back a dangerous invasion well designed to separate and dismember the united Colonies. It was a little army and a little battle, but it was of mighty portent. History has done scant justice to its significance, which rightly should place it beside Lexington, Bunker Hill, Trenton and Yorktown."

President Herbert Hoover,

commemorating the 150th anniversary of the battle

during a speech at Kings Mountain

ACKNOWLEDGMENTS

I am indebted to many people who assisted me with this project by sharing knowledge, correcting wrong assumptions, and providing encouragement. Some of the most helpful included historian Scott Withrow, cartographer John Robertson, and Ambrose Mills—all descendants of participants in the Kings Mountain battle. Also extending exceptional support and insight were Bob Sweeney, Will Graves, Ben Roney, Elaine Bowen and gunsmith Roger Byers. Advice from Paul Carson, superintendent of the Overmountain National Victory Trail, and Chris Revels of the Kings Mountain National Military Park was invaluable. Many others, too numerous to mention, took time to talk and guide me on my quest for information about the era.

Special appreciation goes to the re-enactors from the Overmountain Victory Trail Association who, each year, retrace the historic steps of the overmountain militia from Abingdon, Virginia, and what is now east Tennessee, across two high passes in the Blue Ridge Mountains, and through the western Carolina piedmont to Kings Mountain. These dedicated men and women keep alive the traditions, culture, and sacrifices made by the Liberty Men on both sides of the mountains who left their families in 1780, supplied their own weapons, food and horses; and endured numerous hardships for no pay to succeed against overwhelming odds. The modern-day overmountain men present living history lessons to schoolchildren and anyone else willing to listen about the critical events leading to the battle that President Thomas Jefferson described as *"The turn of the tide of success."*

Mostly, I am grateful to my wife, Dorcas, who put up with me closeting myself for far too many days and who was one of my most critical and constructive editors.

-Joe Epley

CPSIA information can be obtained at www.ICGtesting.com
Printed in the USA
LVOW041915141211

259419LV00009B/17/P

9 781461 075936